# Pass the Poetry, Please!

LEE BENNETT HOPKINS

# Pass the Poetry, Please!

Revised, Enlarged, and Updated Edition

A Harper Trophy Book
Harper & Row, Publishers

*To my Poet-friends*
*who make it all possible*
L.B.H.

Acknowledgments for copyrighted material,
appearing on pages 245 and 246,
constitute an extension of this copyright page.

Library of Congress Cataloging-in-Publication Data
Hopkins, Lee Bennett.
  Pass the poetry, please!

  "A Harper Trophy book"
  Includes bibliographies and indexes.
  1. Poetry—Study and teaching (Elementary)
I. Title
LB1576.H66  1987        372.6'4        86-45758
ISBN 0-06-022602-1
ISBN 0-06-022603-X (lib. bdg.)
ISBN 0-06-446062-2 (pbk.)

# CONTENTS

v

# CONTENTS

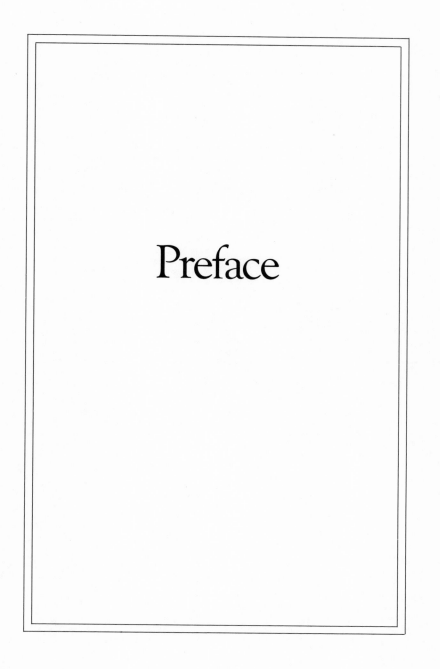

# Preface

This totally revised and expanded edition of *Pass the Poetry, Please!* was completed fifteen years after its first publication in 1972. I have reedited, substantially reorganized, enlarged, and updated each of the chapters in terms of important happenings and events that have occurred in the world of poetry for children since the early 1970s.

It has always been my firm belief that poetry can and must be an integral part of the total school curriculum, weaving in and out of every subject area, as well as playing an important part in children's home lives.

References at the end of each chapter give complete bibliographical information—author, title, illustrator, publisher, and copyright data; books available in paperback editions are also noted. "Appendix 3: Sources of Educational Materials Cited," is included to facilitate ordering, and/or for being placed on mailing lists to receive catalogs, book announcements, and other promotional material to keep abreast of newly published volumes.

A great deal of help was offered to make this new edition possible, and I should like to thank the following individuals, to whom I am greatly indebted: Mary L. Allison, who first believed in this project; Misha Arenstein, who listened for long, long hours; Charles John Egita, whose patience never ceased; Teresa Moogan, editor of this revised edition; Margery Tippie, who copiously copyedited the manuscript; the many people in publishing who shared so much, and Marilyn E. Marlow, for being my sage.

*Lee Bennett Hopkins*
*Scarborough, New York*

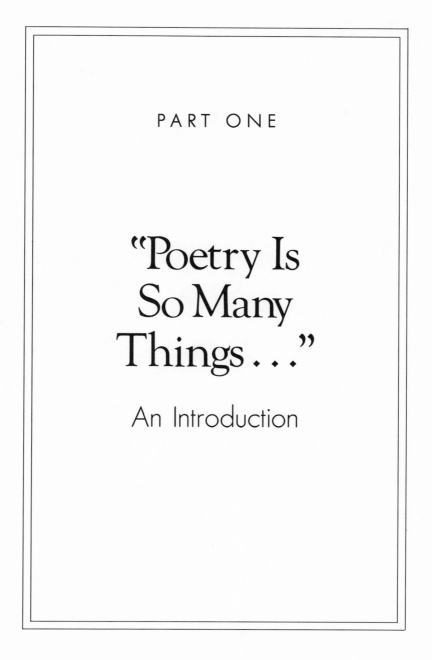

PART ONE

# "Poetry Is So Many Things..."

## An Introduction

An important event in the world of poetry occurred in 1977, when the National Council of Teachers of English (NCTE) established the country's first award for poetry—the NCTE Award for Excellence in Poetry for Children—presented to a poet for his or her aggregate body of work. As of 1982, the award is given every three years. To date, the following poets have received this prestigious honor: David McCord (1977), Aileen Fisher (1978), Karla Kuskin (1979), Myra Cohn Livingston (1980), Eve Merriam (1981), John Ciardi (1982), Lilian Moore (1985). Books by these poets carry the seal pictured below, designed by Karla Kuskin.

New beginnings for poetry for children were also witnessed in the 1980s. For the first time in its history, the John Newbery Medal, an award given annually since 1922 by the American Library Association to the author

of the most distinguished contribution to American literature for children, was presented in 1982 to an original collection of verse—Nancy Willard's *A Visit to William Blake's Inn.* The volume was also named a Caldecott Honor Book for its distinguished illustrations by Alice and Martin Provensen.

Another first for verse came in 1981, when *A Light in the Attic,* by the popular Shel Silverstein, reached number one on *The New York Times Book Review* adult best-seller list. It remained on the list for over three years.

In 1982, T. S. Eliot's *Old Possum's Book of Practical Cats,* upon which the London and Broadway musical productions of the hit show *Cats* is based, reached more readers than it had since it was first published in 1939.

More than ever before, poetry for children has climbed to its proper station. Thank goodness for this trend, for poetry must flow freely in our children's lives; it should come to them as naturally as breathing, for nothing—*no thing*—can ring and rage through hearts and minds as does poetry.

Poetry can work with any grade, any age level. It can meet the interests and abilities of anyone, anywhere, from the gifted to the most reluctant reader; it opens up a world of feelings for children they never thought possible; it is a source of love and hope that children carry with them the rest of their lives.

Children are natural poets. Visit a school playground or park on a spring day and you see youngsters "rhyming." Three children playing jump rope might be exclaiming:

Grace, Grace, dressed in lace
Went upstairs to powder her face.
How many boxes does she use?
One, two, three, four . . .

until one misses, and either this rhyme or another is
recited for the next jumper. Another group of children
beginning a game of hide-and-go-seek or tag may be
deciding who is going to be "it" by chanting:

Eenie, meenie, minee, mo,
Catch a tiger by the toe.
If it hollers, let it go,
Eenie, meenie, minee, mo.

Or:

My mother and your mother were hanging out clothes.
My mother punched your mother right in the nose.
What color blood came out?
R-E-D spells *red* and O-U-T spells *out.*

Still other groups of girls and boys will be bouncing balls,
calling out:

A sailing sailor
Went to sea
To see what he could see, see, see.
And all that he could see, see, see
Was the sea, the sea,
The sea, sea, sea.

Children make up their own nonsense rhymes at play, too:

> Booba, booba, baba, baba,
> Twee, twee, toe, toe.
> I know! I know!

Rhyme is very present in the child's world.

For over twenty-five years, during which poetry and I have intertwined in my work as a teacher, consultant, author, and anthologist, I have listened long and hard to girls and boys. My work has taken me across the United States and Canada, and I have encountered thousands of children in a variety of formal and informal situations. Sharing poetry has always been, and always will be, one of the greatest satisfactions of my life. I have seen children in the early grades naturally "ooh" and "ah" when they heard a poem they liked; I have also seen them wince and screw up their faces when a poem did not please them.

In upper grades, poetry has served as an excellent stimulus to better reading and nurtured a love of words. I have used poetry with slow readers in my classes—readers who could not possibly get through a long story or novel but who could understand and relish the message a poem conveys. Poems, being short, are not demanding or frustrating to these readers. They can start them, finish them, and gain from them, without experiencing any discomfort whatsoever.

Many children in the upper grades, whether slow readers or very good readers, may not be mature enough to tackle the sophisticated prose of some of America's men and women of letters, but they can dip into poetry; they can easily read and understand poems by such masters as Carl Sandburg, Robert Frost, Emily Dickinson, and Langston Hughes. Thus, children's literary horizons can be extended through verses created by some of the finest writers.

Children in the elementary grades are not much different from most adults when it comes to knowing and loving poetry. They have their definite tastes just as adults do.

Poetry is so many things to so many people. The anthologist Gerald D. McDonald stated in the preface to his collection *A Way of Knowing* that:

Poetry can be wittier and funnier than any kind of writing; it can tell us about the world through words we can't forget; it can be tough or it can be tender, it can be fat or lean; it can preach a short sermon or give us a long thought (the shorter the poem sometimes, the longer the thought). And it does all this through the music of words.

The poet David McCord commented to me:

Poetry is so many things besides the shiver down the spine. It is a new day lying on an unknown doorstep. It is *Peer Gynt* and *Moby-Dick* in a single line. It is the best translation of words that do not exist. It is hot coffee dripping from an icicle. It is the accident involving sudden life. It is the calculus of the imagination. It is the finishing touch to what one could not

7

finish. It is a hundred things as unexplainable as all our foolish explanations.

A poem is an experience—something that has happened to a person, something that may seem very obvious, an everyday occurrence that has been set down in a minimum number of words and lines as it has never been set down before. These experiences depend upon the poets: who they are, when and where they live, why and how a specific thing affected them at a given moment.

In a eulogy to William Carlos Williams, John Ciardi wrote:

A good poem celebrates life and quickens us to it. . . . The good poet cannot fail to shame us, for he proves to us instantly that we have never learned to touch, smell, taste, hear, and see. He shames us through our senses by awakening us to a new awareness of the peaks and abysses locked in every commonplace thing. . . . (*Saturday Review*, March 23, 1963, p. 18)

There are as many definitions of poetry as there are poets; their work reflects this diversity, enabling us to choose from a myriad of poems.

Life has produced poets who need the quiet of the country, and they share what their senses reveal. For many the sight of a brook, a reflection in a pond, or "a host of daffodils" inspires fresh images of nature. For others, it is the excitement of the city sidewalks, an image of a fire hydrant, or the city sounds and noises heard that spark verse.

No matter where and when poets live, or where and when they write poetry, all write of everyday happenings from their own points of view about their environments.

Life itself is embodied in poetry, and each poem reveals a bit of life. Good poems make us sigh and say, "Yes, that's just how it is." Or, as Carl Sandburg wrote in his "Tentative (First Models) Definitions of Poetry," thirty-eight gems printed as the preface to *Good Morning, America*: "Poetry is the report of a nuance between two moments when people say, 'Listen!' and 'Did you see it?' 'Did you hear it? What was it?' "

There is really little difference between good poetry for children and good poetry for adults. Poetry for children should appeal to them and meet their emotional needs and interests. We can read about what poetry or a poem *is*, what it *should* do, learn all about meters, rhyme schemes, cadence, and balance; yet all this does not necessarily help to make a poem meaningful. The one criterion we must set for ourselves is that we love the poems we are going to share. If we don't like a particular poem, we shouldn't read it to our children; our distaste will certainly be obvious to them. There are plenty of poems around. Why bother with those that are not pleasing? In the world of poetry almost any theme can be located.

Some people's eyes have flashed at the idea of presenting poetry to children by such greats as E. E. Cummings, Theodore Roethke, or Wallace Stevens, yet it can and has been done successfully. I suppose that once brows were also raised at the thought of bringing "adult literature" into the elementary school or home—books such as 20,000 *Leagues Under the Sea* or *Gulliver's Travels.* We know that these novels have proved to be popular with students. The language and thoughts of poetry written primarily for adult audiences can also appeal to girls and boys.

While working with boys and girls across the country, I have always read a balance of the old and new, poems written "for adults," poems written "for children," and often poems written by children for children.

Many classroom teachers and parents may not want to read "sophisticated" poetry to children, particularly if the poetry is somewhat strange to them. Some adults may never feel comfortable reading, to children of primary or even upper-grade ages, such selections as T. S. Eliot's "The Naming of Cats," which I included in the anthology *I Am the Cat*; this poem does have difficult pacing and hard-to-read phrases such as ". . . rapt contemplation" and ". . . ineffable, effable/Effanineffable/Deep and inscrutable singular Name." Many children, however, relish the challenge presented by the richness of Eliot's language.

Karla Kuskin stated:

There's a line in *The Night Before Christmas* that will stay in my head forever because when I first learned it, I didn't understand all the words.

> As dry leaves before the wild hurricane
> fly,

When they meet with an obstacle, mount
  to the sky,
So up to the housetop the coursers
  they flew,
With a sleigh full of toys,
  and St. Nicholas, too.

I didn't know *hurricane*; I didn't know *obstacle*; I didn't know *coursers*; but I just loved the way they sounded.

Because a particular poem works for me, it doesn't mean it will work for everyone. You know your children and their tastes; moreover, you know what appeals to you. Stay comfortable. If "The Naming of Cats" doesn't please you, look for another cat poem. You will find many. In *Index to Poetry for Children and Young People: 1976–1981,* by the anthologists John E. Brewton, George Meredith Blackburn III, and Lorraine A. Blackburn, you can find listed well over one hundred cat poems, and, if dogs are your favorites, you can find over one hundred poems listed about them here, too! Previous volumes in the series, first published in 1942, are also available.

Bringing children and poetry together can be one of the most exciting experiences in parenting or teaching. Over the years, however, I have noted in too many cases what I have coined the DAM approach—dissecting, analyzing, and *meaninglessly* memorizing poetry to death.

Lee Shapiro, a first-year student teacher in one of my graduate classes in children's literature and storytelling at the City College of New York, wrote me:

The children I work with are 2½ to 3 years old. I feel very unsure of what poems I should select for them, which will be appropriate within their capabilities of understanding.

I have felt for a long time that the structured introduction of poetry which I received in public and high school was frustrating and restricting besides being very painful. Being forced to dissect, analyze, and memorize poetry did not leave me much room for enjoyment. Until very recently I have avoided any kind of poetry. Now I have begun to explore on my own with great satisfaction the world of poetry. How much I missed!

I well remember hating Shakespeare as a high school student. I was forced to dissect, analyze, and memorize some fifteen isolated lines from *Julius Caesar.* The class had a written and an oral test on the "Friends, Romans, countrymen . . ." speech. I received an A on the oral but a C on the written test because I misspelled several words and left out some punctuation marks! The next semester I suffered through a similar experience with Alfred Noyes' "The Highwayman." I, too, soon came to detest the sound of the word poetry. It was not something to be enjoyed—it was a test of endurance and memorization ability.

Looking back on those days, I laugh now, but I still wonder why any student has to suffer through poetry presented in such a dreary, uninteresting fashion, as if it were an exercise in total recall. I cannot even remember poems I *myself* wrote and wouldn't attempt reciting them without the printed words in front of me.

As a young teenager, I wanted adventure, mystery,

murder, passion. It wasn't until my adult years that I realized that Shakespeare and poets like Noyes could have given me what I wanted then. Certainly the tragedies of Shakespeare dealt more passionately and romantically with life than did the drugstore magazines I bought with my weekly allowance. But I wasn't aware of this due to my sour poetic experiences.

Eve Merriam comments: "I want children to love poetry, not memorize it."

In his acceptance speech on receiving the 1982 NCTE Excellence in Poetry for Children Award, John Ciardi remarked:

You can't say, "Memorize . . . and give it back on demand. . . ." You are the ones who must entice the student. If a student can be brought to say, "Wow!" to one poem, he or she can say "Wow!" to another. . . . Unless you and others like you can lead your students to this contact, Pac-Man is going to eat us all.

Unfortunately, there is a steady stream of curriculum guides that advocate dissecting poems to the point of the ridiculous. In one guide, the poem "City" by Langston Hughes is reprinted. The poem, a mere eight lines, beautifully describes a city waking up and going to bed. The guide suggests that after reading the poem aloud to children:

Ask: What is a city? Name some cities. How does a city spread its wings? What does the poet mean when he says, "making a song in stone that sings?" How can a city go to bed? How can a city hang lights? Where would a city's head be?

The guide then suggests that children memorize the poem as a group lesson by rote. After this nonsensical interrogation, billed in the guide as an "appreciation lesson," which I doubt any adult would use, it would take a miracle or a child masochist to ever ask for this, or any other poem, again.

In her article "An Unreasonable Excitement," Myra Cohn Livingston comments on the abuse of her poem "Whispers":

. . . when I find it assaulted in . . . basal readers I want to scream out to well-meaning but misguided educators to cease and desist . . . do not use it to teach about rhyming words or punctuation, do not ask such inane and unanswerable questions as "What does a whisper look like? What color is a whisper?" (*The Advocate,* Spring 1983)

In an article, "A Visit to Robert Frost" by Roger Kahn (*Saturday Evening Post,* November 19, 1980), Frost was asked, "What is the meaning of a poem?" He replied, "What it says." Persisting, the interviewer told Frost, "But we don't know what it means to you." And he answered, "Maybe I don't want you to."

Probably one of the saddest commentaries on the compulsion to analyze in the history of poetry are the endless definitions and interpretations of Robert Frost's most famous, four-stanza, sixteen-line poem, "Stopping by

Woods on a Snowy Evening." Even poet-critics themselves are guilty of endless analysis.

Louis Untermeyer, in *The Pursuit of Poetry,* elaborates
on this tearing apart of Mr. Frost's poem and includes the
poet's own wry reaction to all this:

"I've been more bothered with that one than anybody has
ever been with any poem in just pressing it with more than it
should be pressed for. It means enough without being
pressed." Disturbed by "pressers" puzzling about the snowy
woods and the miles to go, he said that all the poem means
is: "It's all very nice here, but I must be getting home. There
are chores to do." At another time when a critic indicated that
the last three lines implied that the poet longed for an after-life
in heaven, Frost smiled and shook his head. "No, it only
means I want to get the hell out of there."

Children, too, "want to get the hell out of there!"

Long before they enter school, long before they can
read a printed word, children can be heard chanting
familiar Mother Goose rhymes—verses that have come
down through centuries. Young children voluntarily reciting Mother Goose melodies do not stop to ponder
over the meanings of words unfamiliar to them. They do
not know, and may never know, what *curds* or *whey* are;
nor do they know or care about the hidden personages
behind peculiar names such as Wee Willie Winkie, Little
Bo Peep, or the Queen of Hearts. To acquaint very
young children with the fact that Mother Goose rhymes
were political lampoons or satires about such historical
figures as Mary Tudor, Henry VIII, or Mary, Queen of

Scots, would be ludicrous. None of this matters. The children are in love with the easy rhymes, the alliteration, the quick action, and the humor that Mother Goose conveys.

I am often asked, "How do you read a poem aloud to children?" There is no trickery involved in reading poetry aloud. When a poem is read aloud with sincerity, boys and girls will enjoy its rhythm, its music, and will understand the work on their level.

The guidelines below can help those who get butterflies in their stomachs when it comes to presenting poetry. These same points can be shared with children, for they, too, should be reading and sharing poetry aloud.

1. Before reading a poem aloud, read it aloud several times by yourself to get the feel of the words and rhythm. Know the poem well. Mark the words and phrases you would like to emphasize, and then you will read it exactly as you feel it.

2. Follow the rhythm of the poem, reading it naturally. The physical appearance of most poems on the printed page dictates the rhythm and the mood of the words. Some poems are meant to be read softly and slowly; others must be read at a more rapid pace.

3. Make pauses that please you—pauses that make sense. Some poems sound better when the lines are rhythmically strung together. Sometimes great effects can be obtained by pausing at the end of each line. Many of the poems by E. E. Cummings and William Carlos Williams convey greater mood when they are read by pausing at

the end of each short line, as though you were saying something yourself for the first time, thinking of a word or words that will come from your tongue next. Isn't this how we speak? We think as we talk. Sometimes words flow easily—

> other times—
> they
> come
> slowly,
> thinking-ly
> from our
> mouths.

4. When reading a poem aloud, speak in a natural voice. Don't change to a high-pitched or bass-pitched tone. Read a poem as though you were telling the children about a new car, or a television program you saw last night. Again, you must be sincere. A poem must interest you as well as be one that you feel is right for your children.

5. After a poem is read, be quiet. Don't feel trapped into asking children questions such as "Did you like it?" Most girls and boys will answer yes—even if they didn't like it—because *you* selected and read it. And what if they didn't like it? By the time you begin finding out the reasons, the poem is destroyed and half of the class will see why they, too, shouldn't like it anymore.

Another reason children may find poetry distasteful is that it is often taught or presented via a one-week, once-a-year unit approach. There are many places within the day where a poem fits snugly. After all, poetry is not the exclusive property of the language arts. Why not open or close your next mathematics lesson with "Arithmetic," a wonderful free-verse selection that can be found in *Rainbows Are Made: Poems by Carl Sandburg*, which I compiled? Or enhance a spelling lesson with David McCord's "You Mustn't Call It Hopsichord," "Spelling Bee," and "The Likes and Looks of Letters," all in *One at a Time*. The unit approach is good for social studies, science, and mathematics—but not for poetry!

We must do all we can to preserve and nurture the love of rhyme, rhythm, and the feeling for words that young children have in them. They hear jingles on television daily; radios, phonographs, and cassette players blare tunes that either parents, peers, or older siblings play incessantly. As they can with Mother Goose rhymes, four-year-olds can sing lyrics to a popular song without *ever* seeing the words in print. They learn the words by repetition and love of a particular word scheme. And ask the average ten-, eleven-, twelve-year-old or teenager how many popular songs he knows! Young people are entranced, almost mesmerized by their personal poets—today's songwriters.

What is poetry? Perhaps the question is best posed in Eleanor Farjeon's verse "Poetry":

What is Poetry? Who knows?
Not a rose, but the scent of the rose;
Not the sky, but the light in the sky;

Not the fly, but the gleam of the fly;
Not the sea, but the sound of the sea;
Not myself, but what makes me
See, hear, and feel something that prose
Cannot: and what it is, who knows?

Does it really matter what poetry is? It does matter, however, what it should do, what it should evoke in each and every one of us. Poetry *should* make us "see, hear, and feel something that prose cannot."

What is poetry? What is poetry to *you?* When you find it, when you come across the something that makes you say, "I can *see* it! I can *hear* it! I can *feel* it!"—and when you know that neither *you* nor your *children* may ever seem the same again, you will have found out what poetry truly is.

**REFERENCES**

Brewton, John E.; Blackburn, George Meredith, III; and Blackburn, Lorraine A. *Index to Poetry for Children and Young People: 1976–1981.* H. W. Wilson Company, 1983.

Eliot, T. S. *Old Possum's Book of Practical Cats.* Illustrated by Edward Gorey. Harcourt Brace Jovanovich, 1982; new edition; also in paperback.

Hopkins, Lee Bennett (selector). *I Am the Cat.* Illustrated by Linda Rochester Richards. Harcourt Brace Jovanovich, 1981.

———. *Rainbows Are Made: Poems by Carl Sandburg.* Illus-

trated by Fritz Eichenberg. Harcourt Brace Jovanovich, 1982; also in paperback.

McCord, David. *One at a Time: His Collected Poems for the
Young.* Illustrated by Henry B. Kane. Little, Brown,
1977.

McDonald, George (compiler). *A Way of Knowing.* Illustrated by Clare and John Ross. T. Y. Crowell, 1959.

Silverstein, Shel. *A Light in the Attic.* Harper & Row,
1981.

Untermeyer, Louis. *The Pursuit of Poetry.* Simon and
Schuster, 1969.

Willard, Nancy. *A Visit to William Blake's Inn: Poems for
Innocent and Experienced Travelers.* Illustrated by Alice
and Martin Provensen. Harcourt Brace Jovanovich,
1981; also in paperback.

PART TWO

# From Mother Goose to Dr. Seuss– and Beyond

## Acquainting Students with Poets

Perhaps it was the elusive Mother Goose who began poetry for children when she took "Muffet," rhymed it with "tuffet," played around with "thumb" and "plum," and thought up "Hi, diddle, diddle/The cat and the fiddle."

There are many explanations of who the real Mother Goose was. Scholars differ: some claim she was the Queen of Sheba; others say her origin was French, British, or German. The name is *just* a name that originated in Boston, Massachusetts, proclaim many—a moniker that was coined by Thomas Fleet, a well-known Boston printer, whose mother-in-law's name was Elizabeth Vergoose; they say that Fleet printed the very first collection of Mother Goose verses in 1719. Whoever Mother Goose was and wherever the rhymes really originated, they are still an integral ingredient of early childhood and a vital part of world literature.

One of the best reference books on these rhymes of yore is *The Annotated Mother Goose,* edited by William Baring-Gould and Cecil Baring-Gould; this 350-page volume contains rhymes with scholarly explanations and black-and-white illustrations by artists such as Kate Greenaway, Randolph Caldecott, and Walter Crane, along with historical woodcuts. Chapter 1 tells "All About Mother Goose" verses that have become a beloved heritage of "nobody really knows when and where."

Why has Mother Goose had such wide appeal to generation after generation of children? Stop to listen to the
rhymes. See how they awaken responsiveness in children. They are short, fun-filled, dramatic, pleasing to the
ear, easy to remember—and, oh, so hard to forget.

The step from Mother Goose to other forms of poetry
is a small one. Many girls and boys today quickly go from
Mother Goose to the nonsense rhymes of Dr. Seuss—a
man whose language and characters enchant them. We
may never know the true origin of Mother Goose, but
we do know that Dr. Seuss is an American, living in La
Jolla, California. The doctor, whose real name is Theo-
dor Seuss Geisel, was born in Springfield, Massachusetts,
on March 2, 1914. His first book, *And to Think That I Saw
It on Mulberry Street*, was immediately acclaimed. Seussian
characters, thereafter, have captured the hearts of youngsters and their parents as well. His unforgettable characters—grinches, sneeches, drum-tummied snumms, the
Yooks and the Zooks—will probably match Mother
Goose's classic characters—pie-men and pumpkin eaters
and pretty maids all in a row.

Interviewing Dr. Seuss, I asked, "What is rhyme?"
"Rhyme?" he answered. "A rhyme is something without
which I would probably be in the dry-cleaning business!"
The dry-cleaning business lost a great man, but the world
gained from his clever pen.

Many children are raised on Dr. Seuss rhymes. Unfortunately, that is where too many stop, when adults leave
them. Children, given guidance, can learn to love poetry
written by other contemporary poets, many of whom are

discussed within this chapter. Following is a sampling of twenty American poets who have written volumes of original verse and whose works have been widely anthologized. It will serve to introduce the best poetry to boys and girls, motivating them to read the poetry. You can add spice to this information and feed students personal anecdotes about the writers' lives and works.

Throughout this volume I mention titles of many high-quality anthologies; these contain works of both new and older master poets such as A. A. Milne, Walter de la Mare, and others on whom we have all been brought up. It is not my intention to throw away the old, but my desire to bring the new and the now into the lives of children. This leads me to emphasize contemporary poets.

# Arnold Adoff

black   is brown   is tan
is girl   is boy
is nose   is face
is all the colors
of the race
is dark   is light
singing songs
in singing night
kiss big woman   hug big man
black   is brown   is tan . . .

—from BLACK IS BROWN IS TAN

Arnold Adoff's first book, *I Am the Darker Brother: An Anthology of Modern Poems by Negro Americans*, grew from his collecting black American poems for use in his own classroom.

"I began collecting literature for my classes while teaching in the late 1950s and early 1960s in Harlem and the Upper West Side of New York City," he told me. "I have been a poet, deep inside, since I began writing as a teenager. By thirty, I was enough of a man to start to put things together and realize where the thrust should be directed. I wanted to influence the kids coming up—not a small group of academic anemics who try to control aspects of the literature of this country. I felt that if I could anthologize adult literature of the highest literary quality and get it into classrooms and libraries for children and young adults, I could make my share of the revolution. I guess when I realized I was too old to learn how to make bombs, I threw myself full-force into creating books for children."

One volume followed another, and Mr. Adoff burst onto the literary scene like a human being thrust from a circus cannon, to produce outstanding volumes of prose, poetry, biography, and picture books.

In 1973, he completed the comprehensive collection *The Poetry of Black America.*

In the late 1970s, he, his wife, Virginia Hamilton, the acclaimed Newbery Award–winning novelist, and their two children, Leigh Hamilton and Jaime Levi, left New York City to settle in Yellow Springs, Ohio. They built a redwood house behind Ms. Hamilton's mother's house.

Defining poetry, Mr. Adoff told me, "There are as many definitions of poetry as there are different kinds of poems, because a fine poem combines the elements of measuring music, with a form like a living frame that holds it all together. My own personal preference is the music first that must sing out to me from the words. How does it sing, sound—then how does it look?

"I look for craft and control in making a form that is unique to the individual poem, that shapes it, holds it tight, creates an inner tension that makes a whole shape out of the words. I really want a poem to sprout roses and spit bullets; this is the ideal combination, and it is a tough tightrope that takes the kind of control that comes only with years of work."

Mr. Adoff was born in the East Bronx section of New York City. "I was a Cancer crab who was born on a hot July Sunday on the fifteenth in 1915. I grew up in and around the Bronx and all over the city and loved New York and its potential for power, excitement and discovery. There was too much to see, always too much to read, always another place to go. The neighborhood had character—a solid, respectable Jewish middle-class, the butcher, the grocer, my father's pharmacy on the corner, the old ladies sitting in the front of the stoops, mothers waiting with jars of milk for the kids' afternoon snacks after school before running to Crotona Park to play ball.

Books and food, recipes and political opinions, Jewish poetry, and whether the dumplings would float on top of the soup were all of equal importance. And reading, of course. I read everything in the house and then all I could carry home each week from the libraries I could reach on Bronx buses.''

His work is distinctive, diverse, ranging through titles such as *black is brown is tan*, a picture book about an interracial family; *I Am the Running Girl*, depicting a young girl who describes the joy and pride that running gives her; *Friend Dog*, free verse exploring the relationship between a young girl and her dog; *Eats*, reflecting his passion for food and eating; *All the Colors of the Race*, thirty-six stylistic works, written from the point of view of a child who has a black mother and a white father; *The Cabbages Are Chasing the Rabbits*, in which the hunter becomes the hunted on a day in May; *Tornado!*, powerful verses about the destruction and aftermath of a violent storm; *Under the Early Morning Trees*, telling how a young girl enjoys the closeness of nature; *Sports Pages*, thirty-seven verses dealing with the many moods of sports such as soccer, football, gymnastics, track, and tennis.

Other volumes include *Today We Are Brother and Sister*, *Make a Circle Keep Us In*, *Birds*, and *Big Sister Tells Me That I Am Black*.

The poet can be heard reading his works on two cassettes: *Arnold Adoff Reads Four Complete Books: Eats: Poems, black is brown is tan, OUTside/INside Poems, Birds: Poems*; and *Arnold Adoff Reads Four Complete Books: Eats: Poems, I*

*Am the Running Girl, All the Colors of the Race, Johnny Junk Is Dead,* both produced by Earworks.

**REFERENCES**

*I Am the Darker Brother: An Anthology of Modern Poems by Negro Americans.* Illustrated by Benny Andrews. Macmillan, 1968.

*The Poetry of Black America: Anthology of the 20th Century.* Harper & Row, 1973.

*black is brown is tan.* Illustrated by Emily Arnold McCully. Harper & Row, 1973.

*Make a Circle Keep Us In.* Illustrated by Ronald Himler. Delacorte, 1975.

*Big Sister Tells Me That I Am Black.* Illustrated by Lorenzo Lynch. Henry Holt, 1976.

*Tornado! Poems.* Illustrated by Ronald Himler. Dutton, 1977.

*Under the Early Morning Trees.* Illustrated by Ronald Himler. Dutton, 1978.

*Eats: Poems.* Illustrated by Susan Russo. Lothrop, Lee & Shepard 1979.

*I Am the Running Girl.* Illustrated by Ronald Himler. Harper & Row, 1979.

*Friend Dog.* Illustrated by Troy Howell. J. B. Lippincott, 1980.

*Today We Are Brother and Sister.* Illustrated by Glo Coalson. Lothrop, Lee & Shepard, 1981.

*All the Colors of the Race.* Illustrated by John Steptoe. Lothrop, Lee & Shepard, 1982.

*Birds: Poems.* Illustrated by Troy Howell. J. B. Lippincott, 1982.

*The Cabbages Are Chasing the Rabbits.* Illustrated by Janet Stevens. Harcourt Brace Jovanovich, 1985.

*Sports Pages.* Illustrated by Steve Kuzma. J. B. Lippincott, 1986.

# Harry Behn

---

## *CRICKETS*

We cannot say that crickets sing
Since all they do is twang a wing.

Especially when the wind is still
They orchestrate a sunlit hill,

And in the evening blue above
They weave the stars and moon with love,

Then peacefully they chirp all night
Remembering delight, delight . . .

—from CRICKETS AND BULLFROGS
AND WHISPERS OF THUNDER

In an article, "Poetry for Children" (*Horn Book*, April 1966, pp. 163–175), Harry Behn commented on his work:

The poems I shall write about must be mostly my own. They are all I know closely enough. Anything at too great a distance feathers away into a scholarly mist where I am lost and only my intellect can follow, and so all I can do is tell how I happened to write this poem or that—or any at all. I can only guess at what was derived from my own childhood and what I absorbed from my children, and more recently, from theirs.

Mr. Behn was fifty years old before he began writing for children. It began one summer evening when his three-year-old daughter pointed to the stars and said, "Moon-babies." The next day he wrote a poem for her and continued writing poetry until his death in 1973.

Born in McCabe, Arizona, on September 24, 1898, he had the kind of childhood most children today would envy and can only live vicariously via television programs.

"When I was a small boy in Territorial Arizona, in the town of Prescott, in the Bradshaw Mountains, all the boys I played with were influenced by the Native Americans who lived in wickiups on their reservation across Granite Creek. Our parents could still remember mas-

33

sacres or narrow escapes from painted, yelping hostiles and did not love them," he told me.

"The boys were not afraid of the Yavapais. We knew Apaches had been dangerous because they had been treated unfairly. But not even they had been as wicked as gamblers who shot each other once in a while in the bad part of town. . . ."

Upon graduating from high school, he lived one summer with the Blackfeet tribe in Montana, until his parents persuaded him to attend college. In 1922, he received a B.S. degree from Harvard University; the next year he went to Sweden as an American-Scandinavian Fellow; following this he became involved in arts and media, founding and editing *The Arizona Quarterly*, editing anthropological papers, writing movie scenarios, and teaching creative writing at the University of Arizona.

In 1937, he moved to Connecticut to write and travel. He and his wife raised three children.

His first book of poems for children, *The Little Hill*, appeared in 1949, containing thirty poems, many of which have been widely anthologized. Other books include *All Kinds of Time*, an unusual poetic picture book about clocks, time, and the seasons, and *Windy Morning*, a small volume containing many poems about nature and the seasons.

For children in the middle grades, the poet translated Japanese haiku in the volumes *Cricket Songs* and *More Cricket Songs*, with accompanying pictures chosen from the works of Japanese masters.

*The Golden Hive*, for older readers, reflected his joy in nature, his remembrance of his childhood, and his deep sense of the American past. Undoubtedly, his concerns for nature also stemmed from his childhood years.

He commented, "My earliest memory is of a profound and sunny peace, a change of seasons, spring to summer, summer to fall, and the wonder of being alive. Those are the mysteries I later tried to evoke in poems I wrote about my childhood; the imprints of stillness determining which haiku I chose to translate. . . . Like all aborigines, children are accustomed to thinking about the beginnings of things, the creation of beauty, the wisdom of plants and animals, of how alive everything is, like stars, and wildflowers, and how wonderfully different people can be from each other."

The poet also wrote a book for adults, *Chrysalis: Concerning Children and Poetry*, expressing his views on poetry, as well as several novels for boys and girls.

In 1984, *Crickets and Bullfrogs and Whispers of Thunder: Poems and Pictures by Harry Behn* appeared, for which I culled fifty works from five of his earlier, now out-of-print volumes—*The Little Hill, Windy Morning, The Wizard in the Well, The Golden Hive,* and *Chrysalis*.

In an article, "Profile: Harry Behn" (*Language Arts*, January 1985, pp. 92–94), Peter Roop stated about his work:

Fortunately for us he had the ability to capture a few of life's elusive wonders and cage them on a page. Yet, like everything else that slips away when grasped, we can't squeeze these poems too tightly for they might escape. They are the breath beyond what is.

Harry Behn can be heard reading his own poems on the recording *Poetry Parade*, produced by Weston Woods.

**REFERENCES**

*The Little Hill.* Harcourt Brace Jovanovich, 1949.
*All Kinds of Time.* Harcourt Brace Jovanovich, 1950.
*Windy Morning.* Harcourt Brace Jovanovich, 1953.
*The Wizard in the Well.* Harcourt Brace Jovanovich, 1956.
*Cricket Songs.* Harcourt Brace Jovanovich, 1964.
*The Golden Hive.* Harcourt Brace Jovanovich, 1966.
*Chrysalis: Concerning Children and Poetry.* Harcourt Brace Jovanovich, 1968.
*More Cricket Songs.* Harcourt Brace Jovanovich, 1971.
*Crickets and Bullfrogs and Whispers of Thunder.* Harcourt Brace Jovanovich, 1984.

# N. M. Bodecker

*NEW DAY*

Mornings bring
both hope
and curses:
God makes
light,
and I make
verses.

—from PIGEON CUBES

N. M. Bodecker was born on January 13, 1922, in Copenhagen, Denmark.

He states, "When I was a child, a one-legged veteran of the last war with Germany, in 1864, still worked his hurdy-gurdy in the country lanes each spring, and patriotic songs remained current in the nursery, reflecting those last sanguinary battles of my grandparents' youth. My conscious childhood spanned the years 1924–33, that sunny upland where so many of my parents' generation thought the world would remain in an age of peace and reason.

"Instead, a new savagery was building, more fearful than the old; and its clouds and foreshadows touched the rims of even the most jealously guarded nursery. What I have retained of my childhood is perhaps more deliberately sunny, more insistently civilized for that reason."

He went to school in 1933, studying at the Birkerød Kostskole, the year Adolf Hitler became German Chancellor. He graduated in 1939, three months before World War II began. Seven months later, Denmark was invaded and occupied by the Germans.

For five years he studied architecture and art at the Copenhagen School of Commerce. Following this he worked as an illustrator and cartoonist on newspapers and magazines, including the well-known *Politiken*.

He lived at his grandparents' home, and because of his

familiarity with the older, Victorian generation, he says that he is "perhaps a late blooming Victorian—at least artistically."

In 1952, he came to the United States to live, working for sixteen years for the "After Hours" department of *Harper's Magazine.* His illustrations have appeared in many major national magazines, including *Saturday Evening Post*, *Esquire*, and *Holiday*, as well as in many major books.

In 1973, *It's Raining Said John Twaining: Danish Nursery Rhymes*, which he translated and illustrated in full color, appeared.

From the nonsense rhymes he had written over a period of years, *Let's Marry Said the Cherry* was published in 1974, with his drawings, followed by *Hurry, Hurry Mary Dear.*

In *A Person from Britain Whose Head Was the Shape of a Mitten*, Mr. Bodecker turned to writing zany limericks. Other volumes include *Pigeon Cubes* and *Snowman Sniffles.*

"My poetry and verse owe their beginning to the gentle, poetic, but indomitable force that was my mother, a joyous, generous woman, positive and clear in all she did. We read together, sang together, made rhymes together; and together we walked through the fields in the evening. There I learned my botany: cornflower, poppy, pimpernel, bindweed and burr, king's candle, plaintain and cinquefoil, names I could no more forget than my own; and on the sandy slope, just before we turned back in the low, eye-blinding sunlight, wildrose, broom, and Lady Mary's shift sleeve—a poetry all its own," he states.

The poet currently lives and works in Hancock, New Hampshire.

**REFERENCES**

*It's Raining Said John Twaining: Danish Nursery Rhymes.* Margaret K. McElderry Books/Macmillan, 1973.

*Let's Marry Said the Cherry and Other Nonsense Poems.* Margaret K. McElderry Books/Macmillan, 1974.

*Hurry, Hurry Mary Dear.* Margaret K. McElderry Books/ Macmillan, 1976.

*A Person from Britain Whose Head Was the Shape of a Mitten.* Margaret K. McElderry Books/Macmillan, 1980.

*Pigeon Cubes and Other Verses.* Margaret K. McElderry Books/Macmillan, 1982.

*Snowman Sniffles and Other Verses.* Margaret K. McElderry Books/Macmillan, 1983.

# Gwendolyn Brooks

## *SKIPPER*

I looked in the fish-glass,
And what did I see.
A pale little gold fish
Looked sadly at me.
At the base of the bowl,
So still, he was lying.
"Are you dead, little fish?"
"Oh, no! But I'm dying."
I gave him fresh water
And the best of fish food—
But it was too late.
I did him no good.
I buried him by
Our old garden tree.
Our old garden tree
Will protect him for me.

—from BRONZEVILLE BOYS AND GIRLS

Gwendolyn Brooks is the first black woman to win the Pulitzer Prize for Poetry; it was awarded in 1950, for a volume of her adult poems, *Annie Allen.* Most of the poet's work is directed to mature students and adults.

Ms. Brooks was born in Topeka, Kansas, on June 7, 1917. At an early age she moved to Chicago, Illinois, where she still resides. The state of Illinois named her Poet Laureate, succeeding Carl Sandburg. She is the mother of two grown children, Henry and Nora.

Through her poetry, Ms. Brooks speaks of life's realities in vivid, compassionate words about the black experience.

Fortunately, the poet has written one volume of poems for young readers, *Bronzeville Boys and Girls*, a collection in which she set the task of writing "a poem a day in order to complete the book's deadline." Published in 1956, the book presents poignant views of children living in the crowded conditions of an American inner city. Each of the thirty-four poems bears the name of an individual child and is devoted to his or her thoughts, feelings, and emotions. There is "Val," who does not like the sound "when grownups at parties are laughing," and who would "rather be in the basement," or "rather be outside"; "Keziah," who has a secret place to go; "Paulette," who questions her mother's advice about growing up, posing, "What good is sun if I can't run?"; and "Robert, Who Is a Stranger to Himself."

The first time I read "Skipper" in this slim volume, I recalled my childhood—the day when one of my pet goldfish died. I wasn't terribly upset by its death but was rather taken by my Aunt Doris's advice to "flush it down the toilet." I listened and did what she said. But wouldn't the experience have been richer for me if, instead, I had been given a poem such as "Skipper" to read? Perhaps I, too, like the child in the poem, would have buried my fish beneath a tree. And perhaps I would have come to understand much sooner the value of poetry.

*Bronzeville Boys and Girls* is one book that should be in every library, available when you want and need it. And you will—time and time again.

Gwendolyn Brooks' life story is chronicled in *Report from Part One*, telling of her family background, childhood years, her " 'prentice years," marriage, children, contacts with other black writers, and her journey to Africa.

In 1962, she was invited by President John F. Kennedy, along with other leading poets, to read some of her poetry at a poetry festival at the Library of Congress in Washington, D.C. There, just prior to his death, she met Robert Frost, who offered warm praises of her work. In 1985 she was named Consultant in Poetry to the Library of Congress for 1985–1986.

On being a poet, she has stated, "I think a little more should be required of the poet than perhaps is required of the sculptor or the painter. The poet deals in words with which everyone is familiar. We all handle words. And I think the poet, if he wants to speak to anyone, is constrained to do something with those words so that they will 'mean something,' will *be* something that a reader may touch."

Now, most of her time is spent writing poetry, lecturing at colleges, and encouraging young poets. She is at work on the second volume of her autobiography plus a book of poems that she writes on scraps of paper "because I want to carry them in my address book. I'm likely to read them at a moment's notice."

**REFERENCES**

*Annie Allen.* Harper & Row, 1949.
*Bronzeville Boys and Girls.* Illustrated by Ronni Solbert. Harper & Row, 1956.
*Report from Part One.* Broadside Press, 1972.

# John Ciardi

## MUMMY SLEPT LATE AND DADDY FIXED BREAKFAST

Daddy fixed the breakfast.
He made us each a waffle.
It looked like gravel pudding.
It tasted something awful.

"Ha, ha," he said, "I'll try again.
This time I'll get it right."
But what *I* got was in between
Bituminous and anthracite.

"A little too well done? Oh well,
I'll have to start all over."
*That* time what landed on my plate
Looked like a manhole cover.

I tried to cut it with a fork:
The fork gave off a spark.
I tried the knife and twisted it
Into a question mark.

I tried it with a hack-saw.
I tried it with a torch.
It didn't even make a dent.
It didn't even scorch.

The next time Dad gets breakfast
When Mommy's sleeping late,
I think I'll skip the waffles.
I'd sooner eat the plate!

—from YOU READ TO ME, I'LL READ TO YOU

In an article, "Profile: John Ciardi" (*Language Arts*, November/December 1982, pp. 872–876), Norine Odland, Distinguished Professor of Children's Literature at the University of Minnesota, in Minneapolis, wrote:

There is magic in the poetry John Ciardi has written for children. He uses words with whimsical agility. Humor in his poems allows a child to reach for new ways to view ordinary things and places in the world. In a few lines, a Ciardi poem can move a listener from one mood to another; the words tell the reader how the poem should be read.

Born in Boston, Massachusetts, on June 24, 1916, the only son of Italian immigrant parents, John Anthony Ciardi grew up in Medford, Massachusetts, where he attended public school. His father, an insurance agent for Metropolitan Life Insurance Company, was killed in an automobile accident in 1919.

Mr. Ciardi began his higher studies at Bates College in Lewiston, Maine, but transferred to Tufts University in Boston, receiving his B.A. degree in 1938. Then, winning a scholarship to the University of Michigan, he obtained his master's degree the next year, and won the first of many awards for his poetry.

"I always wanted to be a poet," he told me. "I took all sorts of courses in English in college and graduate school," he commented. "John Holmes, a fine poet, and my teacher at Tufts, persuaded me to take poetry seriously in my sophomore year. In graduate school, Professor Roy Cowden gave me great help."

One of America's foremost contemporary poets, Mr. Ciardi, a translator of Dante's work, was an English professor at Kansas City University, Harvard, and Rutgers. After twenty years of teaching, he resigned, becoming poetry editor of *Saturday Review* from 1956 to 1972. He had also served as director of the Bread Loaf Writers' Conference at Middlebury College in Vermont, a group he was associated with for almost thirty years.

After successfully writing adult poetry for some time, he decided to write for children because they were around him.

"I wrote first for my sister's children, from about 1947 to 1953, when my wife and I were living with them. Subsequently, I wrote for my own children as they came along, then for myself. My children [John Lyle Pritchard, Myra and Benn Anthony] were in a hurry to grow up; I wasn't, so I wrote for my own childhood."

His own favorite book, *I Met a Man*, a collection of thirty-one poems, appeared in 1961. "It's my favorite because I wrote it on a first-grade vocabulary level when my daughter was in kindergarten. I wanted it to be the first book she read through, and she learned to read from it. Almost any child halfway through first grade should be able to read the first poems. Any bright child toward the end of the first grade should be able to solve the slightly added difficulties of the later poems."

He had no system of writing. "It's like lazy fishing," he once told me. "Drop a line, sit easy. If a fish bites, play it; if not, enjoy the weather!"

He wrote *The Monster Den* about his own children. "It was a way of spoofing them. Kidding with love and some restraint can be a happy relationship. We were never a somber family."

Many of his poems are spoofs of parent-child relationships. "I often write spoofs. I have written some adult poems *about* children that are *not* for them. The closest I come to pointing out the difference between poetry for children versus poetry for adults is that children's poems are *eternal*; adult poems are *mortal*."

Two of his collections, *The Man Who Sang the Sillies* and *You Read to Me, I'll Read to You*, contain such "eternal" verses as "Some Cook!" and "Mummy Slept Late and Daddy Fixed Breakfast." His last collection of children's verse was *Doodle Soup*, thirty-eight mostly humorous verses with such titles as "The Dangers of Taking Baths," "The Best Part of Going Away Is Going Away From You," and "Why Pigs Cannot Write Poems."

His works for children were based on the premise that "poetry and learning are both fun, and children are full of an enormous relish for both. My poetry is just a bubbling up of a natural foolishness, and the idea that maybe you can make language dance a bit. What is poetry? Poetry is where every line comes to rest against a white space. Being a poet is like being a musician. You get caught up in the music. You're drawn to it. So it is with language. It's an instrument and you can't stop playing."

Recipient of the 1982 NCTE Award for Excellence in Poetry for Children, he can be heard on two recordings available from Spoken Arts. On *You Read to Me, I'll Read to You,* he reads to his three children and they read back to him selections from the book of the same title. After an introduction by the poet, thirty-four poems are presented. On side 1 of *You Know Who, John J. Plenty and Fiddler Dan and Other Poems*, he reads twenty-seven poems from the book *You Know Who.* Selections include "Calling All Cowboys" and "What Someone Said When He Was Spanked on the Day Before His Birthday"—true ear-catchers for youngsters. Side 2, geared to older girls and boys, features several longer poems, including "John J. Plenty and Fiddler Dan" and "The King Who Saved Himself from Being Saved."

The poet died on March 30, 1986. Upon his death, John Frederick Nims, retired *Poetry* magazine editor, stated: "I don't know of another poet who so completely put his life into poetry. I don't know of anyone who talked about poetry in a way that made more sense or put things more strikingly . . . he was a very important influence on the poetry of our time."

**REFERENCES**

*I Met a Man.* Illustrated by Robert Osborn. Houghton Mifflin, 1961.

*The Man Who Sang the Sillies.* Illustrated by Edward Gorey. J. B. Lippincott, 1961; also in paperback.

*You Read to Me, I'll Read to You.* Illustrated by Edward Gorey. J. B. Lippincott, 1962; also in paperback.

*You Know Who.* Illustrated by Edward Gorey. J. B. Lippincott, 1964.

*The Monster Den.* Illustrated by Edward Gorey. J. B. Lippincott, 1966.

*Doodle Soup.* Illustrated by Merle Nacht. Houghton Mifflin, 1985.

# Lucille Clifton

---

### 5

After a little bit of time
Everett Anderson says, "I knew
my daddy loved me through and through,
and whatever happens when people die,
love doesn't stop, and
neither will I."

—from EVERETT ANDERSON'S GOODBYE

Lucille Clifton was born in Depew, New York, on June 27, 1936. She attended Harvard University and Fredonia State Teacher's College. Her own "roots" are detailed in her eloquent memoir, *Generations*, a eulogy to her parents.

In addition to four volumes of adult poetry, she has created several picture books, including her best known "Everett Anderson" verses. The entire series tenderly portrays black experiences—poems telling about six-year-old Everett Anderson who lives in Apartment 14A. Everett plays in the rain, is afraid of the dark, feels lonely at times, and wonders. In 1970, Everett was "born" in *Some of the Days of Everett Anderson*, which she wrote because she "wanted to write something about a little boy who was like the boys my children might know, for my children and others."

Six additional titles appeared featuring the delightful Everett. In 1983, the last of the series, *Everett Anderson's Goodbye*, gave a touching portrait of the young boy trying to come to grips with his father's death. In a sparse amount of words we follow the child's struggle through the five stages of grief—denial, anger, bargaining, depression, and acceptance.

In an article, "Profile: Lucille Clifton" (*Language Arts*, February 1982, pp. 160–167), Rudine Sims, Professor of Education at Amherst in Massachusetts, interviewed the poet. Therein Mrs. Clifton stated:

I never thought about being a writer. I didn't know it was something you could do. I never heard of Gwen Brooks. The only writers I saw were the portraits they have in school. Like Longfellow. Not even Whitman. They were all bearded men —white, dead, old—and none of that applied to me. It was something that never occurred to me. At first I wrote sonnets and things. You know, you write the kinds of things you read. Then I started writing in a simpler kind of voice, and it didn't seem to me to even be real poetry because it didn't look like the kind of poetry I saw.

In August 1979, Mrs. Clifton was named Poet Laureate of the State of Maryland. Currently, she lives and teaches in California. She has six children—Frederica, Channing, Gillian, Graham, Alexia, and Sidney.

"I had six kids in seven years, and when you have a lot of children you tend to attract children, and you see so many kids, you get ideas from that," she told Rudine Sims.

And I have such a good memory from my own childhood, my own time. I have great respect for young people; I like them enormously.

I didn't read children's books that much because there weren't that many, or if there were I didn't know about them. But my family were great readers, despite the fact that neither graduated from elementary school. Both my parents read books all the time, so I grew up loving books. The love of words was something that was natural to me. My mother even wrote poems. And I grew up reading everything I could get my hands on. I was one of those cereal box readers.

Though Everett Anderson is not part of the household, Mrs. Clifton confessed to me that sometimes she feels he does exist. Occasionally, she has even set a place for him at the dinner table!

At the end of Mrs. Clifton's *Generations*, she writes:

Things don't fall apart. Things hold. Lines connect in thin ways that last and last and lives become generations made out of pictures and words just kept . . . our lives are more than the days in them, our lives are our line and we go on.

*Her* lines will continue to go on—and on.

**REFERENCES**

*Some of the Days of Everett Anderson.* Illustrated by Evaline Ness. Henry Holt, 1970; also in paperback.
*Generations.* Random House, 1976.
*Everett Anderson's Goodbye.* Illustrated by Ann Grifalconi. Henry Holt, 1983.

# Beatrice Schenk de Regniers

*KEEP A POEM IN YOUR POCKET*

Keep a poem in your pocket
and a picture in your head
and you'll never feel lonely
at night when you're in bed.

The little poem will sing to you
the little picture bring to you
a dozen dreams to dance to you
at night when you're in bed.

So—
Keep a picture in your pocket
and a poem in your head
and you'll never feel lonely
at night when you're in bed.

—from SOMETHING SPECIAL

Beatrice Schenk de Regniers' books for children run the gamut from stories about giants to poems about cats and pockets.

"All my books have their own way of working themselves out from me, but most of them begin in a meadow," she told me. "I take my notebook and my pencil and go away, alone, to a place where I can be physically in touch with nature. I wander through the countryside and work in a kind of meadow trance.

"I had a difficult time getting away when I worked on *Something Special*, so I got up every morning at five thirty and worked until seven thirty A.M. The dining room table was my meadow for this book. You know how still everything is between five and seven? The house is so quiet."

Her scenery is her apartment furnishings. She and her husband, Francis, live in a stylish New York City apartment in the West Fifties. Plants and flowers sprout all over; modern paintings adorn the walls, along with works by such well-known illustrators as Irene Haas and Beni Montresor. One has the feeling of visiting a carefully selected museum showing. A large fireplace in the living room adds to the atmosphere of a country place right in the middle of one of New York's most bustling areas.

"I'm in a little house of my own here," she stated, borrowing the idea from her book *A Little House of Your Own*, which is her "autobiography." "I love it here. We're only a block from Central Park [where she rides her bicycle], and we're within walking distance of Lincoln Center. Many summer nights have been spent just sitting at the Center and watching the choreography of the fountains in front of the Metropolitan Opera House."

She has had a lifelong interest in dance. "I love to dance!" she exclaimed. Her face lighted up as if in a spotlight. "In my reincarnation I'm going to be a choreographer. My writing is a kind of dance. I want all my books to have a pace, a movement, like a ballet."

The overture to Mrs. de Regniers' life began on August 16, 1914, in Lafayette, Indiana. At the age of seven, she moved with her parents to Crawfordsville, Indiana, where she lived "a wonderful kind of free childhood, where I could gather violets, live in a tree, walk in the woods—*be!*"

She attended the University of Chicago and Winnetka Graduate Teachers College. She has traveled extensively both on her own and as a welfare officer with the United Nations Relief and Rehabilitation Administration (UNRRA) during World War II. After the war, she served as educational materials director of the American Heart Association. "I got sick of health," she commented, "so I left!"

Her first children's book was *The Giant Story*, illustrated by Maurice Sendak. She knows why she did each book and how they came from within her.

About *May I Bring a Friend?*, illustrated by Beni Montresor, winner of the 1965 Caldecott Medal, she told me, "As gay as *May I Bring a Friend?* is, I wept all the while I was writing it. We had two Siamese–alley cats for ten and eleven years. One of the cats died of cancer; he died in my arms. A year later the other was dying, and I was so distressed I decided to write to focus on something else. The book was done in an almost mechanized way. I said, 'I'll write and not think of cats. I'll write verse because it demands concentration.' I didn't know what I was going to write about, but when the book was finished, oddly enough it was filled with animals—but no cats. Beni and I worked closely together on the book. We would call one another and discuss situations on the phone. I wasn't the least bit surprised that it won the Caldecott Medal. I expect all the illustrators of my books to win it; they are all great." (And three of them have—Maurice Sendak, Beni Montresor, and Nonny Hogrogian.)

Her book *Something Special* is just that. The ten rhymes delight young children. "What Did You Put in Your Pocket?" is a chant; "If We Walked on Our Hands" is gay nonsense about a "mixed up/fixed up/topsey turvey/sit-u-a-tion"; "Little Sounds" gives insight into how wonderful our sense of hearing can be.

Other volumes of her poetry include *It Does Not Say Meow*, nine original verses; *A Bunch of Poems and Verses*; *This Big Cat and Other Cats I've Known*; and *So Many Cats*.

For many years, Mrs. de Regniers was the editor of The Lucky Book Club for Scholastic, Inc.

**REFERENCES**

*The Giant Story.* Illustrated by Maurice Sendak. Harper & Row, 1953.

*A Little House of Your Own.* Illustrated by Irene Haas. Harcourt Brace Jovanovich, 1954.

*Something Special.* Illustrated by Irene Haas. Harcourt Brace Jovanovich, 1958.

*May I Bring a Friend?* Illustrated by Beni Montresor. Atheneum, 1964.

*It Does Not Say Meow.* Illustrated by Paul Galdone. Clarion, 1972; available in paperback.

*A Bunch of Poems and Verses.* Illustrated by Mary Jane Dunton. Clarion, 1977.

*This Big Cat and Other Cats I've Known.* Illustrated by Alan Daniel. Crown, 1985.

*So Many Cats.* Illustrated by Ellen Weiss. Clarion, 1986.

# Aileen Fisher

---

## OUT IN THE DARK AND DAYLIGHT

Out in the dark and daylight,
under a cloud or tree,

Out in the park and play light,
out where the wind blows free,

Out in the March or May light,
with shadows and stars to see,

Out in the dark and daylight . . .
that's where I like to be.

—from OUT IN THE DARK
AND DAYLIGHT

61

Aileen Fisher's first book of poetry, *The Coffee-Pot Face*, was published in 1933. Since that date, she has done numerous original collections as well as longer narrative poems dealing with nature, such as *Listen, Rabbit*; *I Stood Upon a Mountain*; and *Like Nothing at All*.

Since the early 1930s, Aileen Fisher, recipient of the 1978 NCTE Award for Excellence in Poetry for Children, has touched thousands upon thousands of boys and girls with her warm, wise, and wonderful writing.

She was born in, and grew up around, the little town of Iron River, on the Upper Peninsula of Michigan near the Wisconsin border. She told me about her early childhood years.

"I was a lucky child. When I was four years old my father had a serious bout with pneumonia. This made him decide to give up his business in Iron River and more or less retire to the country. He bought forty acres near Iron River and built the big, square, white house where I grew up. We called the place High Banks because it was on a high bank above the river—always red with water pumped from the iron mines. Still, the river was good to wade in, swim in, fish in, and skate on in winter. When I was young, there was still quite a bit of logging nearby, and my brother and I used to follow the iced logging roads. There was a big landing for the logs on the railroad about a mile from our house. We had all kinds of pets—cows, horses, and chickens. And we had a big garden each summer. I loved it. I have always loved the country.

"On my eighth birthday a sister was born. I took immediate charge of her because she was, after all, *my* birthday present. Six years later, another sister came along, but by that time my brother and I were almost ready to go to college.

"I went to the University of Chicago for two years, then transferred to the School of Journalism at the University of Missouri. After receiving my degree in 1927, I worked in a little theater during the summer, then went back to Chicago to look for a job. I found one—as an assistant in a placement bureau for women journalists! That fall, I sold my first poem to *Child Life* magazine, a nine-lined verse entitled 'Otherwise.' "

Ms. Fisher commented on the development of the poem, one that remains among her most frequently reprinted works.

"My aim in Chicago was to save every single cent I was able to so I could escape back to the country life I loved and missed. I had to be economical, so I took a cheap, dark, first-floor room in a third-rate hotel on Chicago's South Side. It had only one window, and that opened onto a cement area that led to an alley. Across the panes were bars to keep prowlers away!

"The room was furnished with a steel cot, a wardrobe badly in need of varnish, two chairs, a kitchen table I used as a desk.

"Coming in from work one evening I jotted down some lines I had thought about on the walk from the station. I then went out to dinner at a small, nearby restaurant where I could get a meal for sixty cents. When I got back to my room I liked the nine lines I hurriedly wrote and sent them off, along with several other verses, to Marjorie Burrows, then editor of *Child Life.*

"I always liked to write verse. My mother had quite a flair for versifying, and I was sort of brought up on it. Mother was an ex-kindergarten teacher, which was fortunate for her offspring."

Ms. Fisher continued writing poems for children, and for five years continued working in Chicago, wondering every day how she might get back to the country. In 1932, she adamantly decided to get out of the city and settled in Colorado. The following year her first book was published, *The Coffee-Pot Face,* a collection of verses, about half of which had previously been published in *Child Life.* The volume was selected as a Junior Literary Guild selection.

Ms. Fisher describes her work habits as always being quite methodical.

"I try to be at my desk four hours a day, from eight A.M. to noon. Ideas come to me out of experience and from reading and remembering. I usually do a first draft by hand. I can't imagine writing verse on a typewriter, and for years I wrote nothing but verse so I formed the habit of thinking with a pencil or pen in hand. I usually rework my material, sometimes more, sometimes less. I never try out my ideas on children, except on the child I used to know—me! Fortunately, I remember pretty well what I used to like to read, think about, and do. I find even today that if I write something I like, children are pretty apt to like it, too. I guess what it amounts to is I never grew up."

Ms. Fisher is tall, solidly built, and "decidedly a country person, addicted to jeans and slacks." Currently, she lives in Boulder, Colorado, at the foot of Flagstaff Mountain.

"My house is well back from the street; skunks and raccoons live nearby, and one year I even found a baby porcupine in my yard. In the winter, deer come right down into this end of town, and I often see groups of them on the side of Flagstaff. I must say city living could be a lot worse! But, of course, I can never forget those wonderful years on the ranch when we lived without electricity, central heating, and automatic water. The wood I chopped, the coal I carried, the ashes I took out! I am afraid I am becoming one of those city softies, but those are all pleasant memories, and I'd do it all over again if I had the chance to."

The ranch she refers to is two hundred acres about a twenty-minute drive from Boulder. She designed and built the house with the help of a friend.

"When we moved to the ranch in 1937, no electricity was available, so we organized our lives very happily without it. When we could finally have it, we didn't want it!

"I'm not or ever was a bit gadget-minded. My favorite possessions are books, and interesting pieces of Colorado wood from the timberline, which have been enhanced by wood rasp, chisel, and some sandpaper.

"My pleasures in life are found through animals, especially dogs, mountain climbing, hiking, working with wood, unorthodox gardening, a few people in small doses, and *reading.* I like centrality in my life and peace and quiet, which means that I avoid commercialized excitement, cities, traffic, polluted air, noise, confusion, travel, crowds, and airports. For me early morning on a mountain trail is the height of bliss."

Recently, with a partner, she ventured into real estate, buying a few old houses and restoring them. "It's been fun," she said. "I am sure I was a carpenter in my last incarnation."

Like many authors, Ms. Fisher receives much fan mail, revealing that boys and girls want to know details about everything, "especially pets, weather, electricity, mountains, and cabins."

Regarding poetry, her first love, she stated, "Poetry is a rhythmical piece of writing that leaves the reader feeling that life is a little richer than before, a little more full of wonder, beauty, or just plain delight."

A *must* for classrooms is her bounty of 140 poems, *Out in the Dark and Daylight*, reflecting various moods of the four seasons. Recent titles include *Rabbits, Rabbits* and *When It Comes to Bugs.*

She can be heard reading thirty-one of her poems on the recording *Poetry Parade* (Weston Woods).

**REFERENCES**

*The Coffee-Pot Face.* McBride Company, 1933.
*Listen, Rabbit.* Illustrated by Symeon Shimin. T. Y. Crowell, 1964.

*Like Nothing at All.* Illustrated by Leonard Weisgard. T. Y. Crowell, 1969.

*I Stood Upon a Mountain.* Illustrated by Blair Lent. T. Y. Crowell, 1979.

*Out in the Dark and Daylight.* Illustrated by Gail Owens. Harper & Row, 1980.

*Rabbits, Rabbits.* Illustrated by Gail Niemann. Harper & Row, 1983.

*When It Comes to Bugs.* Illustrated by Chris and Bruce Degen. Harper & Row, 1986.

# Robert Frost

---

## *THE PASTURE*

I'm going out to clean the pasture spring;
I'll only stop to rake the leaves away
(And wait to watch the water clear, I may):
I sha'n't be gone long. —You come too.

I'm going out to fetch the little calf
That's standing by the mother. It's so young
It totters when she licks it with her tongue.
I sha'n't be gone long. —You come too.

—from THE POETRY OF ROBERT FROST

Robert Lee Frost, born in San Francisco, California, on March 26, 1874, did not attend school until he was about twelve years old, and never read a book until he was fourteen.

In *Interviews with Robert Frost*, by Edwin Connery Lathem, a Frost scholar and friend of the poet, the subject commented, ". . . after I had read my first book a new world opened up for me, and after that I devoured as many of them as I could lay my hands on. But by the time I was fifteen, I was already beginning to write verses."

In 1885, after his father's death, he moved with his mother and sister to Lawrence, Massachusetts, his father's birthplace, where in 1890 his first poem, "La Noche Triste," was published in the school paper. Upon graduation from Lawrence High School, he was co-valedictorian. The other student to win this honor was Eleanor White, who became his wife in 1895.

Mr. Frost attended Dartmouth College, but left before taking term examinations to teach in his mother's private school. From 1897 to 1899 he attended Harvard University but left due to illness. After this, as he vacillated between teaching and dairy farming, he grew as a poet.

In 1912, Mr. Frost, with his wife and four children, moved to England, where his first book, *A Boy's Will*, appeared—a collection of thirty poems written between 1892 and 1912. The following year, *North of Boston*, which included his epic work "The Death of the Hired

Man," was published. Mr. Frost, at age forty, had now earned approximately $200.00 from his poetry!

When World War I broke out in 1914, he moved his family back to the United States. Here, at Grand Central Station in New York City, he noticed the *New Republic* magazine; his name and the title "The Death of the Hired Man" were on the cover. He soon found out that Henry Holt and Company was publishing his poetry in the United States; he remained with them for his entire career.

During his lifetime, honor upon honor was bestowed upon him; he was the only person ever to win four Pulitzer Prizes. His own family life, however, was filled with personal tragedies. His sister, Jeanie, became mentally ill and was institutionalized; one daughter, Marjorie, died in childbirth, a year after her marriage; his only son, Carol, committed suicide; another daughter, Irma, was hospitalized as an invalid.

An invitation to participate in the inauguration of President John F. Kennedy was a milestone in his career. Television viewers across the country witnessed an unforgettable incident on this day, January 20, 1961. When the sun's glare and some gusty wind prevented the poet from reading "The Gift Outright," published almost twenty years before the occasion in *The Witness Tree*, he put the sheet of paper in his overcoat pocket and recited the verse from memory.

On March 26, 1962, on his eighty-eighth birthday, Mr. Frost was awarded the Congressional Medal at the White House by President Kennedy. His last book, *In the Clearing*, was published that same year.

He died on January 29, 1963. Upon his death, President Kennedy said, "His death impoverishes us all; but he has bequeathed his nation a body of imperishable verse from which Americans will forever gain joy and understanding."

A biography for mature readers is *A Restless Spirit*, by Natalie S. Bober, which chronicles the poet's life and work.

For adult readers, *Frost: A Literary Life Recommended*, by William H. Pritchard, offers a biography with keen insights into the creative process of the poet and his work.

Robert Frost's poems selected for children appear in *You Come Too*, a collection of fifty-one poems, and in *A Swinger of Birches*, thirty-eight selections, also available on a cassette read by Clifton Fadiman.

In 1978, Susan Jeffers published the first picture-book version of "Stopping by Woods on a Snowy Evening"— a volume to share with all ages.

Robert Frost can be heard on two recordings: *Robert Frost in Recital*, featuring twenty-six selections preserved by The Poetry Center of the 92nd Street YM/YWHA in New York City, which recorded Mr. Frost during three readings given in 1953 and 1954; and *Robert Frost Reads "The Road Not Taken" and Other Poems*, made in his home in Cambridge, Massachusetts, in 1956, containing twenty-three selections. Both recordings are available from Caedmon.

Also available is a twenty-two-minute film, *Robert Frost's New England*, which has garnered a host of media awards, produced by Churchill Films.

## REFERENCES

*A Boy's Will.* David Nutt, 1913.

*North of Boston.* David Nutt, 1914.

*The Witness Tree.* Henry Holt, 1942.

*You Come Too: Favorite Poems for Young Readers.* Illustrated by Thomas W. Nason. Henry Holt, 1959.

*In the Clearing.* Henry Holt, 1962.

*Stopping by Woods on a Snowy Evening.* Illustrated by Susan Jeffers. Dutton, 1978.

*A Swinger of Birches: Poetry of Robert Frost for Young People.* Illustrated by Peter Koeppen. Stemmer House, 1982; also in paperback.

Bober, Natalie S. *A Restless Spirit: The Story of Robert Frost.* Atheneum, 1981.

Lathem, Edward Connery. *Interviews with Robert Frost.* Henry Holt, 1966.

——— (editor). *The Poetry of Robert Frost: The Collected Poems, Complete and Unabridged.* Henry Holt, 1969; also in paperback.

Pritchard, William H. *Frost: A Literary Life Recommended.* Oxford University Press, 1985; paperback.

# Nikki Giovanni

## WINTER

Frogs burrow the mud
snails bury themselves
and I air my quilts
preparing for the cold

Dogs grow more hair
mothers make oatmeal
and little boys and girls
take Father John's Medicine

Bears store fat
chipmunks gather nuts
and I collect books
For the coming winter

—from COTTON CANDY
ON A RAINY DAY

Nikki Giovanni, born on June 7, 1943, in Knoxville, Tennessee, named after her mother, Yolande Corneila Giovanni, was two months old when her family moved to Cincinnati, Ohio, where she currently lives—"sometimes!" She states, "I have one room in New York, three rooms in Cincinnati, and toilet privileges in Seattle, Washington."

At the age of sixteen, she entered Fisk University in Nashville, Tennessee, majoring in history, but did not graduate until eight years later. Upon graduation she did additional graduate work at several schools.

Ms. Giovanni became an assistant professor of English at Rutgers University in New Jersey. She has also held positions as an editorial consultant and columnist for *Encore*, *American*, and *Worldwide News Magazine.*

Her first book of adult poems, *Black Judgement*, was published in 1968 by Broadside Press. Indeed a broadside, this slim, thirty-six-page paperback introduced thirty-six poems. A steady stream of titles followed, each reflecting her deep involvement in the black experience.

Her first book of poetry for children was *Spin a Soft Black Song*, verses resulting from her volunteer activities for the Reading Is Fundamental program. A revised edition of the volume was published in 1985, with new illustrations and a new introduction.

*Ego-Tripping*, published in 1973, contains selected earlier works, with the addition of several new poems written especially for the volume; two of her widely antholo-gized biographical poems, "Nikki-Rosa" and "Knoxville, Tennessee," first published in *Black Judgement*, are included.

*Vacation Time*, her third book for children, appeared in 1980, containing twenty-two new verses.

"My basic philosophy about writing for children—or any other group—is that the reader is both interested and intelligent," she states. "As a lover of children's literature, I always enjoyed a good story, whether happy or sad. I think poetry, when it is most effective, tells of capturing a moment, and I make it the best I can because it's going to live.

"When I think of poems most children read, from Robert Louis Stevenson to some of the modern poets, I think of an idea being conveyed. The image is important but the idea is the heart."

A collection of autobiographical essays, *Gemini*, published in 1971, was a nominee for the National Book Award. The volume explores her own life and times with the fierce intensity of a poet and lover of life.

Nineteen seventy-eight marked her tenth year as a published author with her adult collection *Cotton Candy on a Rainy Day*. The front dust-cover flap sums up a lot of her life and philosophy:

She is a widget, a ball bearing, a tiny drop of oil, a very practical person who does what she does because that's all she can do.

She is a storyteller, believing the function of art is to com-

municate; a poet hoping that poems will help soothe the lone-
liness and fear that life itself brings.

Nikki Giovanni is *Cotton Candy on a Rainy Day.* She thinks
we all are.

She has twice been among the top ten American
women of influence and holds many honorary doctorate
degrees and keys to many cities. When President Jimmy
Carter invited the poet to join the President's Committee
on the International Year of the Child, she replied, "As
a former child, I accept."

The poet loves music and travel, especially to remote
places away from television and the telephone. She is the
mother of a grown son, Tommy.

At the end of *Gemini*, she writes:

I think we are all capable of tremendous beauty once we
decide we are beautiful or of giving a lot of love once we
understand love is possible, and of making the world over in
that image should we choose to. I really like to think a Black,
beautiful loving world is possible. I really do, I think.

The poet can be heard reading selected works for
children on the recording *The Reason I Like Chocolate*
(Folkways).

On the filmstrip set *First Choice: Poets and Poetry* (Pied
Piper), she is seen strolling the streets of New York City,
showing youngsters how the colors, sounds, and rhythms
of sidewalk musicians, vendors, and children's games can
be turned into verse.

In part 2 of the filmstrip, a workshop lesson, she shows

how students can make discoveries for themselves, including sensory descriptions to create a poem about rain or a picnic. Included are a teacher's guide, brief biographical information, and nine poems reprinted from her various works.

**REFERENCES**

*Black Judgement.* Broadside Press, 1968.
*Gemini: An Extended Autobiographical Statement on My First Twenty-Five Years of Being a Black Poet.* Bobbs-Merrill, 1971.
*Ego-Tripping and Other Poems for Young People.* Illustrated by George Ford. Lawrence Hill, 1973.
*Cotton Candy on a Rainy Day.* William Morrow, 1978.
*Vacation Time.* Illustrated by Marisabina Russo. William Morrow, 1980.
*Spin a Soft Black Song.* Illustrated by George Martins. Hill and Wang, revised edition, 1985.

# Langston Hughes

## DREAMS

Hold fast to dreams
For if dreams die
Life is a broken-winged bird
That cannot fly.

Hold fast to dreams
For when dreams go
Life is a barren field
Frozen with snow.

—from SELECTED POEMS

Langston Hughes, a multitalented personality, wrote nonfiction books for children, novels, short stories, plays, operas, operettas, newspaper columns, and a wide variety of poetry.

Mr. Hughes was born on February 1, 1902, in Joplin, Missouri. His childhood was spent shifting from one place to another, from relative to relative. His father, James Hughes, had studied law but because he was black he was refused the right to take his bar examination. Angry and fed up with Jim Crow society, he walked out of the house one day and went to Mexico. Like his father, Langston Hughes endured much racial discrimination.

He attended Central High School in Cleveland, Ohio, where an English teacher, Miss Ethel Weimer, introduced him to the work of poets, among them Carl Sandburg and Robert Frost. In his senior year, he was elected editor of the yearbook and class poet because of his contributions of poems to the school newspaper.

Mr. Hughes went to visit his father upon graduation. On a train heading south for Mexico, he wrote "The Negro Speaks of Rivers," a poem that has become one of his best-known compositions. Later, he sent the poem to Dr. W.E.B. DuBois, an early proponent of black rights, then editor of *The Crisis* magazine, a journal that spoke for an organization that had been recently founded, the National Association for the Advancement of Colored People (NAACP). Printed in *The Crisis*, it was Mr. Hughes' first poem to appear in a magazine for adult readers. The following month, "Aunt Sue's Stories" was published in *The Crisis*. The poem was written about his grandmother, with whom he had lived. She died when he was twelve years old. Mr. Hughes was soon to become known as the Black Poet Laureate, his work appearing frequently in *The Crisis*.

He began a series of wanderings, in manhood, across the world—in parts of Europe, Russia, and Africa. While traveling he worked at a potpourri of jobs, from dishwashing in a Parisian cafe to ranching on his father's Mexican ranch.

His first book of poetry, *The Weary Blues*, was published in 1926 by Alfred A. Knopf. From this date on his works regularly appeared in print, including stories about an important creation, Jesse B. Semple, later known as Simple, a philosophical character with problems typical of those faced by blacks.

Mr. Hughes completed his college education in 1929, graduating from Lincoln University, in Pennsylvania, a college for black men. Later, he moved to Harlem in New York City, where he lived until his death on May 22, 1967.

Four excellent biographies that provide additional background information include a simply written volume for younger readers, *Langston Hughes*, by Alice Walker; *Langston Hughes*, by Elisabeth P. Myers, offering an introduction to the man and his work geared to middle-grade readers; *Langston Hughes*, by Milton Meltzer; and *Langston: A Play*, by Ossie Davis.

Mr. Meltzer, a friend of Mr. Hughes', collaborated with him on two histories: *A Picture History of the Negro in America* and *Black Magic: A Pictorial History of the Negro in American Entertainment*. Mr. Meltzer's biography of the poet was a runner-up for the 1969 National Book Award.

Ossie Davis, a distinguished actor/playwright, was influenced by Mr. Hughes' poems when he first encountered them as a high school student in Waycross, Georgia. He and his wife, actress Ruby Dee, became friends of Mr. Hughes' in the years after World War II when the poet lived in Harlem. Mr. Davis' play about Mr. Hughes is set in the early 1900s, with a cast of nine characters. Excerpts from Mr. Hughes' poems are interwoven with the dialogue.

Three additional adult references are *Arna Bontemps/ Langston Hughes—Letters, 1925–1967*, selected and edited by Charles H. Nichols; *Langston Hughes: Before and Beyond Harlem*, by Faith Berry; and *The Life of Langston Hughes: I, Too, Sing America* by Arnold Rampersad.

Folkways has produced a classic recording, *The Dream Keeper and Other Poems*, featuring Langston Hughes reading selections for young people from the book of the same title. Mr. Hughes shows how his poetry developed from specific experiences and ideas in a warm, witty narrative: A trip to the waterfront inspired "Waterfront Streets"; from an old woman's memory of slavery, he created "Aunt Sue's Stories"; an idea that people should treasure their dreams became his famous poem "Dreams." The narrative by this master poet leads naturally into each of his selections; the script is biographical.

Caedmon has produced *The Poetry of Langston Hughes*, featuring fifty poems read by Ruby Dee and Ossie Davis. This recording, for mature listeners, includes four of the poet's "Madam" poems; his tribute, "Frederick Douglass: 1817–1895"; and "Juke Box Love Song." He can also be heard on *Poetry and Reflections* (also Caedmon), which includes nineteen verses with program notes by Ossie Davis.

The poet's work is widely anthologized. In his poetry he spoke of the elements and emotions of life—love, hate, aspirations, despair; he wrote in the language of today, and he does, and always will, speak for tomorrow.

While traveling around the country as a consultant to Bank Street College of Education, I had the opportunity to read his works to students of various ages and backgrounds. Two years after the poet's death, I selected poems that I had found most meaningful to children. The result became the collection *Don't You Turn Back.* Divided into four sections—"My People," "Prayers and Dreams," "Out to Sea," and "I, Too, Am a Negro"— the works represent a wide range of Mr. Hughes' life experiences, from his first published poem, "The Negro Speaks of Rivers," to "Color," which appeared in *The Panther and the Lash,* published after the poet's death.

Many eulogies have been written about the poet and his contributions to American literature. Perhaps the most tender was one created by a fourth-grade Harlem girl who knew and loved his work. She wrote this poem the day after Mr. Hughes died:

## IN MEMORIAM TO LANGSTON HUGHES

## THE USELESS PEN

A pen lay useless on the desk.
A mother once held a babe on her breast.
Where is the lad this very day?
Down by Poetry Bay they say,
Where the Poets sit and think all day
Of a way to make people happy.
Even though they are not here today
I know they meet by Poetry Bay
Trying to think of a special way
To welcome Langston to Poetry Bay.

**REFERENCES**

*The Weary Blues.* Alfred A. Knopf, 1926.

*The Dream Keeper and Other Poems.* Illustrated by Helen Sewall. Alfred A. Knopf, 1932; reissue 1986.

*Selected Poems.* Alfred A. Knopf, 1959.

*The Panther and the Lash.* Alfred A. Knopf, 1967.

Berry, Faith. *Langston Hughes: Before and Beyond Harlem.* Lawrence Hill, 1983; also in paperback.

Davis, Ossie. *Langston: A Play.* Delacorte, 1982.

Hopkins, Lee Bennett (selector). *Don't You Turn Back: Poems by Langston Hughes.* Illustrated by Ann Grifalconi. Alfred A. Knopf, 1969.

Hughes, Langston, and Milton Meltzer. *Black Magic: A Pictorial History of the Negro in American Entertainment.* Prentice-Hall, 1967.

————. *A Picture History of the Negro in America.* Crown, 1956, 1963.

Meltzer, Milton. *Langston Hughes: A Biography.* T. Y. Crowell, 1968.

Myers, Elisabeth P. *Langston Hughes: Poet of His People.* Illustrated by Russell Hoover. Garrard, 1970; Dell paperback.

Nichols, Charles A. *Arna Bontemps/Langston Hughes— Letters, 1925–1967.* Dodd, Mead, 1980.

Rampersad, Arnold. *The Life of Langston Hughes: I, Too, Sing America.* Oxford University Press, 1986.

Walker, Alice. *Langston Hughes: American Poet.* Illustrated by Don Miller. T. Y. Crowell, 1974.

# X. J. Kennedy

### BLOW-UP

Our cherry tree
Unfolds whole loads
Of pink-white bloom—
It just explodes.

For three short days
Its petals last.
Oh, what a waste.
But what a blast.

—from THE FORGETFUL
WISHING WELL

X. J. Kennedy has been preoccupied with writing since the age of nine or ten. In seventh grade he published homemade comic books on a gelatin-pan duplicator and peddled them for nickels to friends; he also became the editor-in-chief of a woman's magazine with a circulation of one—his mother!

"After college," he states, "I determined on a career as a writer for science fiction magazines, but at the end of six months had sold only two fifty-dollar stories, and so ignobly abandoned the field to Isaac Asimov. After a hitch in the Navy, then a year in Paris studying French irregular verbs on the G.I. Bill, I stumbled into college teaching and eventually became an English professor at Tufts, near Boston, Massachusetts. In 1977, I left teaching to write for a living, and have been doing so happily ever since."

His first adult book, *Nude Descending from a Staircase*, was published in 1961, followed by two more collections, and a volume of selected poems, published in England.

Until 1975, he was best known as a poet who wrote for adults. He also wrote, and continues to write, textbooks and nonfiction, including *An Introduction to Poetry*, which has been used by hundreds of thousands of college students.

For years he wrote verses for children but did little with them. One day, in the 1970s, he received a letter from Myra Cohn Livingston, who liked some of his verses from *Nude Descending from a Staircase*, and wanted to know if he had written verse for children. Via Mrs. Livingston, Margaret K. McElderry, the reknowned editor at Macmillan, heard about him and invited him to do a manuscript of verses for children. The result was *One Winter Night in August and Other Nonsense Jingles*, a rollicking collection of over fifty selections. In 1979, he created *The Phantom Ice Cream Man.*

Nineteen eighty-two marked the publication of *Did Adam Name the Vinegarroon?*, twenty-six alphabet rhymes about mythological and real beasts, featuring such creatures as "Archeopteryx," "Crocodile," "Electric Eel," and "Minotaur." Recent volumes for older readers include *Brats*, forty-two wry poems about nasty children; and *The Forgetful Wishing Well*, containing seventy poems divided into seven sections, featuring ear-catching sounds and fresh word combinations in such poems as the title poem and "Blow-up," from the section "All Around the Year."

He also co-authored *Knock at a Star* with his wife, Dorothy M. Kennedy (see pages 141–42, 159, and 161 for discussion in this volume).

Recently he went from poetry to prose to create his first work of children's fiction, *The Owlstone Crown.*

About his writing he states, "I have never been able to write what is termed free verse. I love the constant surprise one encounters in rhyming things, and the driving urge of a steady beat."

Born in Dover, New Jersey, on August 21, 1929, he

has lived for many years in Bedford, Massachusetts. The Kennedys have five children: Kathleen, David, Matthew, Daniel, and Joshua.

"Our girl and four boys, born from 1963 to 1972, are friendly but supportive critics; and while I subtly urge them to love poetry—anybody's—I have to admit that poetry is a little farther down their ladder of love objects than quarter-pounders, ice skating, electronic rock music, and *The Dukes of Hazzard.* But such is life."

The X in his name was chosen arbitrarily "to distinguish me from the better-known Kennedys!"

**REFERENCES:**

*One Winter Night in August and Other Nonsense Jingles.* Illustrated by David McPhail. Margaret K. McElderry Books/Macmillan, 1975.

*An Introduction to Poetry.* Little, Brown, fourth edition, 1978.

*The Phantom Ice Cream Man: More Nonsense Jingles.* Illustrated by David McPhail. Margaret K. McElderry Books/Macmillan, 1979.

*Did Adam Name the Vinegarroon?* Illustrated by Heidi Johanna Selig. Godine, 1982.

*Knock at a Star: A Child's Introduction to Poetry.* (Selector; with Dorothy M. Kennedy.) Illustrated by Karen Ann Weinhaus. Little, Brown, 1982; also in paperback.

*The Owlstone Crown.* Illustrated by Michele Chessare. Margaret K. McElderry Books/Macmillan, 1983.

*The Forgetful Wishing Well.* Illustrated by Monica Incisa. Margaret K. McElderry Books/Macmillan, 1985.

*Brats.* Illustrated by James Watts. Margaret K. McElderry Books/Macmillan, 1986.

# Karla Kuskin

## HUGHBERT AND THE GLUE

Hughbert had a jar of glue.
From Hugh the glue could not be parted,
At least could not be parted far,
For Hugh was glued to Hughbert's jar.
But that is where it all had started.
The glue upon the shoe of Hugh
Attached him to the floor.
The glue on Hughbert's gluey hand
Was fastened to the door,
While two of Hughbert's relatives
Were glued against each other.
His mother, I believe, was one.
The other was his brother.
The dog and cat stood quite nearby.
They could not move from there.
The bird was glued securely
Into Hughbert's mother's hair.

Hughbert's father hurried home
And loudly said to Hugh:
"From now on I would rather
That you did not play with glue."

—from DOGS & DRAGONS, TREES & DREAMS

Whenever I think of Karla Kuskin's poetry, I think of a teacher I met while conducting a week-long workshop on poetry at the University of Nevada in Las Vegas. It was there the teacher "found" Karla Kuskin and delighted in sharing her humorous poems with the class. Each day she would come into class smiling, with one of the poet's books in her hands. "Do you know 'Hughbert'?" she'd ask. Without waiting for an answer, she would read aloud a poem, then another and another.

Karla Kuskin, a native New Yorker, was born on July 19, 1932, in Manhattan. Her love of verse stemmed from her early childhood years.

"As far back as I can remember," she told me, "poetry has had a special place in my life. As a young, only child, I would make up rhymes, which my mother wrote down and read back to me. And my father wrote verse to and *for* me. As I began to learn to read I was encouraged by my parents to read aloud. I was also fortunate that in elementary school, I had teachers who read poetry aloud and who greatly influenced my love of verse. I guess I grew up with a metronomic beat inside my head, which fortunately never left."

On writing for children she states, "One of the reasons I write for children is to entice some of them into sharing my lifelong enjoyment of reading and writing as my parents and teachers did when they communicated their own love of words to me. Instead of building a fence of formality around poetry, I want to emphasize its accessi-

91

bility, the sound, rhythm, humor, the inherent simplicity. Poetry can be as natural and effective a form of self-expression as singing and shouting."

Her first book, *Roar and More*, published in 1956, began as a project for a graphic arts course she took at Yale University, from which she graduated. Many volumes of verse followed.

The poet's collection *Dogs & Dragons, Trees & Dreams* contains many of her best-loved works, which were written between 1958 and 1975 and illustrated with her lively black-and-white drawings. Through introductions and notes about her poems, she leads readers on an enchanting tour of the world of poetry, telling how and why some of the poems "happened," and how rhythm, rhyme, and word sounds combine to "stick in the mind and stay on the tongue for a lifetime."

One of these notes states:

If there were a recipe for a poem, these would be the ingredients: word sounds, rhythm, description, feeling, memory, rhyme and imagination. They can be put together a thousand different ways, a thousand, thousand . . . more. If you and I were to go at the same time to the same party for the same person, our descriptions would be different. As different as we are from each other. It is those differences that make our poems interesting.

Some of the delights in this volume include "Lewis Had a Trumpet," about a boy who is too fond of the instrument, and "Catherine," a girl who bakes a most delicious mud, sticks, and stones cake. "I Woke Up This Morning," perfect for reading, or even yelling aloud, is three pages long, telling of a young child who wakes up and can do nothing right all day; as the child's frustrations mount, so does the type on the pages, becoming larger and larger, making the poem funnier and funnier.

Of course, there is a serious side to Mrs. Kuskin's work. Many of her poems are tender, thought provoking, reflecting various ages and stages of a child's growing up.

Mrs. Kuskin has written several highly acclaimed picture books, including *A Space Story*, which weaves together a poetic science fiction tale and a factual introduction to the nighttime sky; *The Philharmonic Gets Dressed* delightfully tells how 105 members of an orchestra prepare for an eight-thirty performance.

In 1985, she created the first original collection of verses for Harper & Row's I Can Read Book series, *Something Sleeping in the Hall*, featuring twenty-eight rhymes about various animals.

The poet lives in Brooklyn, New York. She has two grown children, Nicholas and Julia. She designed the official medallion for the NCTE Award for Excellence in Poetry for Children, and received one herself in 1979.

She has stated, "The French critic Joseph Joubert once said, 'You will find poetry nowhere unless you bring some of it with you.' To which might be added that if you do bring some of it with you, you will find it everywhere."

She can be heard reading twenty-four of her poems on

the recording *Poetry Parade* (Weston Woods). Two filmstrip sets featuring the poet are *First Choice: Poets and Poetry* (Pied Piper Productions) and *Poetry Explained by Karla Kuskin* (Weston Woods).

On *Poetry Explained . . .* she describes the principal qualities that distinguish poetry from prose and also responds to the most frequent question, "Where do you get your ideas?" The selections she reads and comments on are from *Dogs & Dragons, Trees & Dreams.*

On *First Choice . . .* her life and work are presented. Part 2 of the filmstrip features a workshop lesson giving children the opportunity to be anything they might like to be—a chair or a strawberry, a curious mouse or a baseball with a headache—and to create rhymed or unrhymed verse about such topics. A teacher's guide, photograph, brief biographic information, and ten poems reprinted from her various books are also a part of the package.

**REFERENCES**

*Roar and More.* Harper & Row, 1956; also in paperback.
*A Space Story.* Illustrated by Marc Simont. Harper & Row, 1978.
*Dogs & Dragons, Trees & Dreams.* Harper & Row, 1980.
*The Philharmonic Gets Dressed.* Illustrated by Marc Simont. Harper & Row, 1982.
*Something Sleeping in the Hall.* An I Can Read Book. Harper & Row, 1985.

# Myra Cohn Livingston

### WHISPERS

Whispers
    tickle through your ear
    telling things you like to hear.

Whispers
    are as soft as skin
    letting little words curl in.

Whispers
    come so they can blow
    secrets others never know.

    —from A SONG I SANG TO YOU

Myra Cohn Livingston, the fourth recipient of the NCTE Award for Excellence in Poetry for Children (1980), is another poet who truly understands childhood experiences. A collection of her books rivals a good course in child development and/or child psychology. Her poems reflect the many moments and moods of growing up; they are filled with laughter, gaiety, curiosity, tenderness, sadness, and exuberance. Whether she is telling of whispers, or the fear of an earthquake in *The Way Things Are*, her use of words, her rhythms, and her various poetic forms evoke sharp moods and vivid mind pictures.

Mrs. Livingston began writing poetry while a freshman at Sarah Lawrence College in New York. She told me, "I turned in some poems, 'Whispers' and 'Sliding' among them, that my professor felt were for children. She urged me to submit them to *Story Parade* magazine; some were accepted. In 1946, 'Whispers' became my first published poem. I submitted a complete manuscript, *Whispers and Other Poems*, to several publishing houses; it was rejected. Margaret K. McElderry [then editor at Harcourt] urged me, however, to continue writing. Twelve years later I sent the manuscript back to her at Harcourt; it was accepted and published in 1958."

Since that time, the poet has created an enormous body of work.

Commenting on her work habits, Mrs. Livingston said,

"My work habits are erratic. Poetry comes in strange ways and never at the moment when one might think it should come. There are poems I have tried to write for twenty years that have never come out right. Others seem to come in a flash. Searching for the right form to express certain ideas takes time. I try to put poems away, once written, and take them out much later. Writing is not easy; it is very difficult work. Nothing that comes easily is worth as much as that which is worked at, which develops through the important process of growing, discarding, and keeping only the best.

"I had one class in creative writing in high school. I studied with Horace Gregory and Robert Fitzgerald, two great poets, while I was in college, and learned my craft well. I have since learned more, but in college I learned to discipline myself to write in forms. One cannot break rules without knowing what they are! I try to impart this same necessity for craft as Poet in Residence of the Beverly Hills School District and to those I teach at UCLA."

She and her husband, Richard R. Livingston, have three grown children, Josh, Jonas, and Jennie, all of whom are involved in the arts. Music is an important part of the family's life.

"One of our closest friends is our neighbor Jascha Heifetz [to whom her book *The Malibu and Other Poems* is dedicated]. This enables us to hear chamber music in the house as it should be heard and to be with many fine, outstanding musicians."

The Livingstons live in a villa built on three levels in the Santa Monica Mountains in California. Their view looks out across Beverly Hills down to the Pacific Ocean. "And on a clear day we can see Catalina!" Mrs. Livingston exclaims.

Her favorite possessions are her books. "I collect Joyce, Yeats, and Caldecott children's books as well as pictures, stories, and items that my children have done for me over the years. I also prize the pictures and prints illustrator friends have given me."

Mrs. Livingston was born on August 17, 1926, in Omaha, Nebraska, and moved to California when she was eleven years old. There she began her creative career as a musician and writer. She studied the French horn from ages twelve through twenty, becoming so accomplished that she was invited to join the Los Angeles Philharmonic Orchestra at the age of sixteen.

"I had an ideal, happy childhood. I had wise and wonderful parents who taught me that a busy creative life brings much happiness. Today, I am a woman with a very full life. I have family, friends, a home I enjoy, a career that enables me to stay home most of the time, the opportunity to live in an exciting community, teach writing, share poetry with children, share my ideas with teachers and librarians, collect books, do bookbinding, and pick flowers—and to keep the joys ahead of the troubles!"

Her first book with Margaret K. McElderry at Atheneum, *The Malibu*, appeared in 1972, followed by *The Way Things Are*, *4-Way Stop*, *A Lollygag of Limericks*, *O Sliver of Liver*, *No Way of Knowing*, *Monkey Puzzle*, *Worlds I Know*, and *Higgledy-Piggledy*.

In addition to writing poetry, she is a highly acclaimed,

indefatigable anthologist. Among her collections are *One Little Room, an Everywhere*; *O Frabjous Day!*; *Callooh! Callay!*; *Poems of Christmas*; *Christmas Poems*; *Easter Poems*; *Thanksgiving Poems*; *Poems for Jewish Holidays*.

In 1982, she teamed up with painter Leonard Everett Fisher to produce such unique works as *Celebrations*, *Sky Songs*, *Sea Songs*, *Earth Songs*, and *A Circle of Seasons*.

Her homage to the great nineteenth-century English humorist Edward Lear appears in *How Pleasant to Know Mr. Lear!*

I have not only read the poetry of Mrs. Livingston but have had the privilege of hearing her read poetry and discuss creative writing on many occasions. When she speaks, she has something important to say. Her poetry and thoughts about poetry are refreshing, contemporary, sometimes controversial. The poet's views and philosophy are expressed in other parts of this volume as well as in her professional volume *The Child as Poet*.

Nineteen eighty-four marked the publication of *A Song I Sang to You*, a rich gathering of over sixty poems culled from her earlier works between 1958 and 1969, with an introduction by David McCord.

A great deal more about her life and work appears in an entertaining, sixteen-page autobiography that appears in *Something About the Author: Autobiography Series, Volume 1* (Gale Research, 1986), edited by Adele Sarkissian.

Nonprint media presentations include *First Choice: Poets and Poetry*, in which she discusses her life and work, making viewers aware of their own varied feelings and how they can be used as a starting point for writing. In part 2 of the filmstrip, a workshop lesson helps young writers to use the couplet form to create a poem based on feelings, such as disappointment. Included are a teacher's guide, a photograph, brief biographical information, and eight poems reprinted from her various books published from 1958 through 1976. On a cassette tape, *Prelude: Selecting Poetry for Young People* (Children's Book Council), she shares thoughts and ideas with educators based on her lifelong experiences of writing poetry and working with boys and girls of all ages. *The Writing of Poetry* (Harcourt Brace Jovanovich) is a set of four boxed, full-color sound filmstrips, created by her, which includes Box A, "An Introduction to Poetry" and "The Tools of Poetry"; Box B, "Traditional Forms of Poetry" and "Open Forms of Poetry"; Box C, "The Voices of Poetry" and "Forms of Poetry: The Limerick." The package, which includes teacher's guides, would be useful to both upper elementary and junior high school students.

**REFERENCES**

*Whispers and Other Poems.* Illustrated by Jacqueline Chwast. Harcourt Brace Jovanovich, 1958.

*The Malibu and Other Poems.* Illustrated by James J. Spanfeller. Margaret K. McElderry Books/Macmillan, 1972.

*The Way Things Are and Other Poems.* Illustrated by Jenni Oliver. Margaret K. McElderry Books/Macmillan, 1974.

*One Little Room, an Everywhere: Poems of Love* (selector). Margaret K. McElderry Books/Macmillan, 1975.

*4-Way Stop and Other Poems.* Illustrated by James J. Spanfeller. Margaret K. McElderry Books/Macmillan, 1976.

*O Frabjous Day! Poetry for Holidays and Special Occasions* (selector). Margaret K. McElderry Books/Macmillan, 1977.

*Callooh! Callay!: Holiday Poems for Young Readers* (selector). Illustrated by Janet Stevens. Margaret K. McElderry Books/Macmillan, 1978.

*A Lollygag of Limericks.* Illustrated by Joseph Low. Margaret K. McElderry Books/Macmillan, 1978.

*O Sliver of Liver and Other Poems.* Illustrated by Iris Van Rynbach. Margaret K. McElderry Books/Macmillan, 1979.

*No Way of Knowing: Dallas Poems.* Margaret K. McElderry Books/Macmillan, 1980.

*Poems of Christmas* (selector). Margaret K. McElderry Books/Macmillan, 1980.

*A Circle of Seasons.* Illustrated by Leonard Everett Fisher. Holiday House, 1982.

*How Pleasant to Know Mr. Lear! Edward Lear's Selected Works with an Introduction and Notes.* Holiday House, 1982.

*Why Am I Grown So Cold? Poems of the Unknowable* (selector). Margaret K. McElderry Books/Macmillan, 1982.

*Christmas Poems* (selector). Illustrated by Trina Schart Hyman. Holiday House, 1984.

*Monkey Puzzle and Other Poems.* Illustrated by Antonio

Frasconi. Margaret K. McElderry Books/Macmillan, 1984.

*Sky Songs.* Illustrated by Leonard Everett Fisher. Holiday House, 1984.

*A Song I Sang to You.* Illustrated by Margot Tomes. Harcourt Brace Jovanovich, 1984.

*Celebrations.* Illustrated by Leonard Everett Fisher. Holiday House, 1985.

*The Child as Poet: Myth or Reality?* The Horn Book, Inc., 1985.

*Easter Poems* (selector). Illustrated by John Wallner. Holiday House, 1985.

*Thanksgiving Poems* (selector). Illustrated by Stephen Gammell. Holiday House, 1985.

*Sea Songs.* Illustrated by Leonard Everett Fisher. Holiday House, 1986.

*Worlds I Know.* Illustrated by Tim Arnold. Margaret K. McElderry Books, 1986.

*Poems for Jewish Holidays* (selector). Illustrated by Lloyd Bloom. Holiday House, 1986.

*Higgledy-Piggledy.* Illustrated by Peter Sis. Margaret K. McElderry Books, 1986.

*Earth Songs.* Illustrated by Leonard Everett Fisher. Holiday House, 1986.

# David McCord

## THIS IS MY ROCK

This is my rock,
And here I run
To steal the secret of the sun;

This is my rock,
And here come I
Before the night has swept the sky;

This is my rock,
This is the place
I meet the evening face to face.

—from ONE AT A TIME

David McCord's poetic subjects range from nature and the country to a trip to the Laundromat. He writes for both children and adults; in an interview, he commented to me on this duality.

"Poetry for children is simpler than poetry for adults. The overtones are fewer, but it should have overtones. Basically, of course, it isn't different. Children's verse sometimes turns out, or is turned out, to be not much more than doggerel—lame lines, limp rhymes, poor ideas. By and large, verse written for children is rhymed; it is nearly always brief, though an occasional poem in the hands of a skilled performer like Ogden Nash, who was a dear friend of mine, may tell a story. But poetry, like rain, should fall with elemental music, and poetry for children should catch the eye as well as the ear and the mind. It should delight, it really *has* to delight. Furthermore, poetry for children should keep reminding them, without any feeling on their part that they are being reminded, that the English language is a most marvelous and availing instrument."

Mr. McCord's first book of poetry for children, *Far and Few: Rhymes of Never Was and Always Is*, appeared in 1952, twenty-five years after his first book of poems for adults was published.

In 1977, the year he became the first recipient of the NCTE Award for Excellence in Poetry for Children, *One at a Time: His Collected Poems for the Young*, was published, a 494-page volume of verse containing works from seven earlier titles. The volume features an introduction by the poet and a very useful subject index. Beloved works such as "Every Time I Climb a Tree," "The Star in the Pail," "This Is My Rock," and "Away and Ago" are contained in this treasury.

Recent offerings include *Speak Up: More Rhymes of the Never Was and Always Is*, a volume of forty poems; *All Small*, featuring twenty-five previously published "small" poems; and a reissue of *The Star in the Pail*, twenty-six poems on subjects ranging from the seashore to the woods to the dentist's office.

Mr. McCord was born on November 15, 1897, near New York's Greenwich Village. He grew up on Long Island, in Princeton, New Jersey, and in Oregon; he was an only child.

"Long Island was all fields and woods when I was a boy," he told me. "We lived next door to a poultry farm and not far from the ocean. My love of nature began there. When I was twelve I went with my father and mother to live on a ranch in the south of Oregon on the wild Rogue River. This was frontier country then; no electric lights, oil, or coal heat. We pumped all our water out of a deep well and pumped it by hand. I didn't go to school for three years, but I learned the life of the wilderness, something about birds, animals, and wildflowers, trees and geology, and self-reliance. I learned to weather seasons of drought and weeks of steady rain. I sometimes panned gold for pocket money—a very pleasing and exciting art once you can control it! I learned to recognize a few of the constellations and to revere the nighttime sky—Orion is still my favorite skymark! I saw and experienced the terror of a forest fire. I can honestly say that I was a pretty good shot with a rifle, but I have never aimed at a living thing since I was fifteen. My love for all life is far too deep for that."

As a child, Mr. McCord was stricken with malaria. Recurring bouts of fever kept him out of school a great deal. This, however, did not stop him from graduating with high honors from Lincoln High School in Portland, Oregon, and from Harvard College in 1921. Harvard, thereafter, became an integral part of his life. Prior to his retirement in 1963, Mr. McCord spent well over forty years at the university, serving in many capacities, but principally as alumni editor and fund raiser. In 1956, Harvard conferred on him the first honorary degree of Doctor of Humane Letters it ever granted. Then-Senator John F. Kennedy received his LL.D. at that same commencement.

The poet told me how he entered the field of children's poetry.

"Two years after I finished my master's degree in English at Harvard—I had previously studied to become a physicist—I wrote a number of poems for children. One was published in the then *Saturday Review of Literature* and got into some anthologies. I seemed to know instinctively that to write for the young I had to write for myself. I write out of myself, about things I did as a boy, about things that are fairly timeless as subjects. I do not believe that one can teach the art of writing. You are born with the urge for it or you are not. Only the hardest self-discipline and considerable mastery of self-criticism will get you anywhere.

"Children still love words, rhythm, rhyme, music, games. They climb trees, skate, swim, swing, fish, explore, act, ride, run, and love snow and getting wet all over; they make things and are curious about science. They love humor and nonsense and imaginary conversation with imaginary things. I pray that I am never guilty of talking down to boys and girls. I try to remember that they are closer to the sixth sense than we who are older.

"Sometimes poems come to me full-blown—nonsense verses in particular. More often I work at them, rewriting for choice of words and smoothness. I never use an unusual word unless I can place it as a key word so that it will make the reader look it up. Poems should open new horizons. They are vistas—familiar as well as strange.

"One of my best high-school teachers once told us, 'Never let a day go by without looking on three beautiful things.' I have tried to live up to that and have found it isn't difficult. The sky in all weathers is, for me, the first of these three things."

He paints watercolor landscapes and has had several individual shows. He was once an avid amateur wireless operator and holds a 1915 first-grade amateur wireless operator's license. Mr. McCord remembers when he heard on a pocket set he had made "one of the original experiments in what we call radio broadcasting—a man playing the banjo!"

Colleagues and critics have showered praise upon his work. Myra Cohn Livingston stated, "[He] has produced a body of work which ranks highest among all poetry for children in this country." Howard Nemerov commented, "It's a rare and wonderful poet who can delight equally . . . the listening child and the reading parent." Clifton Fadiman stated, "He is both an acrobat of language and an authentic explorer of the child's inner world."

In 1983, Simmons College in Boston, Massachusetts, presented him with a Doctor of Children's Literature degree. The citation for the degree reads:

. . . as a poet who has dedicated your life to the creation of poetry which opens the ears of children to the nuances of language and to the splendors of the world which language represents, you have spoken in a unique voice. You have brought to bear upon your work your long and thorough investigation of and fascination with the natural world, the social world, the world of the intellect, and the world of the imagination. Through your writing you have contributed to excellence in literature for children; through your teaching and speaking you have supported the urgent need for such excellence to be available to children. You have helped awaken adults to the sounds of the child's world. With the soul of a naturalist and with the gift of the poet, you have said, 'the world begins in the sweep of eye,/With the wonder of all of it more or less/In the last hello and the first goodbye.' You have conveyed this understanding to adults and to children. The poet John Ciardi has said, 'One is too few of [you] and there is, alas, no second.' It is with great pride that we award you the degree of Doctor of Children's Literature.

Mr. McCord can be heard reading twenty-three of his selected works on the recording *Poetry Parade* (Weston Woods).

On the sound filmstrip *First Choice: Poets and Poetry* (Pied Piper Productions), he discusses his life and work, treating viewers to such beloved poems as "The Grasshopper" and "Every Time I Climb a Tree." A workshop lesson with the poet suggests two topics for writing a poem—a conversation between inanimate objects and writing about being a seagull or an eagle.

**REFERENCES**

*Far and Few: Rhymes of Never Was and Always Is.* Illustrated by Henry B. Kane. Little, Brown, 1952.

*One at a Time: His Collected Poems for the Young.* Illustrated by Henry B. Kane. Little, Brown, 1977.

*Speak Up: More Rhymes of the Never Was and Always Is.* Illustrated by Marc Simont. Little, Brown, 1980.

*All Small.* Illustrated by Madelaine Gill Linden. Little, Brown, 1986; also available in paperback.

*The Star in the Pail.* Illustrated by Marc Simont. Little, Brown. Reissued, 1986; also in paperback.

# Eve Merriam

## A LAZY THOUGHT

There go the grownups
To the office,
To the store.
Subway rush,
Traffic crush;
Hurry, scurry,
Worry, flurry.

No wonder
Grownups
Don't grow up
Any more.

It takes a lot
Of slow
To grow.

—from JAMBOREE

Eve Merriam is a poet, anthologist, playwright, and theater director who writes for all ages. Her play *The Club* received an Obie Award. Most of her poetry for adults is concerned with her major life interests—social and political satire, and the status of women in modern society. She lives in the heart of Greenwich Village's West Side on one of Manhattan's busiest streets.

"I love it here," she says. "I find the ethnic variety of New York thrilling. And everyone is somehow larger than life, so when things go wrong here, they seem worse than they would be anywhere else. People almost take pride in having to cope."

She has two grown sons, Guy and Dee Michel. Guy, an illustrator, provided the artwork for her book of verse *The Birthday Cow*, and did the dust jacket for another, *Rainbow Writing*. Dee is a student of linguistics.

Ms. Merriam, a petite woman, filled with vim and vigor, was born in Germantown, a suburb of Philadelphia, Pennsylvania, on July 19, 1916.

"I remember growing up surrounded by beautiful birch trees, dogwood trees, and rock gardens. I enjoyed watching birds and just walking through the woods. My mother always had a great feeling for nature and gardening. I probably inherited it from her," she commented.

She left Pennsylvania to come to New York City to do graduate work at Columbia University.

"I wanted to get away from home. I wanted to meet poets and be in New York, the literary mecca. I was a born poet. While in school I had my poetry published in various school publications. I began studying for my master's degree, but one day, while taking a walk across the George Washington Bridge, I decided *not* to walk back to Columbia. I quit my studies and decided to find a job. It seemed like a good idea—but what could a poet do? I remembered reading somewhere that Carl Sandburg once worked in advertising, so I would, too. I got a job as an advertising copywriter on Madison Avenue and progressed to become a fashion editor for glamour magazines."

While working full time, she continued to write poetry. "When my first poem was published in a poetry magazine, I could have been run over!" she exclaimed. "It was in a little magazine printed on butcher paper, but it was gold to me!"

In the 1960s, she created a trilogy of books—*Catch a Little Rhyme, It Doesn't Always Have to Rhyme*, and *There Is No Rhyme for Silver*. In 1984, *Jamboree: Rhymes for All Times* appeared, bringing together many of her verses from this earlier trilogy as well as those in *Out Loud*, in a paperback edition. Divided into five sections, *Jamboree* features sixty poems with an introduction by Nancy Larrick, a long-time friend. In 1986, *A Sky Full of Poems*, a second paperback volume, appeared, with seventy-six selections culled from earlier volumes.

About poetry, she states, "I find it difficult to sit still when I hear poetry or read it out loud. I feel a stinging all over, particularly in the tips of my fingers and in my toes, and it just seems to go right from my mouth all the way through my body. It's like a shot of adrenaline or oxygen when I hear rhymes and word play. Word play is really central for me. I try to give young people a sense of the sport and the playfulness of language, because I think it's like a game. There is a physical element in reading poetry out loud; it's like jumping rope or throwing a ball. If we can get teachers to read poetry, lots of it, out loud to children, we'll develop a generation of poetry readers; we may even have some poetry writers, but the main thing, we'll have language appreciators.

"Writing poetry is trying to get a fresh look at something—all poetry is. It's a matter of seeking out sense memories and trying to recapture the freshness of the first time you've experienced things. A poem is very much like you, and that is quite natural, since there is a rhythm in your own body—in your pulse, in your heart beat, in the way you breathe, laugh, or cry, in the very way you speak. What can a poem do? Just about everything."

Recent volumes of her poetry are *A Word or Two with You* and *Blackberry Ink.*

Upon receiving the 1981 NCTE Award for Excellence in Poetry for Children, she offered this advice to aspiring poets of all ages.

"Read a lot. Sit down with anthologies and decide which pleases you. Copy out your favorites in your own handwriting. Buy a notebook and jot down images and descriptions. Be specific; use all the senses. Use your whole body as you write. It might even help sometime to stand up and move with your words. Don't be afraid of copying a form or convention, especially in the beginning. And, to give yourself scope and flexibility, remember: It doesn't *always* have to rhyme."

Eve Merriam can be heard on the recording *Catch a Little Rhyme: Poems for Activity Time* (Caedmon), performing a selection of poems that invite children to respond both verbally and with their whole bodies. Twenty poems are recited from various titles, including *Catch a Little Rhyme* and *There Is No Rhyme for Silver.* Among the delights are "What in the World?" "Alligator on the Escalator," "Mean Song," and "A Yell for Yellow," all of which are included in *Jamboree.*

On the sound filmstrip *First Choice: Poet and Poetry* (Pied Piper Productions), she shows students how to have fun with words. Part 2 of the filmstrip offers a dual workshop lesson—one, an introduction to nonsense words, identifying and using them in a poem; two, an introduction of comparisons via the use of similes. Included are a teacher's guide, a photograph, brief biographical information, and ten poems selected from various books.

On the cassette *Prelude: Sharing Poetry with Children* (Children's Book Council), she offers ways to both share and read poetry aloud.

**REFERENCES**

*There Is No Rhyme for Silver.* Illustrated by Joseph Schindelman. Atheneum, 1962.

*It Doesn't Always Have to Rhyme.* Illustrated by Malcolm Spooner. Atheneum, 1964.

*Catch a Little Rhyme.* Illustrated by Imero Gobbato. Atheneum, 1966.

*Out Loud.* Illustrated by Harriet Sherman. Atheneum, 1973.

*Rainbow Writing.* Illustrated by John Nez. Atheneum, 1976.

*The Birthday Cow.* Illustrated by Guy Michel. Alfred A. Knopf, 1978.

*A Word or Two with You: New Rhymes for Young Readers.* Illustrated by John Nez. Atheneum, 1981.

*Jamboree: Rhymes for All Times.* Illustrated by Walter Gaffney-Kessell. Dell paperback, 1984.

*Blackberry Ink.* Illustrated by Hans Wilhelm. William Morrow, 1985.

*A Sky Full of Poems.* Illustrated by Walter Gaffney-Kessell. Dell paperback, 1986.

# Lilian Moore

---

## *FOGHORNS*

The foghorns moaned
    in the bay last night
  so sad
  so deep
I thought I heard the city
    crying in its sleep.

—from SOMETHING NEW BEGINS

In 1967, Atheneum published Lilian Moore's first book of poems, *I Feel the Same Way*; two years later *I Thought I Heard the City* appeared.

She commented to me, "I think I wrote most of the poems in *I Feel the Same Way* on my way to work each morning. I think of them as my subway songs. Often when I seemed to be staring vacantly at subway ads, I was working intensely on a new idea. And sometimes when it didn't come off, I put it to bed at night, with a profound faith in my unconscious where the special truth I'm seeking usually begins."

Ms. Moore was born in New York on March 17th, St. Patrick's Day.

"Did you know that they have a parade on that day?" she jests. "I feel very modest about it! It's been a birth-date I have always enjoyed because this green holiday trumpets the coming of all greenery of spring and summer. Spring, since childhood, has always been a season of hope to me."

She attended public schools in New York, went to Hunter College, and did graduate work at Columbia University.

"I studied Elizabethan literature," she stated. "I wanted to teach Christopher Marlowe to college freshmen!"

She began teaching in New York City and, due to her skill in working with children who could not read, became a staff member of the Bureau of Educational Research. Here, she worked in reading clinics, wrote professional materials, trained teachers, and did research into the reading problems of elementary school children.

"When did I become a writer? Why, I can't remember when I didn't in some way think of myself as one. One of my earliest memories is of sitting on a big metal box, outside a hardware store on the street where I lived. There was a group of children around me—the friends with whom I went roller skating and sledding—and there I was telling a series of yarns. I can still remember saying, 'To be continued tomorrow!' I wrote the plays I put on in the summers I worked as a camp counselor, and of course, I guess like everyone else, I had half a novel in my drawer that it took me years to bring myself to throw out."

It was while working with youngsters who needed special help in reading that Ms. Moore began to write for children.

"I had been identified for a long time with what are called easy-to-read materials. It's true I learned from the children the basic difference between dense and open material, but I never understood why people thought that easy-to-read material for children had to be clunky and dull. As an editor, I found out later that what I sensed was true; writers often use too many words. On their way to independence in reading, young children often need easy material, sometimes for only a very short time."

Beginning in 1957, for many years she was the editor of Arrow Book Club at Scholastic, Inc., pioneering the development of the club for readers in grades four through six.

"This was one of the most satisfying things I ever did, helping to launch the *first* quality paperback book program for elementary school children throughout the United States. It was a job that brought together my experience as a teacher, my interest in children's books, my work as a writer, and my downright pleasure in the endearing middle-grader. Imagine making it possible for these youngsters to choose and buy good books for the price of comic books! It was years before I could even simmer down. Talking to me about Arrow Book Club is like taking a cork out of a bottle. Even now I remember the endless, wonderful letters from children and teachers. They made it clear we were irrigating a drought area and raising a whole new crop of readers. Whatever I may have contributed to this program was due in part to my almost total recall of the children I had known and taught. They seemed to haunt me and were specters at my side, vigorously approving or disapproving books we chose for them."

Currently, she lives in Kerhonkson, in upstate New York, with her husband, Sam Reavin. She has one grown son, Jonathan.

"I have had the best of both worlds," she says. "I grew up in an exciting city, and now I live on this lovely farm. From time to time, Sam, ex-farmer, writes a children's book, and I, an ex-city woman born and bred, drive the tractor."

In 1982 appeared a volume of her new and selected poems, *Something New Begins*, which includes fifteen new poems as well as poems selected from six earlier collections published between 1967 and 1980. The sampling is wonderful, combining her city/country living, citing images of foghorns in the bay, reflections through store windowpanes, pigeons who never sing, country scenes of chestnuts falling, a Virginia creeper that "reaches out and/roots and/winds/around a tree," and an "Encounter" with a deer.

With Judith Thurman, she compiled *To See the World Afresh*, an anthology of poems giving insight into the earth, creatures of the earth, humans and their poetry. "Section notes" and an index are appended.

The anthology *Go with the Poem* contains some ninety poems divided into ten sections selected with middle-graders in mind. Poems about sports, animals, the city, and more appear by such twentieth-century masters as Lucille Clifton, John Updike, Ted Hughes, and May Swenson.

Lilian Moore is the sixth recipient of the NCTE Excellence in Poetry for Children Award (1985).

**REFERENCES**

*I Feel the Same Way.* Illustrated by Robert Quackenbush. Atheneum, 1969.

*I Thought I Heard the City.* Illustrated by Mary Jane Dunton. Atheneum, 1969.

*To See the World Afresh.* Co-edited with Judith Thurman. Atheneum, 1974.

*Go with the Poem* (selector). McGraw-Hill, 1979.

*Something New Begins.* Illustrated by Mary Jane Dunton. Atheneum, 1982.

# Jack Prelutsky

## *A SNOWFLAKE FELL*

A snowflake fell into my hand,
a tiny, fragile gem,
a frosty crystal flowerlet
with petals, but no stem.

I wondered at the beauty
of its intricate design,
I breathed, the snowflake vanished,
but for moments, it was mine.

—from IT'S SNOWING! IT'S SNOWING!

Jack Prelutsky, prolific writer of light verse, was born in Brooklyn, New York, on September 8, 1940, attended New York City public schools, and graduated from the High School of Music and Art in New York, where he studied voice. After a brief period at Hunter College in New York City, he left to "do his own thing."

While working in a Greenwich Village music store, he began to fill up long hours by writing verses about imaginary animals, strictly for his own amusement. One day, a friend read the poems and urged him to show them to a children's book editor at Macmillan. She encouraged him to write more, but about real animals; eventually, in 1967, *A Gopher in the Garden* was published.

"When I write animal poems, some of the characteristics of the animals are probably me or my friends. I draw on many sources. I'm sure all writers do," he said. "So my sources are autobiographical but they're also from things I read, things people tell me, things I've overheard, things I oversee."

Prior to his becoming a writer of light verse, the list of jobs he held is incredible: cab driver, busboy, photographer, furniture mover, potter, and folksinger. As a tenor, he has performed with several opera companies and choruses; as an actor, he has appeared in the musical comedy/drama *Fiddler on the Roof.* He enjoys bicycling, playing racquetball, woodworking, cooking, listening to classical music and opera. In addition to a collection of almost two thousand volumes of children's poetry, he has an extensive collection of frog bric-a-brac. He and his wife, Carolynn, live in Albuquerque, New Mexico.

Since *A Gopher in the Garden*, he has written a considerable body of work including *Circus*, *Nightmares*, and *The Headless Horseman Rides Tonight*, all illustrated by Caldecott Award winning artist Arnold Lobel.

In 1983, *Zoo Doings* appeared, verses culled from his first three books, *A Gopher in the Garden*, *Toucans Two and Other Poems*, and *The Pack Rat's Day*. He has also done several volumes of holiday verse, *It's Halloween*, *It's Christmas*, *It's Valentine's Day*, *It's Thanksgiving*.

As an anthologist, he created *Read-Aloud Rhymes for the Very Young*, a collection of over 200 poems, and *The Random House Book of Poetry for Children*, which features 572 poems, including 35 of his own verses.

Recent books include *The New Kid on the Block*, *It's Snowing! It's Snowing!*, *My Parents Think I'm Sleeping*, and *Ride a Purple Pelican*.

The poet can be heard reading his own work on two recordings: *Nightmares*, a selection of twenty-four verses from *Nightmares*; and *The Headless Horseman Rides Tonight: People, Animals and Other Monsters*, which features various poems from his published works (both Caedmon).

Available from Random House are three "Holiday Read Along" cassettes featuring his verses from *It's Christmas*, *It's Halloween*, and *It's Valentine's Day*. The cassette *It's Thanksgiving* is available from Listening Library.

## REFERENCES

*Gopher in the Garden and Other Animal Poems.* Illustrated by Robert Leydenfrost. Macmillan, 1967.

*Circus.* Illustrated by Arnold Lobel. Macmillan, 1970; also in paperback.

*Toucans Two and Other Poems.* Illustrated by Jose Aruego. Macmillan, 1970.

*The Pack Rat's Day and Other Poems.* Macmillan, 1974.

*Nightmares: Poems to Trouble Your Sleep.* Illustrated by Arnold Lobel. Greenwillow, 1976.

*It's Halloween.* Illustrated by Marylin Hafner. Greenwillow, 1977; Scholastic paperback.

*The Headless Horseman Rides Tonight: More Poems to Trouble Your Sleep.* Illustrated by Arnold Lobel. Greenwillow, 1980.

*It's Christmas.* Illustrated by Marylin Hafner. Greenwillow, 1981.

*It's Thanksgiving.* Illustrated by Marylin Hafner. Greenwillow, 1982; Scholastic paperback.

*It's Valentine's Day.* Illustrated by Yossi Abolafia. Greenwillow, 1983; Scholastic paperback.

*The Random House Book of Poetry for Children,* (selector). Illustrated by Arnold Lobel. Random House, 1983.

*Zoo Doings: Animal Poems.* Illustrated by Paul O. Zelinsky. Greenwillow, 1983.

*It's Snowing! It's Snowing!* Illustrated by Jeanne Titherington. Greenwillow, 1984.

*The New Kid on the Block.* Illustrated by James Stevenson. Greenwillow, 1984.

*My Parents Think I'm Sleeping.* Illustrated by Yossi Abolafia. Greenwillow, 1985.

*Ride a Purple Pelican.* Illustrated by Garth Williams. Greenwillow, 1986.

*Read-Aloud Rhymes for the Very Young* (selector). Illustrated by Marc Brown. Alfred A. Knopf, 1986.

# Carl Sandburg

---

### *BUBBLES*

Two bubbles found they had rainbows on their curves.
They flickered out saying:
"It was worth being a bubble just to have held that
rainbow thirty seconds."

—from THE COMPLETE POEMS OF CARL SANDBURG

Carl Sandburg, the son of two poor Swedish immigrants, was born on January 6, 1878, in Galesburg, Illinois, a city about 145 miles southwest of Chicago, in Abraham Lincoln country. His father was a railroad blacksmith. Mr. Sandburg was eleven years old when he began combining schooling and jobs, leaving after the eighth grade for one job after the other. He drove a milk wagon, helped in a barber shop, waited at a lunch counter, worked as a farm hand, laborer on the railroad, secretary, newspaper reporter, political organizer, historian, lecturer, and collector and singer of folksongs. He frequently toured the United States; with guitar in hand, he sang folksongs and recited his poems.

Thirty years of his life were spent preparing a monumental six-volume biography of Abraham Lincoln; in 1940 he was awarded the Pulitzer Prize in History for the last four volumes, *Abraham Lincoln: The War Years.* In 1950, he received a second Pulitzer Prize for his *Complete Poems.*

A great deal has been written about him. In 1969, the Library of Congress in Washington, D.C., prepared an eighty-three-page pamphlet entitled *Carl Sandburg* (United States Government Printing Office), which includes an essay by Mark Van Doren and sixty-five pages listing Mr. Sandburg's material in the collection at the Library of Congress.

His first published work appeared in 1904, *Reckless Ecstasy.* Only fifty copies were printed by one of his professors, Phillip Green Wright, who owned and operated a printing press in Galesburg. Three other volumes of work were printed between 1907 and 1910. In 1914, Harriet Monroe, editor of the avant-garde *Poetry: A Magazine of Verse*, received a group of nine poems from Mr. Sandburg. They shocked her. They were unlike anything she was used to reading and/or receiving. Among the nine poems was "Chicago," included in his first book for Henry Holt, *Chicago Poems*, published in 1916. Following this volume, Mr. Sandburg's writings were published at a rapid pace: *Cornhuskers*, *Smoke and Steel*, his writings about Lincoln, his famous *Rootabaga Stories* for children, and his poetry for children, *Early Moon* and *Wind Song*, all reflecting the tempo, life, and language of the everyday people he encountered.

Mr. Sandburg once said, "I glory in this world of men and women torn with troubles yet living on to love and laugh through it all."

In 1970, *The Sandburg Treasury* appeared, which includes the complete *Rootabaga Stories*, *Abraham Lincoln Grows Up*, *Prairie Town Boy*, *Early Moon*, and *Wind Song*, with an introduction by his wife, Paula.

*Early Moon* begins with his must-read "Short Talk on Poetry," a beautiful essay explaining "how little anybody knows about poetry, how it is made, what it is made of, how long men have been making it, where it came from, when it began, who started it and why, and who knows all about it."

*Rainbows Are Made*, seventy Sandburg poems that I selected, is divided into six sections, celebrating human emotions, the magic of everyday objects, nature's face mirrored in small things, wordplay, and the haunting images of the night and the sea. Each section is preceded by one of Carl Sandburg's own definitions of poetry from *Good Morning, America*; for example, "Poetry is a phantom script telling how rainbows are made and why they go away."

Within the volume such favorite poems are included as "Arithmetic," "Paper I," "Paper II," and "Phizzog"— "this face you got"—and "Circles," a seven-line free verse that beautifully sums up the white man's ignorance of the unknown as pointed out by an Indian.

Works of Mr. Sandburg appear in nearly every major anthology of children's poetry. His words are as fresh today as they were decades ago and will continue to be years hence.

The poet died on July 22, 1967, at the age of eighty-nine. Upon his death at Connemara, North Carolina, President Lyndon Baines Johnson issued the statement:

Carl Sandburg needs no epitaph. It is written for all time in the fields, the cities, the face and heart of the land he loved and the people he celebrated and inspired. With the world we mourn his passing. It is our pride and fortune as Americans that we will always hear Carl Sandburg's voice within ourselves. For he gave us the truest and most enduring vision of our own greatness.

Mr. Sandburg's birthplace, 331 East Third Street, in Galesburg, Illinois, stands as a monument to the poet, and in 1968 Connemara Farm, where he spent his last years, became a national historic site, administered by the National Park Service. Located five miles south of Hendersonville, North Carolina, the home and grounds are open to the public. The entire house is exactly as it was when Mr. Sandburg lived there. Each year thousands of adults and children visit these memorials.

Two recordings (both Caedmon) featuring the poet and his work include *Carl Sandburg's Poems for Children*, a reading of forty-six selections, and *Carl Sandburg Reading "Fog" and Other Poems*, recorded during 1951 and 1952; this Grammy nominee includes twenty-nine selections geared toward mature listeners.

**REFERENCES**

*Chicago Poems.* Henry Holt, 1916.

*Cornhuskers.* Henry Holt, 1918.

*Smoke and Steel.* Harcourt Brace Jovanovich, 1920.

*Early Moon.* Illustrated by James Daugherty. Harcourt Brace Jovanovich, 1930; also in paperback.

*Abraham Lincoln: The War Years.* Harcourt Brace Jovanovich, 1939.

*Wind Song.* Illustrated by William A. Smith. Harcourt Brace Jovanovich, 1960.

*The Complete Poems of Carl Sandburg.* Harcourt Brace Jovanovich, 1970.

*The Sandburg Treasury: Prose and Poetry for Young People.* Illustrated by Paul Bacon. Harcourt Brace Jovanovich, 1970.

*Rainbows Are Made: Poems of Carl Sandburg.* Selected by Lee Bennett Hopkins. Illustrated by Fritz Eichenberg. Harcourt Brace Jovanovich, 1982; also in paperback.

# Shel Silverstein

---

## THE SEARCH

I went to find the pot of gold
That's waiting where the rainbow ends.
I searched and searched and searched and searched
And searched and searched, and then—
There it was, deep in the grass,
Under an old and twisty bough.
It's mine, it's mine, it's mine at last. . . .
What do I search for now?

—from WHERE THE SIDEWALK ENDS

With any group of children—anywhere—
all I have to do is mention the name Shel Silverstein, and
many immediately cry out, "Read 'Sarah Cynthia Sylvia
Stout Would Not Take the Garbage Out.' " Or, "Read
'Jimmy Jet and His TV Set.' " Or another or another! If
today's generation of children know of light verse, they
*know* of Shel Silverstein.

Author-illustrator Shelby Silverstein, born in Chicago,
Illinois, in 1932, has had a diverse career. His early
cartoons appeared in Pacific *Stars and Stripes* while he was
a G.I. in Japan during the 1950s. Years later, he was
regularly published in *Playboy* magazine, creating cartoons and offbeat verses.

In 1963, when he was thirty-one, his first book with
Harper & Row, *Lafcadio, the Lion Who Shot Back*, an
amusing fable, appeared. In a rare interview with Jean F.
Mercier, which appeared in *Publishers Weekly* (February
24, 1975, p. 50), he discussed his writing for children.

I never planned to write or draw for kids. It was Tomi
Ungerer, a friend of mine [and a distinguished author/illus-
trator of children's books], who insisted . . . practically
dragged me, kicking and screaming, into Ursula Nordstrom's
office. And she convinced me that Tomi was right; I could do
children's books.

Ursula Nordstrom, the distinguished, now-retired editor of children's books at Harper & Row, was always
right! She sparked the careers of hundreds of authors and

132

illustrators, including Ruth Krauss, Maurice Sendak, Charlotte Zolotow, and countless more.

Following *Lafcadio*, a steady outpour of Mr. Silverstein's best-selling books appeared, including *The Giving Tree* and *A Giraffe and a Half*.

In 1974, *Where the Sidewalk Ends* established the author as one of America's most popular writers of light verse. *A Light in the Attic* appeared in 1981, and sold over 575,000 copies within the first year of publication. In 1985, the volume broke publishing industry records, staying on *The New York Times* best-seller list well over three years—longer than any hardcover book in the list's fifty-year-plus history. Other awards for the book include the 1984 Children's Book Award for nonfiction from the New Jersey Library Association and, in the same year, the William Allen White Award, voted upon by more than 52,000 fourth- through eighth-graders throughout the state of Kansas—the first book of verse to win the White Award in the program's thirty-two-year-old history.

About *A Light in the Attic*, Mr. Silverstein stated, "I like to think of *Light* as not an all-time best seller but as a good book."

A very private person, he has long refused to discuss his books or even allow Harper & Row to release any biographical information about him or photographs. Of course, his picture does appear on the back dust jackets of several of his books.

He lives in as diverse a manner as he writes, dividing his time among Greenwich Village in New York City, Key West, Florida, and a houseboat near Sausalito, California.

"I believe everyone should live like that," he commented. "Don't be dependent on anyone else—man, woman, child, or dog. I want to go everywhere, look at and listen to everything. You can go crazy with some of the wonderful stuff there is in life."

In addition to his books for children and adults, he is also a composer, lyricist, folksinger, and performer. His most popular song, "A Boy Named Sue," was recorded by Johnny Cash. He is also the author of several plays, including his first, *The Lady or the Tiger*, in 1981, and *The Crate*, produced off-Broadway in 1985.

Film buffs can catch his appearance in the 1971 film starring Dustin Hoffman, *Who Is Harry Kellerman and Why Is He Saying Those Terrible Things About Me?*

Mr. Silverstein can be heard on the delightful recordings *Where the Sidewalk Ends* (CBS), which includes thirty-six verses selected from the collection, and which won the 1985 Grammy Award for the Best Recording for Children, and *A Light in the Attic* (CBS), where he performs thirty-nine pieces. Adult listeners can hear him perform thirteen of his ditties on the recording *Songs and Stories*, including such riots as "Never Bite a Married Woman on the Thigh," "The Father of a Boy Named Sue," and "Show It at the Beach," produced by Parachute Records, Inc.

"I would hope that people, no matter what age, would find something to identify with in my books," he comments. "Pick one up and experience a personal sense of discovery."

In an article, "The Light in His Attic," (*The New York*

*Times Book Review*, March 9, 1986), poet Myra Cohn Livingston stated: "Mr. Silverstein's genius lies in finding a new way to present moralism, beguiling his child readers with a technique that establishes him as an errant, mischievous and inventive child as well as an understanding, trusted and wise adult . . . what he says in light verse and drawings to children is of such importance, such urgency that we must be grateful that more than three million copies of his books are being read. In a world that needs a generation of imaginative thinkers, may there be millions and millions more."

Undoubtedly there will be!

**REFERENCES**

*Lafcadio, the Lion Who Shot Back.* Harper & Row, 1963.
*A Giraffe and a Half.* Harper & Row, 1964.
*The Giving Tree.* Harper & Row, 1964.
*Where the Sidewalk Ends.* Harper & Row, 1974.
*A Light in the Attic.* Harper & Row, 1981.

The preceding discussions have been limited primarily to volumes of original verse. Elementary classrooms and homes should contain many volumes of original verse, along with a number of poetry anthologies. Using anthologies is an excellent way to acquaint boys and girls with a wide variety of poets and their different writing styles, and they are convenient to have on hand for children, teachers, and parents, to dip into whenever they feel the need. One of the greatest benefits of a good anthology is that its poems can satisfy many interests and levels and are balanced with work by poets of all genres.

Good anthologists strive for this variety. As the anthologist William Cole wittily remarked to me, "Any anthology done without enthusiasm is like a TV dinner—frozen, tasteless, and quickly forgotten."

Anthologies can be grouped into two categories: One, general anthologies that contain poems on nearly any subject, sometimes arranged or grouped under specific topics; and, two, specialized anthologies that contain poems on one particular subject.

Every home and classroom should have a potpourri of poetry on its bookshelves. Collections of original verse and general and specialized anthologies should be present in number. One good anthology is not enough! With many high-quality anthologies available both in hardcover and paperback editions, children of all ages can enjoy the hundreds of poems and poets tucked inside several volumes. Librarians or booksellers can suggest the more popular anthologies for use with children. But before you choose or buy, decide for *yourself* what is best for you and the children.

## ADDITIONAL REFERENCES

Baring-Gould, William S., and Baring-Gould, Cecil. *The Annotated Mother Goose.* Potter, 1982.

Seuss, Dr. *And to Think That I Saw It on Mulberry Street.* Vanguard, 1937.

# PART THREE

# "Butterflies Can Be in Bellies!"

## Sparking Children to Write Poetry

Once children have been exposed to and enjoyed poetry over a period of time, many will compose poems of their own.

Children should and can write poetry. Children's work is meant to be shared. They can read their works to one another, print it in a class or school newspaper, include it in a play or assembly program, or give it as a priceless gift to someone special.

Often, I receive letters from parents, teachers, and librarians asking me how they can get "Charlie's" poem published. The important thing should be the creation of something from within the child—and that is enough! A child's poem is not any better because it appears in print. We must not feel that everything a child writes is publisher-bound. Poems do not have to appear in print to be heard or be enjoyed by oneself, one's peers, or by an intimate group. We should encourage children to write, play with language, use words in new and special ways, rewrite, and develop their creative potential.

Writing poetry is not easy. Children should be taught to rework their creations—rework them again and again until they "feel" right.

Sound advice regarding children and the poetic experience is offered in Myra Cohn Livingston's *The Child as Poet.*

A fine volume both children and adults will enjoy is *Knock at a Star* by X. J. Kennedy and Dorothy M.

141

Kennedy. Over 160 poems are included by contemporary and past masters, divided into four sections to stimulate the reading and writing of poetry. All types of verse are represented—rhyme, free verse, short-verse forms. The last chapter, "Do It Yourself (Writing Your Own Poems)," gives readers ten suggestions to start them thinking. The "Afterword to Adults" offers suggestions for involving children with poetry.

A third resource is my monthly feature, "Poetry Place," which has appeared in *Instructor* magazine since 1980, containing selected poems on specific themes, a lively illustration, and a special note encouraging students to pick up their pens and pencils to write. One article, "Give Children Poetry" (*Instructor*, March 1982, pp. 36–40), suggests various ways to increase the use and enjoyment of the feature. Some of the ideas are basic; others require a little more time and planning.

## Similes and Metaphors

One way to start children writing is by employing similes and metaphors.

Using similes is a good method of introducing children to techniques for coloring their thoughts; these figures of speech compare two dissimilar objects using *like* or *as.*

Give children phrases such as "as green as ———," asking them to fill in their immediate response. When I suggest this at adult workshops, I ask the audience to give *their* response. Immediately a chorus chants, "As green as *grass*!"

Laughingly, I tell the audience that if their first-, third-, or sixth-grade youngsters said that, they would call them uncreative! Yet this is a perfect response. What is greener than a beautiful patch of grass? To a child "tired answers" are really quite fresh, since every day brings experiences, new reactions, and quite naturally the repetition of many responses we ourselves had as children. To encourage other responses, ask the children to look around the classroom for things that are green, or ask a local paint store for a chart of various colors and shades they carry for the boys and girls to use. Wanda's dress, for example, might be a different shade of green from Donna's; Donald's notebook, the chalkboard, Jennifer's lunchbox, might all contain shades of green. Thus, children begin to see the many uses of shades of green and start to develop broader perspectives.

Now that they have seen green in the classroom, ask, "What else is green?" Allow students to brainstorm until they have exhausted the possibilities. Then, try another simile using something other than color, for example, "as big as ———," "as tired as ———," or "as *anything* as."

Good results can be elicited when girls and boys get, develop, and use new ideas. Things can be poetically compared via the use of similes.

From the *like* or *as* phrases, lead the children into other comparisons. "The house was as ——— as ———," "The rain was like ———," or "The book was like ———."

Third-graders have responded:

The mouse is as small as my hand was on the day I was born.

The giant in the fairy tale is as tall as a basketball player.

The lady is as roly-poly as Santa Claus' Jell-O stomach.

This, then, is a small beginning, a way to start children thinking in terms of poetic imagery, finally setting their thoughts down in pint-sized poems.

In a short but pointed article, "Age and Grade Expectancy in Poetry: Maturity in Self-Expression" (*Today's Catholic Teacher*, September 12, 1969, pp. 18–19), Nina Willis Walter discussed the fact that a child's first attempts at writing poetry are usually very simple. Even high-school students who have not previously attempted a poem may begin to express themselves at a very elementary level of writing. She reports:

The comparison of snow to a blanket is not new, but the following poem was a creative effort by the child who wrote it because the idea of making comparison was new to him and because he was looking at the snow and saying what it looked like to him.

> The snow
> Is like a big white blanket
> On the ground.
>
> —JOEY BARNES, AGE 6

Rather than dismissing Joey's composition as *uncreative*, it would be better to develop with him additional ideas and feelings about snow, using other similes, and leading him into metaphors—figures of speech in which one thing is said to be another.

Metaphors abound in poetry. Share such examples as "The River Is a Piece of Sky" from *The Reason for the Pelican* by John Ciardi; "Some Say the Sun Is a Golden Earring," by Natalie M. Belting in *Piping Down the Valleys Wild*, selected by Nancy Larrick; "The Moon's the North Wind's Cooky" by Vachel Lindsay in *The Moon's the North Wind's Cooky*, selected and illustrated by Susan Russo; or William Shakespeare's "All the world's a stage and all the men and women in it merely players," in Act II, Scene 7 of *As You Like It*.

## Short Verse Forms

Teachers across the country have successfully used short verse forms to call forth novel thoughts from young minds. Popular short verse forms that can be used in elementary grades include haiku, senryu, and tanka, stemming from the ancient Japanese culture; sijo from Korea; and the cinquain that originated in twentieth-century America.

*Haiku* In recent years, poems in haiku form have been read and written in classrooms from coast to coast. There are many reasons for the successful use of haiku with children—the poems are short, the form is easy to remember, and, with practice, enjoyable to construct.

145

The form was invented in Japan centuries ago; it consists of three nonrhyming lines containing seventeen syllables, five-seven-five respectively. Naturally, since the Japanese language differs from English, this form is changed when original Japanese haiku are translated.

The basic requirement of the form is that, in some way, the haiku should relate to nature or the seasons of the year. A good haiku should indicate the season from certain key words that appear within the seventeen syllables.

Another requirement is that the haiku capture a moment or a single image in the busy world of nature. A haiku should strike an image almost as if a slide had been flashed upon a screen in a darkened room.

Children of all ages can try their hands at creating haiku, concentrating and writing about a brief moment; no child, however, should be forced initially into the five-seven-five syllable limitations. I remember receiving a letter from a fifth-grade child in Michigan who was puzzled over "Hokku Poems" by Richard Wright in *The Poetry of Black America*, edited by Arnold Adoff, because two of the verses did not meet up to the "required" seventeen syllables. The required form should be suggested to students, but not rigidly enforced. The world will not be shattered if Mr. Wright's haiku, or any child's, contains eighteen syllables or fifteen! The point is to motivate all children of varying ability to express themselves in a few words and decide which words can be used to communicate poetic ideas.

Before introducing this form, read to the class a variety of haiku that pinpoint the qualities desired.

Excellent examples of haiku appear in *In a Spring Garden,* edited by Richard Lewis, a collection of classic haiku by such master writers of the form as Issa, Bashō, and Buson. The text follows a day of spring, from the early morning admonition to a toad who "looks as if/It would belch forth/A cloud," to the glowing goodnight of a firefly. The master artist Ezra Jack Keats provides vibrant collage illustrations to complement this treasure. *In a Spring Garden* is available as a six-minute film and as a sound filmstrip-book-record combination. Both are narrated by Richard Lewis, and although both are excellent, I have personally found the filmstrip package more successful for use with children in the elementary grades. You can show one, two, or several frames, allow the children to savor the exquisite collage images created by Mr. Keats, and read them the accompanying verse yourself. The film is rather fast paced; very young children might lose the mood you are trying to convey by seeing so much all at once.

There are many volumes explaining the haiku form. The best of the lot is a compact paperbound volume, *Haiku in English* by Harold G. Henderson. This book explains everything you need to know, gives many examples of haiku by master poets, and suggests lesson plans. The volume is one that every teacher should have, ready to be pulled out at a second's notice.

To motivate one lesson in writing haiku, I did the following. I brought to a fifth-grade class a bunch of jonquils and placed them in a clear vase filled with water. Alongside the vase I placed a Mason jar containing a live bumblebee, caught by one of the students in my class—

not by me! This was done prior to the morning admission bell. Several children, upon entering the classroom, noticed the fresh flowers and the bee on my desk. Other children came in and went to their desks without bothering to look at my Tuesday morning display. Soon, however, there was more buzzing in the classroom than any swarm of healthy bees could have produced. When the entire class was settled, I asked them to look at, concentrate on, the flowers and the bumblebee for just three minutes, which can be a long, long time for thirty curious creators. I told them to look at the flowers and bee as they never looked at anything before. At the end of three minutes, I carried the jar to the window, dramatically opened it, and sent Mr. Bumblebee off to freedom. I then asked the class to think about the entire experience—the flowers, the caged-up bee, and my letting it go free. I had provided them with nature, a moment, and an image.

Frieda wrote:

> The bee is set free
> But flowers, you'll only stay
> Alive for a while.

Harriet created:

> Yellow bee, Go to
> The yellow flowers outside
> Where you both are free.

Many simple objects from nature might be used to stimulate youngsters—a twig, a rock, a cricket, or a bunch of leaves. With emphasis on ecology today, haiku is a natural tie-in. Many haiku written by great masters, centuries ago, are more relevant today than they might have been at the time they were written.

*Senryu* Senryu, another popular verse form, is related to haiku. Named for the Japanese poet who originated the form, senryu follows the same five-seven-five pattern of haiku and also concentrates on a single idea or image of a moment. The form differs in that the subject matter is not restricted to nature or the seasons. This form gives students the opportunity to express ideas on any subject—baseball, eating spaghetti, or camping out in the woods. Below is an example of a senryu created by a second-grade child:

> The first day of school.
> Now I know that butterflies
> Can be in bellies.

*Tanka* Tanka are longer in form and again typically deal with nature or a season of the year. Tanka is written in five lines totaling thirty-one syllables, five-seven-five-seven-seven respectively. The first three lines are known as the *hokku*; the last two, the *ageku*. Older students will enjoy experimenting with the tanka form after they have been introduced to, and practiced, haiku.

*Sijo* The sijo (she-jo) verse form is a product of the fourteenth-century Yi dynasty of Korea, a period in Korean history during which science, industry, literature, and the arts developed rapidly.

The form is similar to haiku in several ways: it is based on syllabication, is unrhymed, and usually deals with nature or the seasons. In English, the form is often written in six lines, each line containing seven or eight syllables with a total of forty-two to forty-eight syllables. Originally, sijo verse was written to be sung while the rhythm was beaten on a drum or while accompanied by a lute.

One hot summer, working with a group of students in Hartford, Connecticut, I introduced the sijo form. When I asked what the group might like to write about, two replies came simultaneously: "Somethin' cold," said one child; another replied, "Old Man Winter!" Thus, thoughts of winter were conjured up in sijo form while we all melted away. One child produced:

> Winter is a God-given gift
> It's a pretty good one, too!
> To see the white flakes falling
> And cold, cold wind a'blowin'
> Life seems like the seasons,
> Changing with no reasons.

A boy in the group wrote:

> What a gloomy, snowy night.
> Dull, moody, all the way.
> The ship's crew are all in fright . . .
> The choppy waves roll off the coast . . .
> In the galley, pots are rattling.
> Storm-stopped ships on their way.

In Harlem, a sixth-grade unit on Korea incorporated the sijo form. One boy wrote:

> I wonder what's it like to
> Be a crawling caterpillar.
> They're always so alone
> And ugly and without friends, and sad . . .
> But when the time comes
> Everyone is fooled—a butterfly is born!

Again, it must be emphasized that the strict form should not be a deterrent for some children. In the examples above, you will note that the seven- to eight-syllable count per line does vary now and then.

*Cinquain*   I was first introduced to the cinquain form in the late 1960s while visiting Frances Weissman's fourth-grade class in East Paterson, New Jersey. I immediately became fascinated with both the form and the creations that the boys and girls in her class were producing. This led to a mass of research about the form and its fascinating creator.

Cinquain is a delicately compressed five-line, un-rhymed stanza containing twenty-two syllables broken into a two-four-six-eight-two pattern. The form was originated by Adelaide Crapsey, born on September 9, 1878, in Brooklyn Heights, New York.

Miss Crapsey studied at Kemper Hall in Kenosha, Wisconsin; after graduating from Vassar College in 1901, she returned to Kemper Hall to teach. In 1905, she went to Rome to study archeology. She remained in Italy for one year, returning to teach at Miss Low's Preparatory School for Girls in Stamford, Connecticut (now the Low-Heywood School for girls in grades six through twelve). The remainder of her life she fought a losing battle against tuberculosis.

The years 1913 and 1914 were spent in a sanatorium in Saranac, New York; it was here, in a room that faced an old, sadly neglected graveyard, that she wrote and perfected cinquains. Miss Crapsey termed this plot of land "Trudeau's Garden," after Edward Livingston Trudeau, an American physician who pioneered open-air treatment for tuberculosis at Saranac. This view, plus her prolonged illness, probably inspired her to write verses, both cinquain and other poetic forms, about death. One of her longest poems, "To the Dead in My Graveyard Underneath My Window," was published in 1915, a year after her death, in a slender collection of her work simply titled *Verse*.

In his preface to the 1938 edition of *Verse*, Carl Bragdon wrote of Miss Crapsey: "I remember her as fair and fragile, in action swift, in repose still; so quick and silent in her movements that she seemed never to enter a room but to appear there, and on the stroke of some invisible clock to vanish as she had come."

In my travels around the country, I have introduced this form to many children.

Although the cinquain form has been one of the most popular creative writing assignments given to children, it is also the most abused. Several recently published textbooks, as well as journal articles, pass along misinformation about the form, turning it into an exercise in grammar, writing lists of nouns, adjectives, and participles.

Three examples of perfected cinquain, as well as five cinquain sequences, a form designed by Myra Cohn Livingston, appear in her book *O Sliver of Liver and Other Poems*; fourteen more appear in her volume *Sky Songs.*

David McCord, in *One at a Time*, offers a five-page lesson on the cinquain form for readers and writers.

Like the other verse forms discussed, the cinquain allows children spontaneously to put forth thoughts and feelings in a minimum amount of words and lines. Again, the children's writing should not necessarily have to conform to the formula; overstepping the structured boundaries often enables children to write more freely.

In all these short-verse forms, children can write, experiment, and work toward perfecting poetic imagery. And through short-verse forms a child can play on city streets, bask in the beauty of the countryside, or even go to Neverland Land, as it was called by a child from Julesburg, Colorado.

## Japanese Classifications of Beauty

Before or after students have experimented with and created short-verse forms, have them try their hands at forming word-pictures using the four Japanese classifications of beauty: (1) hade (ha-day), (2) iki (e-kee), (3) jimi (je-me), (4) shibui (she-bu-e).

There is no particular form for children to follow as in the above short-verse forms. The idea is to have children evoke strong imagery through word-thoughts. Students can experiment with the arrangement of words to give their images a more poetic look.

Hade signifies something that is colorful, flashy, or bright. For example:

> Signs on 42nd Street
> flash—
> blue, green, red, yellow,
> looking like fireworks
> fighting hard
> to explode.

Iki should portray something smart, stylish, or chic; for example:

> In the window I saw
> a baby diamond lying on a piece
> of old, soft, blue velvet.

Or:

> The bucket seats
> in my brother's new car
>     were
>     pillow-soft
>     and
>     black-beautiful.

154

Jimi portrays images that are traditional, old-fashioned, or *seemingly* dull and commonplace:

> Knife, fork, and spoon
> set down on the table
> for the hundredth time
> wait for
> the family dinner to begin.

Or:

> Birds left the ground
> and took their proper pattern
> for flying south once again.

Shibui, according to the Japanese, is the highest form of beauty. Here, something dull is written about but in the context of a rich background expressing joy or contrasting brightness:

> The sky was pitch black
> until the lightning bolt
> took over and tore it apart.

Or:

> The purple pansy wasn't noticed
> Until its throat turned bright yellow.

In one fourth-grade class in New York City, a teacher used the four classifications to introduce a two-month writing lesson. Each week the children were told of one classification and were encouraged to write their thoughts. After writing, they mounted their compositions on colored construction paper, illustrated them, and placed them on a bulletin board display.

In lower grades, teachers can encourage a class or small groups of children to do group exercises either independently or via the experience chart approach. In this way, children can brainstorm ideas and work and rework thoughts until perfect images are created.

## Traditional Verse Forms

Children should also be introduced to such traditional verse forms such as the couplet, tercet, quatrain, and limerick.

**The Couplet** The couplet is the simplest form of poetry; it consists of two lines bound together by rhyme. Couplets have been written for centuries and centuries. As early as 1683, couplets were used to teach children both the alphabet and religious morals emphasizing the sinful nature of humankind. Such rhymes appeared in *The New England Primer*:

> A—In Adam's fall
> We sinned all.

> Z—Zaccheus he did climb a tree
> His Lord to see.

Many Mother Goose rhymes appear in couplet form:

> Tommy's tears and Mary's fears
> Will make them old before their years.

> January brings the snow
> Makes our feet and fingers glow.

Students might try writing simple verses about holidays, pets, people, food—anything.

*The Tercet* The tercet, or triplet, is any stanza of three lines which rhyme together. An example by Robert Browning is:

> Boot, saddle, to horse, and away!
> Rescue my castle before the hot day
> Brightens to blue from its silvery gray.

*The Quatrain* The quatrain form is written in four lines and can consist of any metrical pattern or rhyme scheme. In Harlem, one fourth-grader created a poem that tells a great deal about herself, includes excellent word images, and evokes a lot of thought. The child titled her verse "My Seed":

> The seed is growing deep inside
> It cannot hide, it cannot hide.
> It shoves and pushes, it bangs and kicks
> And one day the world will know me.

Ask children to hunt for examples of quatrains written by master poets and read them to the class. A collection of these can prompt discussion about how much can be said in just four lines. Some examples are John Ciardi's "Warning," depicting the dangers of a whirlpool, in *The Man Who Sang the Sillies*, or the Mother Goose rhyme that amusingly sums up the four seasons:

> Spring is showery, flowery, bowery.
> Summer is hoppy, croppy, poppy.
> Autumn is wheezy, sneezy, freezy.
> Winter is slippy, drippy, nippy.

See also David McCord's *One at a Time* for a series of quatrains.

*The Limerick* Limericks immediately bring to mind the poet Edward Lear, who perfected this form to amuse the grandchildren of his friend the Earl of Derby. Lear wrote many limericks, such as:

> There was an Old Man with a beard,
> Who said, "It is just as I feared!
>    Two owls and a hen,
>    Two larks and a wren
> Have all built their nests in my beard!"

The form consists of five lines. Lines one, two, and five rhyme; lines three and four may or may not rhyme.

After hearing many limericks written by Lear and others, children will want to create their own. To help them, you might try this: Write one line on the chalkboard, for example, "There was a man with 33 shoes." Encourage children to make up a list of all the words they can think of that rhyme with "shoes." Then they can suggest a second line for the limerick, ending with one of their words. This line is also written on the chalkboard. Next, the children can think of a third line following the thought of the limerick but not ending with a rhyming word. Now they can make a second list of words rhyming with the last word in the third line and use this as a resource to finish line four. Line five can end with a rhyming word from the first list they prepared.

The limerick form gives children an opportunity to use interesting-sounding words, experiment with language, and have fun in clever word-ways.

Collections of limericks abound. In *They've Discovered a Head in the Box for the Bread and Other Laughable Lyrics*, collected by John E. Brewton and Lorraine A. Blackburn, you will find many of Edward Lear's limericks, along with others by such notables as John Ciardi, Eve Merriam, and Ogden Nash.

*Knock at a Star*, by X. J. Kennedy and Dorothy M. Kennedy, presents an introduction to the form, including examples.

In Myra Cohn Livingston's *A Lollygag of Limericks*, the poet created many limericks while being enchanted by such unusual place names as Needles-on-Storr, Stroud-and-Straw-on-the-Wold, discovered on a summer trip to England. Her fine volume *How Pleasant to Know Mr. Lear!*, a tribute to the great nineteenth-century English humorist, contains a scholarly selection of Lear's story poems, limericks, notes, and artwork, divided into eleven sections. Mrs. Livingston's introduction details

Lear's life and work. Appended is the informative "Notes on the Sources of the Poems, Further Fax, and Speculations About Old Derry Downs Derry," plus an index of titles and first lines.

Twenty-seven of Edward Lear's nonsense verses are delightfully performed on side 2 of the recording *Nonsense Verse of Carroll and Lear* (Caedmon). They are read "nonsensically" by three top star-talents, Beatrice Lillie, Cyril Ritchard, and Stanley Holloway.

Arnold Lobel's *The Book of Pigericks*, original limericks in a beautifully designed volume, can further motivate writing lessons based on other animals. Can you just envision a bulletin-board display proudly touting cat-ericks, dog-ericks, horse-ericks—animal-ericks of all kinds—along with children's artwork? *The Book of Pigericks* is also available as a "Children's Literature Read Along" book/cassette package from Random House.

## *Parody*

Children can have a great deal of fun experimenting with parodies. Limericks and Mother Goose rhymes are popular forms to use to introduce parodies. Why not have children set some of the Mother Goose rhymes in an amusement park, as Hollywood or television personalities, or at the seashore? One fourth-grader offered:

Little Boy Blue, come blow your horn.
The sheep's in the meadow, the cow's in the corn.
Where is the boy that looks after the sheep?
He's down at the seashore buying hot dogs cheap!

A fifth-grader came up with:

> There was an old woman
> Who lived in a shoe.
> She had so many children . . .
> That she looked in the Yellow Pages
> And called a Real Estate Man.

Ellyn Roe, a teacher at Cedar Heights Junior High School in Port Orchard, Washington, reports on how she uses Elizabeth Barrett Browning's, "How Do I Love Thee?" with her students on Valentine's Day.

I read it aloud and students offer interpretations of the more difficult lines. Next the kids copy the poem's first line and proceed to list attributes of a beloved person or object. For example:

> How do I love thee? Let me count the ways.
> I love the way thee runs to greet me after school.
> I love the way thy coat gleams in the afternoon sun
> As I run my fingers through its furry softness . . .

Other examples of parodies can be found in *Knock at a Star* by X. J. Kennedy and Dorothy M. Kennedy.

Unfortunately, one of the finest volumes of parodies, *Speak Roughly to Your Little Boy*, edited by Myra Cohn Livingston, is out of print. If you can track it down in a school or public library, do so! In this spirited volume, Mrs. Livingston presents a wide array of poems followed by a parody and/or burlesque. Thus you will find the cumulative nursery rhyme "The House That Jack Built," followed by G. E. Bates' "Pentagonia," a clever parody about the building of the Pentagon in Washington, D.C. The poems and parodies have been largely drawn from the work of English and American poets—Edward Lear, Edgar Allan Poe, Lewis Carroll, William Carlos Williams, David McCord, and Phyllis McGinley.

Lewis Carroll was a master of parody and burlesque. In both his classics, *Alice's Adventures in Wonderland* and *Through the Looking Glass, and What Alice Found There*, many parodies appear. For example, the theologian Dr. Isaac Watts had written a four-stanza verse, "Against Idleness and Mischief," published in 1715 in *Divine Songs Attempted in Easy Language, for the Use of Children.* The verse begins:

> How doth the little busy Bee
>     Improve each shining Hour,
> And gather Honey all the Day
>     From ev'ry op'ning Flow'r.

> How skillfully she builds her Cell!
>     How neat she spreads the Wax;
> And labours hard to store it well
>     With the sweet Food she makes.

In *Alice's Adventures in Wonderland*, Lewis Carroll turned this into:

> How doth the little crocodile
>     Improve his shining tail
> And pour the waters of the Nile
>     On every golden scale!

162

How cheerfully he seems to grin,
How neatly spreads his claws,
And welcomes little fishes in
With gently smiling jaws!

There are many parodies in Lewis Carroll's writings, including the wonderful verse beginning "You are old, Father William," in *Alice's Adventures in Wonderland*, which is a close and ingenious parody of "The Old Man's Comforts," by Robert Southey.

Don't miss sharing with children of all ages the delightful recording *Nonsense Verse of Carroll and Lear* (Caedmon), performed by Beatrice Lillie, Cyril Ritchard, and Stanley Holloway. Side one consists of ten selections, including "Father William," read by Mr. Ritchard, and the wonderful interpretation of "Jabberwocky" read by Miss Lillie.

## Concrete Poetry

Concrete poetry, or shape poems, are picture poems made out of letters and words; they are strongly visual, breaking away from any and all traditional poetic forms —poetry to be seen and felt as much as to be read or heard.

In Lewis Carroll's *Alice's Adventures in Wonderland*, when the mouse is telling Alice that his is "a long and sad *tale*," and she is looking down at him agreeing that his is indeed "a long and sad *tail*," her idea of the *tale* comes out this way:

Fury said to a
mouse, That he
met in the
house,
"Let us
both go to
law: *I* will
prosecute
*you*. Come,
I'll take no
denial; We
must have a
trial: For
really this
morning I've
nothing
to do."
Said the
mouse to the
cur, "Such
a trial,
dear Sir,
With
no jury
or judge,
would be
wasting
our
breath."
"I'll be
judge, I'll
be jury,"
said
cunning
old Fury:
"I'll
try the
whole
cause
and
condemn
you
to
death!"

*Seeing Things,* written and designed by Robert Froman, with lettering by Ray Barber, contains fifty-one selections arranged on the pages in shapes appropriate to their subjects. One clever bit, entitled "Graveyard," shows ten tombstones with one lettered word on each, reading: "A nice place to visit but you wouldn't live there."

## REFERENCES

Adoff, Arnold (selector). *The Poetry of Black America: Anthology of the 20th Century.* Harper & Row, 1973.

Brewton, John E., and Blackburn, Lorraine A. (selectors). *They've Discovered a Head in the Box for the Bread and Other Laughable Limericks.* Illustrated by Fernando Krahn. T. Y. Crowell, 1978.

Ciardi, John. *The Man Who Sang the Sillies.* Illustrated by Edward Gorey. J. B. Lippincott, 1961; also in paperback.

————. *The Reason for the Pelican.* Illustrated by Edward Gorey. J. B. Lippincott, 1961.

Crapsey, Adelaide. *Verse.* Alfred A. Knopf, 1915.

Froman, Robert. *Seeing Things.* T. Y. Crowell, 1974.

Henderson, Harold G. *Haiku in English.* Charles E. Tuttle Company, 1967.

Kennedy, X. J., and Kennedy, Dorothy M. (selectors). *Knock at a Star: A Child's Introduction to Poetry.* Illustrated by Karen Ann Weinhaus. Little, Brown, 1982; also in paperback.

Larrick, Nancy (selector). *Piping Down the Valleys Wild.*

Illustrated by Ellen Raskin. Dell Publishing Company, reissued 1985; also in paperback.

Lewis, Richard (selector). *In a Spring Garden.* Illustrated by Ezra Jack Keats. Dial Press, 1965; also in paperback.

Livingston, Myra Cohn. *The Child as Poet: Myth or Reality?* The Horn Book, Inc., 1984.

————. *A Lollygag of Limericks.* Illustrated by Joseph Low. Margaret K. McElderry Books/Macmillan, 1978.

————. *O Sliver of Liver and Other Poems.* Illustrated by Iris Van Rynback. Margaret K. McElderry Books/Macmillan, 1979.

————. *Sky Songs.* Illustrated by Leonard Everett Fisher. Holiday House, 1984.

———— (selector). *How Pleasant to Know Mr. Lear!* Holiday House, 1982.

————. *Speak Roughly to Your Little Boy: A Collection of Parodies and Burlesques, Together with the Original Poems, Chosen and Annotated for Young People.* Harcourt Brace Jovanovich, Inc., 1971.

Lobel, Arnold. *The Book of Pigericks: Pig Limericks.* Harper & Row, 1983.

McCord, David. *One at a Time: His Collected Poems for the Young.* Illustrated by Henry B. Kane. Little, Brown, 1974.

Russo, Susan (selector and illustrator). *The Moon's the North Wind's Cooky: Night Poems.* Lothrop, 1979.

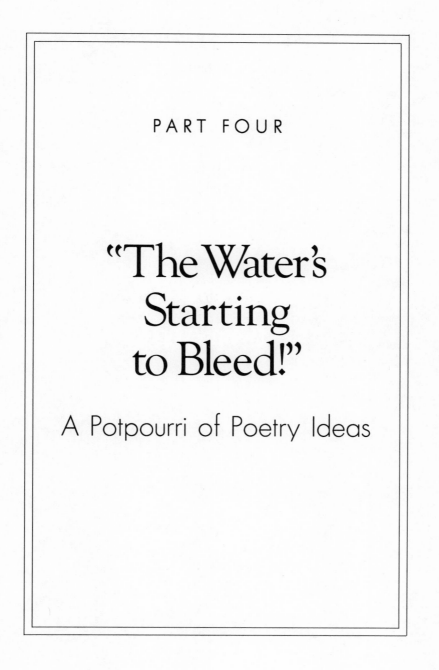

PART FOUR

# "The Water's Starting to Bleed!"

A Potpourri of Poetry Ideas

This section offers dozens of ideas for motivating and appreciating poetry at home, in classrooms, or libraries. No attempt has been made to assign age levels to these projects; they can be, and have been, used effectively or adapted to fit any age level. A variety of themes tie in with children's interests and curricula. None of the projects demand excessive time or unusual materials. Items like shoeboxes, string, and Styrofoam can often be more valuable than expensive commercial kits of materials. With a little bit of imagination, and an occasional trip to Woolworth's, you will find that children will be passing the poetry often with pride and pleasure.

## Mother Goose Grows and Grows

As well as being an important part of our literary heritage, Mother Goose rhymes also serve as an excellent introduction to poetry. The powerful rhythm and highly imaginative, action-filled use of words, the wit, ideas, and compact structure of the rhymes aid children in developing a lifelong interest and appreciation of verse.

A trip to almost any library will supply countless Mother Goose collections, illustrated by master artists. Not-to-be-missed volumes are listed in the "Mother Goose Collections" on pages 243–44.

Boys and girls of all ages can have a great time with the melodies, rhythm, and language, and will find that the Mother of us all can provide innumerable opportunities for many imaginative and creative activities.

*Creating a Mother Goose Village* After children are familiar with a variety of Mother Goose collections, begin planning a Mother Goose village. Children can be asked which rhymes they would like to dramatize, what costumes, props, and scenery will be needed. Once the projects have been chosen, the village can be mapped out. Street signs such as "Jack Horner's Corner" or "King Cole's Court" can be made by the children and placed around the room to show the locations of the various projects.

The entrance to your classroom can become a giant shoe. Let the children help decide what measurements are needed for the shoe; sketch an outline of it, and the doorway, on a large piece of brown wrapping paper for the children to paint and cut out. After the shoe is framed around the doorway, it can be decorated with photographs of the children—the inhabitants and stars of the Mother Goose Village. A sign that says "Welcome to Mother Goose Village" can provide a final touch.

For Contrary Mary's garden, paper flowers created by the children can be attached to sticks and planted in Styrofoam-filled shoeboxes, which can be set "all in a row" and covered with green crepe-paper borders. The garden can also become a birthday garden if you have the girls and boys draw daisies with brightly colored petals on plain white paper plates. The eye of each daisy can contain a child's name and birthdate. Each can be attached to a stick or colored straw and planted.

A large, rectangular cardboard box can easily serve as Humpty Dumpty's wall. Children can draw or paint bricks on the box, and Humpty can be fashioned from a large balloon. Paint on facial features with a felt-tip pen. Use cellophane tape to add a hat and a paper necktie, and then tape Humpty to the wall to await his fate. When the moment for the great fall comes, a child can pierce the balloon with a pin. Be sure that you have an extra balloon on hand as an understudy just in case Humpty explodes before his cue!

A cockhorse for the Lady of Banbury Cross can be made from a broom. A paper-bag horse face can cover the straw. Rags, crepe paper, or colored yarns can be tied around the end of the stick to make a tail.

What rhymes take place in the country? What rhymes take place in the city? Two backdrops can be planned to provide extra space for performers. A "rural mural" can include a haystack for Little Boy Blue, a meadow, a barn for the cow, and so on. A "city mural" might include some of the shops mentioned in the rhymes.

*Creative Dramatic Techniques* There are many ways to dramatize Mother Goose rhymes. Some can be recited by one child or a chorus; others can be sung by the children using traditional music or their own melodies. The abilities and needs of the children and the rhymes themselves will dictate the most appropriate form.

171

Short, familiar rhymes such as "Jack and Jill," "Little Miss Muffet," or "Humpty Dumpty" are easy to pantomime as the audience guesses the name of the rhyme depicted.

Longer narrative rhymes such as "Old Mother Hubbard" or rhymes that can be expanded, such as "Tom, Tom, the Piper's Son," can be enacted with puppets. For "Old Mother Hubbard," one child might narrate while others recreate the action and improvise dialogue for the puppet characters.

Involve one group of children in a "countdown for a cow." The cow is leaving for the moon. Present at the countdown are the Cat and the Fiddle, the Dish and the Spoon, and other animals and objects invented by the children, who can dress up in paper-bag masks. What are the reactions of the citizens of Mother Goose Village? Will the cow make it? Live interviews can also be successful with such characters as Humpty Dumpty, and the Queen of Hearts, as well as many others.

A first-grade class in Harlem produced "Mother Goose Comes to New York," in which they created their own parodies based on the popular rhymes. A third-grade class in Virginia staged a Mother Goose festival; a sixth-grade class in New Jersey held an extraordinary Mother Goose pageant, enjoyed by the entire school in the assembly hall.

*Language Arts and Critical Thinking* Mother Goose rhymes are full of lost or missing things—lost sheep, lost mittens, lost mouse tails. There are also many things that could be missing—Jack Horner's plum or Miss Muffet's spider, for instance. The children can draw missing objects or write the words for them on a piece of paper. These can then be placed in a coffee can or a cardboard well made from a milk carton. Each boy or girl can fish out a slip of paper and match the object with the Mother Goose character who lost it. Other children might prefer writing lost and found ads—for example, "Lost—24 blackbirds. Last seen in the King's backyard."

Many foods are mentioned in the rhymes. A classroom Mother Goose market could advertise and sell curds and whey, hot cross buns, and pease porridge hot and cold— with reduced prices for the "nine-day-old" variety! The children can make signs listing the items and prices as well as for things out of stock, such as "Sorry—No Bones Today."

What are some jobs mentioned in the rhymes? Do any exist today? What are they called? In a job-hunting game, set at a modern "employment agency," boys and girls can apply for jobs as cobblers or piemen. Can jobs be found to match their skills?

Little Miss Mouse sat on a ————. Children can create original rhymes, perhaps creating Mother Goose–type verses about their favorite television or cartoon characters.

To enhance mathematics lessons, have students note the rhymes containing numbers, encouraging them to make up individual word problems for classmates to solve. For example: How many men went to sea in a bowl? (Three.) Add that number to the number of bags of wool the black sheep had. What is the answer? Six. With numberless rhymes, children can have great fun studying various illustrators' interpretations. For example, how many silver bells and cockle shells can they find in this picture of Contrary Mary's garden? How many in that? How many children lived in each version of the old woman's shoe?

Visual literary skills are enhanced as well when students look at various illustrators' interpretations of Mother Goose characters. Which picture of Little Miss Muffet and the spider that sat down beside her is your favorite? Why?

*Culminating Activities* A "pat-a-cake party" can be planned when the show is over. Children can help bake cakes and put alphabet letters on the frosting or decorate store-bought cupcakes to serve at the party.

A picture map can be assembled from drawings made by the children of the various areas of Mother Goose Village. The finished map can be placed on a dittoed program sheet and distributed to visitors as a memento of the village. Map skills can be reinforced by asking questions: How can we get from one area of the village to another? What places do we have to pass? What is the best route?

*Mother Goose in Recordings and Multimedia Sets*
Mother Goose has been treated in a number of unique ways in media. The following materials are those that have proved to be most effective with children.

Caedmon features the recording *Mother Goose*, starring three luminaries from the entertainment world, Cyril Ritchard, Celeste Holm, and Boris Karloff, who perform sixty-nine verses and songs. Both familiar and lesser-known selections are included.

Folkways has produced *Nursery Rhymes*, a recording with Ella Jenkins, the distinguished folksinger, who performs twenty-two favorite verses.

Zaner-Bloser's "Nursery Rhyme Mats" includes a boxed set of fifteen large (17½" × 11¾"), durable, plastic-laminated pupil mats with a different rhyme on each mat, illustrated in full color by Anthony Rao; the reverse side of each mat features the Zaner-Bloser Manuscript Alphabet and cardinal numbers from 1 through 10. A teacher's mat features all of the nursery rhymes on the pupils' mats. A hardcover volume, *The Highlights Book of Nursery Rhymes,* also illustrated by Anthony Rao, completes the package.

The mats can also be ordered in sets of five; *The Highlights Book of Nursery Rhymes* can also be ordered separately.

Silo's *Mainly Mother Goose Songs and Rhymes for Merry Young Souls* is a recording featuring traditional Mother Goose rhymes as well as favorite childhood songs. More than seventy selections are accompanied by combinations of fiddle, guitar, dulcimer, even knee-slapping and whistling.

Spoken Arts has produced two recordings entitled *Treasury of Nursery Rhymes.* The selections are sung, read, and arranged by Christopher Casson, the son of Dame Sybil Thorndike and Sir Lewis Casson. Volume one contains forty-two rhymes; volume two contains over fifty selections. To enhance the songs, Mr. Casson uses an Irish harp and recorder for pleasing backgrounds.

*The Mother Goose Book* filmstrip series produced by Random House is based on the magnificent illustrations from *The Mother Goose Book* by Alice and Martin Provensen. Six filmstrips with recordings, activity sheets, a music sheet, poster, and a hardcover edition of the book comprise this treasury.

Weston Woods features *The Mother Goose Treasury*, a filmstrip with illustrations by Raymond Briggs in full color.

## Poetry Activities for All Ages

In addition to Mother Goose, try the following activities to involve children in all kinds of poetic experiences.

*Best Poem of the Month* At the beginning of each month, encourage students to find poems characteristic of that month. In February, for example, children might find poems entitled "February," or discover poems about Lincoln's Birthday, Valentine's Day, George Washington's Birthday, or a poem by a black poet to commemorate Black History Month. Time can be set aside each week for children to read aloud those they have found, telling why each was chosen. The poems can be written out and tacked onto a bulletin board or hanging display.

During the last week of the month, the class can vote on the Best Poem of the Month and select several runners-up. The winners can be kept in a shoebox poetry file that can serve as a good place for children to find favorite poems to read again and again. The file can also be used year after year, providing an excellent resource for future classes.

In one Texas classroom, a teacher used this idea and correlated it with a hanging calendar—a clothesline stretched across the back of the room. When the children brought in poems relating to special events—holidays, children's birthdays, local events—they were placed upon the line and labeled with specific dates. General poems about the month, such as seasonal pieces, were also attached to the line.

Another teacher using this technique held a poetry festival at the end of each month. Each of the poems selected by the class was once again read aloud—but this time to another class. Children practiced their selections; several acted them out; others used simple props for their poetry reading; and some did projects to accompany the poems.

Often, when this idea is tried, the unexpected happens. In one class, six children had April birthdays. During that month many boys and girls brought in birthday poems. The best poem in the opinion of that classroom was Aileen Fisher's "Birthday Present" in *Out in the Dark and Daylight.*

In another classroom, during December, to the hustle and bustle of the holiday season, a first snowfall, two birthdays, and several other miscellaneous events was added the acquisition of a pet hamster—and guess what poem was selected as the best? One youngster found Marci Ridlon's delightful "Hamsters" reprinted in my anthology *Surprises*, to delight both the members of the class and the teacher.

**Boo Poems to Be Scared By** Halloween is one of the favorite holidays on the school calendar. Children can be "safely scared" by reading poems about ghosts, goblins, witches, wizards, and other eerie creatures and characters that make appearances during the Halloween season.

Several excellent collections of "boo" poems to share with readers are available.

*Hey-How for Halloween*, twenty poems that I selected, pays tribute to the spine-tingling season with works by E. E. Cummings, Carl Sandburg, Myra Cohn Livingston, John Ciardi, and others. Janet McCaffery's black-and-white illustrations capture the Halloween mood. A double-page spread within the text depicting a flock of bats flying from the moon can be used to spark children's original verse. Place the spread on an opaque projector to motivate young writers.

*In the Witch's Kitchen*, compiled by John E. Brewton, et al., is a gathering of forty-six poems. Ghouls, ghosts, skeletons, and spooks parade through the pages in works by X. J. Kennedy, Shel Silverstein, Theodore Roethke, Lilian Moore, and others.

*Shrieks at Midnight*, selected by Sara and John E. Brewton, contains poems about restless spirits roaming the earth and modern ghosts who were "done in" for daring to fold up an I.B.M. card. Poems by Lewis Carroll, John Ciardi, and Langston Hughes scare readers of all ages.

Eight delightful verses by Lilian Moore can be found in *Something New Begins*.

Thirteen easy-to-read poems appear in *It's Halloween* by Jack Prelutsky. "Skeleton Parade," "Bobbing for Apples," and "The Haunted House" are among the offerings.

Although not specifically Halloween in theme, readers will be spooked by Jack Prelutsky's *Nightmares* and *The Headless Horseman Rides Tonight.* Twelve poems appear in each volume, versifying such creatures as "The Dragon of Death," "The Bogeyman," "The Poltergeist," and "The Zombie."

*Creatures*, my volume, offers eighteen poems, including "The Old Wife and the Ghost" by James Reeves, "The Dracula Vine" by Ted Hughes, and "The Seven Ages of Elf-Hood" by Rachel Field.

A must for mature readers is Myra Cohn Livingston's *Why Am I Grown So Cold?* In her brief introduction, Mrs. Livingston states: "Science has many explanations for many phenomena, but it has yet to unravel many mysteries. And these mysteries are the blood and bone of this anthology." Over one hundred fifty poems give a wide array of verse dealing with the supernatural. Titles of the twelve sections are intriguing unto themselves—for example, "Enchantment, Witchery, Sorcery, Allurement, and Necromancy"; "White Wands, a Haunted Oven, The Mewlips, and Other Strange Matters." The book's title stems from "The Warning," a cinquain written by Adelaide Crapsey in the early 1900s. Indexes of titles, first lines, authors, and translators are appended.

Play a recording of some eerie music on Halloween Day with the lights turned out and a candle flickering on your desk to bring on delightful shivers.

*Boxes and Poetry* The sides of a small cardboard box provide ample opportunity for displaying children's interpretations of favorite poems. Secure the cover on the box with tape. Children can paint the surface or decorate the box with cloth or paper. After they have selected a poem, they can mount illustrative material on all six sides of the box. One sixth-grade student brought in a commercial photo cube, an inexpensive plastic cube available in most novelty stores. A Polaroid camera was used to shoot photographs of a New York harbor, and the finished pictures were placed in the photo cube to dramatically depict "Waterfront Streets" by Langston Hughes from *Selected Poems.*

To enrich a unit on the zoo, a second-grade teacher used shoeboxes to represent animal habitats. The insides of the shoeboxes were painted, interesting paper provided collage landscapes, and, finally, animal drawings were put into the shoeboxes. Several of the children's works were very humorous. Henry's giraffe, for example, projected through a slit in the top of the shoebox that insured room for Mr. Giraffe's very long spotted neck; Edith's elephant's trunk was far too long for the shoebox —thus it protruded through the side of the box; Roy's lion's tail stuck out through a slit in the side of the box, and a tiny paper mouse rested on the tail.

Poems about the various animals were found and placed alongside the children's artwork.

During various box-projects, be sure to share Carl Sandburg's delightful free verse "Boxes and Bags," in *Rainbows Are Made: Poems by Carl Sandburg,* in which

"Elephants need big boxes to hold a dozen handkerchiefs."

*Poems about Building*  A New Jersey teacher correlated poetry and art for a unit on community planning and construction. The poems included Eve Merriam's "Bam, Bam, Bam," from *Jamboree*, and "Construction Job" and "A Time for Building," both from *A Song I Sang to You*, by Myra Cohn Livingston.

The teacher encouraged the children to bring back to class a variety of materials gathered at a nearby building site. Bricks, scraps of wood, nails, and plaster were used by the class to construct sculptures and collages. Finished projects were put together in a hall display.

A trip to any community site—even a junkyard—can spark children to create poetry. Sharing a free-verse poem such as "Passing by the Junkyard" by Charles J. Egita, from my collection *A Song in Stone*, can start you thinking about "heaps" of possibilities.

*Choral Speaking*  Choral speaking is an activity that can contribute to the appreciation and enjoyment of poetry as well as provide worthwhile learning and listening experiences.

The easiest form of choral speaking is the refrain, where children merely repeat the refrain of a frequently repeated line of a longer poem. After hearing a selection several times, children quickly note that the line will appear and reappear, and they will wait anxiously for their cue to participate.

I have used, for example, Shel Silverstein's "Peanut Butter Sandwich" from *Where the Sidewalk Ends* with boys and girls in preschool and kindergarten classes. Each of the twelve stanzas ends with the words "peanut butter sandwich." Before reading the selection, I ask them to shout out the three words. I next tell them that when I raise my hand this is the cue for them all to shout "peanut butter sandwich." It has never failed me. With the availability of the recording based on the book (CBS), children can shout out the words along with Mr. Silverstein, if you don't want to read it aloud.

A second type of arrangement is two-part speaking. Two groups of children take a part of the poem. An example is the nursery rhyme:

## *RIDING*

| | |
|---|---|
| This is the way the ladies ride: | GIRLS |
| Tri, tre, tre, tree: tri, tre, tre, tree! | ALL |
| This is the way the ladies ride: | GIRLS |
| Tri, tre, tre, tree: tri, tre, tre, tree! | ALL |
| | |
| This is the way the gentlemen ride: | BOYS |
| Gallop-a-trot, gallop-a-trot! | ALL |
| This is the way the gentlemen ride: | BOYS |
| Gallop-a-trot, gallop-a-trot! | ALL |
| | |
| This is the way the farmers ride: | BOYS |
| Hobbledy-hoy, hobbledy-hoy! | GIRLS |
| This is the way the farmers ride: | BOYS |
| Hobbledy-hoy, hobbledy-hoy! | GIRLS |

Line-a-child arrangements are somewhat difficult, yet give each child a chance to speak one or more lines alone. The difficulty arises from the necessity for precision of delivery.

In part-speaking, varied groups of children take parts of the selection. The teacher has the responsibility of knowing which child can handle the various speaking assignments. One example:

### IF YOU'RE GOOD

| | |
|---|---|
| Santa Claus will come tonight | BOYS |
| If you're good | ALL |
| And do what you know is right | GIRLS |
| As you should. | ALL |
| Down the chimney he will creep, | SOLO |
| Bringing you a wooly sheep | SOLO |
| And a doll that goes to sleep | SOLO |
| If you're good. | ALL |
| | |
| Santa Claus will drive his sleigh | BOYS |
| Through the wood | ALL |
| But he'll come around this way | GIRLS |
| If you're good. | ALL |
| With a wind-up bird that sings | SOLO |
| And a puzzle made of rings, | SOLO |
| Jumping jacks and funny things. | ALL |
| If you're good. | ALL |
| | |
| He will bring you cars that go | BOYS |
| If you're good | ALL |
| And a rocking horsey, oh, | GIRLS |
| If only he would! | SOLO |

| | |
|---|---|
| And a dolly that can sneeze, | SOLO |
| That says, "Mama!" | |
| when you squeeze | SOLO |
| He'll bring you some of these | SOLO |
| If you're good. | ALL |
| | |
| Santa grieves when you are bad, | BOYS |
| As he should: | ALL |
| But it makes him very glad | SOLO |
| When you're good; | SOLO |
| He is wise and he's a dear | SOLO |
| Just do right and never fear | SOLO |
| He'll remember you each year— | SOLO |
| If you're good! | ALL |

The most difficult type of choral speech is unison speaking, for it involves all students speaking at the same time. Perfect timing, balance, phrasing, inflection, and pronunciation are required, which takes much practice and is quite time-consuming.

Programs of choral speaking can be planned and enhanced with lighting effects and with interesting staging techniques, such as having children stand in a semicircle, scattering them around the stage, or interspersing simple dance and mime with their readings.

Choral speaking helps develop good speech, provides the timid child with a degree of self-confidence, and gives many pleasurable moments.

*Circus! Circus!* Who can resist the magic of the circus? Color, lights, action, music, clowns, acrobats, animals, and a host of other sights and sensations constitute a circus atmosphere full of many poetic images. If your students have never seen a real three-ring entertainment, you can bring it alive in the classroom.

Jack Prelutsky's *Circus* contains poems about aerial acrobats, monkey bands, equestrians, and clowns that prance through the pages as "the circus parade goes marching."

More fun and rhymes are available in *If I Ran the Circus* by Dr. Seuss, and *You Think It's Fun to Be a Clown!* by David Adler. Don't miss Ray Cruz's full-color pictures in this volume featuring clowns that leap from the pages. The witty, surprise ending is a special treat.

Add musical zest to circus festivities by using selected songs from the Broadway musical *Barnum*, available at your local record shop on a CBS recording.

For additional ideas on using the circus theme, write for *Circus—A Teaching Unit*, a twenty-four-page booklet that provides background information and a variety of teaching suggestions that cover all curriculum areas. Single copies are available free from Ringling Brothers and Barnum and Bailey Circus, Department of Educational Services, 3201 New Mexico Avenue, N.W., Washington, D.C. 20016.

Blow up some balloons, pop some popcorn, put out some clown makeup, play *Barnum*, and display the books of circus poems to let the world know that the circus is coming to your classroom.

*Collage Poetry Balls* After children have selected a favorite poem, encourage them to create a collage poetry ball. Children's collages interpreting the poem can be placed on large circles cut from oaktag or construction paper. Photographs from newspapers or magazines, cloth, realia, various sizes of print or type, and original drawings can be the raw material for depicting the poem's meaning.

Shirley McCammon, an English teacher, used a variation of this idea to encourage her students to write poetry. "I Am" collages motivated students to ask themselves, "Who am I? Where am I going? Where did I come from?" After the collages were completed, students wrote several sentences about themselves, leading to the creation of free verse after they had worked and reworked their original lists. One example follows.

List of Sentences:

> I am inhibited to degrees.
> Filled with mixed emotions.
> Unhappy at times, full of life.
> Lonely but popular.
> I am one and the same.
> I am unique.
> I am ME!

The verse:

> Inhibited, filled with emotions,
> Unhappy at times,
> Though full of life.
> Lonely, yet popular,
> I am uniquely ME.

Children can create collages focusing on their homes, families, special interests, hobbies, pets, peers, or aspirations; they can then try writing poems about themselves and their collage constructions.

These can also be turned into poetry wall hangings. Children can mount wallpaper on large, rectangular pieces of cardboard and then illustrate their interpretation of poems with collage materials. The panels can be used for hall or classroom bulletin board displays, and later taken home by students to share with families.

*Color Me Poetry* There are a number of successful ways to involve children with finding or writing poems about color. One teacher placed a bright array of colored wrapping tissue on a bulletin board display with the caption "Find a Poem About Me."

A dramatic technique for stimulating children to think about color is to use an overhead projector. Place a clear bowl of water atop the projector—a plastic turtle dish or a clear glass pie plate works best. By dropping a few drops of food coloring in the bowl, magical things happen on the screen. The coloring can be stirred around or blown to create movement, or colors can be mixed together to make new color combinations.

In a kindergarten class where this was done, one small lad remarked, "Oh, my! The water's starting to bleed!"

The movement of the color can be enhanced by the playing of a musical selection or can be combined with dance and rhythm movements.

Paint blots is another technique that works well. Chil-

dren can drop a few blobs of tempera paint on construction paper and carefully fold the paper in half. When it
is opened, they will find an interesting paint blob, à la
Rorschach. Within the next few days they can give a title
to their creation and look for appropriate poems that best
illustrate their blots. The results will be surprising.

In *Hailstones and Halibut Bones* by Mary O'Neill,
twelve poems about various colors appear, each asking a
question: "What Is Gold?" "What Is Red?" "What Is
Orange?" The poems not only tell about the color of
objects but touch upon the ways color can make us feel,
for example: "Orange is brave/Orange is bold"; "Gold
is feeling/Like a king"; "Blue is feeling/Sad or low."

The poems stir our senses and make us want to look
around carefully to see everyday colors we have taken for
granted and see them anew in fresh, poetic imagery. To
further encourage children to create color images, bring
to class specific objects—a rose, a bunch of colored
leaves, or a black ant; their physical presence will awaken
mental images.

A Las Vegas, Nevada, teacher asks her students to
describe thoughts about colors, not often written about.
She asks, "How do certain colors make you feel?" Several responses include:

Aqua makes me feel like a mermaid dancing in the sea.

Bronze makes me feel like a dead statue.

Amber makes me feel like millions of waves of grain.

Color is around and about us. Use it to broaden children's writing.

**Fingers on Hand** Boys and girls can try creating poems about their fingers or fingers of friends, relatives, or pets. In a New Jersey classroom, a third-grade teacher did a bulletin-board display entitled "Our Fingers." Children traced the outline of one hand on a piece of construction paper. Their poems were printed on the outline and pasted onto the display. The following example is an unsophisticated verse, but a good one considering it came from a child who had never written poetry before:

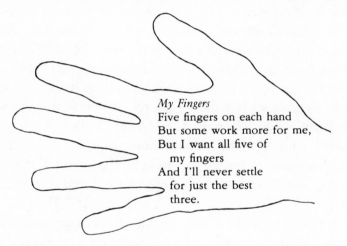

*My Fingers*
Five fingers on each hand
But some work more for me,
But I want all five of
    my fingers
And I'll never settle
    for just the best
    three.

**Globe-trotting with Poetry** Poetry reflects people, their lifestyles, experiences, dreams, feelings, ideas. It is a universal form of creative communication, yet each poem has a unique "personality." By learning what poets from all over the world have to say, children can better understand how all people are alike and yet different.

A world-poetry hunt is a good way to start globetrotting. Post a map of the United States and the world on a bulletin board. Underneath, set up a table display of books featuring poetry of both American and foreign poets. As the children find, read, and share the selections, they can mark off places on the maps where the verses originated.

Encourage each student to research the part of the country that his or her favorite poet comes from. Sometimes this information is readily found on book jackets. As children's repertoires grow, they will begin to see that poets come from all walks of life and environments. Some leading American poets they will want to encounter are David McCord from Massachusetts; Eve Merriam, New York; Gwendolyn Brooks, Illinois; Aileen Fisher, Colorado; Myra Cohn Livingston, California.

Poetry that can help children gain new insights about world neighbors and their cultures can be found in *Have You Seen a Comet?*, edited by Anne Pellowski, et al., which contains poems, letters, anecdotes, stories, essays, and illustrations by children and teenagers from the United States and foreign countries—Liberia, Czechoslovakia, Turkey, Costa Rica, Malaysia, and Poland.

Another attractive combination of language and verse is *Chinese Mother Goose Rhymes*, selected and edited by Robert Wyndham. Designed to read vertically, Chinese calligraphy ornaments the margins of each page. Forty traditional rhymes, riddles, lullabies, and games that have amused children for generations are included.

Perhaps groups of children would like to design and make mini-anthologies as gifts to next year's incoming class, the school library, or parents. One group might plan a poetry atlas featuring poems from continent to continent and illustrate them with original drawings and appropriate sections cut from world maps.

*Growing with Poetry* A primary teacher in Trenton, New Jersey, uses a chart titled "I Am Getting Bigger" in her classroom. Inches are marked off on the chart, and a space alongside the numbers records the children's names. Once a month, each child is measured to record growth. The chart contains a variety of pictures and poems to be read to or by boys and girls while their heights are being recorded. Poems might include Karla Kuskin's "The Question" in *Dogs & Dragons, Trees & Dreams*, the section "Mostly Me" in Myra Cohn Livingston's *A Song I Sang to You*, the section "Children" in Eve Merriam's *Jamboree*, or the section "At the Top of My Voice" in my collection *Surprises.*

*A Line of Poetry* A New York City teacher devised a good way to prompt children to search for poems by stringing a clothesline across the classroom and attaching brown manila envelopes to it with clothespins. Pictures were pasted to the face of each envelope—a picture of a boy, a girl, or an animal, or a photograph depicting a particular season of the year. Class members were encouraged to look for, or write, poems about the illustrations on the envelopes and put them into the envelopes. A poetry clothesline can become a permanent fixture in the classroom and be changed as often as needed to tie in with specific lessons.

*A Peephole Poetry Display* Students can let their imaginations run wild when creating peephole poetry displays, working individually or in groups. After a poem has been selected, a hole about the size of a pencil should be punched in one end of a shoebox, while the other end is cut out completely and covered with cellophane. The children then construct a diorama inside the box interpreting the poem selected. When the display is completed, the boxtop is put on and the light from a flashlight is projected through the cellophane. As one child reads the poem, or it is read on a commercial or class-made recording or tape, another can peep through the hole and view the diorama.

*People Poems* Poems about people of every size, shape, and form are indeed plentiful in the world of children's poetry.

Readers can encounter friends such as Sarah Cynthia Sylvia Stout, who "would not take the garbage out," or Benjamin Bunnn, "whose buttons will not come undone" in Shel Silverstein's *Where the Sidewalk Ends.*

Lewis, who "had a trumpet," Hughbert, and Alexander Soames, a child who speaks only in rhyme, are three characters in Karla Kuskin's *Dogs & Dragons, Trees & Dreams.*

For mature readers, Nancy Larrick offers a bountiful collection, *Crazy to Be Alive in Such a Strange World.*

Famous people are also the subjects of many poems. An excellent collection to have on hand is Rosemary and Stephen Vincent Benét's *A Book of Americans,* featuring such personalities as Johnny Appleseed, Dolly Madison, P. T. Barnum, and the Wright Brothers, perfect for enhancing American history lessons.

In the section "Grownups" in Eve Merriam's *Jamboree*, we meet Abraham Lincoln, George Washington, and King Solomon.

After hearing and reading a variety of people poems, students might think of people they would like to meet and write about—the school custodian, a favorite teacher, the local pet shop owner, a pizza maker—anyone, either famous or not. Finished poems might be given to favorite people as a gift.

*Personal Poetry Anthologies* Dianne Weissberger, a teacher in Germantown High School, Germantown, Pennsylvania, excited her students by sending them on a poetry hunt. The students selected a theme, finding ten related poems; these were transcribed into booklets, illustrated with appropriate pictures. On the last page of each booklet, the students wrote a concluding paragraph explaining why they had chosen a particular theme and how they felt about it while working on the project. Ms. Weissberger reports: "The summary paragraphs proved to me that students gained much insight into themselves and actually found poetry fun!"

The number of poems selected can depend on age level. Third-graders, for example, might choose only three or four poems relating to a specific topic.

The basic objective is to get children to think through the whys, whats, and hows of the project. Why did they choose the theme they did? What sources did they draw from? What relationships did they see between the selections? How did they benefit from the project? Choosing poems helps children focus attention on what they are reading and feeling!

Illustrations can be original drawings or pictures collected from a variety of sources. Artwork for booklets might also be created by older students, or even someone from the child's immediate family. Finished booklets might include an attractive cover containing a good title for the work and the name of the compiler and artist. A table of contents can be included as well as an index of titles, first lines, and poets, all reinforcing important language arts skills. To add to this project, students might include a brief biographical sketch of each poet. The last page can contain a photograph of the compiler along with a composition explaining the work.

*Pet a Poem* Set up a class pet shop. Have children bring in stuffed toys or, under supervision, a live pet. Students can find poems to honor favorite pets, or create original poems.

Poems about pets abound. Cat lovers will find a host of feline favorites in two books of original verse by Beatrice Schenk de Regniers, *This Big Cat and Other Cats I've Known* and *So Many Cats.*

Mature readers will want to read the classic cat-of-cats book, T. S. Eliot's *Old Possum's Book of Practical Cats*, or listen to the cassette produced by Caedmon with readings by Sir John Gielgud and Irene Worth.

Twenty-four selections by nineteen poets appear in my compilation *I Am the Cat*, following the feline's life from the birth of a kitten to cats in old age.

*A Dog's Life* also presents a life cycle from puppyhood to a dog's death; twenty-three poems, selected by me, depict a wide array of breeds. William Cole's *Good Dog Poems* contains eighty-eight verses divided into ten sections.

Horses are heralded in *My Mane Catches the Wind*, for which I selected twenty-two poems showing life cycles from the birth of a foal to an aged horse. *The Poetry of Horses*, selected by William Cole, features 111 selections, divided into nine sections.

A pet mouse will become more alive by sharing various poets' thoughts about mice. A rich gathering of fifty poems appears in Vardine Moore's *Mice Are Rather Nice*.

All four creatures are celebrated in Part 8 of Nancy Larrick's *Piping Down the Valleys Wild*, via twenty-two selections. Parrots, monkeys, turtles, and goldfish are also mentioned.

*A Picture for a Poem* Dig into your own personal picture file and post an interesting photograph or picture on the bulletin board. Students can hunt for poems they feel fit the mood or describe the illustration. Catchy titles add to such displays. For example, the caption "Sneak into This Haunted House," under an illustration of an old house—the "hauntier" the better—might elicit original poems, or a poem such as "The Haunted House" in *Nightmares*, by Jack Prelutsky, might be shared.

Other pictures and captions might deal with nature, the environment, space, sports, or the sea.

*A Pocketful of Poems* Cut out several large pocket shapes from medium-weight cardboard or oaktag. These pockets can be painted with tempera or covered with patterned fabric or construction paper. Label each pocket with a category such as "Me," "The City," "Insects," or "Animals." Leaving the tops open, secure the pockets to a bulletin board by stapling around the edges. Insert several poems in each pocket and encourage the children to pick out and read a poem whenever they have some free time. Near the bulletin board, place a copy of Beatrice Schenk de Regniers' "Keep a Poem in Your Pocket," from her book *Something Special.* The poem is reprinted on page 56.

Children can be encouraged not only to pick the pockets but to fill them once in a while, too!

*A Poem for a Picture* Students are often asked to illustrate poems they have read or heard. You might try turning this idea around by encouraging boys and girls to draw or paint a picture first, then find a poem that goes with it. Several children can look for poems they feel appropriate for a classmate's drawing. If they cannot find a suitable poem, they may decide to write their own. In any case, the children will have looked at a variety of poems, and the next time they paint they may remember just the right verse to accompany their pictures.

**Poems to Satisfy Young Appetites** A bulletin board can feature the question "What's for Lunch?" A table setting can be depicted by stapling a paper tablecloth on the bulletin board for a background along with paper plates, cups, and plastic cutlery. The latter can be mounted with double-faced masking tape or strong glue.

On each plate a food poem can appear. One might describe eating an ice cream cone on a hot summer's day, another might mention the spicy taste of chili con carne or relishes on a hot dog. Before lunch hour, either a child or the teacher can read a selection from the plate. The poems can be changed as regularly as children's tastes.

Three volumes of poems about food are *Eats: Poems*, an original book of verse by Arnold Adoff, which includes poetic morsels on Chinese food, chocolate, and apple pie; my collection *Munching: Poems About Eating*, featuring such tasty delights as "Bananas and Cream" by David McCord, "Turtle Soup" by Lewis Carroll, and "The Pizza" by Odgen Nash; for older readers, *Poem Stew*, selected by William Cole, offers a feast of funny poems from the creased prune to rhinoceros stew, with works by Kaye Starbird, Richard Armour, and six by Mr. Cole himself.

**Poems to Celebrate** Holidays hold a special place in all of our hearts, each rich in tradition. Both Thanksgiving, inherited from the Pilgrims, and Independence Day, commemorating the birthday of our country, provide us with a sense of being, connecting us with our early history and customs; Christmas and Easter are joyous days that are shared with people the world over; St. Valentine's Day and Halloween, though not considered legal holidays, bring to us hundreds of years of culture and custom, wit and wisdom, folklore—and fun!

Luckily, poetry about these and other major and minor holidays abounds. Here is a holiday potpourri sampling for you to share with students of all ages.

Harcourt Brace Jovanovich Holiday Poetry series includes six collections compiled by me: *Beat the Drum, Independence Day Has Come*; *Easter Buds Are Springing*; *Good Morning to You, Valentine*; *Hey-How for Halloween*; *Merrily Comes Our Harvest In: Poems for Thanksgiving*; *Sing Hey for Christmas Day*.

Myra Cohn Livingston's collections for holidays include *Callooh! Callay! Holiday Poems for Young Readers* and for middle-graders, *Christmas Poems*, *Easter Poems*, *Thanksgiving Poems*, *Poems of Christmas*, *Poems for Jewish Holidays* and *O Frabjous Day! Poetry for Holidays and Special Occasions*. All ages will enjoy her original creations, representing sixteen landmark days on the calendar, in *Celebrations*, including "Martin Luther King Day," "Saint Patrick's Day," "Passover," and "Birthday."

Jack Prelutsky's original verses appear in *It's Halloween, It's Christmas, It's Thanksgiving, It's Valentine's Day.*

Through such volumes, readers will meet works by "old-timers" such as Joyce Kilmer, William Shakespeare, and Stephen Vincent Benét; they'll find the contemporary voices of David McCord, Aileen Fisher, and Shel Silverstein; they'll weave in and out of old-new voices, too—poets who have been read by generation after generation of children and still speak to us today, such treasured poets as Langston Hughes, Carl Sandburg, and Dorothy Aldis.

Holiday celebrations can be enhanced when girls and boys design their own greeting cards. Appropriate poems can be selected or written, illustrated, and sent on such occasions as birthdays, Mother's Day or Father's Day—ideal times to write and illustrate greeting card verses for special friends and relatives.

*Poet of the Month* Being introduced to new poets and their work can be stimulating for children. Use a bulletin board and tabletop display to highlight a particular poet of the month. The bulletin board can feature biographical information along with several of the poet's poems printed on oaktag. If possible, a photograph of the poet can be included. A table display can feature volumes of the poet's work, and, if available, a recording of his or her voice or that of another person reading from the poet's works.

Each day, read a selection or two from the featured books and play the recordings. Encourage children to look for additional biographical information on the poet, or to search out more examples of his or her work. Build up a "poet's file" by having the boys and girls write letters to publishers or to living poets themselves requesting additional information. In the latter case, the children's letters should be sent in care of the publishing house along with a self-addressed stamped envelope; they will be forwarded to the poet by the editor. Students can also look for information in books and periodicals.

Below is a listing of poets and their birthdates. All of

these individuals are perfect choices for your students' poet of the month:

| | January | | July |
|---|---|---|---|
| 6 | Carl Sandburg | 15 | Arnold Adoff |
| 13 | N. M. Bodecker | 17 | Karla Kuskin |
| 18 | A. A. Milne | 19 | Eve Merriam |

| | February | | August |
|---|---|---|---|
| 1 | Langston Hughes | 16 | Beatrice Schenk de Regniers |

| | March | 17 | Myra Cohn Livingston |
|---|---|---|---|
| 2 | Dr. Seuss | 19 | Ogden Nash |
| 17 | Lilian Moore | 21 | X. J. Kennedy |
| 26 | Robert Frost | | |

| | April | | September |
|---|---|---|---|
| 22 | William Jay Smith | 8 | Jack Prelutsky |
| 26 | William Shakespeare | 9 | Aileen Fisher |
| | | 24 | Harry Behn |

| | May | | October |
|---|---|---|---|
| 12 | Edward Lear | 14 | E. E. Cummings |
| 17 | Eloise Greenfield | 29 | Valerie Worth |
| 25 | Theodore Roethke | | |
| 31 | Elizabeth Coatsworth | | November |

| | June | 13 | Robert Louis Stevenson |
|---|---|---|---|
| 6 | Nancy Willard | 15 | David McCord |
| 7 | Gwendolyn Brooks | | |
| 7 | Nikki Giovanni | | December |
| 24 | John Ciardi | 10 | Emily Dickinson |
| 26 | Charlotte Zolotow | | |
| 27 | Lucille Clifton | | |

*A PoeTree* Branches can be arranged to create a "Poe-Tree" by attaching them to a wall, hung from the ceiling like a mobile, or placed in a pail or flowerpot filled with sand, earth, or styrofoam. Spray paint can change the color of the branches from time to time.

As children select and illustrate favorite poems, they can be attached to the branches for others to read. The PoeTree can tie in with specific curriculum subjects or have a theme assigned to it.

A New York City teacher combines this idea with Poet of the Month (see page 199). Atop the tree the poet's name is printed on oaktag; when available, a picture of the poet is added. The branches of the tree are then filled with poems by the poet being honored.

The PoeTree can also be a seasonal tree. At Christmastime, for example, Christmas or winter poems might appear; in February, the PoeTree can help celebrate Black History Month by featuring poems by or about famous black personalities.

In New Jersey, a fourth-grade teacher has each child create mini-PoeTrees as gifts for Mother's Day. Each child decorates a cardboard milk carton, fills it with earth, and places a small twig firmly inside. A poem or two is attached to the twig. At the top of the branch some children place pictures of their mothers or themselves. The mini-PoeTrees are unique, unusual, inexpensive, and very effective presents.

*A Poetry Animal Fair* Use a corner of the room to set up a poetry animal fair. Hang a mobile from the ceiling featuring pictures of animals. Place a large wooden box under the mobile to hold books of poems about animals together with models of animals that children bring into class.

After the boys and girls have read many poems about animals, have them select a favorite. Drawn or cut-out pictures of animals can be pasted to cardboard and attached to sticks to make hand puppets. Children can work the puppets while reading their favorite poem about the animal of their choice.

A similar idea was carried out by a first-grade teacher in California. She used the theme "Fish for a Poem" and featured a fish mobile. The mobile contained several poems about fish. Underneath the mobile a fishbowl with two goldfish was placed on a box. A second box was gaily decorated and contained poems about fish and the sea, which had been mounted on pieces of cardboard. A small hole was punched in each piece of cardboard, through which a paper clip was slipped. Children could take their "fishing poles"—long sticks with magnets attached to the ends—and literally fish for poetry.

*Poetry Face to Face* A mirror can be used to help introduce a variety of poems. Attach one to a bulletin board or hang one on a wall; around it place several poems about one's face or oneself. Near the mirror place several volumes of poetry. Poems might include "Robert, Who Is a Stranger to Himself" by Gwendolyn Brooks in *Bronzeville Boys and Girls*, or Carl Sandburg's "Phizzog" in *Rainbows Are Made: Poems by Carl Sandburg*, selected by me. The display might also contain pictures of the children in the class or baby pictures for peers to guess who *was* who!

*Poetry Happenings* A group of children can plan poetry happenings or dramatic readings of several poems relating to a specific subject. Poems can tie in with curriculum, specific interests such as sports or hobbies, or a subject—rocks, the city, famous people, or music. When they have a final selection, they can present a poetry happening for the class and for other classes in the school. To enhance the happening, simple props or creative dramatics can be employed.

Recently, I was invited to an elementary school in Westchester County, New York, where a group of fourth-graders presented a lavish production based on my collection *A Dog's Life.* The children wore masks they had made depicting various breeds of dogs. The simple staging on stools and ladders was enhanced by spotlights. One group taped sounds of dogs barking and howling for background effects; another group set Karla Kuskin's "Full of the Moon," which is included in the collection, to music. To see and hear nine-year-olds perform works by Carl Sandburg, Robert Frost, Harry Behn, and Gwendolyn Brooks was pure magic. The tender "For Mugs" by Myra Cohn Livingston, about a dog who has just died, brought chills to the entire audience.

Any grouping of poems lends itself to a multitude of production ideas. Try it!

*A Poetry Jar* An elementary teacher in Las Vegas, Nevada, devised a clever way to motivate her students to read poetry. A clear glass jar becomes the Poetry Jar. At the beginning of each week an object is placed in the jar.

Children then become poem hunters, seeking poetry that mentions or describes the object.

Objects might be toy models of cars or animals, realia such as a leaf, rock, or flower, or sometimes a live specimen such as an ant or a guppy. A larger container such as a fish tank might feature turtles, horned toads, or interesting fish.

Alongside the jar or tank leave a pencil and a pad of paper for those who want to sit, observe, and create poetry. The girls and boys might also try creating a variety of short verse forms based on the objects in the Poetry Jar.

*A Poetry Weather Calendar* Younger boys and girls will enjoy a poetry weather calendar. Use a large piece of oaktag for each month. List the month, weeks, and days of the week, along with the question "What is the weather like today?"

On the bottom of the chart attach several large brown envelopes labeled "Sun Poems," "Wind Poems," "Cloud Poems," "Rain Poems," or "Snow Poems." Collected poems can be placed within appropriate envelopes, which can be added to and used year after year. When the month, date, and day of the week have been discussed, a child can volunteer to tell what the weather is like, then choose an appropriate poem from an envelope to read or have read to the class. Weather combinations, such as "sunny and windy," can also be used.

Girls and boys can be encouraged to add to the envelopes as they find various weather poems throughout the year.

An excellent resource to use is Maurice Sendak's *Chicken Soup with Rice*, wherein the acclaimed author/illustrator sings praises of his favorite soup in gay themes and pictures for each month of the year. *Chicken Soup with Rice* is also available as a filmstrip set from Weston Woods, and as a book and cassette package from Scholastic, Inc.

Other sources to seek out include the section "Sun and Rain and Wind and Storms," in Myra Cohn Livingston's *A Song I Sang to You*; the section "Weather and Seasons" in Eve Merriam's *Jamboree*; the section "Rain, Sun, and Snow" in *Surprises*, selected by me; and Part 3, "I like it when it's mizzly . . . and just a little drizzly . . ." in Nancy Larrick's *Piping Down the Valleys Wild*.

*Prose and Poetry* Prose and poetry go well together. After children have read a favorite book or listened to one read aloud, follow it up with a poem.

Story hours provide wonderful opportunities to introduce poetry. After reading a book to students, follow with a poem that has the same theme. For example, if you read a book such as *The Snowy Day* by Ezra Jack Keats, you can add depth to the moment with a poem such as "Cynthia in the Snow" by Gwendolyn Brooks, in *Bronzeville Boys and Girls.* This enables children to hear a Caldecott Award–winning volume and a Pulitzer Prize–winning poet—all tucked into a ten- or fifteen-minute time period.

Older students can combine poetry with other forms of literature, too. After they have finished reading a novel, ask them to find a poem that reflects the book's subject or theme. For instance, after reading a Marguerite Henry or Walter Farley novel about horses, have them look for a poem about horses. A story such as *The Mouse and the Motorcycle* by Beverly Cleary is sure to send all those who like rodents scurrying for a poem that expresses feelings about mice.

Nonfiction can be dealt with in the same way. After boys and girls have read a book about dinosaurs, for example, have them look for a dinosaur poem to share. *Dinosaurs* features poems about the beasts of yore, by poets such as Patricia Hubbell, Myra Cohn Livingston, Lilian Moore, and Valerie Worth, selected by me.

Misha Arenstein, a fourth-grade teacher in Scarsdale, New York, uses this technique for book-sharing: He has students tuck a poem related to a book inside the cover so that when others read it they already have a poem on hand to read, too. He then encourages readers to add another poem. Within months, one novel might have three, four, or more verses relating to the plot, characters, or setting inside the cover for this and future classes to enjoy.

Another idea to spark the use of poetry with prose is by having children read or re-read favorite fairy tales and introduce them to humorous verses about characters, plots, or situations. For example, after discussing the plot of "Cinderella," children will enjoy hearing such verse as "... And Then the Prince Knelt Down and Tried to Put the Glass Slipper on Cinderella's Foot" by Judith

Viorst in *If I Were in Charge of the World and Other Worries*, briefly relating how Cinderella has changed her mind about the handsome prince the day after the ball; the untitled verse encouraging Cinderella to *use* her wits which begins "Look Cinderella" in *A Song I Sang to You* by Myra Cohn Livingston; and the irreverent "Cinderella" in Roald Dahl's *Revolting Rhymes*.

*Season Songs* Scientists have set approximate dates for the arrival of each season in the Northern Hemisphere: autumn, September 21; winter, December 21; spring, March 21; summer, June 21. Check the correct dates and times in your local newspaper. The summer and winter dates, marking the days of longest and shortest daylight, are called "solstices." Spring and autumn occur when the sun is directly over the equator; these times are called equinoxes.

Mark the arrival of each season by taking the class on a neighborhood field trip. Let students look for the first signs of the season and perhaps collect some materials for a science table display. Time might also be set aside for some brainstorming in which students list words to describe the coming season. The words can be copied and/or mimeographed for each child to have and to use in writing his or her experiences.

Poetry reflecting the various seasons is abundant. For younger readers you might use *The Sky Is Full of Song*, selected by me, which contains thirty-eight poems celebrating the seasons.

Middle-graders will enjoy any of the five following titles:

Barbara Juster Esbensen's *Cold Stars and Fireflies* is a sparkling collection of forty-three original poems about nature and the changing seasons, with evocative illustrations touched with reds and grays.

Myra Cohn Livingston's *A Circle of Seasons* is an original thirteen-stanza poem following the cycle of the seasons.

Two anthologies include *Moments*, selected by me, containing fifty selections; Part 6, "I wonder what the spring will shout . . . ," in Nancy Larrick's *Piping Down the Valleys Wild* includes seventeen verses hailing the season.

Aileen Fisher's *Out in the Dark and Daylight* provides an abundance of original verses about the year and its many seasonal moods.

For additional references see "Poems to Celebrate" (pages 197–99), and "Poet of the Month" (pages 199–200).

***See the Sea in Poetry*** A Las Vegas, Nevada, teacher uses a tabletop display entitled "Our Home—The Sea" to tie poetry into science, art, and literature. She covers a table with sand, a variety of seashells, and starfish. The display also contains a toy shovel and pail, which serves as a container for sea poems the students in her class find or write. Behind the display she places prints of great seascape paintings to further motivate youngsters to look at, feel, and write their own thoughts about the sea.

*Sea Songs*, a collection of original poems by Myra Cohn

Livingston, can be displayed, along with three anthologies: *The Ice-Cream Ocean and Other Delectable Poems of the Sea*, selected and illustrated by Susan Russo; *The Sea Is Calling Me*; and Section 5 of *Rainbows Are Made: Poems by Carl Sandburg*, both selected by me.

Once boys and girls have been exposed to various poets' work, they can be further encouraged to create original verse. The children's creations can be placed in the pail on the display. At the end of a given time both the poems the students found and the ones they themselves created can be bound into a scrapbook and illustrated with original drawing or pictures clipped from magazines and newspapers.

*The Senses and Poetry* Children can be sparked to create poems after they have had a variety of planned sensory experiences. One way to motivate boys and girls to use their senses is to take them for several walks around the neighborhood. Be specific on each walk. Tell the class, "Today we are going on a *hearing* walk to record only the various sounds we hear." On a second walk, children can record all that they see; on a third, all that they smell, and so on. During each walk the class can record all the various sounds they hear, sights they see, and so forth in a notebook.

A second-grade class went to visit a nearby pond for a "seeing" walk. The children saw many things but were fascinated by the many seed pods that appeared on the bank. After bringing the pods back into the classroom, several boys and girls wrote the following:

Seed pods when they break look like bombs exploding.

Seed pods sail like parachutes when they open.

The pods look like cotton candy when they are put together.

I could eat it, but I won't.

After several such walking trips, plans can be made for a sensory field trip. Visit an area the children have never seen before; a trip to a museum or a bakery, or even a ride on a train or merry-go-round, can produce excellent results when boys and girls are offered the opportunity to open up their senses.

A third-grade teacher in Indianapolis, Indiana, has her class listen to nature by providing them with imaginative questions. She asks: "How does a brook sound?" "What song does a cricket sing?" "What tool do you think of when you hear a woodpecker?" "How do raindrops sound against your umbrella?" "You are on a buffalo hunt with Indian friends. What sounds do you hear as the herd draws near?"

Such questions are good ones to ask before taking the class on a walking trip.

Sounds can arouse young writers. Another idea to inspire writing is to record or have students record a variety of sounds—bacon frying, the ticking of a clock, a slamming door, a baby crying, a typewriter or electric razor in action. After discussing sounds and noises and actually hearing them, a fourth-grade class in Harlem composed the following:

## NOISE

Noise, noise everywhere
What to do! It's always there.
Bang! Pow! Zoom! Crunch!
Buzz! Crack! Crack! Munch!

In the air, on the ground,
Noise, noise all around.
Dogs barking, cars parking,
Planes flying, babies crying.

Sh . . . sh . . . time for sleep.
Not a single little peep.
Oh no—through the door—
Comes a noisy, awful snore.

Tick-tock—stop the clock.
Stop the yelling on my block.
Close the windows, shut them tight.
Cotton in ear—nighty-night.

Suzanne Hunsucker, a teacher at the Riverton High School in Wyoming, offered this idea for "sensational writing":

I bombarded [the children's] senses as they walked into the classroom . . . music was playing, crepe paper hanging. I passed out chocolate kisses and small pieces of material to feel, and I sprayed the air with spice room deodorizer. All this launched a good discussion of the senses. . . .

To develop the sense of touch, we blindfolded some volunteers and had them describe objects they were feeling without actually naming them. For sound, we wrote thoughts to music and tape recorded sounds. For development of sight, I first prepared a slide show of famous paintings and described how to look for such elements as shape, design, perspective, texture, movement, lighting, and color. Students began to really look at and analyze these works with a critical eye . . .

Nancy Larrick suggests additional ways to involve children in the sensory approach to writing poetry:

Often it helps to bring in familiar objects which children can handle and then record their thoughts about . . . anything small enough to pick up and see from every angle. One group of fifth-graders soon set up what they called a "junk tray" from which they chose the inspiration for poetic images, even short poems . . .

In another class, wire coat hangers were twisted into modern sculpture, which led to poetry writing.

After children have had such sensory experiences, they can be encouraged to look for poems that deal with the senses and, of course, write their own verse.

*Sing a Poem* Music and poetry! Isn't that the perfect combination?

Several excellent collections of poems set to music get students singing, playing musical instruments, or experimenting with musical forms.

*Lullabies and Night Songs*, edited by William Engvick, with music by Alec Wilder and magnificent, full-color illustrations by Maurice Sendak, is as perfect now as when it first appeared in 1965. Forty-eight melodies appear in this oversized volume, including many Mother Goose rhymes and such gems as James Thurber's "The Golux's Song," Lewis Carroll's "The Crocodile," William Blake's "Cradle Song," and Robert Louis Stevenson's "Windy Night." A recording of the book, performed by Jan DeGaetani, is available from Caedmon.

Wonderland can be made a wee more wondrous with Lewis Carroll's *Songs from Alice.* Nine songs from *Alice's Adventures in Wonderland*, and ten from *Through the Looking Glass, and What Alice Found There*, are set for piano, guitar, and additional parts for violin, flute, or recorder. "Father William," "Turtle Soup," and "Jabberwocky" are among the familiar Lewis Carroll classics.

A handsome, eighty-page symphony, *The Moon on the One Hand* by William Crofut, with arrangements by Kenneth Cooper and Glen Shattuck, contains fifteen poems, most about nature and animals and including delights such as "in Just-" by E. E. Cummings; "The Chipmunk's Day," "The Mockingbird," and "Bird of the Night" by Randall Jarrell; and "Eletelephony" by Laura E. Richards. Arrangements include a variety of styles and instrumental possibilities—from piano to flute or the human voice.

Volumes such as these will lead students to set other poems to music, either those found in books or ones they have composed.

They can also be used to stage a classroom or assembly poetry musicale.

**Sports in Poetry** A sixth-grade teacher whets his students' poetry appetites with a sports in poetry bulletin board display.

A photo montage about a specific sport (baseball, football, water skiing), along with several related sports poems, is created by students. On the bulletin board is the following suggestion: "Make a photo montage about a sport you like. Find a poem about the sport. Or write one yourself."

Underneath the bulletin board is a tabletop display of books containing sports poems. Resources include two original books of verse by Lillian Morrison, *The Sidewalk Racer and Other Poems of Sports and Motion* and *The Break Dance Kids.* An anthology of poems selected by Lillian Morrison is *Sprints and Distances.*

Arnold Adoff's *Sports Pages* reflects the experiences and feelings of young athletes involved in various sports.

***Styrofoam and Space Projects*** A study of space can tie in with current events and humankind explorations while presenting some excellent poetry. After the children have heard, read, or written poems about space, encourage them to do a display. Give the children small Styrofoam balls that they can paint with tempera paint. Next, provide them with round, colored toothpicks that can be inserted into the Styrofoam. Finished projects can be attached to a bulletin-board display featuring poems, current events clippings from newspapers and magazines, and students' original artwork. Several of the balls might be strung together to create hanging mobiles.

*Poems About Outer Space* is a boxed set, which I designed, that includes paperbound anthologies, eight spiritmaster activity sheets, four posters, and "I Love Poetry" stickers. A teachers' guide offers many further ideas to rocket your children into a study of outer space. The kit is available from Sundance Distributors.

# What Is Poetry?

In addition to the many quotes about poetry that appear throughout the volume, here are some others that can be used as bulletin board sparklers for a variety of occasions or shared with students to evoke discussion:

Poetry is the most effective way of saying things. —Matthew Arnold

You may not shout when you remember poems you have read or learned, but you will know from your toes to your head that something has hit you. —Arna Bontemps

One of the skills of a good poet is to enact experiences rather than to talk about having had them. "*Show* it, don't *tell* it," the poet says, "make it happen, don't talk about its happening." —John Ciardi

Poetry is beautiful shorthand. —William Cole

A lot of people think or believe or know they feel—but that's thinking or believing or knowing; not feeling. And poetry is feeling—not knowing or believing or thinking. —E. E. Cummings

Poetry makes possible the deepest kind of personal possession of the world. —James Dickey

If I read a book and it makes my whole body so cold that no fire can ever warm me, I know that is poetry. If I feel physically as if the top of my head were taken *off*, I know that is poetry. These are the only ways I know it is. Is there another way? —Emily Dickinson

A poem . . . begins as a lump in the throat, a sense of wrong, a homesickness, a lovesickness. —Robert Frost

The basis of literary education is poetry. Poetry is rhythm, movement. The entering of poetic rhythm into the body of the reader is very important. It is something very close to the development of an athletic skill and, as such, it can't be rushed. —Northrop Frye

Poetry is comment on the world by people who see that world more clearly than other people and are moved by it. —Phyllis McGinley

Poetry is speaking painting. —Plutarch

Poetry is a sequence of dots and dashes, spelling depths, crypts, cross-lights, and moon-wisps. —Carl Sandburg

Poetry is a record of the best and happiest moments of the happiest and best minds. —Percy Bysshe Shelley

## *Poetry in Nonprint Media*

This selected listing of audiovisual materials includes programs that have been used and enjoyed by a variety of educators and children to enhance poetic experiences. Items mentioned in other parts of this volume are not described again below.

*Recordings The* source to consult for recordings is *International Index to Recorded Poetry*, compiled by Herbert H. Hoffman and Rita L. Hoffman, a guide to over 1,700

phonodiscs, tapes, cassettes, and filmstrips. The compilers have attempted to include every poetry recording released through 1980, anywhere in the world, in any language. Some 2,300 poets are represented by about 15,000 poems, in more than twenty languages. The compendium is divided into six sections: author index, title index, first line index, reader index, a register of poets by language of composition, and a list of recordings analyzed.

Caedmon offers a variety of poetry recordings. *A Gathering of Great Poetry for Children*, edited by Richard Lewis, is a four-set package, featuring the work of contemporary and classic poets, ranging from A. A. Milne to Gwendolyn Brooks. Several poems are read by the poets themselves—Carl Sandburg, Robert Frost, T. S. Eliot; others are read by Julie Harris, Cyril Ritchard, and David Wayne.

Caedmon has also produced *Silver Pennies* and *More Silver Pennies*, a two-record set narrated by Claire Bloom and Cyril Ritchard, containing selections from the books of the same title, edited by Blanche Jennings Thompson, published in 1925 and 1930. Many poems in the first album deal with fantasy and imaginative creatures—fairies, elves, goblins; the second album examines people's feelings and values.

*Filmstrip Sets* Guidance Associates features *A Pocketful of Poetry*, a set of two filmstrips and cassettes, designed to introduce children to writing poetry, and *Poems for Glad, Poems for Sad*, two filmstrips and cassettes dealing with emotions.

Mature students can be introduced to classic poets and poetry via nine filmstrip sets in the *Living Poetry* series, produced by McGraw-Hill. Original artwork and music enhance dramatic readings, encouraging students to read the original verses. Titles in the series include "Hiawatha's Childhood," part 3 of Henry Wadsworth Longfellow's twenty-two-part *The Song of Hiawatha*, which begins after the birth of Hiawatha, continuing to his entrance into manhood; "The Deacon's Masterpiece," Oliver Wendell Holmes' poem about the "one-hoss shay . . . it ran a hundred years to a day"; "Casey at the Bat" by Ernest Lawrence Thayer, which depicts the excitement and tension of the Mudville nine's valiant try for victory in the bottom of the ninth, with two away, two men on, and the mighty Casey coming to bat; *Poems of Lewis Carroll*, featuring three poems, "Father William," "The Walrus and the Carpenter," and "The Gardener's Song"; "Paul Revere's Ride" by Henry Wadsworth Longfellow, which captures the urgency and magnitude of Revere's mission when "the fate of a nation was riding that night . . ."; *Poems of Tennyson and Browning*, including Robert Browning's "Incident of the French Camp" and Tennyson's "The Charge of the Light Brigade," along with a guide providing brief historical backgrounds to the incidents on which the poems were based; *Poems by Walt Whitman*, featuring "I Hear America Singing," "Miracles," "When I Heard the Learn'd Astronomer," and "O Captain! My Captain!"

Random House has produced *Pick a Peck o' Poems*, six filmstrip sets that I edited featuring poems by contemporary poets that are woven into a narrative, defining poetic terms in simple language. *What Is Poetry?* introduces rhyme, free verse, and imagery, showing similarities and differences; *Sing a Song of Cities* features poems about how people travel, shop, play, and build on city streets; *Animals, Animals, Animals* includes poems about pets in houses, jungles, zoos, and museums; *When It's Cold, and When It's Not* depicts weather and the four seasons; *Our Earth to Keep* is a plea for keeping the earth beautiful; *A Poem Belongs to You* encourages writing poetry. Included is a teacher's guide with reprints of the poems heard on the recordings.

Also from Random House is Nancy Willard's *A Visit to William Blake's Inn: Poems for Innocent and Experienced Travelers*, a filmstrip set based on the author's 1982 Newbery Award–winning volume. Using the Caldecott Honor Book illustrations by Alice and Martin Provensen, this adaptation further enhances the mood of the verse with the addition of a musical score. A complement to the set is the filmstrip *Meet the Newbery Author: Nancy Willard.*

SVE's four-filmstrip set portrays *Animals in Verse.* Titles include "Animal Mothers and Babies," "Animals in the City," "Animals in the Zoo," and "Animals on the Farm." Outstanding photography and original music and lyrics highlight the presentations; a teacher's guide is included.

Also from SVE is *Seasons of Poetry,* a set of four filmstrips depicting the changing seasons; a teacher's guide is included.

*Professional Cassettes* In *Take a Poetry Break: Making Poetry Come Alive for Children*, produced by the American Library Association and distributed by PBS Video, Caroline Feller Bauer addresses a group of educators, quickly dispelling the myth that poetry is dull or boring. She talks about some of America's top poets for children and presents a host of ideas meshing poetry and media.

Tapping into children's interests in such topics as animals, food, humor, and money, she demonstrates how poetry can enhance every area of the curriculum. The cassette is perfect to share at faculty meetings, at in-service programs, or with parent groups. Write to PBS Video for costs of buying and/or renting the cassette.

Also consult Ms. Bauer's professional books, *This Way to Books* and *Celebrations*, for further ideas on presenting poetry.

**REFERENCES**

Adler, David A. *You Think It's Fun to Be a Clown!* Illustrated by Ray Cruz. Doubleday, 1980.

Adoff, Arnold. *Eats: Poems.* Illustrated by Susan Russo. Lothrop, Lee & Shepard, 1979.

———. *Sports Pages.* Illustrated by Steve Kuzma. J. B. Lippincott, 1986.

Bauer, Caroline Feller. *Celebrations.* H. W. Wilson, 1985.

———. *This Way to Books.* H. W. Wilson, 1982.

Benét, Rosemary, and Benét, Stephen Vincent. *A Book of Americans.* Illustrated by Charles Child. Henry Holt, 1933, 1961.

Brewton, John E.; Blackburn, Lorraine A.; and Blackburn, George M. III (compilers). *In the Witch's Kitchen: Poems for Halloween.* Illustrated by Harriet Brown. T. Y. Crowell, 1980.

Brewton, Sara, and Brewton, John E. (compilers). *Shrieks at Midnight.* Illustrated by Ellen Raskin. T. Y. Crowell, 1969.

Brooks, Gwendolyn. *Bronzeville Boys and Girls.* Illustrated by Ronni Solbert. Harper & Row, 1956.

Carroll, Lewis. *Songs from Alice.* Music by Don Harper. Illustrated by Charles Folkard. Holiday House, 1979.

Cole, William (compiler). *Good Dog Poems.* Illustrated by Ruth Sanderson. Scribner's, 1981.

———. *Poem Stew.* Illustrated by Karen Ann Weinhaus. J. B. Lippincott, 1981; also in paperback.

———. *Poetry of Horses.* Illustrated by Ruth Sanderson. Scribner's, 1979.

Cleary, Beverly. *The Mouse and the Motorcyle.* Illustrated by Louis Darling. William Morrow, 1965; Dell paperback.

Crofut, William. *The Moon on the One Hand: Poetry in Song.* Arrangements by Kenneth Cooper and Glenn Shattuck. Illustrated by Susan Crofut. Atheneum, 1975.

Dahl, Roald. *Revolting Rhymes.* Illustrated by Quentin Blake. Alfred A. Knopf, 1982.

de Regniers, Beatrice Schenk. *So Many Cats.* Illustrated by Ellen Weiss. Clarion, 1986.

———. *Something Special.* Illustrated by Irene Haas. Harcourt Brace Jovanovich, 1958.

———. *This Big Cat and Other Cats I've Known.* Illustrated by Alan Daniel. Crown, 1985.

Eliot, T. S. *Old Possum's Book of Practical Cats.* Illustrated by Edward Gorey. Harcourt Brace Jovanovich, 1982; revised edition; also in paperback.

Engvick, William (editor). *Lullabies and Night Songs.* Music by Alec Wilder. Illustrated by Maurice Sendak. Harper & Row, 1965.

Esbensen, Barbara Juster. *Cold Stars and Fireflies: Poems of the Four Seasons.* Illustrated by Susan Bonners. T. Y. Crowell, 1984.

Fisher, Aileen. *Out in the Dark and Daylight.* Illustrated by Gail Owens. Harper & Row, 1980.

Hoffman, Herbert H., and Hoffman, Rita L. *International Index to Recorded Poetry.* H. W. Wilson, 1983.

Hopkins, Lee Bennett (selector). *Beat the Drum! Independence Day Has Come.* Illustrated by Tomie de Paola. Harcourt Brace Jovanovich, 1977.

————. *Creatures.* Illustrated by Stella Ormai. Harcourt Brace Jovanovich, 1985.

————. *Dinosaurs.* Illustrated by Murray Tinkleman. Harcourt Brace Jovanovich, 1987.

————. *A Dog's Life.* Illustrated by Linda Rochester Richards. Harcourt Brace Jovanovich, 1983.

————. *Easter Buds Are Springing.* Illustrated by Tomie de Paola. Harcourt Brace Jovanovich, 1970.

————. *Good Morning to You, Valentine.* Illustrated by Tomie de Paola. Harcourt Brace Jovanovich, 1976.

————. *Hey-How for Halloween.* Illustrated by Janet McCaffery. Harcourt Brace Jovanovich, 1974.

————. *I Am the Cat.* Illustrated by Linda Rochester Richards. Harcourt Brace Jovanovich, 1982.

————. *Merrily Comes Our Harvest In: Poems for Thanksgiving.* Illustrated by Ben Shecter. Harcourt Brace Jovanovich, 1978.

————. *Moments: Poems About the Seasons.* Illustrated by Michael Hague. Harcourt Brace Jovanovich, 1980.

————. *Munching: Poems About Eating.* Illustrated by Nelle Davis. Little, Brown, 1985.

————. *My Mane Catches the Wind: Poems About Horses.* Illustrated by Sam Savitt. Harcourt Brace Jovanovich, 1979.

————. *Rainbows Are Made: Poems by Carl Sandburg.* Illustrated by Fritz Eichenberg. Harcourt Brace Jovanovich, 1982; also in paperback.

————. *The Sea Is Calling Me.* Illustrated by Walter Gaffney-Kessell. Harcourt Brace Jovanovich, 1986.

————. *Sing Hey for Christmas Day.* Illustrated by Laura Jean Allen. Harcourt Brace Jovanovich, 1975.

————. *The Sky Is Full of Song.* Illustrated by Dirk Zimmer. Harper & Row, 1983; also in paperback.

————. *A Song in Stone.* Illustrated by Anna Held Audette. T. Y. Crowell, 1983.

————. *Surprises.* An I Can Read Book. Illustrated by Megan Lloyd. Harper & Row, 1983; also in paperback.

Hughes, Langston. *Selected Poems.* Illustrated by E. McKnight Kauffer. Alfred A. Knopf, 1966.

Keats, Ezra Jack. *The Snowy Day.* Viking, 1962; also in paperback.

Kuskin, Karla. *Dogs & Dragons, Trees & Dreams: A Collection of Poems.* Harper & Row, 1980.

Larrick, Nancy (selector). *Crazy to Be Alive in Such a Strange World: Poems About People.* M. Evans, 1979.

————. *Piping Down the Valleys Wild.* Illustrated by Ellen Raskin. Doubleday, 1985; revised edition; Dell paperback.

Livingston, Myra Cohn. *Celebrations.* Illustrated by Leonard Everett Fisher. Holiday House, 1985.

————. *A Circle of Seasons.* Illustrated by Leonard Everett Fisher. Holiday House, 1982.

————. *Sea Songs.* Illustrated by Leonard Everett Fisher. Holiday House, 1985.

————. *A Song I Sang to You.* Illustrated by Margot Tomes. Harcourt Brace Jovanovich, 1984.

———— (selector). *Callooh! Callay! Holiday Poems for Young Readers.* Illustrated by Janet Stevens. Margaret K. McElderry Books/Macmillan, 1978.

————. *Christmas Poems.* Illustrated by Trina Schart Hyman. Holiday House, 1984.

————. *Easter Poems.* Illustrated by John Wallner. Holiday House, 1985.

————. *O Frabjous Day! Poetry for Holidays and Special Occasions.* Margaret K. McElderry Books/Macmillan, 1977.

————. *Poems for Jewish Holidays.* Illustrated by Lloyd Bloom. Holiday House, 1986.

————. *Poems of Christmas.* Margaret K. McElderry Books/Macmillan, 1980.

————. *Thanksgiving Poems.* Illustrated by Stephen Gammel. Holiday House, 1985.

————. *Why Am I Grown So Cold? Poems of the Unknowable.* Margaret K. McElderry Books/Macmillan, 1982.

Merriam, Eve. *Jamboree: Rhymes for All Times.* Illustrated by Walter Gaffney-Kessell. Dell paperback, 1984.

Moore, Lilian. *Something New Begins: New and Selected Poems.* Atheneum, 1982.

Moore, Vardine. *Mice Are Rather Nice: Poems About Mice.* Illustrated by Doug Jamison. Atheneum, 1981.

Morrison, Lillian. *The Break Dance Kids: Poems of Sport, Motion and Locomotion.* Lothrop, 1985.

————. *The Sidewalk Racer and Other Poems of Sports and Motion.* Lothrop, Lee & Shepard, 1977.

———— (selector). *Sprints and Distances: Sports in Poetry and Poetry in Sports.* Illustrated by Clare and John Ross. T. Y. Crowell, 1965.

O'Neill, Mary. *Hailstones and Halibut Bones: Adventures in Color.* Illustrated by Leonard Weisgard. Doubleday, 1961.

Pellowski, Anne; Sattley, Helen R.; and Arkhurst, Joyce C. *Have You Seen a Comet? Children's Art and Writing from Around the World.* John Day, 1971.

Prelutsky, Jack. *Circus.* Illustrated by Arnold Lobel. Macmillan, 1974; also in paperback.

————. *The Headless Horseman Rides Tonight: More Poems to Trouble Your Sleep.* Illustrated by Arnold Lobel. Greenwillow, 1980.

————. *It's Christmas.* Illustrated by Marylin Hafner. Greenwillow, 1981.

————. *It's Halloween.* Illustrated by Marylin Hafner. Greenwillow, 1977; also in Scholastic paperback.

————. *It's Thanksgiving.* Illustrated by Marylin Hafner. Greenwillow, 1982; also in Scholastic paperback.

————. *It's Valentine's Day.* Illustrated by Yossi Abolafia. Greenwillow, 1983; also in Scholastic paperback.

————. *Nightmares: Poems to Trouble Your Sleep.* Illustrated by Arnold Lobel. Greenwillow, 1976.

Russo, Susan (selector). *The Ice-Cream Ocean and Other Delectable Poems of the Sea.* Lothrop, 1984.

Sendak, Maurice. *Chicken Soup with Rice: A Book of Months.* Harper & Row, 1962; also in paperback.

Seuss, Dr. *If I Ran the Circus.* Random House, 1956; also in paperback.

Silverstein, Shel. *Where the Sidewalk Ends.* Harper & Row, 1974.

Viorst, Judith. *If I Were in Charge of the World and Other Worries.* Illustrated by Lynne Cherry. Atheneum, 1981; also in paperback.

Wyndham, Robert (editor). *Chinese Mother Goose Rhymes.* Illustrated by Ed Young. Putnam, 1982; also in paperback.

# A Brief Afterword

In A. A. Milne's delightful classic *The House at Pooh Corner* (Dutton, 1928), the renowned Winnie-the-Pooh sums up the creation of poetry in one line. He tells his friend Piglet, "It is the best way to write poetry, letting things come."

Letting things come is the way of poetry, for poetry can help life along no matter what age or stage of development we are at:

> Poetry can—
>
> Make you chuckle,
> or laugh, or cry,
> make you dance
> or shout, or sigh.

Why? Because poetry, like life, comes about naturally. For each step we take, each decade we live, poetry can weave

> in and out
>    and
> up and down
>    and
> around and around
> us—just like life itself.

Letting things come, letting poetry come into the lives of children, is one of the best things any of us can do as adults. And we can help by taking the poetic advice of Beatrice Schenk de Regniers when she tells us to "keep a poem in your pocket" (see page 56).

So—*keep* a poem in your pocket—or pocketbook, or briefcase, or shopping bag. Pull it out when needed or wanted and spread it around freely. In short—pass the poetry—*please!*

# Appendixes

# Appendix 1
## *Poetry Reflecting Contemporary Issues*

Two important contemporary subjects for today's child are the city and multi-ethnic experiences.

This selected list cites some of the best collections of original poems and anthologies containing poems about these topics.

### *The City*

Brooks, Gwendolyn. *Bronzeville Boys and Girls.* Illustrated by Ronni Solbert. Harper & Row, 1956. See pages 41–44.

Hopkins, Lee Bennett (selector). *A Song in Stone: City Poems.* Illustrated by Anna Held Audette. T. Y. Crowell, 1982.

> This American Library Association Notable Book of 1983 features twenty selections, including works by Patricia Hubbell, Judith Thurman, and Norma Farber, illustrated with black-and-white photographs.

Janeczko, Paul (editor). *Postcard Poems: A Collection for Sharing.* Bradbury Press, 1973.

> Several city images appear in this volume of 109 poems for mature readers such as "On Watching the Construction of a Skyscraper" by Burton Raffel, "Street Windows" by Carl Sandburg, and "Blue Alert" by Eve Merriam.

Kennedy, X. J. *The Forgetful Wishing Well: Poems for Young People.* Illustrated by Monica Incisa. Margaret K. McElderry Books, 1985.

> Part 6 of this volume, "In the City," contains eight selections including "Boulder, Colorado," "Forty-Seventh Street Crash," and "Flying Uptown Backwards."

Larrick, Nancy (editor). *Piping Down the Valleys Wild.* Illustrated by Ellen Raskin. Delacorte, reissued 1985; also in paperback.

> Part 14, "The City Spreads Its Wings," from Langston Hughes'

poem "City," contains eleven poems such as "Mrs. Peck-Pigeon" by Eleanor Farjeon, "Concrete Mixers" by Patricia Hubbell, and "City Lights" by Rachel Field.

Moore, Lilian (selector). *Go with the Poem: A New Collection.* McGraw-Hill, 1979.

Part 6, "The City: We Call It Home," contains eleven selections, including "Rain" by Adrien Stoutenberg, "The Yawn" by Paul Blackburn, and "New York in the Spring" by David Budbill.

————. *Something New Begins.* Illustrated by Mary Jane Dunton. Atheneum, 1982.

Although not all of the selections in this volume are city-oriented, there are enough here to share, including such gems as "Pigeons," "Foghorns," and "Mural on Second Avenue." See also pages 19–20.

## The Black Experience

This selected list cites volumes published between 1956 and the present. Although the poems are mainly geared toward mature readers, you will find some within the volumes that can be used with younger children.

Adoff, Arnold.

For titles of Mr. Adoff's books dealing with black and multiracial experiences, see pages 27–31.

Brooks, Gwendolyn. *Bronzeville Boys and Girls.* Illustrated by Ronni Solbert. Harper & Row, 1956. See pages 41–44.

Bryan, Ashley (selector). *I Greet the Dawn: Poems by Paul Laurence Dunbar.* Atheneum, 1978.

Following a brief introduction of Paul Laurence Dunbar (1872–1906) and his work, Mr. Bryan presents six sections of the poet's work. Although much of the poet's work was written in dialect, such as these first lines from "Little Brown Baby":

> Little brown baby wif spa'klin eyes,
> Come to yo' pappy an' set on his knee . . .

Mr. Bryan has selected poems in standard English, leaving in a few dialect poems. The volume is illustrated with black-and-white drawings by the compiler.

Clifton, Lucille. See pages 53–55.

Giovanni, Nikki. See pages 74–77.

Greenfield, Eloise. *Honey, I Love and Other Love Poems.* Illustrated by Leo and Diane Dillon. T. Y. Crowell, 1978; also available in paperback.

Fifteen poems appear in a small-size format with delightful illustrations. Excerpts from the book appear on the recording of the same title (Caedmon), performed by the author and friends and enhanced by a lively jazz accompaniment.

Hughes, Langston. See pages 79–83.

McKissack, Patricia C. *Paul Laurence Dunbar: A Poet to Remember.* Children's Press, 1984.

A biography of the poet for mature readers.

## American Indians and Eskimos

Bierhorst, John (editor). *In the Trails of the Wind: American Indian Poems and Ritual Orations.* Farrar, Straus & Giroux, 1971.

Translated from over forty languages, this collection of 126 poems represents the best-known Indian cultures of North and South America. Omens, battle songs, orations, love lyrics, prayers, dreams, and mystical incantations are included, beginning with the origin of the earth and the emergence of humans through to the apocalyptic visions of a new life. Detailed notes appear on each of the selections along with suggestions for further reading and glossary of tribes, cultures, and languages, which give insight into the poetry. The volume is illustrated with black-and-white period engravings.

———. *The Sacred Path: Spells, Prayers and Power Songs of the American Indians.* William Morrow, 1983.

As in the above title, this volume draws upon classic sources, representing the many cultures of North, South, and Central America, incorporating material unavailable until the 1970s and 1980s. The anthology is arranged as a progression—from "Birth and Infancy" to "For the Dying and the Dead." Selections used in rituals by such tribes as the Cherokee, Aztec, and Chippewa are associated with love, sickness, weather, farming, and hunting. Notes, sources, and a glossary of tribes, cultures, and languages are appended.

————. *Songs of the Chippewa.* Adapted from collections of Frances Densmore and Henry Rowe Schoolcraft and arranged for piano and guitar. Illustrated by Joe Servello. Farrar, Straus and Giroux, 1974.

Authoritatively edited and with the inclusion of lavish paintings, this volume contains seventeen chants, dream songs, medicine charms, and lullabies, collected near the western shores of the Great Lakes by Frances Densmore during the 1900s, and by Henry Rowe Schoolcraft more than one-half century earlier. An introduction and section of notes appear.

Jones, Hettie (compiler). *The Trees Stand Shining.* Illustrated by Robert Andrew Parker. Dial Press, 1971; also in paperback.

This volume will appeal to younger children because of its format—a large picture book containing beautiful full-color paintings. The anthologist arranged this collection to trace a journey through two days' time; she tells the reader that "the poems . . . are really songs. In their songs, American Indians told how they felt about the world, all they saw in the land, what they did in their lives." The songs are from such tribes as the Iroquois, Teton Sioux, Chippewa, and Papago.

# Appendix 2
## *Poetry in Paperback: A Selected List\**

Ciardi, John. *Fast and Slow.* Illustrated by Becky Gaver. Houghton Mifflin.

Thirty-four early poems are featured in this volume of humorous and nonsense verse.

\*————. *The Man Who Sang the Sillies.* J. B. Lippincott.

Cole, William. *A Boy Named Mary Jane and Other Silly Verse.* Illustrated by George MacClain. Avon.

Twenty-four original, humorous poems, including "Banananananananana," about a boy who loses the spelling bee because he cannot stop spelling "banana"; "Snorkeling," and "Piggy."

\*————. *Poem Stew.* Harper & Row.

\*de Angeli, Marguerite. *Book of Nursery Rhymes and Mother Goose Rhymes.* Doubleday.

deGasztold, Carmen Bernos. *Creature's Choir.* Illustrated by Jean Primrose. Viking.

Translated from the French by Rumer Godden, this volume includes poems about various animals, such as "The Snail," "The Centipede," "The Whale," and "The Fly."

————. *Prayers from the Ark.* Illustrated by Jean Primrose. Viking.

Translated from the French by Rumer Godden, this volume features prayers uttered by various animals—"The Prayer of the Little Ducks," "The Prayer of the Elephant," "The Prayer of the Little Pig."

Dickinson, Emily. *I'm Nobody! Who Are You? Poems of Emily Dickinson for Children.* Illustrated by Rex Schneider. Stemmer House.

---

\*Titles marked with an asterisk are discussed within the the text of this volume.

Forty-five selections culled from the works of Emily Dickinson (1830–1866), including "There Is No Frigate Like a Book," "A Word Is Dead," and "Dear March, Come In."

*Eliot, T. S. *Old Possum's Book of Practical Cats.* Illustrated by Edward Gorey. Harcourt Brace Jovanovich.

*Frost, Robert. *A Swinger of Birches: Poems of Robert Frost for Young People.* Illustrated by Peter Koeppen. Stemmer House.

Greenfield, Eloise. *Honey, I Love and Other Love Poems.* Illustrated by Diane and Leo Dillon. Harper & Row.

*Hopkins, Lee Bennett (selector). *Rainbows Are Made: Poems by Carl Sandburg.* Illustrated by Fritz Eichenberg. Harcourt Brace Jovanovich.

*———. *The Sky Is Full of Song.* Illustrated by Dirk Zimmer. Harper & Row.

*———. *Surprises.* Illustrated by Megan Lloyd. Harper & Row.

*Jones, Hettie (selector). *The Trees Stand Shining.* Illustrated by Robert Andrew Parker. Dial.

*Larrick, Nancy (selector). *Piping Down the Valleys Wild.* Illustrated by Ellen Raskin. Dell.

*McCord, David. *All Small.* Illustrated by Madelaine Gill Linden. Little, Brown.

*———. *Every Time I Climb a Tree.* Illustrated by Marc Simont. Little, Brown.

Nash, Ogden. *Custard and Company.* Illustrated by Quentin Blake. Little, Brown.

Ogden Nash's nonsense verses are included, featuring eighty-four selections from the various published works of the poet, from the early 1930s through to the early 1960s.

*Merriam, Eve. *Jamboree: Rhymes for All Times.* Illustrated by Walter Gaffney-Kessell. Dell.

*———. *A Sky Full of Poems.* Illustrated by Walter Gaffney-Kessell. Dell.

*Prelutsky, Jack. *It's Halloween.* Illustrated by Marylin Hafner. Scholastic.

*———. *It's Thanksgiving.* Illustrated by Marylin Hafner. Scholastic.

*———. *It's Valentine's Day.* Illustrated by Yossi Abolafia. Scholastic.

*Sandburg, Carl. *Early Moon.* Illustrated by James Daugherty. Harcourt Brace Jovanovich.

*————. *Wind Song.* Illustrated by William A. Smith. Harcourt Brace Jovanovich.

Smith, William Jay. *Laughing Time: Nonsense Poems.* Illustrated by Fernando Krahn. Dell.

A host of humorous poems, perfect for reading aloud, is offered in this whimsical collection of light verse.

Viorst, Judith. *If I Were in Charge of the World and Other Worries.* Illustrated by Lynne Cherry. Atheneum.

Forty-one humorous verses appear with such titles as ". . . And Then the Prince Knelt Down and Tried to Put the Glass Slipper on Cinderella's Foot," and "Thoughts on Getting Out of a Nice Warm Bed in an Ice-Cold House to Go to the Bathroom at Three O'Clock in the Morning." The volume is divided into ten sections with headings such as "Fairy Tales," "Wicked Thoughts," and "Cats and Other People."

*Willard, Nancy. *A Visit to William Blake's Inn: Poems for Innocent and Experienced Travelers.* Illustrated by Alice and Martin Provensen. Harcourt Brace Jovanovich.

*Wyndham, Robert (selector). *Chinese Mother Goose Rhymes.* Illustrated by Ed Young. Putnam's.

# Appendix 3
## Sources of Educational Materials Cited

American Library Association, 50 E. Huron St., Chicago, IL 60611
Atheneum, 115 5th Ave., New York, NY 10003
Avon Books, 959 8th Ave., New York, NY 10019
Bradbury (see Macmillan)
Bobbs-Merrill, 4300 W. 62nd St., Indianapolis, IN 46206
Broadside Press, 12651 Old Mill Pl., Detroit, MI 48238
Caedmon, 1995 Broadway, New York, NY 10023
CBS Records, 51 W. 52nd St., New York, NY 10022
Children's Book Council, 67 Irving Pl., New York, NY 10003
Churchill Films, 662 N. Robertson Blvd., Los Angeles, CA 90069
Clarion Books, 52 Vanderbilt Ave., New York, NY 10017
T. Y. Crowell (see Harper & Row)
Crown, 225 Park Ave. S., New York, NY 10016
John Day, 257 Park Ave. S., New York, NY 10010
Delacorte, 245 E. 47th St., New York, NY 10017
Dell (see Delacorte)
Dial, 2 Park Ave., New York, NY 10016
Dodd, Mead, 79 Madison Ave., New York, NY 10016
Doubleday, 245 Park Ave., New York, NY 10017
Dutton (see Dial)
Earworks, Arnold Adoff Agency, Box 293, Yellow Springs, OH
    45387
M. Evans, 216 E. 49th St., New York, NY 10017
Gale Research, Book Tower, Detroit, MI 48226
Garrard, 1607 N. Market St., Champaign, IL 61820
David Godine, 306 Dartmouth St., Boston, MA 02116
Greenwillow, 105 Madison Ave., New York, NY 10016
Guidance Associates, Pleasantville, NY 10570

Farrar, Straus & Giroux, 19 Union Square W., New York, NY
 10003
Folkways Records, 43 W. 61st St., New York, NY 10023
Harcourt Brace Jovanovich, 1250 6th Ave., San Diego, CA 92101
Harper & Row, 10 E. 53rd St., New York, NY 10022
Hill, Lawrence (see Farrar, Straus & Giroux)
Hill and Wang (see Farrar, Straus & Giroux)
Holiday House, 18 E. 53rd St., New York, NY 10022
Henry Holt, 521 5th Ave., New York, NY 10175
Houghton Mifflin, 2 Park St., Boston, MA 02107
Alfred A. Knopf, 201 E. 50th St., New York, NY 10022
J. B. Lippincott (see Harper & Row)
Listening Library, 1 Park Ave., Old Greenwich, CT 06870
Little, Brown, 34 Beacon St., Boston, MA 02106
Lothrop, Lee & Shepard (see Greenwillow)
Macmillan, 866 3rd Ave., New York, NY 10022
McGraw-Hill, 1221 Ave. of the Americas, New York, NY 10020
William Morrow (see Greenwillow)
National Council of Teachers of English (NCTE), 1111 Kenyon
 Rd., Urbana, IL 61801
Oxford University Press, 200 Madison Ave., New York, NY 10016
Parachute Records, Inc., 8255 Sunset Blvd., Los Angeles, CA
 90046
PBS Video, 475 L'Enfant Plaza, S.W., Washington, D.C. 20024
Pied Piper Productions, Box 320, Verdugo City, CA 91046
Clarkson M. Potter (see Crown)
Prentice-Hall, Englewood Cliffs, NJ 07632
G. P. Putnam's, 51 Madison Ave., New York, NY 10010
Random House (see Alfred A. Knopf)
Scholastic, Inc., 730 Broadway, New York, NY 10003
Scribner's (see Atheneum)
Simon and Schuster, 1230 Ave. of the Americas, New York, NY
 10020
Spoken Arts, P.O. Box 289, New Rochelle, NY 10820
Stemmer House, 2626 Caves Rd., Owings Mills, MD 21117
SVE, 1345 Diversey Parkway, Chicago, IL 60614
Charles Tuttle, Rutland, VT 05701

United States Government Printing Office, Superintendent of Documents, Washington, D.C. 20401

Viking, 40 W. 23rd St., New York, NY 10010

Weston Woods, Weston, CT 06880

H. W. Wilson, 950 University Ave., Bronx, NY 10452

Zaner-Bloser, 2300 W. 5th Ave., P.O. Box 16764, Columbus, OH 43216.

# Appendix 4
## *Mother Goose Collections*

de Angeli, Marguerite. *Book of Nursery and Mother Goose Rhymes.* Doubleday, 1954; also in paperback.

This Caldecott Honor Book contains 376 rhymes, with over 260 full-color and black-and-white illustrations.

de Paola, Tomie. *Mother Goose.* Putnam's, 1985.

Over 200 Mother Goose rhymes illustrated with vibrant, full-color paintings.

―――. *Mother Goose Story Streamers.* Putnam's, 1984.

This set of four streamers, perfect for bulletin-board displays, includes "Baa, Baa, Black Sheep," "Hey Diddle Diddle," "Jack and Jill," and "Little Miss Muffet."

Hague, Michael. *Mother Goose: A Collection of Classic Nursery Rhymes.* Holt, Rinehart & Winston, 1984.

Over forty-five rhymes illustrated in full color.

Lobel, Arnold. *Gregory Griggs and Other Nursery Rhyme People.* Greenwillow, 1978.

Thirty-four nursery rhymes about lesser-known but colorful ladies and gents such as "Hannah Bantry," "Terrance McDidler," and "Little Miss Tucket" (who sat on a bucket), each illustrated with lush, full-color drawings.

―――. *The Random House Book of Mother Goose.* Random House, 1986.

Over 300 nursery rhymes selected and illustrated by the Caldecott Medalist.

Provensen, Alice and Martin. *The Mother Goose Book.* Random House, 1976.

More than 150 rhymes beautifully illustrated in full color.

Tripp, Wallace. *Granfa' Grig Had a Pig and Other Rhymes Without Reason from Mother Goose.* Little Brown, 1976; also in paperback.

This host of rhymes is whimsically illustrated in full color.

# ACKNOWLEDGMENTS

*Thanks are due to the following for the use of the copyrighted selections listed below:*

Atheneum Publishers, Inc. for "New Day" from *Pigeon Cubes* by N. M. Bodecker. Copyright © 1982 N. M. Bodecker (A Margaret K. McElderry Book); "Blow-Up" from *The Forgetful Wishing Well* by X. J. Kennedy. Copyright © 1985 X. J. Kennedy (A Margaret K. McElderry Book); "Foghorns" from *I Thought I Heard the City* (1969) in the compilation *Something New Begins* by Lilian Moore. Copyright © 1982 by Lilian Moore. All reprinted with the permission of Atheneum Publishers, Inc.

Beatrice Schenk de Regniers for "Keep a Poem in Your Pocket" from *Something Special.* Copyright © 1958 by Beatrice Schenk de Regniers. Reprinted by permission of the author.

Harcourt Brace Jovanovich, Inc. for "Bubbles" from *Wind Song* by Carl Sandburg. Copyright © 1960 by Carl Sandburg. Reprinted by permission of Harcourt Brace Jovanovich, Inc.

Harper & Row, Publishers, Inc. for "Skipper" from *Bronzeville Boys and Girls* by Gwendolyn Brooks. Copyright © 1956 by Gwendolyn Brooks Blakely; "Out in the Dark and Daylight" from *Out in the Dark and Daylight* by Aileen Fisher. Copyright © 1980 by Aileen Fisher; "Hughbert and the Glue" from *Dogs & Dragons, Trees & Dreams: A Collection of Poems* by Karla Kuskin. Copyright © 1964 by Karla Kuskin; "The Search" from *Where the Sidewalk Ends: Poems and Drawings of Shel Silverstein.* Copyright © 1974 by Snake Eye Music, Inc.; "Mummy Slept Late and Daddy Fixed Breakfast" from *You Read to Me, I'll Read to You* by John Ciardi (J. B. Lippincott). Copyright © 1962 by John Ciardi; "Poetry" from *Eleanor Farjeon's Poems for Children* (J. B. Lippincott). Copyright © 1938, renewed 1966 by Eleanor Farjeon; first ten lines from *black is brown is tan* by Arnold Adoff. Copyright © 1973 by Arnold Adoff. All reprinted by permission of Harper & Row, Publishers, Inc.

245

## ACKNOWLEDGMENTS

Henry Holt and Company, Inc. for the six-line excerpt from *Everett Anderson's Goodbye* by Lucille Clifton. Copyright © 1983 by Lucille Clifton; "The Pasture" from *The Poetry of Robert Frost,* edited by Edward Connery Lathem. Copyright 1939, © 1967, 1969 by Holt, Rinehart & Winston, Inc. Reprinted by permission of Henry Holt and Company, Inc.

Alfred A. Knopf, Inc. for "Dreams" from *The Dream Keeper and Other Poems* by Langston Hughes. Copyright 1942 by Alfred A. Knopf, Inc. and renewed 1970 by Arna Bontemps and George Houston Bass. Reprinted by permission of Alfred A. Knopf, Inc.

Little, Brown and Company, Inc. for "This Is My Rock" from *One at a Time* by David McCord. Copyright 1929 by David McCord. First appeared in *Saturday Review.* Used by permission of Little, Brown and Company, Inc.

William Morrow & Company, Inc. for eight lines from "Winter" in *Cotton Candy on a Rainy Day* by Nikki Giovanni. Copyright © 1978 by Nikki Giovanni; "A Snowflake Fell" from *It's Snowing! It's Snowing!* by Jack Prelutsky. Copyright © 1984 by Jack Prelutsky. By permission of Greenwillow Books (A Division of William Morrow & Company, Inc.). Both reprinted by permission of William Morrow & Company, Inc.

Marian Reiner for "Crickets" from *Crickets and Bullfrogs and Whispers of Thunder: Poems and Pictures* by Harry Behn, selected by Lee Bennett Hopkins. Copyright 1949, 1953, © 1956, 1957, 1966, 1968 by Harry Behn. Copyright renewed 1977 by Alice L. Behn. Copyright renewed 1981 by Alice Behn Goebel, Pamela Behn Adam, Prescott Behn and Peter Behn; "Whispers" from *Whispers and Other Poems* by Myra Cohn Livingston. Copyright 1958 by Myra Cohn Livingston; "A Lazy Thought" from *Jamboree: Rhymes for All Times.* by Eve Merriam. Copyright © 1962, 1964, 1966, 1973, 1984 by Eve Merriam. All rights reserved. All reprinted by permission of Marian Reiner for the authors.

246

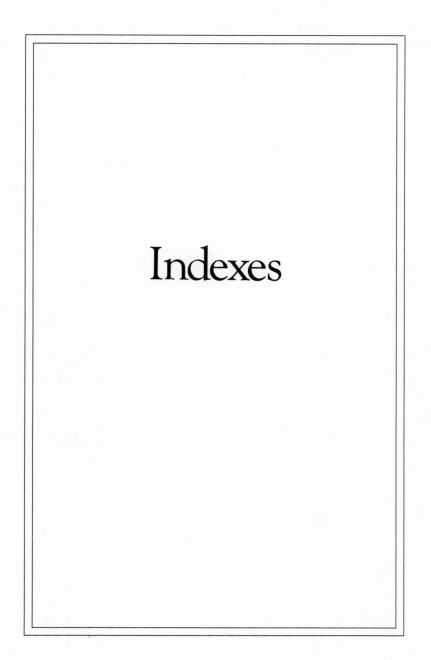

# Indexes

# Author Index

Adler, David, 185
Adoff, Arnold, 26–31, 146,
  197, 200, 214
Aldis, Dorothy, 199
Armour, Richard, 197
Arnold, Matthew, 215

Baring-Gould, Cecil, 23
Baring-Gould, William, 23
Barnes, Joey, 144
Bates, G. E., 161–62
Bauer, Caroline Feller, 220
Behn, Harry, 32–36, 200, 203
Belting, Natalie M., 145
Benét, Rosemary, 192–93
Benét, Stephen Vincent,
  192–93, 198
Berry, Faith, 81
Blackburn, George Meredith,
  III, 11
Blackburn, Lorraine A., 11, 159
Blake, William, 212–13
Bober, Natalie S., 71
Bodecker, N. M., 37–40, 200
Bontemps, Arna, 215
Bragdon, Carl, 152
Brewton, John E., 11, 159,
  178
Brewton, Sara, 178

Brooks, Gwendolyn, 41–44,
  54, 190, 200, 203, 205, 217
Browning, Elizabeth Barrett,
  161
Browning, Robert, 157, 218

Carroll, Lewis, 160, 162–64,
  178, 197, 212, 213, 218
Ciardi, John, 3, 8, 13, 45–51,
  108, 145, 158, 178, 200, 215
Cleary, Beverly, 206
Clifton, Lucille, 52–55, 120,
  200
Coatsworth, Elizabeth, 200
Cole, William, 195, 197, 215
Cooper, Kenneth, 213
Crapsey, Adelaide, 151–52,
  179
Crofut, William, 213
Cummings, E. E., 9, 16, 178,
  200, 213, 215

Dahl, Roald, 207
Davis, Ossie, 80, 81
de la Mare, Walter, 25
de Regniers, Beatrice Schenk,
  56–60, 194, 196, 200, 230
Dickey, James, 215
Dickinson, Emily, 7, 200, 215

# AUTHOR INDEX

# Title Index

# Index of Poets, Poems, and First Lines
## Appearing in Part Two

261

# Digital Photography

# Digital Photography

**99 easy tips**

to make you look like a pro!

**Ken Milburn**

**McGraw-Hill** Osborne

New York Chicago San Francisco Lisbon
London Madrid Mexico City Milan New Delhi
San Juan Seoul Singapore Sydney Toronto

**McGraw-Hill/**Osborne
2600 Tenth Street
Berkeley, California 94710
U.S.A.

To arrange bulk purchase discounts for sales promotions, premiums, or fund-raisers, please contact **McGraw-Hill/**Osborne at the above address. For information on translations or book distributors outside the U.S.A., please see the International Contact Information page immediately following the index of this book.

**Digital Photography: 99 Easy Tips to Make You Look Like a Pro!**

1234567890 CUS CUS 0198765432

ISBN 0-07-222793-1

| | |
|---|---|
| **Publisher:** | Brandon A. Nordin |
| **Vice President &** | |
| **Associate Publisher:** | Scott Rogers |
| **Acquisitions Editor:** | Marjorie McAneny |
| **Project Editor:** | Janet Walden |
| **Acquisitions Coordinator:** | Tana Allen |
| **Technical Editor:** | Rowena White |
| **Copy Editor:** | Lisa Theobald |
| **Proofreader:** | Paul Tyler |
| **Indexer:** | David Heiret |
| **Computer Designers:** | Kelly Stanton-Scott, Jean Butterfield |
| **Illustrators:** | Lyssa Sieben-Wald, Michael Mueller |
| **Series Design:** | Mickey Galicia, Peter Hancik |
| **Cover Design:** | Pattie Lee |

This book was composed with Corel VENTURA™ Publisher.

## Dedication

I would like to dedicate this book to
Janine Warner, without whom
none of this would have
happened.

## About the Author

**Ken Milburn** started taking pictures the year he entered high school and was working professionally as a wedding photographer by the time he graduated. He has been involved with photography both as a hobby and professionally ever since, and he has worked in advertising, travel, and fashion photography. He has been working with computers since 1981 and has written hundreds of articles, columns, and reviews for such publications as *Publish*, *DV* magazine, *Computer Graphics World*, *PC World*, *Macworld*, and *Windows* magazine. He has published 10 other computer books, including the first edition of *The Digital Photography Bible*, *Master Visually Photoshop 6*, *Master Photoshop 5.5 VISUALLY*, *Cliff's Notes on Taking and Printing Digital Photos*, and *Photoshop 5.5 Professional Results*. Ken also maintains a practice as a commercial photo-illustrator and has become internationally known for his photopaintings, which have been featured twice in *Design Graphics* magazine, in the all-time best-selling poster for the 1998 Sausalito Arts Festival, and in the 1999 American President Lines calendar.

# Contents at a Glance

# Contents

# Acknowledgments

If it weren't for Gene Hirsh, my friend and the co-author of our *Photoshop Elements: The Complete Reference*, it is unlikely that this book would have made it to press on time. When illness and deadline pressures from other projects got to me, Gene gave it his all to make sure that the project happened. Gene, you're the man. Thank you and God bless.

I also want to thank my brilliant and charming acquisitions editor for her persistent calm, sense of humor, and practical approach to life. Margie McAneny belongs in the top rung of acquisitions editors. Tana Allen is equally diligent and conscientious, not to mention great to work with. I also want to extend a warm thanks to Rowena White, Janet Walden, and Lisa Theobald for their skillful editing. Bravo to Peter Hancik for a great design and also to Pattie Lee for an eye-catching cover. Finally, I extend big thank you to my long-time agent, Margot Maley Hutchinson, for all her work in making this project a reality.

Lots of companies helped us out with review copies of their software and with review units of their cameras. You'll see photographs and mentions of these products throughout the book. Copious thanks to all of these companies for their help! Without it, we wouldn't have been able to gather nearly as much valuable information. I'd also like to make special mention of Nikon and Olympus; both companies made sure we were kept up-to-date and were especially quick to respond to our needs. And special thanks also to the people at TechSmith for the constant updates to SnagIt! (which created all of the screenshots in this book) and Camtasia, a program that's great at capturing the screen in motion.

# Introduction

You've done it! You finally went out and bought that digital camera you've heard so much about and now you're staring at it, wondering how to make the thing work. It can be a bit intimidating at first. Do you find yourself pondering all those buttons, screens, and dials and scratching your head? Where do you put in the film anyway? It's OK, though, because you did one thing right. You purchased this book, which places you firmly on the path to shooting digital photographs like a pro.

This book was conceived with the novice digital photographer in mind. For that reason, I have kept the language in plain English; where technical terms are used, they include a clear, concise, no-nonsense explanation. The digital camera is complex enough without making you learn a whole new technical language. So rest assured that this book will make your life a bit easier by demystifying the subject as much as possible, making it possible for you to easily grasp this content and make it work for you.

Much of the knowledge in this user-friendly book was gained over my years of hard-knocks experience. The 99 tips herein will help you take control of your camera, compose better photos, and will then launch you into the power of digital editing.

My hope is that you will find this book a helpful companion in introducing you to the tools and techniques that pros use to get dramatic results. The only difference between an amateur and a pro is knowledge and experience. I plan to convey to you the essential knowledge that will make the experience a rewarding one and start you on your way to more accomplished work.

Digital photography is a new invention, so practically everyone is a novice—or was one not so long ago. I wanted to mention this so you will feel comfortable and encouraged in your pursuit of this fascinating new aspect of photography. You have lots of company in this pursuit, because we are all, even the pros, learning what digital photography can do. Think of this as the "Digital Photography Gold Rush"—you, too, can stake out your claim!

I have worked hard to devise a format for this book that will be easy to use. The information presented in the tips follows a general structure of *what* is it?, *why* do you need it?, and *how* do you do it? This allows you to get at the information you want quickly, without having to sift through pages of text. I think you will find this a useful guide to stash in your camera case and to use for reference again and again. I wish I had this book when I started out. Perhaps that's why I wrote it.

I have chosen to use Adobe Photshop Elements to demonstrate many of the image-editing techniques in this book, because I feel it is one of the most robust image editors to hit the market at a low price. Adobe Photoshop Elements was fashioned after Adobe Photoshop, a professional-level image editor. By using Elements, which actually shares many of the same features as Adobe Photoshop, you can get a good sense of and feel for what professionals use everyday. If you want to try out Adobe Photoshop Elements, you can download a free demo version at http://www.adobe.com/products/photoshopel/.

# Make This a Better Book: Talk to the Author

I may not be able to answer all the e-mail I get, but I'll certainly read them and your voice will have an influence on future editions. Unfortunately, if I'm up against paying deadlines when you write, it may not be practical to get back to you right away. Please don't let that discourage you from letting me know what you think—especially if you have constructive suggestions for improving this book. Immediately following the completion of this book, my Web site was thoroughly redesigned. One of the new features is a gallery of photos with "How I Did It" tips attached. Watch the site for frequent updates and news and reviews of breaking developments in the digital photography field. My Web site address is http://www.kenmilburn.com. You can reach my e-mail address through the Web site.

*–Ken Milburn*

# Part I

# Taking Full Advantage of Your Camera

# Chapter 1

# How Does a Digital Camera Work?

Anyone, and that includes professionals, who first picks up a digital camera can be a bit intimidated—all those new buttons, screens, and dials. I am here to demystify the device so you harness the power the digital camera gives you. Understanding how a digital camera works at the functional level establishes the foundation you need to take good photographs. The camera is your tool in capturing your vision and, as any craftsman will tell you, knowing your tools is key to creating high-quality work. In this chapter, I will go over all the parts of the camera, explain their functions, and familiarize you with their unique features and terminology.

## 1. The Basic Parts of a Digital Camera

First, you must get familiar with the basic components of a digital camera, which have many features that you won't find on conventional cameras and some that you will. Figure 1-1 illustrates the typical location and configuration of the components on most digital cameras. Your camera may vary in the exact location, so also refer to your manual if you need further clarification.

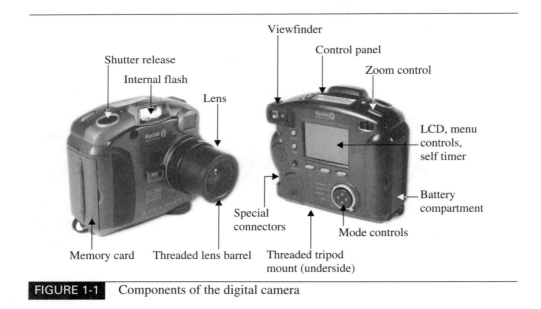

**FIGURE 1-1**    Components of the digital camera

## Battery Compartment

This is the slot where you install your camera's batteries. The batteries may be rechargeable or standard types and come in various sizes. Most digital cameras hold multiple batteries.

## Control Panel

The control panel is "information central." This is a small LCD display, usually located on the top of the camera or on the topside of the back of the camera, that displays the current settings, battery life, number of images remaining to be taken, and mode operation of the camera. The symbols and items displayed vary with different manufactures, but these are slowly becoming standardized.

## Internal Flash

The internal flash is a built-in electronic strobe-type flash that is timed to go off with the release of the shutter. It can also be suppressed, forced, or delayed via menu controls for various shooting conditions (see Chapter 5).

## LCD

LCD stands for *liquid crystal display*. This is a reference to the type of technology that was used in the early flat-panel video displays. Many technologies are used now, but LCD has become a generic term for a flat video display. Think of it as a small television screen on the back of your camera and sometimes in the viewfinder. It displays what the lens "sees" (as opposed to the slightly offset and distorted view that an optical viewfinder provides), shows previews of the shots that you have taken, and displays the camera's interactive menus in color. You can even see motion video on the LCD—if your camera supports that feature.

## Lens

The lens is a piece of ground glass or plastic that focuses the light on the sensors. It is mounted in a cylindrical housing, which is attached to the front of the camera. The lens (or some of the elements within it) moves within the housing closer or nearer to the image sensors, which allows the image to focus. Some lenses are permanently mounted to the camera and others are detachable and interchangeable. The lens is your primary eye on the world in photography, so lens quality is very important. A significant portion of what you pay for in a camera should be due to the quality of the optics.

## Mode Controls

Mode controls can be in the form of dials or buttons on the top or back of the camera. They allow you to switch between various basic shooting modes so that your camera can be made to adapt quickly to the conditions of the shoot. Examples of such mode controls are programmed or automatic, aperture-priority, and shutter-priority. Although many other types of mode settings are available, these choices vary wildly from one camera model to another. (See Chapter 3 for more information on modes.)

## Menu Controls

You'll find the menu controls on the back of the camera, shown on the LCD in the form of an interactive video display. You can change a wide range of camera options using these controls.

## Memory Card Compartment

The memory card compartment is a small door or slot in the side or on the bottom of the camera that allows for the insertion of a memory card or disk. Images are stored on the memory card. (See Tip 10 in Chapter 2 for more on memory cards.)

## Viewfinder

The viewfinder is a small eyepiece located on the top part of the camera. Viewfinders come in three varieties—optical, electronic, and through-the-lens (see Tip 24 in Chapter 4). Viewfinders are designed to simulate what the lens is seeing to enable you to frame your picture.

## Self Timer

The self timer allows you to set a timer so that you can walk away from the camera and have it take the photo after a short delay. A few digital cameras also come with wireless remote switches that can trigger the camera to take a photo from a distance. Self timers are often used in place of cable releases to keep the camera from jiggling and blurring the photo when the shutter release is pressed.

## Shutter Release

The shutter release is a multifunction button, usually found on the top right part of the camera. It is used in its half-pressed mode to set metering and focus. In its fully pressed mode, it releases the shutter to expose the electronic image sensors and capture the image.

## Special Connectors

Special connectors are extra outputs and inputs that allow for the attachment of external power, external flash, audio, video, and computer connections. Because not all cameras include all of these connections, you should shop carefully to make sure that those connections you need are included on the camera.

## Threaded Lens Barrel

If the front of the lens barrel is threaded, it can accept a wide variety of color-balancing, special-effects, and close-up filters. It is also much more able to adapt to supplementary telephoto and wide-angle lenses. You can spot a threaded lens barrel by looking at the inside rim of the metal that surrounds the front lens element. If you see screw threads, obviously the barrel is threaded. Some cameras require you to push on nonthreaded adapters, increasing the chances that a supplementary lens could be accidentally knocked from its perch. Unthreaded barrels are most often found on cameras whose lenses retract into the camera body or on low-priced cameras.

## Threaded Tripod Mount

The threaded mount is a bolt hole in the bottom of the camera that accepts the mounting screw for tripods, camera stands, external flash units, and other types of camera mounting hardware. The screw size and thread are nearly always one-quarter inch in diameter. Some larger, more expensive, and sturdier tripods and accessories use a one-third-inch mounting screw, but users of consumer-level digital cameras seldom need be concerned with these.

## Zoom Control

If your camera has a zoom lens, it will have a control that widens or narrows the angle of view. The control, in the form of a toggle switch, is usually found on top of the camera. Zooming allows you to move closer to your subject without changing your position.

# 2. The Basic Differences Between Conventional and Digital Cameras

Even though conventional cameras have been including more and more electronic features, the primary operation of the camera is mechanical. To take a photograph, the shutter has to open to expose the film inside. Digital cameras have almost completely eliminated the mechanical aspect of photography. About the only place that moving parts still exist in digital cameras is in the focus and zoom functions of the lenses.

If you have operated a single-lens reflex (SLR) camera, you will find that using a digital camera is similar in a lot of ways. SLRs are typically 35mm film cameras that let you see directly through the lens via a mirror that reflects the image to the viewfinder. The mirror moves out of the way when the shot is taken.

The following is a comparison list pointing out some of the basic differences between digital and conventional cameras:

| Digital Cameras | Conventional Cameras |
| --- | --- |
| Memory cards can be reused | Hand-loaded film—needs processing |
| Can view shots immediately on LCD | Have to wait for processing (except for Polaroid—60 sec.) |
| Can preview a catalog of shots in memory | No preview |
| Can take shots over again many times and not use more memory | No way to reuse film after it has been exposed |
| Low to good resolution | Good to excellent resolution |
| Can record motion sequences (some models) | Can't record video |
| Can record audio (some models) | Can't record audio |
| Batteries must be recharged often | Small batteries last a long time (except motor-drive cameras) |
| Swiveling LCD allows framing from odd angles (some models) | Need to frame through the viewfinder |
| Zoom lenses | Zoom lenses |
| Detachable lenses only on most expensive models | Detachable lenses on all but least expensive models |
| Few to no moving parts | Many moving parts |

## 3. Know Your Resolution

*Resolution* in digital photography refers to the number of individual *pixels* (discrete picture elements) that are used to define the detail in the image. Think of pixels as tiny, solid-color square tiles in a very large mosaic tabletop picture. Image size is defined by pixel dimensions, as in 640×480, which refers to the number of horizontal (640) and vertical (480) pixels in the matrix that makes up the picture. The higher the resolution, the clearer and more detailed the picture appears.

Inside your digital camera are specialized light-sensitive chips, called *image sensors*. Image sensors use either Complementary Metal Oxide Semiconductor (CMOS) or Charge-Coupled Device (CCD) technology. (Ironically, only the newest and highest definition or the cheapest and lowest definition cameras currently use CMOS technology.) These chips are made up of arrays of image sensors. Each sensor translates the light falling on it into electronic signals, which define color and intensity. This information is stored as digital data in a computer data device that's built into the camera or as flash memory on a removable card. The data on these cards is translated by computer programs and displayed as color pixels on a computer screen or the camera's LCD.

Figure 1-2 shows the same image displayed at low resolution and high resolution. You can see how the pixels appear more "blended" at a higher resolution.

You will notice that each camera comes with a pixel rating, such as 1.3 megapixels (million pixels) or 3.2 megapixels on up to 6 megapixels in the newest models. More megapixels translate to more individual light sensors on the image chip, which translates to higher image definition, which translates to sharper, clearer pictures. Your camera's megapixel rating determines how much detail can be captured in the highest resolution setting. You can usually blow up standard 35mm film to 8×10, 11×14, and in some cases 16×20 without seeing too much loss in quality, but go any further and the quality starts to go downhill.

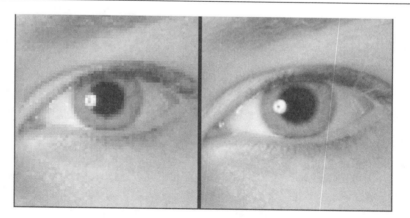

Resolution at 1 megapixel          Resolution at 3 megapixels

**FIGURE 1-2**    You can see the difference in image quality between low resolution (left) and high resolution (right) digital cameras.

With digital cameras, the resolution of the image sensor determines the detail, so if you want the ability to blow up your pictures to any great degree, you will need to use a higher resolution mode. The 5- and 6-megapixel digital cameras are the first to produce images with quality similar to that of film. Popularly priced 2-megapixel digital cameras will allow for passable inkjet or photographic prints of up to 8×10 in size, comparable to machine-made prints available from consumer-level one-hour photo labs.

On the other hand, if your image is targeted for online display, such as the Web, video, or animation, the need for resolution will be much lower. The best advice is to buy the highest capacity memory cards you can afford and shoot all your pictures at the highest resolution your camera will allow. You may think you have a good reason to shoot at a lower resolution, but the only really good reason is if you just have no other way to get the shots you want to take without running out of memory before you can download the images off the memory card and start over. After all, it's always better to have *some* picture of something that's important to you than no picture at all. It's equally important to remember that if detail and quality don't exist in the image you shoot, you are never going to be able to restore it later. Remember that you can never take exactly the same picture twice. (Well, almost never. Still-life photos taken under controlled studio lighting conditions are the one exception I can think of.)

## Try This:  Up Close and Personal with Pixels

If you have the ability to load your camera's images onto your computer, you might use your image-editing software to zoom in on a part of the image to get a closer look at the pixel structure. Try doing test shots of the same scene or object at various resolution settings to see the differences. If you can look at film under magnification, you will see the grain structure—and a lot of similarities between pixels and grain. Although film is often referred to as *continuous tone*, that is not factually correct. Film has discrete color elements that are similar to pixels. The big difference is that the film's elements have a random shape and size whereas digital pixels are uniform squares in a grid—with no empty space in between them. So, in a sense, digital images are grainless.

## Why Is Resolution Important?

The more resolution (pixels) your camera can capture, the finer the detail in the photograph and the more information you have to work with later in editing or printing the image. Due to the rapid advancements in digital technology, today's digital cameras are approaching the quality of conventional film—and may soon surpass it. Higher resolution means sharper and more detailed pictures.

The resolution ultimately affects output (this applies to printers, film recorders, video, or the Web). Every type of output demands a certain amount of information from the images that it uses for input (the image stored on the memory card in pixels). Prints and slides demand a significantly larger number of pixels (about 240 to the printed inch) to produce good quality. (See Chapter 14.) Video and the Web require much less (between 72 pixels and 96 pixels to the displayed inch). (See Chapter 7.)

Cropping a part of a photo throws away pixels and, therefore, affects resolution. You can't replace that resolution if you then enlarge the cropped image. Understanding what your target output is going to be will help you choose the appropriate resolution settings and help you learn how to frame your image to maximize results. However, as I mentioned earlier, the simplest way to deal with this is to capture every image with as much resolution as your camera can accommodate.

## How Do I Adjust Resolution?

Most cameras provide multiple resolution settings. You can access the menu for selecting the resolution options through your LCD menu options panel. The exact pixel dimensions of each resolution setting will vary according to the megapixel rating of the camera. It is a very good idea to keep the camera set at its highest quality, highest resolution setting until you have a critical need to capture more pictures than that setting will allow. Remember, once you've taken the picture, you can never increase its quality. Nor can you retake the picture.

NOTE    *It's a good idea to check your camera's control panel after you change resolution settings to see how many shots you can store on your memory card. This will allow you to gauge your shoot.*

The following table provides a comparison chart to indicate the range of output capabilities that are practical for the resolution rating of the camera. The higher resolution cameras give you the greatest range and flexibility.

| Camera Resolution Ranges* | Up to 8×10 Prints | 8×10–11×14 Prints | Poster-Sized Prints | Inkjet Prints | Web Graphics |
|---|---|---|---|---|---|
| 1 megapixel range—very low 640×480 to 1024×768 | | | | | x |
| 2 megapixel range—low 1280×960 | x | | | x | x |
| 3 megapixel range—medium 1200×1600 | x | x | | x | x |
| 4 megapixel range—high 2272×1704 | x | x | x | x | x |
| 5+ megapixel range—very high 3008×1960 | x | x | x | x | x |

*The resolutions indicated represent an average for the range in that category. Actual resolutions may vary somewhat according to manufacturer and model.

## About Image Quality Settings

In addition to giving you a choice of resolution settings, most digital cameras let you choose what they call "image quality." Why provide two settings that seem to amount to the same thing? Because they are really two independent factors, each of which contributes to overall image quality. Resolution is one of these factors. The degree of "lossy" compression used in writing the file to JPEG (for Joint Photographic Experts Group) format is the other.

JPEG is the image file format that is most often used by digital cameras, because it saves space and allows you to record more images on the memory card. It accomplishes this by "reinterpreting" the picture so that it doesn't have to record exact data for every pixel in the image. Instead, you decide how much compression you want to use. The lower the image-quality setting you use, the more compression the camera's processor uses in saving the image to memory— and the more information is irretrievably lost (and replaced with little color anomalies that seem to resemble film grain).

The first time a high-quality JPEG image is saved and then opened for viewing, it is difficult to tell that any information has been discarded at all. However, each subsequent file save recalculates the amount of data to be thrown away, and the same amount of data that was discarded in the first instance is discarded again. So the first thing you need to know about JPEG images is that when you open them, you must subsequently save them to a "lossless" format, such as TIFF (for Tagged Image File Format), or to your image editor's proprietary file format (such as Photoshop's PSD format) if you want to prevent continued image degradation.

As far as lower quality settings, the most important thing for you to remember about them is that you can never recover the image information that was lost. Each time you lower the quality setting, you raise the level of image compression—which is nothing more than further data loss. So you have to remember the same lesson you learned about reducing resolution. Once you've discarded image quality, you can never get it back, and you can almost never replace the picture you took in the first instance. Again, the only reason you should be willing to lose image quality is if your camera or computer doesn't have the capacity to store many more pictures (and you haven't had the foresight to buy extra memory cards).

Some of the more advanced digital cameras will also let you save files in either TIFF or RAW image file format. TIFF records every pixel in the exact shade of the 16 million possible colors that the image sensor could capture. Some of the best sensors can actually record a lot more than 16 million colors, thus allowing them to capture a range of brightness values closer to those found in bright, natural sunlight. That is why some cameras even let you record your images to a format called RAW (referring to untouched data as it comes directly off the sensors). RAW image files can contain as much data as your camera is designed to capture (higher cost digital cameras typically record 12 to 16 bits of information per pixel instead of the usual 8 bits per pixel). RAW image files produce extremely high-quality images, but they also create data files that are eight to sixteen times as large as those recorded for a Super High Quality (SHQ) JPEG image. You must also have (or be willing to wait for) an image editor that will allow you to process image files that contain more than 8 bits of information per pixel.

# Chapter 2

# Taking Care of Your Camera

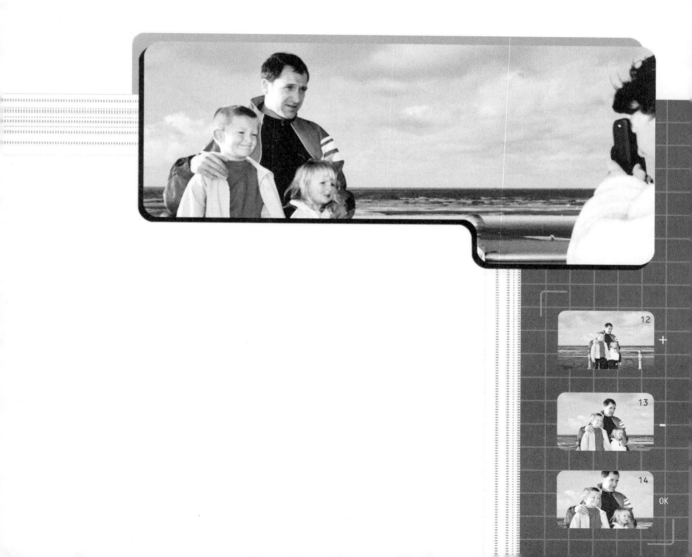

Because a digital camera is a significant investment, it's well worth the time to learn the proper care and maintenance so your camera will continue to take good pictures over the course of its lifetime. A digital camera is a delicate piece of equipment that must be handled and maintained properly to keep it functioning correctly. This chapter covers the basic methods for caring for your camera and provides tips and pointers from an experienced user, to help you avoid learning camera care "the hard way." Just a few good habits and a bit of extra caution can save you tons of grief and make your picture-taking experience a rewarding one.

## 4. Keep Your Camera Handy—Safely

When you are moving about with your camera, you need to know the best ways to protect it while still allowing for convenient access. You may often need to travel over some rough terrain—from an overcrowded gathering to an overgrown path in a forest—to get the shot you want. If your camera is not protected properly, it can suffer some serious damage. Take some simple precautions, and you'll be prepared to deal with almost any situation.

Having your camera easily accessible will give you an advantage when the unexpected shots pop up. You'll want to be able to grab your camera and shoot in just a few moments, so you should have it stored in a way that allows for that. "Be prepared" should be the photographer's mantra. If you're not prepared, you just don't get the picture.

### How Do I Store My Camera Properly?

Use a moisture-resistant padded case that is insulated to protect against bumps, bangs, and rapid temperature changes. Velcro-adjustable, padded partitions will keep your camera's parts and accessories from moving around as you move. You want the camera and any other breakable parts to fit snugly inside the case. If you want to carry an extra lens or other accessories, such as an external flash, find a case that provides compartments that these items fit into properly. The case should have enough room for extra batteries, memory cards, cleaning aids, and any other accessories you regularly carry. If you plan on moving about, keep your case as compact as you can, so it doesn't become cumbersome.

Keep the camera in the case when you are carrying it or storing it. If the camera is hanging around your neck it can get caught on protruding objects, take a bad knock if you slip, and swing out of control—causing damage to the camera or to you or someone close by. You want to avoid having to make the choice of protecting the camera or yourself. You can hang your camera from a belt, so you are sure you know where it is and so it won't swing around as you move.

If you are in a situation that requires you to grab shots as the moments present themselves, you should wear your camera on a neck strap. Always place the strap around your neck, or better yet, sling it over your head to the opposite shoulder like a seat belt, which is much more secure. Never, ever sling it over only your shoulder, because a practiced thief can steal it in an instant. At the least it will surely plunge disastrously to the pavement as soon as you're distracted or you take another bag off your shoulder. Digital cameras are even less forgiving than film cameras with this sort of treatment—even though you paid three or four times as much for the digital variety.

**NOTE** *Better camera cases provide many compartments so you can get to needed items quickly and without rummaging. Take the time to choose a case that suits your needs and properly fits your camera and your accessories. It is a good idea to take your camera and accessories with you when you purchase a case, so you can test to see that it all fits. You don't want to leave essential pieces behind for lack of room.*

## 5. Keep It Dry, Cool, and Clean

Your digital camera is a delicate piece of electronic equipment and needs to be treated with respect if you are going to maintain it in good working condition. Developing good habits to start with will assure that it stays operational. One of the main threats to electronics is the environment. Severe heat and cold, rain, and dust can wreak havoc on your camera and need to be protected against.

### How Do I Protect My Camera?

Common sense tells you that it's a good idea to bring an umbrella if you think it might rain. If you must, shoot only when the precipitation is fairly light and predictable, unless you have an underwater camera housing. If the wet weather is light and predictable, you'll capture the mood and atmosphere that comes with all that dampness.

When you're shooting in light precipitation, it's a good idea to invite someone along to hold the umbrella for you so your hands can be free to shoot (and to tuck the camera away if the wind shifts). If you don't have an assistant and a umbrella, look for anything that can provide temporary cover while you take the shot, such as a piece of cardboard or a newspaper—or just pull your coat over your head and camera for a makeshift hood.

Failing all that, try to find places that are covered but still provide an open view to the subject, such as a porch, large tree, or overhanging ledge. Keep your camera in its bag until you're under such protective covering. You can take nice rainy-weather shots from inside your car, either through the wet windshield or with one of the side windows opened just enough for the camera to peek past.

Severe heat and cold can cause cameras to malfunction, and in some cases damage can result. It is never a good idea to leave a camera in a car where it can be exposed to extremes of hot or cold for long periods of time. If you have to leave the camera in the car, make sure it is stored in a well-insulated case and away from direct sun (and out of sight). In extreme cold conditions, you will want to warm up the camera before switching it on. A good way to do this is to put it inside your overcoat and let your body heat do the job. If you are hiking about in cold or hot weather, it is good practice to keep the camera in its case when it is not in use.

Keeping the lens and LCD clean is the best way to keep your camera in good working order and get good, clear images. Don't use off-the-shelf cleaning solutions, your clothes, or your fingers to clean the lens or LCD. It will only make matters worse and may damage the lens. Use only supplies—tissues and a brush to wipe off dust and grime—designed for lens cleaning. You can purchase these from a camera store and you should keep them with you at all times. Actually, the best and most affordable lens-cleaning kits are those made for eyeglasses. You can buy the cloths and the lens-cleaning solution at most opticians and camera stores.

Dust and other airborne material can be hazardous to your camera. Keep the lens covered (see Tip 8, later in this chapter) and the camera in its case when dirt or debris is flying. One of the worst places you can take a camera is to the beach, especially on a windy day. Sand particles can tear up a lens or LCD in no time. If you have to shoot in such conditions, make sure you use a haze (UV) filter (see Tip 8, later in this chapter) to protect the lens, and cover the LCD with a piece of clear vinyl. Fine sand can also work its way into your camera's mechanical parts, such as the lens mount and shutter release. If this happens, it is wise to take your camera into a professional service for cleaning.

## 6. Make a Raincoat for Your Camera

A camera raincoat is a homemade waterproof covering for your camera that allows you to shoot in inclement weather without exposing your camera to adverse conditions.

## Why Does My Camera Need a Raincoat?

Photos taken in bad weather are often dramatically striking—precisely because we don't often see such photos. Using your camera in inclement weather can be dangerous to your camera if you are not careful. If you want to capture a great shot in bad weather, though, you'll need to get out of the shelter and into the middle of things. If you are intending to shoot in wet weather, you need to take some precautions to protect your equipment. The best protection is an underwater housing, but they're not available to fit all digital cameras and they can cost as much as the camera. The next best thing is a raincoat made from a plastic bag.

## How Do I Make a Raincoat for My Camera?

You will need a 2-gallon "ziplock"-type plastic bag, a haze (UV) filter, and a sunshade (always a good idea anyway because it protects your camera's lens).

1.  Lay the bag flat and place the sunshade on the bag so that exactly half the shade straddles the bottom edge of the bag.

2.  Trace around the sunshade with a felt-tip pen to make a half circle. Keeping the bag flat, use an Xacto knife, scissors, or a utility knife to follow the traced half circle and cut out an opening for the sunshade through both layers of the bag. After you have cut the half circle, open up the bag and you will see that it forms a full circle.

3.  Now place the UV filter over the lens and screw it in. Then screw the sunshade onto the filter.

4.  Place the camera inside the plastic bag and push the sunshade through the hole in the bottom.

5.  Tape the plastic bag to the sunshade so that water or debris can't leak in.

These steps, and the finished raincoat, are shown in Figure 2-1.

While you're carrying the camera, keep the bag zipped shut. When you reach your location and you're ready to shoot, hold the camera so the rain won't come into the back of the bag, unzip it, and reach inside to hold the camera. Be sure to pull the bag back over your wrist. You can make a few of these raincoats ahead of time and keep them handy.

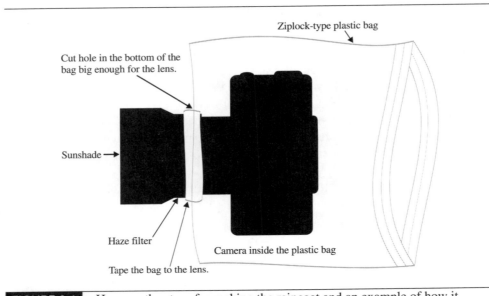

Ziplock-type plastic bag

Cut hole in the bottom of the bag big enough for the lens.

Sunshade →

Haze filter

Tape the bag to the lens.

Camera inside the plastic bag

**FIGURE 2-1**    Here are the steps for making the raincoat and an example of how it should look on the camera.

**NOTE**    *It's a good idea to slide a big, loose rubber band over the bag and around your wrist so the wind can't suddenly blow the bag over the camera, thus exposing it to the rain.*

## 7. Take Care of the LCD

Figure 2-2 shows an example LCD. LCDs are usually made of glass and scratch easily, so you should take care to avoid any type of impact or abrasion to that area of your camera. They are often coated with thin films to make them more viewable in glare situations, and that coating is also sensitive. You should treat the LCD as you would a pair of expensive glasses.

### Why Is the LCD Important?

As emphasized in Chapter 1, the LCD is your camera's "window to the world." That wonderful little display monitor on the back of your camera provides you with a view of what your lens sees, as well as menu commands, and previews. It is an essential part of your camera, so you want to keep it in good working order. It is also one of the most vulnerable parts of your camera besides the lens.

**FIGURE 2-2**    The LCD is your electronic window to the world.

### How Do I Protect the LCD?

Keep it clean. Use the same cleaning equipment you use on your lens. Put a piece of smooth cardboard over it with a rubber band if it doesn't have a built-in cover or protective case. Leaving a Hoodman (a cowl that you attach to the back of the camera with Velcro or an elastic strap to shade the LCD from the sun; see Chapter 15) attached can also be effective. Avoid leaving your camera in your car for extended periods of time, unless it is stored in an insulated bag or case that protects it against extreme temperatures. Glove compartments and trunks are solar ovens that can reach temperatures several times that of the outside temperature. Exposure to too much bright sunlight or extremes in temperature can also damage LCDs.

## 8. Keep the Lens Covered

The lens cover is a plastic or metal piece that covers and protects the lens when you are not shooting pictures. Tethers are available at camera supply stores to keep the lens cover with the camera so that it doesn't get lost in the haste of removing it from the camera. A tethered lens cap is also a good reminder to make sure the lens cover is on the lens when it is not in use. Never store the camera without making sure the lens cover is securely in place. This will keep it clean and protect it from damage. Remember, just a small impact with any hard object can permanently damage your lens.

### What Kinds of Lens Covers Are Available?

Lens covers come in a few varieties:

**Built-in Lens Covers**    Many low-end to midrange cameras with fixed lenses come with a mechanical door that slides back to reveal the lens as soon as you turn on the camera. This is a nice feature because it automatically closes when you turn off the camera, so you'll never forget to put the lens cover back on or lose it.

**Plastic Snap-on Covers**    These covers are designed to fit your particular lens and have spring-loaded catches that fit into the screw threads on the inside rim of the lens. This type of lens cover tends to pop off when you unexpectedly give a fairly light nudge to one of the release handles. On the other hand, the quick-release mechanism lets you get the cover on and off quickly.

**Rubber or Plastic Slip Covers**    These are designed to slip snugly over the outside of the rim of your lens and must be fitted to your particular lens. These are good covers if they fit tightly enough so they don't slip off when you don't want them to.

**Metal Screw-on Covers**    These are the best kind of covers for absolute protection, and most professional photographers use them. They are made of tough metal and screw into the inside lens threads, making it virtually impossible for them to detach unexpectedly. Of course, your camera must have a threaded lens barrel to use a screw-on cover.

**UV Filter Protection**    A glass UV filter screws on the front of your lens to protect it from being scratched. After all, you can affordably replace a UV filter. If you scratch your lens, you may have to replace the entire camera. This filter has little effect if you're shooting indoors, but outdoors it has the added benefit of reducing ultraviolet haze that often softens landscape photos.

## 9. Keep Fresh, Quality Batteries on Hand

Cameras use either a proprietary rechargeable battery that must be purchased through the camera's manufacturer or standard AA batteries, which are readily available in many stores. You won't have much luck using standard alkaline batteries—they don't hold enough charge and thus have to be purchased more frequently (often for more than a roll of film costs).

It's a good idea to purchase a camera that uses rechargeable batteries. A number of rechargeable battery types are available, as discussed in the following sections.

**Nickel Cadmium (NiCaD)**   These types of batteries are the most common, but they are not necessarily the best for a couple of reasons:

- They are not environmentally friendly.

- NiCad batteries suffer from memory effect.

*Memory effect* is the process of a battery reducing its ability to hold a full charge when it is repeatedly recharged before it has been fully discharged. This effect increases every time the battery is recharged prematurely. It is a common problem with NiCad batteries and can render the batteries useless over time.

**Nickel Metal Hydride (NiMH)**   NiMH batteries are the best type of battery for use with digital cameras. They can be recharged at any time with no performance loss. They also tend to have higher power-rating capacities. They can be recharged many times before burnout. Finally, they can be recycled without damage to the environment.

**Lithium Ion (LiON)**   LiON batteries are mostly used in external power packs and are not readily available in AA size. They provide much more power than the other types of rechargeable batteries, so these batteries might play an important roll in future camera models.

## Why Do I Need Fresh, Quality Batteries?

Keeping well-charged, high-quality batteries on hand is an important issue with digital camera use. Digital cameras draw a lot of power, because almost everything about them is electronic. You can run through batteries pretty fast if you are using a lot of the features—like the LCD, flash, and zoom lens.

It's a good idea to have at least one set of extra batteries on hand to ensure that you can make it through a normal day of shooting. You can always recharge your batteries overnight so you're good to go the next day. Of course, if you're a pro or just a fanatical hobbyist, you might want to get several sets of batteries. You can buy them at your local discount warehouse for about $20 for a set of four. Look for the power rating on the batteries. If it's not printed on the batteries, you can bet that the manufacturer isn't proud of the rating. A rating of 1600 MaH is good. Anything higher is excellent.

## How Do I Tell Whether the Batteries Are Charged?

All digital cameras provide battery-life indicators on their control panels—an example is shown in Figure 2-3. The indicator is usually a symbol that looks like a battery and graphically indicates in quarter steps how much charge is left in the installed batteries.

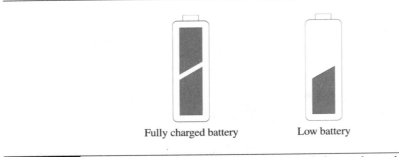

Fully charged battery                    Low battery

 **FIGURE 2-3**    The battery indicator on the control panel shows charged and low battery views.

Stay aware of the battery power level and check it at power-up and at regular intervals while you shoot, especially if you are using a lot of the electricity-hogging features like the LCD and flash. You want to be prepared so the big shot doesn't find you holding a dead camera.

## How Do I Change or Recharge the Batteries?

Most digital cameras come with a battery charger, like the one shown in Figure 2-4, but this inclusion is beginning to disappear as camera prices come down. Most of the chargers that are included take a long time to recharge batteries, which is inconvenient if you use your camera a lot. Worse, if you leave the batteries in the charger for too long, they will be damaged unless the charger is smart enough to turn itself off.

Proprietary battery sizes and shapes—that is, special batteries that can be used for a single camera model only—are becoming more common. You're better off buying a camera that uses standard AA batteries, if you can. One set of proprietary batteries (an "invisible" excuse for fattening the camera manufacturer's profit margins) costs roughly twice as much as a set of four conventional AA batteries. Furthermore, if you run out or lose proprietary batteries while traveling through the Amazon, you're not going to be able to buy new ones.

It's a good idea to buy a one-hour charger and one or two extra sets of batteries. The charger device plugs into a regular wall socket and has compartments to receive the batteries. Make sure you get a charger that will receive a full set of batteries at one time. This will allow the charger to charge one set of batteries while you're using the other set. Don't leave batteries in the charger for extended periods of time beyond when they are fully charged, because they will overheat, shortening their life

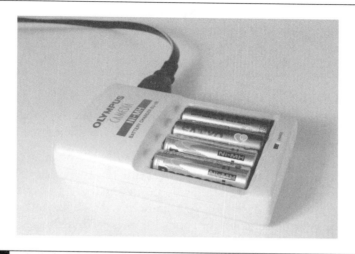

**FIGURE 2-4**    A typical battery charger often comes with the camera.

span. The best chargers will automatically turn themselves off as soon as the batteries are fully charged.

NiMH batteries can lose some of their charge over time, even when they are not in use, so you may need to recharge them periodically to keep them optimal. Make sure you place the batteries in the charger properly or they will not charge.

**NOTE**    *Remember that batteries are the lifelines for your camera, and without good power, you are dead in the water.*

## 10. Using and Caring for Memory Cards

Memory cards are the digital equivalent of the removable film in a conventional camera. When images are exposed on the image sensors, they are converted to electrical signals that are stored on solid-state flash memory media that take the form of small cards or disks that can be easily inserted and removed from the camera. You can keep additional cards with you to store images, should one card become full. No developing is necessary and the cards are reusable after erasing or reformatting—just like a floppy disk. They come in a range of memory capacities (which equates to the number of shots they can hold) according to the card type. The brand of camera you have will determine which type of memory card it uses.

Memory cards work with card readers, which can be attached to a computer to allow the transfer of images to other devices. Also, most current digital camera models can be attached to the computer via a USB cable so that the images can be transferred directly to the computer.

## What Types and Sizes Are Available?

Various types of memory cards (see Figure 2-5) can be purchased with a variety of storage limits. The available types are explored in the following sections.

**CompactFlash Types I & II**     CompactFlash (CF) cards are the most popular type in use today—but only by a small margin over SmartMedia cards. CF cards are reasonably small and lightweight, fit nicely inside small digital cameras, and come protectively encased. Type I CF cards currently have an upper limit of 512MB of storage space, which is enough for about 144 Super High Quality (SHQ) 5-megapixel JPEG images.

Type II CF cards are basically the same as Type I, with the only significant difference being the thickness of the card. The Type II card is thicker to accommodate higher storage capacity or truly miniature hard drives (that actually fit right inside the card). Some CF II cards and drives will hold 1GB of memory. That's enough to get most pros through a full day of shooting without ever having to stop and download, but these cards are still rare and, as a result, they cost about $600.

**FIGURE 2-5**     Memory cards come in a variety of types.

**SmartMedia**    These are the thinnest and lightest of the memory cards. This was accomplished by taking some of the technology off the card and placing it in the camera itself. The disadvantage of the SmartMedia arrangement is that when storage capacity ability advances, the camera may not be able to use it. You can purchase cards of up to 128MB. At present, these are the second most popular memory cards—by a close margin.

One of their advantages is that, like CF cards, you can buy them almost anywhere. The other advantage of popularity is cost-per-megabyte, which is just pennies higher than the cost-per-megabyte of CF cards and significantly lower than that of the memory cards discussed in the following sections.

**MemoryStick**    MemoryStick is a compact memory card created by Sony and used almost exclusively in Sony products. Sony has locked its proprietary memory-card format across almost all its electronic devices, so if you buy a Sony handheld computer, you are probably more inclined to buy Sony cameras or MP3 players—just so you can use MemoryStick in all the equipment. If you don't want to be forced into making your memory choice based solely on the type of memory card used, keep the issue of exclusivity in mind.

**PCMCIA PC Card**    Personal Computer Memory Card International Association (PCMCIA) is a bus format invented for laptop computers. PCMCIA storage cards are only one type of device that will fit into PCMCIA slots. Digital cameras that support PCMCIA cards can also accept other types of memory media by using an adapter. PCMCIA memory cards are typically found in older, high-end, professional digital SLRs and studio-type cameras, because their large physical size allows more room for the bulkier memory card. They provide a wide range of storage capacity of up to several gigabytes.

**Computer Disks**    This type of camera memory is identical to the standard 3.5-inch or mini CD disks you use in the computer. The advantage is instant transferability of the camera's images to virtually any computer. The disadvantage is that the storage media will hold a limited number of pictures and is comparatively slow at both recording and transferring images. It is also impractical to store high-resolution images on floppies. Even at a relatively low JPEG quality setting, a floppy disk could barely hold one 5-megapixel image.

NOTE    *If you use more than one digital camera, it's a good idea to use the same memory type in both so you can interchange the cards.*

## Why Do I Need a Memory Card?

Some low-end digital cameras can't handle memory cards. They store everything on built-in memory chips instead. This means that when the internal memory is filled, the images must be downloaded or erased before shooting can continue. Of course, that's not convenient if you're in the middle of a hike, at a wedding, or in any other situation where downloading just isn't an option.

Memory cards, on the other hand, allow you to shoot as many photos as you have cards. When you run out of space on one card, you just swap it for another.

## How Do I Use Memory Cards?

Memory cards are easy to use. Check your camera's manual to make sure you get the right type.

On cameras that accept them, memory cards are installed via a small door or slot on the camera, as shown in Figure 2-6. Don't ever force the card into the slot. If you cannot easily insert it, either you have aligned it incorrectly, something is already in the slot, or the card is damaged.

**FIGURE 2-6**    The memory card fits into a slot in your camera.

You should never insert or remove a memory card while the camera's power is turned on, or you may damage either the data or the card. After the card is inserted properly, you can close the door and power on the camera. Some cards must be formatted the first time they are used. You will find formatting commands on your LCD menu display. After the card is formatted, it is empty and ready to take the maximum number of pictures that your camera's resolution and quality settings will allow.

# Chapter 3

## Understanding Shooting Modes

The advanced electronics of today's digital cameras perform automatically many of the tasks necessary for taking a photograph. The automatic or programmed mode is always a good starting point for any shot. However, as good as these automatic functions are, they are not a foolproof system. The alternative shooting modes allow for a higher degree of control, giving you options that automatic mode cannot offer in many situations. If you want to maximize your ability to capture almost any shot that comes your way, you'll need to master all the modes of your camera.

## 11. Understand the Shutter Release Button

The shutter release button is found on the top of the camera, typically on the right side. This button has two functions:

- Pressed halfway, it locks in the focus and exposure on the area you designate by centering it in the viewfinder.

- Fully pressed, it releases the shutter to expose the image.

If you're already familiar with photography and own a camera that automatically focuses and sets exposure, partially pressing the shutter release button is probably familiar to you. This function is exactly the same on digital cameras as it is on film cameras.

### Why Do I Need to Use the Dual Modes of Operation?

Understanding the focus and exposure lock mode will let you determine exactly what part of the picture should have the sharpest focus, whether or not that object is centered in the viewfinder. Usually the object that is to be in sharpest focus is the one that needs to be best exposed, too.

### How Do I Use the Shutter Release Button?

A mark, or target, in the center of your camera's viewfinder or (more often) LCD monitor indicates what object the camera is targeting to set its focus and exposure. The shape of the mark varies from camera to camera—it may be a circle, a pair of facing square brackets, or a small plus sign. (Figure 3-1 shows an example target hovering over a scene.)

You use the dual mode shutter release button in conjunction with the target to set the camera's focus and exposure. In this first exercise, I am assuming that the target of exposure and focal point are in the same place. (I will tell you how to set it up if they are not in the same place in the next exercise.) Here's how it works:

**1.** Place the mark in the camera's viewfinder on the spot where you want the focus to be sharpest and the exposure to be the picture's midtone. (A good midtone would equate to an average skin tone or middle to light gray. Remember that *tone* refers to the light and dark values, not the color.) When you set the exposure in this way, it will have the effect of lightening dark objects, such as shaded objects, and darkening light objects, such as a midday sky.

NOTE    *To get accustomed to seeing tonal values over color values, compare color and black-and-white photographs of the same subject. You will be surprised at how some colors vary in brightness in the color photo, yet look almost identical in black and white.*

**2.** Without moving the camera, press the shutter release button halfway. Both focus and exposure will stay locked. Keep the shutter release button in this halfway position until you're ready to take the picture.

**3.** Reframe the picture so it includes the elements you want and excludes anything that's not important to the picture. (Chapter 4 offers more tips on image composition and framing a shot.)

**4.** Fully press the shutter release button to take the picture.

Figure 3-1 shows an example of using the target to set the shot's proper focus and exposure, and then reframing the shot for the final composition.

FIGURE 3-1    Locking the target (left) and then moving off center (right) as a way of adjusting composition

There are (rare, to be sure) times when the point of sharpest focus and the center of interest are in two different places. Here's how you work around that situation:

1. Frame your picture, placing the focus target on the object that's most important to expose correctly.

2. Press the shutter release button halfway to lock the exposure settings, and then take a look at the camera's control panel (the little LCD near the top of the camera) and make a mental note of the exposure settings shown there.

3. Change your picture-taking mode to manual and set the shutter and aperture to the same settings you saw on the control panel.

4. Now aim the target at the center of focus, press halfway to set the focus, reframe your picture so it's framed in the way that pleases you most, and press the shutter release button all the way down to take the picture. The exposure will be correct because once you've set it manually, the camera can't automatically reset the exposure.

NOTE    *Not all digital cameras feature the ability to use full manual exposure control. A few cameras, however, let you set focus and exposure separately. Since there's no hard-and-fast rule for how they all do this, you'll just have to check your camera's manual.*

Once you've taken a picture (or a series of pictures if you're in a situation where you have to shoot fast), use the LCD screen to review them. Then if you've goofed, you can immediately reshoot. It's doubly important to do this until you're pretty sure of your ability to set the camera properly, because some photo ops simply can't be re-created.

---

**Try This:  Practice Makes Perfect Timing**

The difference in time between the instant the button is fully pressed and the instant you hear the "shutter sound" (or the LCD screen is temporarily blanked) is known as *shutter lag time*. If you want your digital photos to capture the very instant when a picture is taken, you need to practice anticipating the shutter lag. Practice clicking, waiting, and hearing the click until you feel you've formed the habit of shooting at just that fraction of a second before you really need to.

## 12. Get the Correct Color Balance

You can achieve natural-looking skin tones and other colors by using the camera's white balance controls. *White balance* is a system of balancing color components to simulate pure white under various lighting conditions so that all other colors are correctly calibrated for that condition.

Most cameras set white balance automatically as one of the options, but sooner or later, some extraneous light will "fool" the camera into setting the wrong color balance. If you preview the shot, you'll know immediately if this is the case. If so, pray that your camera lets you set white balance for a specific color of light. Daylight, indoor incandescent, indoor fluorescence, halogen lamps, and even overcast skies have unique color signatures and can be handled in cameras with white balance presets that cover these categories. Check your camera to see what presets are available. Most digital cameras that sell for over $300 will let you force a particular color balance mode.

### Why Does White Balance Need to Be Set Correctly?

You need to set the white balance because different lighting sources are more intense in certain parts of the color spectrum. The type of light you're shooting in can translate to unnatural-looking colors in your photographs. For example, incandescent light gives the scene an overall yellow tint and fluorescent lights produce a blue, green, or violet cast. Light coming through clouds is bluer (cooler) than pure daylight. The light at sunset is much warmer than it is at midday. Our eyes and brain are exceptionally good at subconciously compensating for most such color casts. Your eyes rebalance the scene under given lighting conditions to look as it would look if you viewed it in daylight conditions. Technology, however, hasn't yet invented a way of printing a picture so that it rebalances the color as you view it in different lighting conditions.

The digital camera needs to know what pure white is in relation to the lighting in the scene so it can balance the colors correctly. Most of the time, this is handled automatically by the camera's electronics, but in some cases you might want to set it manually if you are still getting inappropriate color shifts in your photos.

NOTE

*If you do capture color shifts in your camera, your image-editing software can do wonders in correcting them—sometimes even automatically. The only problem with this, however, is that making these corrections online takes more of your valuable time and is one more thing to learn. Otherwise, your image-editing software can probably do a better job than the camera can because it's running on a much more powerful computer than the one built into your camera.*

## How Do I Set White Balance?

Most of the time, the camera gets white balance right automatically under normal conditions, as long as you make sure the camera is set for automatic white balance. However, a large area of a specific man-made color or a mixture of two different types of prevailing light (like fluorescent and incandescent in the same room) can throw the camera way off.

Some cameras give you only the option of choosing the type of lighting source as a *category*—the most typical setting categories being auto, sunlight, cloudy, incandescent, and fluorescent. If the automatic mode is not working well, select one of the categories (LCD menu options) that most closely relates to the lighting condition you are in. Take a test shot to determine whether the camera corrects the color shift. You want the photo to appear as close as it can be to the way your eye sees it, and that should be your basis for comparison. You might need to experiment with the settings to get the best results for odd lighting situations. If you find you cannot get it perfect, you may be able to make some adjustments in an image-editing program.

Cameras that have more advanced manual white balance, referred to as *white preset*, are more adaptable to all lighting situations. This allows the camera to set the exact color "temperature" from reading off a white source such as a white piece of paper or a white wall. If the camera has this type of manual white balance setting, aim the camera at a white card or piece of typing paper held close to the principal subject and take a reading. This will assure 100 percent correct white balance. It's a good idea to keep a white card (or better, a Kodak 50 percent gray card) with you for this purpose since a pure white source may not always be on hand. A 50 percent gray card is a better choice because it's not as likely to be outside the range of the camera's exposure setting, and you can also use it to substitute for an incident light meter because it's neutral in both color and brightness—the perfect situation for reading with a spot meter.

## 13. Use Automatic and Programmed Modes

Understanding how to use the exposure modes is probably the trickiest thing you will need to learn to take great photographs. Tackle this one, and it's all downhill from there. Basically, two camera functions control the exposure of a photograph: the amount of light you let in through the lens at any given moment and the amount of time you let light come through the lens. *Aperture* controls the amount of light, and the *shutter* controls the amount of time.

## What Are Automatic and Programmed Shooting Modes?

In automatic mode, the camera automatically calculates and chooses the best settings for the scene you are about to shoot; you don't need to do anything more than press the shutter release button. This is why automatic mode is often referred to as the "point-and-shoot mode."

Programmed mode is often used as a substitute for automatic mode, but it can mean more. Some cameras, such as the Nikon series, let you preprogram a number of settings, such as resolution, quality, white balance, or preset aperture or shutter (but not both), and you can save these settings to a programmed folder. That way, you can set up your own programs for situations you often encounter—such as shooting action or shooting in a backlit setting, or even for those situations best for making instant catalog photos for a commercial Web site. Other manufacturers, such as Olympus, provide a whole series of preprogrammed modes aimed at solving the problems encountered in certain typical shooting situations. Commonly found preset mode settings include night scenes, snow scenes, backlit scenes, and action (sports) scenes. Then, if you're going to shoot in one of those situations, you just set the camera's mode dial or make a choice on the LCD menu. As long as you're shooting fast-action sports and your camera is in action mode, you're likely to get a high percentage of well-exposed photos without having to give it any further thought at all. Ideally, it's nice to have a choice between both methods of mode setting. Custom mode setting (exemplified by the Nikon approach mentioned previously) is terrific for special situations that are unique to your personal needs.

## Why Do I Need to Use Automatic Mode?

Using modes cuts the time it takes for you to set and balance your camera's settings when shooting in situations that are common but that require a different set of exposure settings than the "ideal" or "normal" situation (bright sunlight coming from behind your shoulder, is considered "normal" by camera manufacturers). Instead of having to study what to do, you just turn the dial or click the menu button to choose the situation you're in. That gives you the best chance of getting a good shot quickly (for shots like the one shown in Figure 3-2).

Eventually, you should learn how to adjust your camera's settings yourself, because exceptions to the camera's preset modes do occur and because settings for one type of situation can be perfect for other situations. Automatic mode is not a cure-all, so it's good for you to understand the shutter and aperture *priority* modes (see Tips 15 and 16 later in this chapter) that can offer more optimal results when you have the time to use them. *Shutter-priority mode* lets you choose a specific

**FIGURE 3-2**    Photographing an animal is the kind of spontaneous shot that leaves you with no time for complex setup.

shutter speed while the camera chooses the correct aperture for proper exposure. *Aperture-priority mode* lets you choose the exact aperture you want while the camera chooses the shutter speed. You use shutter-priority mode when you know you want to freeze motion or intentionally blur it. You use aperture-priority mode when *depth-of-field* (the distance over which everything is in sharp focus) is the most important consideration. In sports photography, shutter priority is virtually indispensable. In portraiture, aperture priority is needed because you want to force the background to blur by using the widest available aperture (f-stop).

## How Do I Use the Camera in Automatic (Point-and-Shoot) Mode?

Some cameras allow you to use automatic mode by selecting a position on the mode switch, and others require that you select the mode from the LCD menu. Most cameras will default to automatic mode unless you specifically set the camera to not do so. The camera uses its sensors to make its best guess at the proper *f-stop* (denoted as f-2.8, f-3.5, and so on) and shutter speed required for a good exposure. All you have to do is point and shoot.

> **NOTE**
>
> *Always return your camera to automatic mode before you move on to the next shooting location. You'll then have the best chance of getting at least an acceptable picture when there's no time to prepare.*

## 14. Use Manual Mode

In manual mode, the aperture and exposure controls are set entirely by the photographer. The camera can't change these settings on its own. If you want to set focus manually, that's usually a separate operation and the ability to do that is even rarer than the ability to set exposure in full manual mode. The purpose of manual mode is to give you complete control over exposure.

### Why Do I Need Manual Mode?

Manual mode is most appropriate for situations in which you want to use a particular aperture or shutter speed and also want to overexpose or underexpose the image deliberately. An example for using manual mode would be shooting a high-key glamour portrait. You want to use the camera's maximum aperture to keep depth-of-field as shallow as possible. At the same time, the shot should be "overexposed" by one or two stops so that skin tones are lighter and more delicate than usual and the eyes are brighter, more piercing, and more sensitive looking than usual. Another instance in which full manual mode is required is the situation in which it is impossible for the camera to calculate the proper exposure automatically, such as in the fireworks photo shown in Figure 3-3. Most of the area in the photo is of the night sky, but the point of interest is the bright light from the fireworks, which would have hardly registered on the camera's built-in meter. Also, a long exposure was required to give the fireworks time to create a light trail.

Using manual mode is also a good way to teach yourself how to master the camera. You can easily experiment with what happens when you vary the combination of aperture and shutter speed. Best of all, most digital cameras place extensive image information (called EXIF data) in the header of each

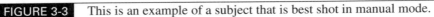

**FIGURE 3-3**     This is an example of a subject that is best shot in manual mode.

JPEG file—so it's easy to use your camera's image transfer software, an image-cataloging program, or the browser in either of the current versions of Photoshop (7 and Elements 2.0) to show you the image, while providing the specifications on how that image was shot. In other words, you can compare what it took to blur the flying hair in one shot to what it took in another that is perfectly exposed but features razor-sharp strands of flying hair and a background that is out of focus. Taking the time to learn manual mode operation can spell the difference between a snapshot and a great photograph, and it gives you the power to tackle any situation.

## How Do I Use the Camera in Manual Mode?

1. Take a meter reading for the overall brightness of your subject by shooting a test shot in automatic mode.

2. Preview the test shot on your LCD monitor. Most cameras will show the exposure that was used superimposed on the image.

**3.** Use the mode switch on your camera to put the camera in manual mode. Some cameras allow you to do this with a simple position on the mode switch and others require that you select it from the LCD menu.

**4.** After you set up manual mode, use the jog control and/or the mode dial to adjust the shutter speed and f-stop to the desired levels. You'll have to check your camera's manual to see how your particular model works.

**5.** Check your camera's control panel. If your camera was well designed, you will be able to preview the effect of the manual settings in the LCD. If not, simply shoot a test shot and then review it to see how close your settings come to the effect you want.

The following list provides manual setting guidelines that work for a range of typical situations. These guidelines will give you a good starting point. You can then fine-tune the settings to meet specific requirements.

- **To stop motion**   Set the camera to the highest shutter speed that will give you a correct exposure at or near the widest possible aperture (smallest f-stop number).

- **To blur motion**   Set your camera at a fairly slow shutter speed, but not too much slower than 1/60.

- **To blur the foreground and background**   Use the widest aperture and then raise your shutter speed to compensate.

- **To maximize the overall sharpness of the image from as close to the camera as possible to as far from the camera as possible**   Use the smallest f-stop (largest number) to narrow the aperture as much as possible. Most digital cameras will not step down their apertures to an opening smaller than f-11.

You can keep the exposure level constant by reducing the f-stop by one setting each time you increase the shutter speed by one setting—and vice versa. This counterbalancing of aperture and shutter speed settings allows you to choose between controlling depth-of-field (aperture) or stop action or blurred motion (shutter speed) while maintaining a balanced exposure.

The following table shows settings that cameras typically use for shutter speed (top row) and f-stop settings (bottom row). The settings are often slightly more or less than a full setting (called an *exposure value* or EV) because of the mechanics traditionally used in the manufacture of 35mm cameras.

| Shutter speed (in seconds) | 1/4 | 1/8 | 1/15 | 1/30 | 1/60 | 1/125 | 1/250 | 1/500 | 1/1000 |
|---|---|---|---|---|---|---|---|---|---|
| f-stop (aperture) | f-1.5 | f-2.0 | f-2.8 | f-3.5 | f-5.6 | f-8 | f-11 | f-16 | f-22 |

A nice thing about digital cameras is that they let you see the effects of changing the setup in your LCD preview. The LCD preview will show the changes in exposure so you can easily see the optimal settings in advance. Using film is much trickier and requires a lot of experience to get it right (plus, it's not immediate). If the subject doesn't move or can be posed, even expert film photographers will take a range of exposures (called *bracketing*) to make sure they get the shot that's most favorable to the subject. Remember, however, that sometimes the "wrong" exposure is the happiest of accidents. Digital cameras eliminate a lot of the guesswork, but you can still take all the credit for the "perfect" exposure.

## 15. Set Aperture Priority

The aperture controls the amount of light that comes through the lens at any given instant. Within the lens of the camera is a diaphragm called an *iris* that opens and closes according to automatic or manual settings. It is named after (and is much like) the iris in your eye. The size of the iris's opening is referred to as the *aperture*. Changing the aperture settings adjusts the size of the opening and thus the amount of light the lens passes through to the image sensor.

### What Is Aperture-Priority Mode?

When you lock in the aperture setting as a priority, the camera is forced to adjust the shutter speed relative to the aperture setting. This is called *aperture-priority mode*. This is different than fully automatic mode, in which the camera determines both the aperture and shutter speed for you.

### Why Do I Need to Use Aperture-Priority Mode?

Aperture priority is used when you want to be able to control depth-of-field or ensure either the fastest (by opening the aperture as far as possible) or the slowest (by closing the aperture as much as possible) shutter speed. Higher f-stop numbers indicate a smaller aperture, smaller f-stop numbers indicate a larger aperture. Go figure, but that's just the way it is.

**Control Depth-of-Field**   Depth-of-field is the distance between the closest sharply focused object to the lens and the farthest sharply focused object from the lens. Smaller apertures (higher f-stop numbers) create greater depth-of-field. Wide apertures create very shallow depth-of-field.

The other factor that influences depth-of-field is the focal length of the lens. The focal length of digital camera lenses, as stated on the lens barrel, is misleading because it is almost always stated as the equivalent of the focal length of a 35mm camera. This relation works as far as the equivalent angle of view is concerned. However, it is the actual distance of the camera lens to the film plane that determines depth-of-field. The shorter the focal length, the greater the depth-of-field. The size of the image sensor in most digital cameras is between one-half and one-quarter that of a 35mm film frame. As a result, the lens must be one-half to one-quarter the distance from the film plane in order to get the same angle of view. At the same time, you get two to four times the depth-of-field. If you have a camera that gets less than 3 megapixels of resolution and your lens is zoomed to about 50mm (normal field of view) equivalency, focusing on an object 10 feet away will put everything in focus from about 3 feet to infinity. If you are shooting close-ups or portraits and want to blur the background at all, you must shoot at the widest possible aperture. It's also a good idea to zoom out as far as possible.

The latest generation of very high resolution digital cameras have image sensors that are about two-thirds the size of a 35mm film frame. These cameras will give you quite a bit more aperture control over depth-of-field because their lens focal lengths have to be longer in order to accommodate the larger physical image size.

NOTE   *You also can change apparent depth-of-field after you've shot the picture by using your image-editing program's selection tools and blurring filters (see Tip 64 in Chapter 9).*

Learning to control depth-of-field gives you one method of isolating the subject from its background. Sometimes, for example, you want to blur the background and focus in on the nearer subject (as shown in Figure 3-4). At other times, you want everything you are viewing to be in clear focus. The aperture setting will give you at least some control over depth-of-field.

**Ensure the Fastest or the Slowest Shutter Speed**   Because the aperture can limit the amount of light that gets in through the lens, you must adjust the camera's exposure times to compensate. Opening the aperture wide will allow for the fastest possible shutter speed in any given lighting condition. Faster shutter speeds will accommodate stop-action photography or provide a steady shot when conditions make it impossible to hold the camera still.

NOTE   *Remember that the aperture settings are inverse to the size of the aperture. Larger f-stops produce smaller openings for light.*

**FIGURE 3-4**    Changing depth-of-field can be used to blur unwanted detail in the background.

## How Do I Use Aperture-Priority Mode?

1. Set the camera to aperture-priority mode by using the mode control or selecting aperture-priority mode from the LCD preview menu.

2. Use the appropriate knob, jog control, or menu selection to change the aperture setting or f-stop up or down, depending on your focus and shutter speed requirements.

**NOTE**    *Another way to affect the speed of exposure is to change the camera's ISO (International Standards Organization) rating. Digital ISO numbers are designed to be equivalent to film ISO speed ratings (for example, ASA 100, 200, and so on). This is a way of changing the image sensors' sensitivity to light. In the digital world, higher ISO settings increase the voltage noise and pictures appear grainier. So when the need for fast shutter speed is not an issue, a lower ISO is better. That is why most digital cameras default to their lowest ISO settings. On the other hand, faster film is also grainier—so the viewing audience is used to seeing this condition when candids are shot in dim lighting conditions. You can change the ISO settings through the LCD menu.*

## **16.** Set Shutter Priority

You can manually set the shutter speed to have the camera calculate the appropriate aperture setting.

### Why Do I Need to Use Shutter Priority?

Shutter priority will allow you to control how you photograph objects in motion. Shutter priority is the mode to use when you want to increase or reduce the amount of blurring in the picture that's due to the movement of either the subject or the camera. You can achieve some interesting special effects by slowing the shutter speeds to blur moving objects (such as water in a waterfall) while the surroundings remain in sharp focus. This adds a suggestion of motion that can be very dramatic. By using shutter priority with higher speed settings, you can freeze moving objects, as is often the case in sports photography. Not setting the shutter speed high enough can result in blurred shots, as Figure 3-5 shows.

**FIGURE 3-5**   Shooting photos while you are dancing is not advised unless you have the shutter speed maxed.

### How Do I Use Shutter-Priority Mode?

1.  Set the camera to shutter priority by moving the mode control to the appropriate position, or choose priority mode from an LCD menu.

2.  Use the appropriate knob, jog control, or menu selection to change the speed settings, which are designated in fractions of seconds or in full seconds (which is usually reserved for evening or nighttime photography).

3.  If, for example, the display shows 1/250, this means it is set at one two-hundred-and-fiftieth of a second, which is a safe speed for most handheld shooting. Set the camera at the highest possible shutter speed that's consistent with the brightness of the prevailing light. Make a test shot to see what that is.

Many cameras can go up to 1/1500 and higher, which can stop a race car in its tracks. A setting of 1/4 is good for blurring swift-moving water, but you will have to shoot with your camera on a tripod in order to keep the surrounding landscape sharp. If you go beyond a setting that the camera can adjust for with the aperture, you will most likely see a flashing red light close enough to the viewfinder that your eye pressed against it can see it. The flashing red light is warning you that the picture you are about to take is either overexposed or underexposed. Warnings are a help, but you need to learn to trust your own judgment more than the camera's.

## 17. Use Macro Mode for a Closer Look

Macro focusing refers to a camera's ability to focus at very close distances (3 feet or less) and magnify a small part of an object or scene so that it fills the entire image sensor, much like a magnified image fills the view while you're using a low-power microscope.

Digital cameras vary in their ability to take macro shots, so if you like close-up photography, the closest possible distance at which the subject can be in focus is something to consider when choosing a camera. Most digital cameras can focus to distances closer than are typical with film cameras, because a digital camera's sensors are typically one-third to two-thirds (for cameras starting at 4-megapixel resolution) the size of a 35mm frame. As a result of the small sensor size, the lens must be much closer to the sensor to provide a "normal" field of view. The closer the lens is to the sensor, the greater the depth-of-field. Most digital cameras, regardless of price, focus down to between 2 and 4 feet. However, some digital cameras, such as those in the Nikon Coolpix series, can shoot at distances well under 1 inch from the lens, which can make a fly look like a prehistoric monster. Figure 3-6 shows a close-up shot.

## Why Do I Need Macro?

There is an old saying in photography: "If you think you are too close, get closer." The macro is your chance to get even closer. The most common error made by amateur photographers is failure to move in on their subjects to fill the frame with only the details they need for the shot. Close-up shooting is a good way to break this habit and discover a wonderful world of details that most of us overlook (or can't see). Macro mode is extremely valuable if you like studying the abstractions inherent in close-ups and is often helpful for recording small details used in scientific research, police evidence, or printed documents.

**FIGURE 3-6**    This macro shot gives you the bee's eye view.

### How Do I Use Macro Mode?

1. Read your camera's specifications to determine what macro ranges it can handle.

2. Turn on macro mode. Some cameras force you to enter macro mode from the camera's LCD menu. Most cameras come with a macro button. Toggling the macro button to its on position increases the distance of the lens from the sensor, which lets the camera achieve closer than normal focusing.

3. You can usually tell when macro mode is turned on by looking for a flower icon on the camera's control panel LCD.

4. Turn on your camera's LCD and move in on your subject as close as necessary. Then partially press the shutter release button. If the camera won't focus, either you're outside macro focusing range or you've turned off autofocus.

5. Once the image is focused, you may discover you'd like to change the framing. You may be able to move in even closer and get sharp focus. If not, back off a bit.

NOTE  *When using macro mode, it's a good idea to work in aperture-priority mode so that you can use a small aperture to increase depth-of-field. Remember that lower aperture means slower shutter speeds, so you might need to use a tripod. This is especially important because at close distances, small camera movements can dramatically change your framing.*

If you're shooting outdoors, use something as a windbreak, because any movement in close-up shots is hard to deal with, as everything, including movement, is amplified. A piece of cardboard, such as the sun protector in your vehicle, can work well as a windbreak. In a pinch, use your own body as a windbreak by putting your back to the wind while shooting. Check your focus in the LCD and take test shots.

## 18. Use Burst Mode to Capture the Moment

Burst mode (also called rapid sequence or continuous) allows the camera to record a rapid sequence of still shots (usually at the rate of two to five shots per second) by storing them directly to the camera's internal memory and not onto the memory card. The amount and the speed at which this can happen is determined by

- The size of your camera's memory

- The speed of data transfer

- Your currently chosen resolution

Obviously, smaller images use less data space, so they can be recorded much faster. You will need to check your camera's specifications to determine its specific burst mode capabilities.

Figure 3-7 shows a series of shots taken of a subject in motion in burst mode.

## Why Do I Want to Create a Rapid Sequence?

One of the best reasons for shooting in rapid sequence is to help you capture the peak moment in an action shot. Remember the shutter lag time mentioned in Tip 11 earlier in this chapter? The workaround is to put your camera in burst mode and start shooting about half a second before the peak of the action will occur

FIGURE 3-7    This series of shots was taken of a skateboarder as she moved across the parking lot. I followed her motion with the camera in burst mode.

(think of the moment the bat hits the ball). By shooting at 1/3 second intervals, you're more likely to catch that peak.

Burst mode also avoids another significant lag time associated with normal shooting modes—the time between shots as the camera offloads the images to the memory card. Burst mode bypasses that action and postpones storing the images to the card or disk until the whole sequence is finished. In Las Vegas terms, when you use burst mode, you are hedging your bet.

Before you get too excited about burst mode, check your camera's specifications to determine whether burst mode is available. Also, the more images you can shoot with one burst and the shorter the interval between individual frames, the better your chances of capturing that peak moment. (See Chapters 7 and 13 for more information on shooting in burst mode.)

### How Do I Use Burst Mode to Shoot a Rapid Sequence?

1. Choose the resolution at which you want to shoot in burst mode. If you want the best resolution for the frame you finally select, it's worth considering a compromise at the second highest quality setting for JPEG compression. Keep your image resolution at the maximum your camera can shoot. If capturing the peak moment is more important than getting the best quality, lower both the quality and resolution by as much as you think you can tolerate.

2. To shoot, you need to get the camera in a stable position, so a tripod is a good idea. Any movement in the camera will make the sequence jumpy if you later want to use it in an animation. Half press the shutter release button to lock in focus and exposure. When you are ready to shoot the sequence, press the shutter release all the way down and hold it until the burst is complete.

3. At the end of the burst, the warning light near your viewfinder will start flashing as the camera offloads the sequence to your memory card. When the flashing stops, you can jog through the images in preview mode. If you don't like what you see, erase those images and try again.

## 19. Use Time-Lapse Mode

Most of us have seen time-lapse photography in all those wonderful nature films that show a flower opening up or a butterfly emerging from a cocoon. These are motion sequences shot over a long period of time and then shown in rapid succession to give the illusion that the transformation is happening in real time. Time-lapse mode is the opposite of burst mode. Time-lapse compresses slow motion into a smaller window of time, whereas burst mode captures microseconds of very fast motion as a series of stills.

## Why Should I Use Time-Lapse Mode?

Time-lapse photography can give you a clearer look at things that move slowly when contrasted with the hyperactivity that usually surrounds us. If you want to demonstrate how something changes over an extended period of time, this is a mode you'll appreciate. Figure 3-8 shows an example.

NOTE *You don't need a time-lapse mode on your camera to capture action over extended periods of time. Richard Misrach, a photographer in Berkeley, California, made an astonishing series of photographs by shooting a picture once a week of the view from his second-story deck in the hills overlooking San Francisco Bay (Richard Misrach: Golden Gate. Arena Editions, 2001).*

## How Do I Use Time-Lapse Mode to Create a Sequence of Shots Over Time?

Many cameras have built-in technology that helps greatly with producing time-lapse sequences. The computer in the camera is used to set a fixed time interval between shots. The feature is similar to the self-timer, except it keeps repeating shots. The camera will shoot automatically according to how you set it or until it runs out of storage or batteries. Once again, you will need to use a tripod to steady the camera while the sequence is being shot.

FIGURE 3-8    Time-lapse photography closely connects events that happen over an extended period of time.

Because the time interval for the total sequence can be extensive, you need to pay attention to the environmental conditions. The lighting, weather, or position of the subject may change over time. You will need to take that into consideration and apply the controls as needed to maintain a consistent environment over the length of the shoot—which can be minutes, hours, days, or longer. You may need special lighting or protection from wind, for example. How you handle this depends on how ambitious you are. Most of all, you will need patience. Time-lapse photography is challenging, but it's also rewarding, and the photographs you take will certainly get compliments.

NOTE
*Many digital cameras ship with, or can be used with, an AC adapter. If your time-lapse sequence will take place over more than 24 hours, you'd best plug in your camera with an AC adapter so that you don't run out of battery power. If you're out in the wilderness, you can use an external battery pack. These typically sell for around $50 and last about four times longer than the camera's internal batteries.*

## 20. Use Video and Audio Modes

In these modes, the camera acts as a video camera or voice recorder for short periods of time. Some cameras have only video capabilities. For audio, the camera must be equipped with a microphone. The video and audio are typically about half the quality of movies shot on an old-fashioned, low-tech camcorder. However, it is rare that you can shoot sequences that last more than a minute. The best use for these "video-ettes" is for Web or e-mail animation, or you can insert them into presentation programs, such as Microsoft PowerPoint.

Shooting digital video is much like shooting in burst mode, except video mode uses much lower resolution images so that it can shoot at a much higher frame rate than burst mode. Standard video will shoot at 30 frames per second to be able to fool the eye into seeing a continuous motion without any perception of individual frames. Digital still-camera videos, on the other hand, typically record at 10 to 15 frames per second. However, at the small maximum size in which they're usually filmed, the motion in digital format seems reasonably smooth and natural.

Most cameras record to one or more of the following file formats: MPEG (Motion Picture Experts Group), AVI (the Windows movie standard), or MOV (QuickTime). (See Chapter 7 for more on moving pictures.) All these formats have a strong following and support, but QuickTime files are definitely the most Web and cross-platform friendly. These file formats have built-in compression algorithms that reduce the amount of information needed to be stored for each frame. Much of the resulting loss of quality is hidden by the fact that the viewer sees each frame for too short a time to register small defects on the mind's eye.

## Why Do I Need to Record Video or Audio?

The low quality of digital videos shot by most digital cameras is actually perfectly appropriate for motion sequences that are to be used as attention-catchers on Web sites or PowerPoint presentations. That is because the lower quality results in smaller files that can load and play faster over Internet connections, and that take up a smaller part of the Web page display. These same qualities make still-camera videos ideal for e-mailing a baby's first steps or the first kiss of newlyweds.

Also, digital cameras have the convenient feature of writing the video directly into digital video format, saving them as QuickTime or MPEG files. It is much easier to place these preformatted files into a presentation or onto a Web page. Let's face it, if you're shooting video with a digital camera, you are probably not trying to make an edited film. You simply want some simple motion that calls attention to whatever is being presented or that demonstrates a process that's difficult and boring to explain in words. If the camera records audio, you can even say a personal hello to your Web site's visitors.

## How Do I Set Up and Record Video and Audio?

1. It is best to use the highest-capacity memory card you can afford so that you have room to shoot scenes more than once. Movies devour card storage space.

2. Place the camera in video mode via the control mode selector or the LCD.

3. Half press the shutter release button to lock in the autofocus and exposure. Then fully press the shutter and hold it down to start recording.

4. The display will let you know how much time you have left to record with a countdown meter.

5. You can stop the recording at any time by letting up on the shutter release button.

6.  As soon as you end the recording, the camera will begin offloading the video frames to your memory card. This may take a few seconds, so don't turn off the camera while the transfer to the memory card is taking place.

## 21. Photograph Documents and Artwork

Documents and artwork are flat, two-dimensional material that is textual or graphical in nature. This could be documents like letters, signs, and books, or graphics pieces like drawings, paintings, and illustrations.

### Why Does Shooting Documents and Artwork Need Special Consideration?

If the piece you want to shoot is not set up properly—in terms of orientation to the camera and lighting—your shot will suffer from *keystone distortion,* in which the edge farthest from the camera appears smaller than the closer opposite edge; poor focus; color distortion; and almost certainly lighting glare on the surface of the document.

### How Do I Set Up and Shoot Documents and Artwork?

1.  Be sure your camera has a macro mode if you are shooting pieces that are closer to the camera than its normal focusing distance permits. This will usually be the case if you are copying small documents such as postage stamps or business cards.

2.  If your camera's macro mode doesn't allow you to focus close enough, check the Web site of a major online camera store (such as http://www.bhphoto.com) for supplementary macro lenses that are compatible with your camera. These are usually quite reasonable in cost.

3.  Mount the camera on a tripod and make sure the camera is parallel to the document in the vertical and horizontal directions. It is a common mistake to lean a work against the wall and not realize that the angle of the lean will cause keystone distortion if you do not tilt the camera at the same angle.

4.  If possible, set the color balance manually. If that is not possible, set the preset closest to the lighting you are using.

5.  For shooting documents, use a high-contrast document mode or (second best) a black-and-white mode if one is available on your camera. Light

evenly from both sides of the document. The lights should be matched lights at 45-degree angles to the document surface and at equal distances from the center of the piece. The light distribution should be even across the document. If you are shooting small art, another good solution is to buy an inexpensive copy stand from a professional photography store. This will allow you to lay the document flat and also provides brackets for mounting your camera lights.

**6.** A polarizing filter may help to kill reflections. Don't use glass over your artwork unless you are willing to polarize all your lights and your camera lens, which can be quite a project and quite an expense for an inexperienced shooter.

Figure 3-9 shows the copy stand setup for photographing documents.

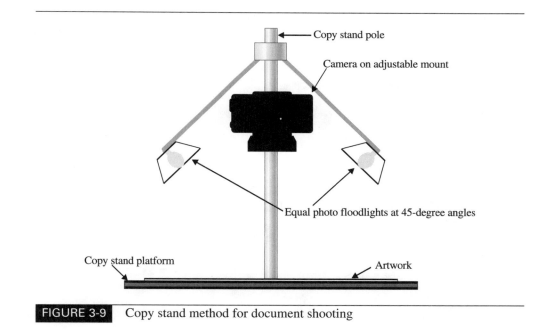

Copy stand pole

Camera on adjustable mount

Equal photo floodlights at 45-degree angles

Copy stand platform

Artwork

**FIGURE 3-9** Copy stand method for document shooting

# Chapter 4

# Composing, Focusing, and Metering

This chapter shows you some of the optimal procedures for ensuring that you get the best pictures out of whatever photo opportunity happens to present itself. Remember, the prime photo ops often come when you least expect them. So if you know the basic rules for composing your photo, if you focus on what you want to be the center of attention, and if you use proper metering to make sure your picture isn't too light or too dark—you'll have done most of what you need to do to ensure a winner. The only remaining trick is learning to capture exactly the right 1/100 of a second.

## 22. Understand How Good Composition Holds Viewer Interest

*Composition* refers to how the elements of an image fit together. Finding a good subject to photograph is not enough in itself. Shooting it in a way that is original, cohesive, attractive, and powerful is what will make the photograph memorable. The process is called *image composition*, but is generally referred to simply as composition.

In Figure 4-1, you can see that the photograph of the waterfall on the left is cut off on every side so your eye keeps moving to the edges in an attempt to see what was not included. The image seems incomplete, which produces a tension within the viewer. On the right is a well-composed photo of the same waterfall. There is a clear foreground, middle ground, and background. The water can be seen in its entirety, and the view is contained by the cliffs which draw your eye to the waterfall as the center. This photograph allows the viewer to relax and focus on the cascading water.

FIGURE 4-1    By looking at these two shots of the same subject, you can see the photo on the right is a more dynamic composition.

## Why Do I Need Good Composition?

Achieving good composition is not a trivial accomplishment and is extremely important in producing an excellent photograph. Good composition focuses the viewer's attention and interest and provides a visually dynamic experience.

The best compositions work on multiple levels, so that color, light, shapes, and subject matter all work together as a whole. We've all spent hours looking at the usual family snapshots, and we understand the difference between a good photograph and a lackluster one. Subject matter, body language, facial expression, the backdrop or setting, and the play of light are all important contributors to the greatness of a photograph—but in most cases, the deciding difference is composition.

## How Do I Achieve Good Composition?

You need to consider a number of factors when setting up a composition: the selection and arrangement of the elements, the framing of the elements, the shot's focal point, and the symmetry of the photo.

Artists use the Rule-of-Thirds to produce dynamic compositions. The rule is based on the ancient Greek concept of the "golden rectangle"—basically the same shape as a normal photograph. To use the rule, draw two imaginary vertical and two imaginary horizontal lines in the rectangle of the frame to divide it into thirds, both horizontally and vertically. By placing the elements in the composition on each of the grid intersections, a pleasing and balanced arrangement results. Figure 4-2 shows a good example of the Rule-of-Thirds in a photograph. After a while, you'll develop an intuitive sense for this kind of balance if you are aware as you practice.

**Selecting the Essential Elements**    The essential elements of a shot are the objects or settings that relate to your subject. Try to pare down your subject matter to the bare essentials. Everything in a photograph should be included for a reason, not just because it was there. Although you can remove or alter certain details later with image-editing software, you need to understand what you are shooting and try to frame it in a way that captures the most concise image to express that understanding. If there are elements in the background or foreground that you want to be sure to include or exclude, adjust your depth-of-field to bring them in or out of focus. Change the orientation of the camera to vertical if that frames the scene better. Get close in and fill the frame with the subject or parts of the subject. The best way to capture the essentials in a photo is to experiment—move around and explore your options. Take a number of photos using different compositions, because there is never just *one* solution. Remember, taking extra digital photos costs you absolutely nothing and it is the best and quickest route to learning to

**FIGURE 4-2**   Notice how the photo is composed so that the important elements align with the thirds of the grid.

be a good photographer. The best photographers are those who know what to throw away.

**Arranging the Key Elements**   The key elements of the composition need to be arranged in relation to the whole frame and to each other. This includes the relationship of objects, background, light, and color. The arrangements in a shot can be considered on both a two-dimensional plane (strictly as flat shapes on paper) or in three-dimensions (foreground, middle, background, and perspective). The orientation of the camera can play a factor here, too. Study the composition of professional photographs and see how they balance all of these elements in unconventional ways.

Most of us, when starting out, tend to place the focal point at the center of the frame and not give too much consideration to other elements surrounding it. Try to give every element of a photo an equal level of importance, and a major door of perception will open for you. Don't be afraid to try unique approaches to taking your photos that might involve shooting from odd angles, adjusting the lighting, shooting at different times of day, or getting very close to the subject—to name a few. Swiveling LCD viewfinders give digital photographers unique opportunities for unusual viewpoints.

**Framing the Photo**    The frame represents the extent of the image that will be captured by the camera's image sensors. What you see when you look through the viewfinder will tell you the extent of the frame in most cases.

Optical viewfinders can suffer from parallax problems at close shooting distances, which can skew the frame boundaries up, down, or sideways. (See Tip 24 later in the chapter for more information on parallax problems.) Some cameras give you an indication of the shift to help you compensate, but some don't do this, so you need to learn how to accommodate parallax problems through experience. For close-ups, you may find it more accurate to use the LCD to frame your shots.

Pay careful attention to any subject matter that is intersected by the frame boundary. The human eye tends to suppress detail at the periphery of vision, so it is common for new photographers not to notice the frame edges when shooting a photograph, only to be surprised later when they see how much detail was lurking in those portions of the picture. Be aware that the camera registers more than you do, so you need to look at all parts of the frame carefully to set up composition correctly.

**Finding the Focal Point of the Picture**    The focal point is the main point of interest in the photo composition. This is *not* necessarily the center of the frame. (See the information on the Rule-of-Thirds in the section "How Do I Achieve Good Composition?" earlier in this chapter.)

Two things—clear focus and position—define the focal point. The eye will move to the sharpest detail in the photograph first. Then the eye will move through the image guided by placement, color, contrast, perspective, and visual connections. You want the viewer's eye to stay within the composition at all times, so be careful of elements that carry the eye out of the frame. Try using the focus lock to move the focal point off center and balance that with other elements on the opposite side. This creates a more dynamic and exciting image. Few things in life are perfectly symmetrical on a one-for-one basis—not even the human face. So if you center objects, the composition usually feels unnatural. While that might be okay if you intended it and it helps the shot, centering the main point of interest often tends to make the image static—unmoving and boring.

Figure 4-3 shows how elements of perspective can draw the viewer to a focal point of the bird, then up and out into the sky. The movement of your eye mimics the motion of the roller coaster, giving the viewer a visceral connection with the subject.

**FIGURE 4-3**    All the visual elements should work to support the focal point of the photograph. In this image, the perspective draws you into the composition.

**Using Symmetry in the Arrangement**    Symmetry comes in two basic forms: *static* symmetry is balanced around a central axis, and *dynamic* symmetry uses proportional arrangement to create a less obvious solution. Both produce a stable, balanced image, but static symmetry has a more graphical feel. Dynamic symmetry has greater flexibility and a more natural look.

Again, you should try to overcome the tendency to place the focal point of the photo dead center in the frame. Lock on your target and then try moving the camera off the focal point to develop a dynamic symmetry with the subject matter.

## 23. Understand Focus

Focus is the ability of the camera lens to bring to clarity the most important part(s) of an image's detail (see Chapter 3).

## What Are the Types of Focusing Systems?

Most cameras offer three types of focusing systems:

- **Autofocus** A system for adjusting focus automatically by means of a sensor on the front of the camera and a motor for moving the lens in the camera in and out. This is a hands-free solution to focusing and it works amazingly well most of the time.

- **Manual focus** Focus is achieved manually by you either turning the lens (on cameras that provide this), adjusting a menu distance slider, or selecting a fixed distance.

- **Fixed focus** Allows for focus at one preset distance. It is limited to low-end cameras, such as those throwaway point-and-shoots that get left at the processing lab. Lately, some low-resolution, under-$50 point-and-shoot digital cameras have begun to appear that have fixed-focus lenses.

## Why Do I Need to Pay Attention to Focus?

Since focal points in a photo are most commonly delineated by sharp focus, it is paramount to control which areas of the picture are in focus and which ones are not if you care about the quality of your photos. The human eye is constantly scanning and readjusting focus, which produces the impression that everything is in focus all the time. In actuality, however, we focus only on a small part of our visual field at any instant. This dictates how we view photographs, because a human viewer will naturally fix on the sharpest detail immediately. The camera does not have that luxury, so you will need to understand and control what the camera is focusing on. Sometimes, intentionally blurring objects in a shot can be a nice effect, especially in foregrounds and backgrounds or to create a motion effect.

Figure 4-4 shows examples of how focus can affect an image. Clockwise, the motorcycle riders are blurred in a way that indicates motion, the leaf shows the sharp detail of a close macro shot, the sharper focus in the center draws you to the eye and holds you there, and finally the use of background blurring accentuates the larger flower.

**FIGURE 4-4**    Examples of how focus can affect an image

## How Do I Focus the Camera Properly?

You focus the camera in three basic ways: via autofocus, manual focus, and fixed focus. Autofocus and manual focus are most pertinent to digital photographers. Only the very cheapest of digital cameras have fixed focus. These cameras have such extreme depth-of-field that it is almost impossible to get anything out of focus.

Autofocus is achieved in one of two ways:

- **Continuous autofocus**    Doesn't lock when you lock the exposure, and the camera follows focus, regardless of how rapidly the subject moves and changes position. Continuous autofocus is absolutely necessary when shooting fast-moving subjects. Otherwise, they won't be in the same position when the shutter is fired as they were in when you first pressed the shutter button to focus. Continuous autofocus is also used for making movies and shooting sporting events.

- **Locked autofocus**    The focus remains set at the focusing distance set by the camera when you put the camera in lock mode by partially pressing the shutter release button.

**Try This:** **Getting Around Tricky Autofocus Situations**

If you are shooting through some close-up object, such as branches, a fence, or blinds, the autofocus sensors will be confused. Bright or fast-moving objects can also confuse autofocus sensors. If you find that your camera is arbitrarily changing focus, try to find a nearby object that is the same distance from the camera as the object you want to focus on; then half press the shutter release button to lock the focus, keep the shutter button partially pressed, and aim at the scene you want. This will lock in the proper focus distance and ignore any interference that may lie between you and the subject.

**Shooting in Locked Autofocus**    Locked autofocus works well for almost every shooting situation. Here's how you use locked autofocus:

1.  Check to see whether your camera lets you choose between locked autofocus and continuous autofocus. If it does, turn off continuous autofocus (or at least make sure continuous autofocus is not turned on).

2.  Look through the viewfinder and align the focus/spot metering target on the object or scene you want to focus on.

3.  Since the target is in the center of the frame, it may be necessary for you to lock the focus and move it to adjust your composition. If so, press the shutter release button halfway. A small motor in the camera moves the lens in response to input from the sensor until the targeted image is in focus.

4.  While holding the shutter to maintain the lock, rotate the camera to frame the image as you want.

5.  Press the shutter button completely to take the picture.

NOTE    *Most cameras provide continuous autofocus without saying so. As you move the target to other objects at greater or lesser distances, the camera will adjust the focus automatically. If you want to use continuous focus, all you have to do is not lock the focus. Just fully press the shutter release button to shoot.*

**Focusing in Manual Mode**　If you can't find anything in the shot to lock into focus, you can switch to manual focus mode and set the focus for the correct distance. Most cameras let you switch off autofocus and then choose a preset distance from the LCD menu or rotate the lens by hand.

> **NOTE**　*If you're focusing manually by the menu method, you won't be able see focus corrections in the optical viewfinder. You will have to use the LCD.*

Cameras equipped with an electronic or through-the-lens (TTL—as is SLR, single-lens reflex) viewfinders will have a much easier time focusing in manual mode, because they display exactly what the lens is seeing and are much easier to view than an LCD in bright light conditions. A few higher-end SLR digital cameras let you focus manually the old-fashioned way: you twist the lens barrel while watching the focus change on the camera SLR viewfinder's ground glass.

1. On most digital cameras, you can go to the LCD menu and choose the manual focus option. This turns off the autofocus sensors.

2. Use the jog control to select your focus from a list on the LCD menu.

3. If you know the distance to the object you want to focus on, you can set that value and shoot.

4. If you're not sure whether you set the correct distance, switch the LCD out of menu mode and aim the camera at the subject. The only way you'll know if your focusing guess was right will be to view the LCD. If you're in bright sunlight, you'll need an LCD hood (such as one made by Hoodman; see Chapter 15), or you can just throw a jacket or a piece of dark cloth over your head and the camera.

**Fixed Focus**　Low-end cameras can have fixed lenses that are preset to a specific focal length. When you are using a camera like this you will have clear focus from a few feet away to infinity. Check your camera's specifications for the minimum distance. These cameras cannot focus for close-up shots and cannot adjust for depth-of-field. Fixed focus is designed to take a standard snapshot and to keep the cost of the camera low.

## 24. Use the Two Viewfinders

The viewfinder is the optical or electronic window that you look through to compose a shot. It is the connection between your eye and the camera's eye, so in that sense it is a very important device. Virtually all digital cameras have two viewfinders—some sort of optical or SLR viewfinder that you view by putting your eye up to a window, and the LCD preview monitor on the back of the camera.

### What Types of Eyepiece Viewfinders Are Available?

Within the eyepiece category are three types—optical, electronic, and through-the-lens (TTL) viewfinders.

**Optical Viewfinders**   The optical viewfinder is the simplest and most error-prone of the three types of eyepieces. It is a separate optical device that gives you a view that's more or less parallel to the view the lens sees.

Because an optical viewfinder provides only a facsimile of the lens view, the closer your shot is to the camera the greater the offset between what the viewfinder sees and the framing of the photo that the camera would actually take at that moment. This disparity is technically known as *parallax error*. To ensure against accidental cropping due to parallax error, you should know that most optical viewfinders are designed to see about 85 percent of the total image area that will be recorded. You should accommodate for this. Most digital cameras that sell for under $1000 use optical viewfinders because they cost much less to build than TTL or electronic SLR viewfinders.

### Try This:   Learn to Compensate for Parallax

Take a photograph of something that has a uniform gridlike structure, such as a window with equal panes or a brick/cement block wall. Make a note of where you line up the edges when you look through the viewfinder. Take the shot. Look at the shot after you take it and you will clearly see how far the image shifted from where you lined it up. Take other test shots from closer and then farther away and you will see how the shift changes as you get closer and how it is diminished by distance. Familiarize yourself with the shift in your camera so you can compensate when shooting.

Optical viewfinders do have a couple of advantages: You can see what you're aiming at under any type of lighting conditions. They are also the preferred type of viewfinder for fast action because you can frame the picture quickly.

Figure 4-5 shows the disparity between what the viewfinder shows and what is actually captured in the photograph.

**NOTE** *Optical viewfinders usually come with a diopter adjustment for photographers who wear glasses. This is a small dial next to the optical viewfinder that allows you to adjust the focus to compensate for your eyeglasses. They usually have a limited range and don't work for every case.*

**Electronic Viewfinders**    An electronic viewfinder is a step above an optical viewfinder because it more accurately shows you what the lens is seeing and doesn't result in parallax errors. It does this by placing a tiny LCD display within the eyepiece that gives you the same view as the standard LCD display. The size of the viewfinder dictates that it be fairly low resolution, so seeing minute detail can be a problem, especially when you're trying to focus manually. It also represents a power drain and will run down batteries quickly. On the other hand, if you are not using the larger LCD as a viewfinder, you are saving considerable battery power.

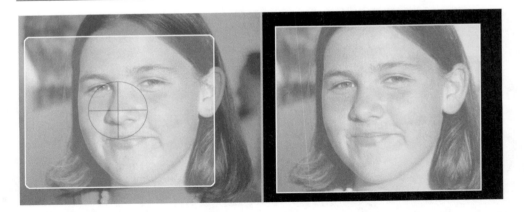

**FIGURE 4-5**    You can see the viewfinder view (left) and the obvious shift in the photograph (right).

**Through-the-Lens Viewfinders**    The TTL viewfinder is by far the best solution for accurate framing, because it allows you to view your shot through the lens itself. Found in traditional SLR cameras, TTL viewfinders use mirrors or prisms to divert the light passing through the main camera lens onto ground glass. A prism then inverts the picture to its normal orientation and you view it through an optical eyepiece.

This system is expensive and is found only on digital cameras in the $1000-plus consumer/professional price range.

## What Types of LCD Viewfinders Are Available?

LCD viewfinders are found on all but the smallest and cheapest digital cameras. They are even beginning to show up on a few film cameras—proof that anybody can benefit from a good idea.

LCD monitors perform multiple tasks, one of which is to act as a viewfinder. The LCD display is basically a small laptop monitor located on the back of your camera that projects an accurate view of what your lens is seeing. The LCD provides the best approximation of how the final photograph will be framed, because it shows you the same picture that is recorded by the image sensor chip. The picture you see (provided it's not washed out by bright surrounding light or darkened by viewing it from an angle) is exactly how the sensor is interpreting the current camera settings. It's as if you've gotten the film back from the lab before you've even taken the picture—like having a darkroom with you in the field.

As for the drawbacks of LCD viewfinders, they are hard to see in bright light situations and they use a lot of power. If you are doing most of your shooting outdoors, get an LCD hood or carry around a square yard of black felt that you can throw over your head when it's critical to be able to prejudge exposure. Hopefully, somebody will find a way to make LCD displays usable in all lighting conditions, because they do provide some profound advantages over other types of viewfinders.

NOTE    *When you use your LCD monitor as your viewfinder, you must take extra precautions to steady your camera, because it is not braced against your cheek and because you are probably holding the camera with outstretched arms. Use higher shutter speeds if possible. Also, put the neck strap around your neck or chest and stretch it as tightly as possible with your arms. The tension takes away unsteadiness in your grip.*

### How Do I Use the Different Viewfinders?

The following chart indicates the best use for each type of viewfinder. As you can see, the LCD is by far the most versatile.

| Condition | Viewfinder Types | | | |
| --- | --- | --- | --- | --- |
| | Optical | Electronic | TTL | LCD Display |
| Distant shots | X | X | X | X |
| Close shots | | X | X | X |
| Need for accurate framing | | X | X | X |
| Shooting angles that make looking through the eyepiece difficult | | | | X |
| Candid shooting | X | | X | |
| Stop action | X | | X | |
| Need to see color cast | | | | X |
| Need to see exposure settings | | | | X |
| Need to see depth-of-field | | | X | X |
| Need to preview shots | | | | X |
| Need to conserve power | X | | | |
| Reduce shutter lag | X | | | |
| Bright sunlight | X | X | X | |
| Low lighting | X | | X | X |
| Normal lighting | X | X | X | X |

## 25. Using the LCD in Bright Sunlight

The light used to illuminate LCDs is pretty weak and was originally designed to be used in controlled lighting conditions, which can be dimmed to make viewing the LCD easy. (For more information on LCDs, see Tip 7 in Chapter 2.)

### Why Is Using the LCD in Sunlight an Issue?

Most of us have experienced the frustration of having surrounding bright light make it difficult to read an LCD display. Until the technology is improved so outside viewing is not a problem, you will need to use some shading device in bright conditions, or you have to use your optical viewfinder exclusively to frame shots. Although it's usually the other way around, some low-end cameras don't have viewfinders, so you are forced to use the LCD.

### How Do I Set Up and Use the LCD in Sunlight?

An LCD could almost be a substitute for an SLR—if only you could see it in lighting conditions where it was bright enough to take a picture without supplemental lighting. Actually, all you need is a $2 handheld, plastic slide viewer or a nylon and Velcro accessory called the Hoodman, which sells for $20 (see Chapter 15). The Hoodman is also excellent protection for the LCD when the camera is in its carrying case. LCD hoods are also available through some camera manufacturers as accessories.

Finally, you could make your own hood device with a dollar's worth of black felt board, a straight edge, an Xacto knife, and some black masking tape. Or, the best device of all is to use a square yard (bigger is even better) of cheap black felt—just drape it over the camera and your head. You'll be able to see the LCD perfectly, but watch out for speeding cyclists (and unsolicited comments on your sense of fashion)!

## 26. Understand Metering Options

Photographs have *everything* to do with light. Light is what we are trying to capture and record on the image sensors in the most accurate manner possible. Light meters are designed to help you analyze the intensity, contrast, and even color of the light that is collected by the lens. This will allow you or the camera to set the exposure levels properly and capture as much detail as possible. Light meters are not a perfect science, although they are getting more sophisticated and accurate all the time. You should realize that no metering system is foolproof, and only experience and sometimes trial and error will prevail.

### What Types of Light Meters Are Available?

Two types of light meters are available: *incident* and *reflective*. Incident light meters read the light inside of a frosted ball located within the meter, resulting in an accurate measure of the intensity of the light *falling onto* the subject, rather than the intensity of light *being reflected* from the subject. This is the best way to measure light so that objects that are predominantly lighter or darker than 50 percent gray (reflectively neutral) don't misguide the reading by fooling the meter into thinking that the overall scene is darker than it really is. Wise use of incident light meters takes some training and experience. You also need to hold the meter directly in front of the subject if you want to get the most accurate readings.

You'll encounter reflective meters much more frequently. Most of these are built into your camera. Many built-in meters read the light directly through the lens, which is the most accurate method. Some cameras have a separate miniature lens used by the built-in meter. Although these are generally okay, you should make sure that you don't cover the meter lens with your finger while you're shooting. Also, don't let it get struck by direct sunlight or your reading will be disastrously skewed.

When a reflected light meter is built into the camera, the camera's electronics use the exposure data generated by the meter to set the proper exposure (aperture and shutter speed) according to the other parameters you've set (such as bracketing settings).

A number of metering methods provide different results in various lighting conditions. Few cameras feature all these options, so refer to your camera's specifications to see which options are available with your camera.

Figure 4-6 shows how different light-metering systems analyze the area of the frame to determine the correct exposure.

**Average Center Weighted Metering**    The most common metering system in digital cameras, average center weighted metering takes 60 to 80 percent of the reading from the center third of the image. Its advantage is that it modifies the center readings with some averaged information about the rest of the scene. This type of metering assumes that the focal point of the scene is always at the center. This, of course, is seldom true. It works best if the camera lets you target what you want to get a reading on, lock it in, and then realign the shot. Because the target area is much more general than a spot meter, center weighted metering is more likely to be "good enough" when you don't have time to be accurate with where you aim it.

NOTE    *A few of the newest and most expensive professional 35mm SLR film cameras have meters that follow your eye in order to place the focus spot. You never have to reposition the camera. You can bet that eventually this technology will find its way onto digital cameras, but don't wait until then to buy one.*

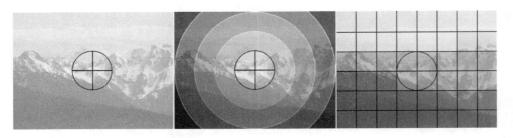

FIGURE 4-6    Common metering options, from left to right: spot, average center weighted, and matrix

**Spot Metering**    Spot metering takes the entire reading from a small circle—usually 3 to 15 percent of the entire image. Most cameras let you lock the spot meter in the same way you lock focus with a half shutter press. This allows you to take a reading, hold it, and then realign the shot. Spot metering lets you take readings on specific objects and ignore everything else. This guarantees that you get a good exposure on that targeted object, but it may result in unpredictable exposures in other parts of the scene. Because it ignores all but the most important area of the scene, spot metering is particularly appropriate for shots with back lighting, spot lighting, highly contrasting backgrounds (such as snow and black velvet), and macro shots. Spot meters require fairly accurate aiming, so you should be careful that you target an area that represents an average brightness of the subject.

NOTE        *You can't get built-in incident light meters, but you can get the same results by spot metering a matte-surfaced object that is 50 percent gray. You can buy 50 percent gray cards from any professional photographer's store for a few dollars.*

**Matrix Metering**    Matrix metering divides the scene into a number of grid segments (the number of segments varies with the type of camera) and calculates the brightness and contrast levels separately for each segment. The information about brightness and contrast is used to analyze the proper exposure based on a database of information derived from thousands of photographs and stored in the camera's computer memory. This advanced type of metering is good at avoiding extreme or unusual lighting conditions from being averaged into the exposure settings and throwing them off. It can decide when to discount the sky or a bright candle in a dark room, for example, and to guess at which areas are the most important in the picture—some cameras even let you pick which matrix areas to emphasize (a Nikon strong point). This is the most advanced type of metering.

## Why Do I Need Metering Options?

Every metering option has strengths and weaknesses. Having options allows you to optimize the way you take light readings based on your shooting conditions. So far, no single metering method can provide a foolproof way of getting the exposure perfect every time. You will sometimes need to switch the way your camera takes readings if you want the greatest capability under all conditions. Advances are being made, and these point to a more advanced matrix system becoming the standard in cameras in the future.

### How Do I Choose the Right Metering Option?

The camera you own will sometimes limit the type of metering options you have available. High-end cameras will almost always offer more options. Familiarize yourself with what your camera offers.

The matrix system offers the best all-around performance but is currently available only on high-end cameras. The low-range to midrange cameras will most likely have average center weighted and spot metering options, which work pretty well, especially since most digital cameras allow you to lock the meter target with the focus. Use the average center weighted method for conditions in which lighting is more evenly distributed and not too extreme. This will most likely be the default method for your camera, but check your manual to be sure. Use the spot meter method when you have a backlit subject, high-contrast lighting, or a macro shot—or when you want accurate incident light metering by reading a gray card or other neutral-brightness object (such as skin tones).

Remember the advantage of digital is that you have infinite test-shot capability, so if it's critical, take a few test shots for exposure. If the automatic metering is not providing what you want, use the exposure compensation or priority modes to correct it. With film, this is not so easy.

## 27. Keep It Steady

*Steady* in the world of photography is the relationship between the movement of the camera and the speed of the shutter. Keeping the camera steady means not letting it move at all while the shutter is open. And the slower the shutter speed, the stiller the camera needs to be.

### Why Is Keeping It Steady Important?

If the movement of the camera is faster that the shutter speed, the image will be blurred (to put it another way, less than sharp). This effect is commonly called *camera motion blur*. Unlike the motion blur that results when the subject is moving too fast for the camera shutter to stop it, camera motion blur rarely produces a photograph that one would consider to be of acceptable quality.

### How Do I Keep the Camera Steady in Different Situations?

The best way to keep your camera steady is to place it on a platform that is stable. A tripod is the most typical platform used by photographers, but single pole supports (called monopods) work well and are more compact and portable.

If a camera stand is not available, you can use any solid object with a flat surface large enough to accommodate the camera, such as a fence post, a rock, or your car.

Wind can often make it difficult to steady a camera, and it can knock a camera from a perch if the camera is not securely attached. If you are shooting with another person, your assistant can stand in a position to block the wind or hold up a windbreak of some sort. Another difficult situation is in crowds, where you may get nudged and jostled. Shoot with your back against a wall so you are not pushed from behind. Putting obstacles, like chairs or an assistant, around you can divert traffic momentarily while you take the shot. If you are the outgoing type, you can announce that you want to take a shot and people will sometimes stop to give you some elbow room (but that's an approach that often makes subjects self-concious when you're trying for spontaneity in a candid photo).

## **28.** Make Test Shots

The test shot becomes the proving ground for your theories about how your photograph is going to look when you press that shutter release button. Never fear; you will find yourself getting it right more often as you get used to your camera and how to control it.

### Why Should I Take Test Shots?

With digital cameras, test shots are totally painless, unless you are far from a store and dangerously low on battery power. Digital "film" can be used over and over, so you can take as many shots as you want without running to the store to buy film and waiting to get prints back.

The camera's LCD becomes your test track, and you can send images out for a spin as often as you like. If you don't like an image, you can just erase it and try again. Obviously this is not possible for every situation, but when you can, it is good practice to test your shots. Besides, the more you practice this way, the sooner your instincts will be able to take over and produce the results you want. When you are learning, test shots are an invaluable tool that can help you discover what you and your camera can do.

Those of us who are traditional photographers using mechanical cameras venture forth with the best of intentions, and then we forget to take notes to keep track of the settings we used for test shots. By the time the film comes back from the lab, we've forgotten all about what it took to get those shots. Once again, the digital camera comes to the rescue. Unbeknownst to many, most cameras automatically record just about everything you might care to know about how you shot any digital picture. This information is stored in something called an EXIF file, which is actually a small part of the data recorded into your camera's RAW, TIFF, or JPEG file. The image browser in the latest versions of Photoshop 7 and Elements 2.0 will automatically show you the EXIF information any time you select a file's thumbnail.

Figure 4-7 shows a series of test shots taken with various settings. Taking such test shots with various camera settings is called *bracketing* and is discussed in Tip 38 in Chapter 6.

## How Do I Take a Test Shot?

If you're going to be making a critical shot or shooting a series of shots in the same situation, or if you have to shoot in other than average lighting conditions, you can take the shot, preview it on your LCD screen, and then adjust the exposure accordingly and reshoot.

With a digital photo, you should always expose for the highlights and then correct for the shadows later in an image editor. (See Tip 61 in Chapter 9 for more information.) Using the LCD as your viewfinder, you can also see the exposure settings change as you adjust them, to get a sense of the proper settings before you take the shot. This is a big advantage over a conventional mechanical camera. It is always a good idea to shoot a range of settings to have a basis for comparison and to understand more about the range of possibilities available. You may discover effects that you couldn't have guessed just by trying something a little out of the ordinary.

**FIGURE 4-7**    Which test shot would you choose as the keeper?

# Chapter 5

# Lighting Techniques

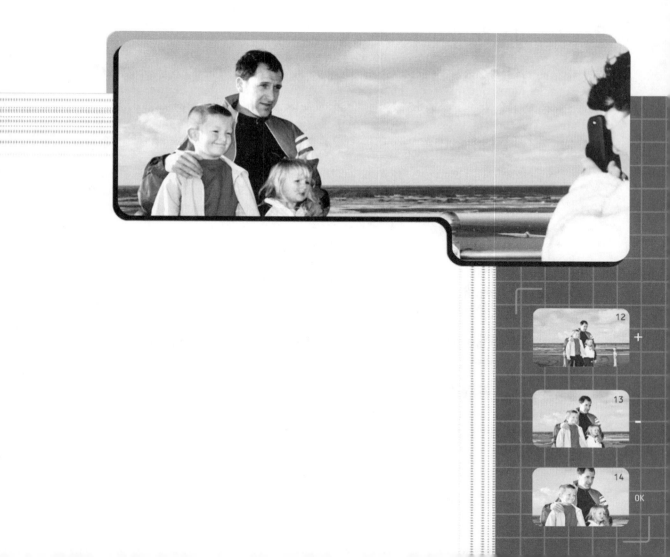

Photography is ultimately about understanding light. What we see and photograph is actually nothing more than the prevailing light that is reflected from the surfaces of the things around us. It is the color and intensity of that reflected light that forms the picture—both in our heads and in the camera. So obviously, becoming a master of controlling and capturing light is at the heart of good photography. In this chapter I will give you some insights into how to work with and control the lighting so that your camera can capture the best image possible. You will learn how to use available lighting and artificial lighting, and how to overcome some common problems associated with lighting. Learning good lighting techniques is a fundamental piece of knowledge that will set a solid foundation for your photographic endeavors.

## 29. Use the Built-in Flash

Almost all digital cameras come with an electronic flash that is built into the camera body and is triggered by the shutter release button. The flash is programmed to fire automatically when the light sensors indicate that available light is insufficient for a good exposure. You can also manually force it to fire or suppress it.

The flash is a strobe-type light and can be fired again and again as long as your camera has enough power. To achieve an appropriate level of exposure, the camera has to build up to a prescribed voltage. This eats battery power and forces you to wait while the charge is being renewed before you can take the next shot. A light indicator near the eyepiece tells you when the flash has power and is ready to fire again. If you are planning to use your flash a lot, it's wise to have extra batteries or an external battery pack, or be connected to an AC adapter that's plugged in.

If it's the only light source, the built-in flash is better than nothing—and at least you'll be able to get the picture—but the direction of the flash's light can't be controlled by the photographer, and it usually produces unflattering shadows and overbright highlights. Flash has limited range and cannot get you a reasonable exposure of anything much farther away than 10 to 12 feet. The cure is easy and can cost you less than $100: Buy an automatic external flash that is brighter than the internal flash. (See the next tip in this chapter for more information on using external flashes.)

### Why Do I Need to Use a Built-in Flash?

Almost any situation in which flash is needed or desired can be better served by an external flash than an internal flash. There are, however, two exceptions: fill flash and the times when the built-in flash is the only choice you have.

**Fill Flash**   One of the best uses for built-in flash is for shooting pictures (especially of people) in bright sunlight. This is called a *fill flash* because it helps reduce the harsh contrast of direct sunlight by filling in shadow with light. The result is a more evenly exposed image. When using the built-in flash as a fill, the existing light will have to be brighter than the flash. Since the camera is ordinarily programmed to use the flash only when the lack of available light leaves you no other choice, you will have to use a setting that forces the flash to fire under any conditions. It's even better if your camera has a fill flash setting, because the camera will then use the brightness of the existing light as a gauge for how bright the flash fill should be and will automatically set the flash accordingly.

**Dim or Dark Lighting Conditions**   Built-in flashes are used when not enough light is available to get a good exposure. In low light conditions, the camera will automatically kick in the flash to compensate if it cannot find an exposure setting that will work with available light. If you don't want the flash to fire in these conditions, you will need to suppress it manually. Generally, this is a matter of toggling a flash button on the camera so that the flash symbol changes on the control panel LCD.

Fill flash                     No flash

**When Time Is of the Essence**   Some shots do not leave you any time to set up or experiment with a flash. This is when you will want to use the camera in full automatic mode and let it do the best it can—with or without automatic flash. With more time, you might do better, but if you need the photo as a record, a shot produced in this way is better than no shot at all.

**Nighttime Shots**   Remember that the flash has a limited range, so if you're taking night shots, be aware that the background beyond the flash range will appear black, as shown in Figure 5-1. On many cameras, the flash has a "slow" mode that can be used for properly exposing night shots by freezing the subject with flash while using slow shutter speed to bring out the background with a longer exposure. (See Tip 31, later in this chapter.) Unless you intentionally want to blur the background as an effect, use a tripod.

**FIGURE 5-1**   This is a good use of an internal flash where the moment was at hand and light was limited.

**Moving Objects in Low Light**   Capturing moving objects requires a fast shutter speed, so you will need a fair amount of available light to allow such a shutter speed. In low light conditions, the flash will stop the action at close range. The flash is a valuable tool for journalists and close-up nature photographers, for instance. If you have to use the built-in flash as the only light source for subjects more than ten (or so) feet away, raise the ISO rating in your camera. You'll find that adjustment in your camera's LCD menu. Each doubling of the ISO rating will add about five feet to your maximum range.

## How Do I Set Up and Use the Built-in Flash?

The camera's default is to put the flash in auto flash mode, so that every time you partially press the shutter button (which turns on the light meter), the sensors are reading the available light and determining whether the flash should fire. If you have set the camera so that the flash will fire, an indicator will tell you when the flash is ready. If you shoot before you get that signal, it's likely that your flash will underexpose the subject. The camera will also determine the brightness and/or the duration of the flash based on the autofocus distance from the subject. In auto flash mode, this indicator will work only when the light levels are low enough to require the flash.

The following camera settings (modes) determine whether the flash fires and how the flash calculates its duration (exposure).

**Auto Flash**     The camera defaults to this setting. To switch back to auto flash mode from another flash mode, press the flash mode button on your camera until the appropriate symbol is displayed on the control panel.

**Fill Flash**     Fill flash is a useful option (but fairly rare) that's well worth looking for. Press the flash mode button until the fill flash symbol appears on the control panel. In this mode, the flash will fire regardless of available light, and it will be adjusted to be a lower intensity flash so it doesn't overpower available light. This is the subtle but important difference between a fill flash setting and a forced on setting. Set your metering target on the subject in the shadow and lock it to get a proper exposure with a half press of the shutter.

An example of what the fill flash can do is shown in Figure 5-2.

**Red-Eye Reduction**     Press the flash mode button until the red-eye reduction symbol appears in the control panel. In this mode, a short flash will fire ahead of the shutter release to reduce the effect of red eye. (For more information, see Tip 33, later in this chapter.)

NOTE      *Image-editing software will do a far better job of red-eye reduction than the camera will. In fact, I'd suggest not using the camera's red-eye reduction feature at all. It works by firing a preflash that causes the subject's pupils to shrink. It also causes the subject to blink and causes external slave flashes to fire at the wrong time.*

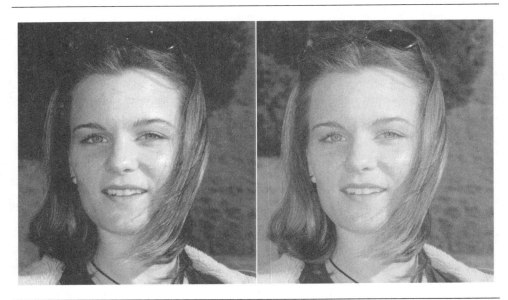

**FIGURE 5-2**    You see how well the shadows were balanced with the high contrast light on this subject by using a fill flash (right), as opposed to the photo with no fill (left).

**Slow Synchronization**    This mode will give you a more balanced exposure between foreground and background in night shots. Check your camera's manual to determine how to set slow sync flash. (It is usually set on the LCD menu.) You will want to steady the camera on a stable object or tripod before you shoot, as the slow shutter speed will cause the background to blur if the camera isn't rock steady. (For more information, see Tip 31 later in this chapter.)

## Try This:    The Kleenex Cure for an Internal Flash

If your camera doesn't have a fill flash setting, you can tape a layer or two of Kleenex or use a neutral-density filter over the flash so that the actual brightness of the flash will be a stop or two lower than the camera calculates. The Kleenex trick has the added advantage of diffusing the light from the fill flash—and is a good idea for indoor candid photos. If you use it indoors, you'll need to compensate for slight underexposure when you process the image in your image editor, which you can do with an auto-correct command in a single button-click.

**Off** Press the flash mode button until the manual off symbol appears in the control panel. In this mode, the flash is prevented from firing. This is good for situations in which you don't want a flash even in low light because:

- You'd rather risk a little blur or ISO-boost noise than lose the atmosphere provided by available light.

- You want to reduce shutter lag.

- Battery power is low.

- Flashes are prohibited.

Sometimes shooting with natural light is the only way to go, even if it's a low light situation. If you want to convey a cozy mood like the one shown in Figure 5-3, for example, you wouldn't want the flash to brighten up the picture too much.

 Natural lighting is often the best way to capture the subtleties of mood.

## 30. Use an External Flash

It's a good idea to use an external flash in addition to or instead of your built-in flash. The external flash can be connected to your camera via a hot shoe, a sync cord, or a *slave* unit (an electronic sensor that fires the flash it's attatched to when it sees the flash from another unit or receives a radio signal). It can attach to the camera with a mounting bracket, or it can be handheld or mounted on a separate stand. If you don't have experience with using external flashes, start with an inexpensive one that features automatic exposure calculation and a built-in slave unit. Sunpak and Vivitar (among others) make units that sell for less than $100.

The advantages of the built-in slave control is that you don't need cords, so you don't have to worry about the sync cord pulling the flash or the camera to the pavement if a passerby happens to bump into it.

### Why Do I Need to Use an External Flash?

An external flash is superior to a built-in flash in every way except cost and portability. The external flash

- Makes it possible to bounce light, scattering it so that it can illuminate a much larger area evenly and greatly soften the edges of shadows.

- Illuminates a much larger area, which will extend the depth of your shot.

- Eliminates red eye because it doesn't fire directly into the subject's pupils. (See Tip 33, later in this chapter.)

- Makes it possible to use multiple external flashes so that you can light several areas of the photo (for example, background and foreground) at once. This is almost imperative if you have to shoot crowds, events, or interiors.

### How Do I Set Up and Use an External Flash?

Attach the external flash to your camera via the sync cord or the hot shoe, depending on what's available with your camera. Some flash units have a mounting bracket that attaches to the mounting screw on the bottom of the camera. If you're using a flash with a built-in meter, the flash will calculate its own exposure, even if you bounce or diffuse it. If you use a significantly more expensive unit that receives instructions from your camera, the flash exposure setting will be set through the camera's built-in meter, which can be even more accurate.

Your camera should be set to aperture-priority mode and to the manufacturer's recommended aperture for your external flash. For even more control over exposure, you can set your flash and camera to manual mode and calculate detailed settings for your shot.

If you use a slave-style flash, make sure the slave unit is positioned to see the primary flash. If you use a built-in slave that faces forward, you may need to use a small pocket mirror to catch the light from the primary (cue) and bounce it back into the slave sensor. When using an external flash, the internal flash can serve as a fill. If you don't want the internal flash to serve as a fill, you'll need at least one external flash that is hard-wired to the camera. The hard-wired external flash either can be your sole light (which can be bounced for broader, softer coverage) or can serve as the cue light for another, slave-fired, external flash.

A number of common external flash configurations will be useful in most shooting situations:

- Handheld portrait (an arm's length away, at a 45-degree angle from the camera). This can also be used in conjunction with the built-in fill flash to soften shadows.

- Bounced off a white wall, ceiling, or card to provide general, natural looking lighting for large areas.

- As a key light with the built-in flash used as fill. The key light is the dominant light sources. Two light sources are usually better than one. A second flash or other light source will dramatically increase your ability to control the contrast of the light and produce properly contoured objects with good detail in the shadows.

## Try This:   Turn Your Internal Flash into an Invisible Remote

You can hide the light from the internal flash and still use it to fire a slave unit. Just tape a piece of fully exposed and developed color transparency film over the built-in flash's lens. The flash will then transmit only invisible infrared light, which happens to be visible to slave sensors. This is a great way to use external flashes with cameras that don't have any kind of connector for an external flash.

NOTE  *Most digital camera flash connectors are made to be used with flashes that are manufactured specifically for one brand or range of cameras. Camera manufacturers generally make their connectors so that they will work only with their own brands of flash, which, of course, cost about twice as much as generic automatic external flashes. Because camera-specific flashes are often made to set themselves according to a meter reading taken through the camera's lens or sensor, they tend to be more accurate than the generic models. However, the generic models I've tested from Sun and Vivitar have proven to be amazingly accurate, extremely easy to use, and affordable, and they have built-in slave sensors.*

## 31. Keep the Background Bright and Naturally Lit with Slow Sync Flash

This is a function of the built-in flash and has everything to do with timing. When selected, the slow sync flash will go off early in a long exposure shot to illuminate nearby objects while letting background areas expose at a slower rate, which helps balance the overall exposure. The flash is synchronizing with the total exposure time by firing selectively at the start or end of the time exposure shot. It is designed to help you take better shots in low light conditions. It can also produce unique blurring effects on moving objects with lights at night.

### Why Do I Need to Use Slow Sync Flash?

One of the problems with using flash, especially if it's built-in, is that anything more than a couple of feet behind the subject tends to look very dark in the shot. If you're shooting outdoors (especially at night), the background will simply go black.

Figure 5-4 shows an example of this. The picture on the left is a slow sync shot. The image on the right was shot with a straight flash.

### How Can I Use Slow Sync Flash to Improve the Exposure?

You can work around the problem of dark backgrounds when using the flash in low light by keeping the shutter open long enough to expose the background properly to bring it into view.

The camera should be mounted on a tripod to keep it steady during the long exposure times. The flash will fire when the shutter is released, but the shutter will remain open for a bit longer.

**FIGURE 5-4**   You can see a lot more detail behind the foreground figures in the slow sync shot on the left, as opposed to the blacked-out background on the right.

## 32. Lighting Portraits

A portrait photograph is a photograph with one or two people as its primary focal point or predominant subject. An example of a portrait is shown in Figure 5-5.

### Why Do I Need Special Lighting for People?

The human eye and brain are particularly sensitive to the physical details of people images, so it's worth your time to take extra care when photographing people so they look "real" (if that's the look you want). For example, if skin tones or hair colors are off, the whole perception of the subject is affected, because our powerful preconceived image of what people are supposed to look like takes over.

The human form is complex and has many shapes, colors, and textures that reflect light and cast shadows in varying ways. Getting the reflection in someone's glasses to disappear or eliminating red eye requires special lighting.

### Try This:   See It Now or See It Later?

Some cameras allow you to set a slow sync flash to go off at either the beginning or the end of the longer exposure. Each produces a different blurring effect on moving objects. Experiment with it and see which one you prefer.

**FIGURE 5-5**    An example of a well-lit portrait

Portrait photography is particularly demanding, because you are "freezing" the subject at a particular point in time. Most of us rarely sit as still as we appear in a portrait. In addition, we viewers don't normally stare at people—as we do at a portrait. It's impolite, for one thing. Part of the fascination of portrait photography is that we can stare at it and see every detail. This is why detail in the picture must be as exceptional as it can be. Lighting plays a key role in that endeavor.

Lighting can also be used to indicate a person's mood, environment, and even emotion. For example, taking a picture in the early morning when the sun is weak can produce a cool light that will give the effect of a cool environment. Put that together with a person bundled in warm clothing, and you have a convincing cool-weather shot, even though it may have been taken in August.

## How Do I Set Up and Use Lighting to Improve Portrait Photos?

In outdoor settings, soft diffused light is best—it reduces the effect of harsh shadows because the light is scattered, much like the effect of a lampshade or a frosted bulb. Get into shooting in shade or shoot on cloudy days. North light (indirect sunlight) is ideal. Try to shoot at the beginning and end of the day if you can. Face the subject so that the light is coming from behind the camera (avoiding backlighting). If you must shoot in bright sunlight, check out the sections on using fill flash in Tip 29 at the beginning of this chapter.

If you're shooting indoors, you can use a main light (a key light) that is roughly 1/3 brighter than the fill light. You generally want this light to be located about a foot above the camera and a foot to the left for glamour portraits, and higher and further to the left for more traditional portraits. We read from left to right so our eyes tend to move naturally in that direction and follow the light. Use a second light for fill. Diffuse light sources are generally better for shooting women and older people (for softer contouring of features and minimization of wrinkles and eye bags). Use higher contrast lighting for men and for characters (for a more angular, hard-edged rendering of features).

## 33. Control Red Eye

When the pupils in someone's eyes appear unnaturally red in the photograph, it is referred to as *red eye*.

### Why Does Red Eye Occur?

Red eye occurs when you use a straight-on flash, such as a built-in flash. The light actually goes into the pupil of the subject's eye and bounces off the retina and back into the camera lens after being tinted red by the blood in the eye. (Pretty gross, huh?)

### How Do I Minimize Red Eye in My Photos?

Most digital cameras have a red-eye reduction mode. It works by firing a preflash to cause the subject's pupils to get smaller in reaction to the initial bright light, so that there's less chance of reflecting light from the back of the eyeball during the actual flash. This technique works, but it causes a couple of undesirable problems:

- The preflash causes the subject to blink, and the end of the blink, when the eyes are reopening, occurs just when the real flash occurs and the shutter clicks. So the subject looks drugged, because the eyelids are half open.

- This kind of shot increases shutter lag by a factor of two to three, because the camera has to wait for the preflash to complete before the flash and the shutter can fire—so you almost always miss the critical moment.

Your best bet is to turn off red-eye reduction and fix the red eyes in your image editor. The exception, of course, is when you're making shots that you want to transmit immediately to another source or place on the Web.

## 34. Use Reflectors to Fill in Shadows in Sunlight

An alternative to using fill flash when you're shooting portraits or still lifes in bright sunlight is to use a reflector to bounce light from the sun back into the shadow areas. You can use any white or silver reflecting surface. Reflectors are much better than fill flash for filling shadows in indirect lighting, such as shady situations or cloudy days.

A reflector is any surface that bounces light. Light, neutral-colored surfaces, preferably smooth white or silver, do the best job of reflecting light. Foam board is readily available in art supply stores and is often used for that purpose. Another readily available and portable reflector is one of the folding reflectors that are used to keep the temperature down in parked cars (also a good idea for protecting your camera gear from extreme temperatures when it's locked in the car). The metallic car reflectors are very bright.

---

### Try This: A Good Reflection on Your Photos

Try using the folding reflector that you place in your car windshield for a reflector. They're sold at flea markets for next to nothing. Some come with a different color on each side, so you can create effects by bouncing a blue or gold light from the reflector into the shadow areas. Try projecting reflected light through different kinds of translucent or perforated material to get patterns of light effects.

## Why Do I Need to Use a Reflector to Light a Scene?

When photographing in bright sunlight, you can often get harsh shadows in your shot. Reflected light can provide another light source to help mitigate this harsh shadow effect. Reflected light can also be used as a special effect to increase shadow effects or to cast another colored light on a subject. Reflectors are much better than fill flash for filling shadows in contrasting lighting, but not as easy to manage without a helper. In indirect lighting, such as shade or cloudy days, reflectors are the only affordable and portable way to fill shadows.

## How Do I Set Up and Use Reflectors?

Positioning is the key to making reflected light work properly. The reflectors need to be facing into the sun at an angle that bounces the light back at the subject. It helps if you have a friend along to hold the reflector. You can also use light reflected off existing structures, such as a white building wall, a white sand beach, or water. The most important factors to watch out for in positioning reflectors are

- Don't position the reflector so close or use one that's so bright it causes cross shadows.

- Try to avoid shining into the subject's eyes, which may cause squinting.

- Don't aim it directly at the camera or you risk having it shown in the background or creating unwanted lens flare.

- Don't position it so that its light casts a shadow on the subject.

## 35. Use Inexpensive Lighting for Extreme Close-ups (Macros)

When shooting extreme close-ups (also known as *ECUs* or *macros*), you often want to be able to control the direction and brightness of the light so that you can shoot at a small enough aperture to give you maximum depth-of-field.

## How Do I Set Up and Use the Lighting to Optimize Close-ups?

The lights need to be placed fairly close to the subject at angles that won't reflect directly back into the lens. If the subject has shiny surfaces, be aware of how those surfaces are picking up the light. Don't position the lighting gear in such a way that the lighting equipment's mirrored image is reflected from the surface of a shiny subject and is seen by the camera.

Lights can get hot, so if your subject is sensitive to heat, you can either move your lights to a safe distance or turn them on only for the time it takes to actually shoot the picture. Finally, be sure your camera isn't so close to the subject that it casts shadows on the subject. If that's the case, move the lights.

## Try This: Available Lighting

The household-variety reflector flood lamps with frosted lenses can be placed into any standard lighting sockets and perform fairly well as close-up lights. Gooseneck floor lamps make affordable light stands for these lamps. If color accuracy is important to you, visit your local photo store and buy blue lamps that have been prebalanced for daylight. This will help you shoot in a room with lots of window light. If you want a soft light source for still-life subjects, make a tent from a clear frosted shower curtain liner, or better, use flexible frosted sheets of plastic and then shine the lamps through the tent. You can also use light diffusers that are made for ceiling fluorescent lights.

Lighting is also important in bringing out surface texture, which can be one purpose of shooting extreme close-ups. Getting the light angled to cast shadows that accentuate the surface can produce a much more dramatic image, as you can see in Figure 5-6. Macro images can also be backlit to produce a glowing effect, like sun through the petals of a flower or an ice crystal pattern on a window.

**FIGURE 5-6**    The effect of proper lighting on a macro shot

# Chapter 6

# Overcoming Difficult Situations

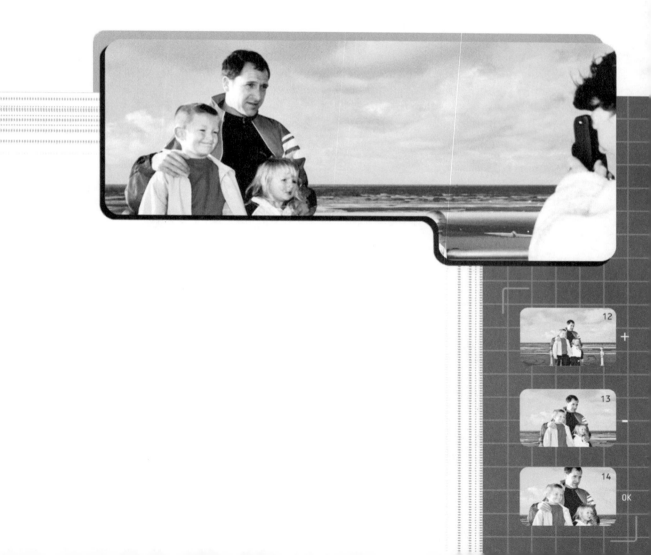

In the course of shooting you will come across situations that demand extra knowledge and experience to deal with them properly. Previously you may have passed up shooting in these situations because it seemed too daunting. Now it is time to break into some new territory. In this chapter I will give you some inside information on how to deal with those shots that take a bit more thought to capture but are really not that difficult once you know how to make your camera do the work. Freezing fast action, creating power motion effects, and shooting at night are all within your reach.

## 36. Freeze Fast Action

The terms *freeze* and *stop action* in photography refer to a single-frame photo that captures a clear image out of a sequence of motion. So much of modern life occurs in fast motion—cars, sports, people all hurrying about in the course of a day. If you want to capture clear images of life in motion, such as the image shown in Figure 6-1, your camera's shutter speed needs to be fast enough to capture the subject before it moves any perceptible distance or the image will be blurred. The faster the subject is moving, the faster the camera shutter needs to open and close to freeze it in motion.

FIGURE 6-1    You can "freeze" activities in a photograph that you might never get a good look at in real life.

## Why Do I Need to Freeze Moving Subjects?

You need to learn how to shoot to freeze motion so you don't end up with blurry action shots. Freeze motion shots can be dynamic and exciting and are definitely a step up from static snapshots. Because you don't have much time to pose action shots, you need to be prepared to capture the perfect shot when it happens. This is a "get-it-while-you-can" mode, so learning how to be in the right place at the right time with the right settings is the name of the game.

## How Do I Set Up the Camera to Take Fast Moving Shots?

The faster the shutter speed, the faster the action you will be able to stop. With a traditional camera, shutter speeds of 1/250 and 1/500 of a second are typically used to freeze a shot. With a high-end digital camera, you can shoot at speeds as fast as 1/5000 of a second. That is fast enough to stop a bullet midflight. More typically, 1/1000 of a second is considered very fast.

To set up a camera to freeze a shot, adjust the mode switch and LCD menu to put the camera in shutter-priority mode. Otherwise, the camera may make the correct exposure but choose a shutter speed that is too slow to stop the baseball or the ski jumper. Using the jog control and/or the mode dial, set the shutter at its fastest available speed—usually 1/500 of a second or greater. You should be able to see the shutter speed on the control panel at or near the top of your camera.

Take a test shot if you can, to determine whether the shutter speed you set eliminates blurring in the shot. If you can't get a proper reading at the highest shutter speed, increase the camera's ISO setting on the LCD menu. This is the equivalent of loading faster film in a conventional camera. If you still can't get the shot without blurring, use a flash—preferably an external flash (because they're brighter and you can determine the angle of light). It is best to mount the flash on a bracket attached to the camera so that it will follow the motion of the subject as you move the camera. If you use an external flash in otherwise dim lighting conditions (rather than as fill flash), you don't need to worry about the shutter speed—the duration of all electronic flash units is typically somewhere between 1/1000 and 1/10,000 of a second, which is faster than any shutter.

Shoot at the peak of the action—when the subject is moving the least and the shot looks the most exciting. If you have to choose, exciting is better than slow. Take a number of shots in sequence to maximize your chances of getting the best shot.

Make sure your camera is set for autofocus. If your camera has a continuous autofocus option (a special focus ability that lets you focus on-the-fly as images are changing), use it. If not, don't partially press the shutter button before you shoot or you'll lock focus on the subject before it reaches the point at which you want to take the picture. If the subject is moving toward or away from you, locking the focus will focus on the wrong spot, as the subject will have moved out of range.

## 37. Follow Motion to Blur the Background

Motion blur is the effect caused by moving the camera so the image is blurred on the image sensors. It is often the result of jittery camera handling on slower shutter speeds, but motion blur can have dramatic results when it's used intentionally with moving subjects.

### Why Would I Want to Blur My Photograph?

Ideal subjects for a motion-blurring technique could be a coasting cyclist or skateboarder, a moving car, or a jet. Your objective in such a shot is to get the background to blur while keeping the focal point subject in sharp focus. This creates a visual illusion of the subject in motion that is more believable than just a freeze frame (see the previous tip). You can also use the inverse—freeze the background and let the moving subject blur. The resulting shot has a ghostly feel to it.

Figure 6-2 shows the motion-blurred scenery behind the person in a moving car.

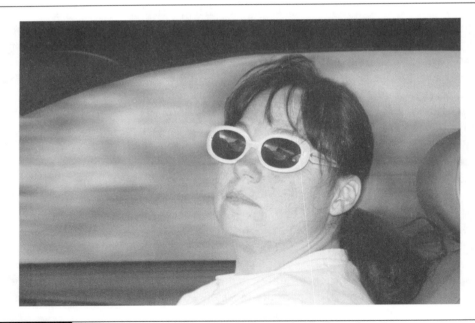

**FIGURE 6-2**    The effect of motion blur accentuates the feeling of motion.

## How Do I Use the Camera to Achieve This Effect?

Using a high shutter speed isn't the only way to freeze the target in motion—especially if that motion is primarily progressing across the image plane and isn't complex, like leaping in the air, twirling, or rapidly moving toward and away from you.

Shoot through the viewfinder, use continuous autofocus if it's available, and keep the focus target aligned with a specific feature of the subject, such as an article of clothing, so you can track it as you move the camera. Move the camera in a way that precisely follows the motion of the subject, keeping the camera's viewfinder aligned so that the subject maintains a constant position relative to the frame.

To get a smooth motion, you can use a panhead tripod. This is a tripod with a horizontally swiveling head that allows you to swivel the camera fluidly to follow motion, while other camera motion is locked in place. If you are going to shoot by hand, you can hold your arms rigidly next to your body while swiveling your torso to pan the shot. This will minimize vertical movement. You can also shoot from a moving vehicle that is pacing alongside a subject. (Make sure someone else is driving, of course, or you may be taking dramatic vehicle accident photos for the evening news!)

Motion blur can also be achieved in the inverse by setting your shutter speeds slower than 1/60 of a second so that the static background will be in sharp focus while the subject that is moving blurs.

You can also add motion blur later in image-editing programs (see Chapter 9).

## 38. Take Night Shots

A night shot is taken in dark conditions, such as outside in the evening or at night, in a dark room, or in a subway or other dark place. What I'm referring to as a night shot applies to any situation that has unusually low levels of light rather than the time of day. Taking a picture in a dark cave poses demands similar to those for taking pictures outside at night. Nighttime shooting conditions could actually be brightly lit or have high degrees of contrast—such as fireworks, nighttime sporting events, or city traffic.

Figure 6-3 is a shot that conveys the fantasy feeling of lights at night. Capture the urban world at night to produce some rewarding photographs.

### Why Take Shots at Night?

Half (or more) of our lives takes place after the sun goes down, and some of the most exciting images are revealed at night. This is the mysterious time when people celebrate and socialize. This is also the time that architecture and the natural environment come alive with amazing displays of shadow and light. Some of the most dramatic photographs are taken in low light conditions, so learning to take night shots will expand your repertoire significantly.

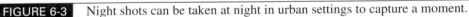

**FIGURE 6-3**    Night shots can be taken at night in urban settings to capture a moment.

## How Do I Take Night Shots?

You can shoot photos in the dark in two ways: with artificial light and with available light. Artificial lighting most typically involves using a flash or multiple flash units. It may also involve setting up key lights to illuminate certain parts of the scene. This tip focuses on shooting with available light, as flash shooting is covered in Chapter 5.

**A Sturdy Tripod or Support Is Essential**   When shooting at night with available light, you need to keep the camera steady. Because of the limited light, you will need to take *time exposures,* which involve keeping the shutter open for extended periods of time to gather more light—from a fraction of a second to a minute or more. The camera needs to be absolutely still during these long exposures, and this is impossible to do without a tripod or other steady camera support.

**The Best Time to Shoot**   Dusk, dawn, or in full moonlight, when there's a good balance between ambient (the general atmospheric light) and artificial lighting, make for some of the best shooting times. The darker the whole scene, the longer the exposure time necessary, which increases the possibility of movement in the scene, which produces streaks and blurs (although sometimes these can contribute interestingly to a night shot). Shooting in darkness will also tend to overexpose any bright lights. Early evening shots, like those shown in Figure 6-4, can produce dramatic results.

**FIGURE 6-4**   The moon's reflection illuminates the water and adds a whole new dimension (left), while early evening provides a backdrop for detail and good contrast for the lights (right).

You can capture a more evenly exposed scene at dusk and then darken it later with image-editing software much more effectively (see Chapter 9) than you can on the spot with your camera. In fact, you can even turn daylight photos into nighttime shots by manipulating an image with software. Don't boost your camera's ISO, because that increases image noise (graininess). Long exposures will also increase image noise. It is possible to eliminate some of this noise after the fact, but only by using professional image-editing software such as Photoshop 7 and specialized third-party programs.

**Setting the Proper Exposure**    Place your camera in spot meter mode if it's available, and half press the shutter release button to lock in a reading from the part of the image where you want to capture the most detail. This is especially important if you want detail in the brightest objects, such as a full moon or the detail inside a lighted building at night.

If you don't have a spot meter mode, zoom to telephoto, aim at the most important part of the scene, and half press the shutter release button to lock the reading. Then note the shutter speed and aperture displayed on the LCD and write down these settings. Switch to manual mode and set the shutter speed and aperture as you noted. Because you are shooting in manual mode, the settings won't change when you compose your shot.

If your camera doesn't have a manual mode, you can try a technique called *bracketing*.

1. Place the camera on a tripod. With the camera in autofocus mode, lock in your focus and meter, compose it, and take the picture.

2. Without changing modes, proceed to take several more pictures while using the jog control to adjust the exposure value (EV) to −.5, −1, +.5, and +1.

3. Preview the shots as you take them and discard those that don't work.

4. Keep adjusting the EV as necessary to get a good exposure.

Many digital cameras have a function called auto-bracketing, which will automatically take two extra pictures of both a higher and lower EV value in addition to the original shot. You can set this mode from the LCD menu. Use a slow sync flash to balance the exposure of background and foreground in night shots (see Chapter 5). If you bracket night shots with the camera on a tripod, you will be able to use parts of all three exposures when you are working in an image editor that supports layers, such as Photoshop Elements, Paint Shop Pro, or PictureIt!

## 39. Steady Handheld Shots in Dim Light

*Handheld* shots refer to shots taken while holding your camera in your hands instead of mounting it on a tripod or other device. You are the support for the camera while the shot is being taken.

### Why Is It Important to Keep It Steady?

Unless you like blurry photographs, keeping the camera steady is essential to clear, sharp images. This is especially true in low light conditions when you are working with slower shutter speeds. Most photographers cannot hold a camera completely motionless. This is not a problem as long as the shutter speeds are above 1/60 of a second. If you are steady as a rock, you might be able to shoot down to 1/30, but at that speed the slightest breeze or nervous jitter will cause the camera to move and blur the image.

As mentioned earlier, blurring shots can create exciting and provocative photographs, but sometimes blurring just looks bad, as the shot in Figure 6-5 demonstrates.

FIGURE 6-5    Bracing the camera on the shoulder of the person nearby might have saved this shot.

### How Do I Take a Good Handheld Shot in Dim Light?

You will often find yourself in situations in which the light levels fall and you don't have your tripod on hand. The first order is to set the shutter speed as high as you can by using aperture-priority mode; set it to fully open. If you are still in the danger zone, try looking for something you can use to brace the camera against—like a tree limb, fence post, or even your car. Any solid object will do.

Rest the camera on the object and set up your shot. With some type of support, you can adjust your camera's shutter and aperture to take the best shot. I have even used the back of a companion when I had to! Bean bags (any fabric sack filled with styrofoam pellets) will let you level the camera when bracing it on a slanted or irregularly shaped support, such as a banister or car hood.

If you are absolutely in a pinch and can't find anything to assist you, try using this stance to get as steady as you can: Kneel down with one knee on the ground and place the elbow of the arm holding the camera on the raised knee as support. This gives you a direct line of support to the ground and takes the weight off the arm. It isn't too comfortable, but it works. Or, if you want to add an unusual point of view (or if your subject is a child or pet), lie down in the prone rifle position that is used by so many sharpshooters to steady their aim.

# Chapter 7

# Things You Don't Do with Your Film Camera

The invention of digital technology has opened the door to new functionality never imagined in the days of conventional photography. Today's digital cameras can perform a wide range of tasks giving you a creative freedom that is really quite astounding. All packed in this marvelous little box of electronics is the ability to take 360-degree panoramic shots, create animation, and even shoot video clips, in addition to the traditional single-shot function. This chapter takes a closer look at this bag of tricks.

## 40. Make Panoramas

A panoramic shot is made up of a number of photographs that, when combined using specialized software, take in a wider or taller view than you could with a single normal-sized shot. The sequence of photographs is pieced back together into one larger picture using a software technique called *stitching*. In motion pictures, *panning* means moving the camera in a continuous motion from side to side or up and down to give the viewer a broader view of the scene. You are doing essentially the same thing with a sequence of stills when you take a panoramic shot.

### Why Do I Need Panoramic Shots?

The process of panoramic shooting allows you to broaden your photographic horizons, literally. You can capture the expansiveness of the central plains, a magnificent city skyline, a complete shot of the world's tallest tree, or that endless stretch of shoreline. It is even possible to capture a 360-degree view. Figure 7-1 shows the difference between a regular shot and a panoramic shot.

When you look through your viewfinder, you'll notice that your view of the scene is limited only to what your lens can see. This is often disconcerting, because your eyes' peripheral vision is always much broader than the camera's. Of course, you can always pull back as far as the next county, but that shot won't show much detail. What do you do when you want to be closer and still get the whole vista in the picture? Creating a panoramic shot is the answer.

### How Do I Set Up and Take a Panoramic Shot?

To shoot a panoramic sequence, you will need to overlap your shots, maintain a consistent focus distance from the subject in all your shots, keep the camera level, maintain a constant exposure from shot to shot, and transfer the images to a computer for merging into a panorama.

**FIGURE 7-1**    The view with a normally framed shot (top) and the same view shot as a panorama (bottom)

**Overlap Your Shots**    Shoot a number of pictures whose frames overlap by at least 30 percent—that is, the last 30 percent of the shot you just took should be the first 30 percent of the next shot, and so on. Try to find visual reference points before you shoot to guide you in overlapping the next shot. This will also give you cues to help you piece together the shot later when you're using image-editing software. Although the number of pictures you take is not fixed, some software applications have memory limitations regarding panorama merging, so don't take more shots than you need to cover your subject with the proper overlap. Some cameras have a panoramic mode, which will show you overlap guides on the LCD.

**Maintain a Consistent Focal Distance**    It's important that you keep the camera the same focal distance from your subject so that the perspective and proportions remain constant from shot to shot. Do not use the zoom lens or change the camera's position or center of rotation until the sequence of shots is complete. Be aware of moving subjects, especially when they are in the overlap area. If the subject is in the overlapping part of one frame and not the adjacent frame, it will confuse the stitching software.

**Keep It Level**    Keep the camera on a level track as you move through the sequence to make it easier to fit the pictures together with a minimum amount of distortion. The easiest way to do this is to use a tripod with a rotating head. Some come with degree markings that let you be precise. In the absence of a tripod, try to find a visual cue to guide you through the sequence, such as a horizon line. In fact, if you don't have a tripod, you're probably not going to get an acceptable stitch because very little affordable stitching software is good enough to "second-guess" the lack of consistency in camera position and rotational axis.

**NOTE**    *The most seamless panoramas are those shot by mounting the camera on a special tripod rig that rotates the camera about its absolute optical axis, which is usually somewhat in front of the camera's tripod thread—in fact, about halfway between the front element of the lens and the image sensor (digital "film"). It also helps to have a system for rotating the camera when it's set in a vertical orientation and a way of moving it in exact degrees of rotation. Several manufacturers make affordable versions of such rigs for a variety of digital cameras. The best known of these manufacturers is Kaidan.*

**Maintain a Constant Exposure**    If you are using a camera with automatic exposure, it will read and adjust the exposure with every shot. In a panoramic shot, you want to maintain a constant exposure to eliminate mismatches in color and brightness from one frame to another. You should use manual mode and lock in the exposure for all the shots in the sequence. (See Tip 14 in Chapter 3 for more information on manual mode.)

**Select Panoramic Mode**    If your camera has it, use panoramic mode. This mode allows you take a sequence of shots with a fixed exposure and often provides guides to help you overlap the shots correctly.

**Transfer the Files to a Computer**    You can use any number of software programs designed to combine your sequence of images into a single panorama. (See Chapter 8 for more information on moving images to your computer.) Adobe Photoshop Elements comes with a built-in stitching program call Photomerge, and it is amazingly easy to use.

Following are the basic steps involved in using Photomerge to produce a panorama:

1.  Open the program, and you are prompted to add the sequence of files you downloaded from your camera. The default for the program is to attempt to stitch the photos automatically, which works pretty well if you've used one

of the tripod heads made for shooting stitched panoramas. If that's not the case, try unchecking the option Attempt To Automatically Arrange Source Images under Settings and then choose OK.

2. The Photomerge screen appears with thumbnails of your images in the upper window.

3. Choose the thumbnail of your first image and drag it into the lower window. Then do the same with the second image. You will notice that the second image becomes semitransparent as you move it over the first image (see Figure 7-2). This allows you to visually align similar features from both images.

4. Line up the two images as best you can and the program will do the rest. It seems like a bit of magic as they merge, but the program actually uses blending algorithms to stitch them together.

**FIGURE 7-2**   In Elements' Photomerge you can drag the thumbnails to the lower window and match up the edge details.

5. Repeat this process with as many images as you have in your sequence. When you are done, choose OK and the program will render the final panorama.

6. Now you can use the Photoshop Elements tools to crop, adjust color, and touch up the new panoramic image as necessary.

## 41. Shoot Movies

As you learned in Tip 20 in Chapter 3, switching your camera to video mode enables it to shoot short video clips that can be played back on your camera's preview, your computer's media player, or on the Web. You can even record them to tape or DVD and include them in your personal archive. If you only need short movies, then you may be able to save yourself the expense of a separate video camera. Try out your camera's movie-making abilities and see what you can do.

### Why Would I Shoot a Movie?

As the old saying goes, "A picture may be worth a thousand words, but a movie has thousands of pictures." Because a movie captures a larger slice of time than a single frame is able to, it is particularly suited for recording something that is changing over time, such as the scoring moment in a sports event or a child's first steps. And although you may already own a video camera, you may find there are times when it isn't practical to carry it with you. The advantage of a digital camera is that by switching it from single-shot to video mode, you can still capture important events with motion and sound, producing a priceless record. (Try that with your conventional camera!) You can download those movie files into your computer, and then e-mail them to relatives and friends or publish them on your Web page.

Videos also can be a practical tool to use for business purposes. For instance, shooting a quick tour through a property can be helpful to a real estate agent and can show much more than static photos. The same files can be exported to a database, displayed on a business Web site, incorporated into a presentation, or transmitted via e-mail to other offices or directly to a client. Or you could record a demonstration of how to attach two components and post for viewing by service reps in the field. The ability to shoot short movies adds another dimension to your picture-taking experience, making your digital camera your portable multimedia production facility.

## How Do I Set Up and Shoot a Movie with a Digital Camera?

The rules for shooting a movie with a digital camera are pretty much the same as for a standard video camera, only simpler. Following are some guidelines for setting up and shooting a proper movie.

**Set Up the Shot**    First, you need to know in advance what you want to shoot and make sure it will fit into the time duration limitations imposed by your camera. If the subject matter you want to shoot takes 2 minutes and your camera only can shoot video for 30 seconds, you are obviously not going to get it all. The video time duration limitations are listed in your camera's manual. The camera will also display a countdown meter to tell you how much shooting time you have left. The average maximum shooting time for a single movie sequence is about 30 seconds. If possible, do a quick run-through before you record the shot. This will help you avoid excessive reshoots.

Be aware of your lighting situation over the course of the entire shooting time. Your flash will not be operational when you are shooting a movie (it can't recycle fast enough), so you have to work with available light or have other external light sources. When you're shooting inside, you will need a fairly bright and consistent lighting source to get a good exposure. You can set up external floodlights to brighten the environment.

Finally, try to place yourself in a good position relative to what you want to shoot so you won't need to move during shooting.

**Setting Up the Camera**    Place the camera in video mode (see Tip 20, in Chapter 3); if your camera doesn't have video mode, you can use burst mode (see Tip 18, in Chapter 3). If you are using burst mode to capture a series of still pictures, you can download the individual frames and use a video-editing program to turn them into a movie. The movie won't have the smooth motion of a video, however, and will be more jerky, like a flip-card animation.

**Shooting the Movie in Video Mode**    Try to remain in a fixed position throughout the shot. Holding a digital camera steady while walking about is next to impossible, and you'll end up with something that looks like a *Blair Witch Project* effect (jumpy and rough). In addition, avoid rapid camera movements unless you want your audience to get queasy. The slower frame rates of MPEG movies also increase the negative effect of rapid movement by making the movie jerky. If you want to move the camera, pretend you are moving in slow motion or use a video-style tripod that allows for smooth panning and tilting.

Relating to movement, use your zoom feature sparingly. One of the most common errors the beginner makes in shooting movies is to zoom in and out constantly. If it is important to zoom, do it as slowly as you can and only do it once. All movement should be subtle.

If you are staging the movie, use a signal to begin and end action. When you are shooting for such a short duration, you don't want to waste valuable seconds.

Be sure to keep the action within the frame. Because LCD screens often refresh too slowly to show a movie sequence smoothly, it is best to use your camera's optical viewfinder. Also, be careful of bright backlighting created by windows or lamps, for example, which can throw off your exposure and silhouette your subject.

If you are recording sound, try to keep a constant distance from the sound source so you don't get big changes in the sound levels. If you want to say something while you are shooting, just realize that you are close to the microphone, so talk softly.

Finally, remember that you can erase any movie and shoot it over if you need to.

## 42. Shoot Animation for the Web

*Animation* covers a broad spectrum of style and technique. Everything from flip-page stick figures to Disney-style animated movies. One thing is for sure: digital techniques are becoming a common part of all animated works. This section covers animation as it relates to Web production.

We have all seen short animation pieces when we surf the Web. They often appear in banner ads and on portal pages. Web animation uses a special file format called GIF (Graphics Interchange Format) that allows a sequence of images to be played with definable parameters that control certain aspects of display. You can produce these animation files in a number of ways, and you can use any number of image sources. In this tip, I'll explain how shooting a sequence of movements can be converted into an animation that you can play on the Web.

### Why Would I Want to Shoot a Web Animation?

Movement can be an irresistible attention-getter if it isn't so big or pervasive that it becomes annoying. Animations are eye-catching and can relate a lot of information in a short time. Adding animation to a Web site can bring new life to the media and guide the viewer's eye to points of particular interest. Animations also can be used to demonstrate something that is hard to convey with words or still pictures alone—such as the proper tennis swing or how to prune a tree. Such a process or gesture is best understood by seeing it in motion.

### How Do I Use a Photographed Sequence to Produce Animation?

Burst and time-lapse mode sequences (see Tips 18 and 19 in Chapter 3) can provide a foundation for building many sorts of animation; just make sure that all the images are the same size and format. Animation files for the Web are usually in the form of GIF files. The GIF format allows a sequence of image files of the same size to be stacked up, so to speak, and played in succession, thus creating an animation. The individual images are most dramatic when they re-create a simple sequence of motion—such as someone walking, a ball bouncing, or a butterfly flapping its wings.

You can approach shooting for animation in a number of ways:

- You can use the object animation technique. You make small changes to the scene, photograph each change, and then put them together in an animation file, such as the series of clock hands in motion over an hour depicted in Figure 7-3. To execute this technique successfully, the camera must be fixed in one position—and it requires a lot of patience on your part. Claymation is another example of object animation technique; think of *Gumby*, the "Wallace and Gromit" movies, and the California Raisins ads.

- You can use a burst mode sequence for capturing a series of short-interval time slices of motion. This is good for depicting an average motion, such as walking—you can capture a model walking down the runway, for example. If you want really smooth motion from a burst mode series, have your subject move in slow motion so that there's not too much movement between shots.

**FIGURE 7-3**    A sequence of shots can be combined to produce an animation.

■ If you're more interested in a slideshow than a movie, you can use a series of images that don't have any inherent animated connection to create a slideshow effect. They could be a series of faces, travel shots, or artworks. Many of the programs that do GIF animation will let you time the duration of each frame in the sequence.

GIF animations are produced by specialized software applications, or in some cases, as a routine in your image editor. (See Tip 90 in Chapter 13 for more on using an image editor to create GIF animations.) A number of good programs let you create GIF animations from a sequence of photographic images. Ulead GIF Animator, Microsoft GIF Animator, GIF Construction Set, and Animagic, to name a few, will automate the process.

# Part II

# Digital Darkroom Magic

# Chapter 8

# Moving and Managing
# Your Pictures

So far I have focused on what you can do with your digital camera. Now I will shift the focus to that other wonderful invention, the computer. This chapter will concentrate on the process of moving images from your camera to the computer so you can begin the process of editing your photos in the digital darkroom. I will also present the best methods for managing your collection of digital photographs so you can store and catalog them correctly, giving you easy access anytime you need it. Learning good image-management techniques first will make your experience with editing photographs later more rewarding.

## 43. Transfer Images Directly from Camera to Computer

Now that you have filled up your camera's memory card with stunning pictures, you'll need to transfer those images to your computer to manage, edit, and print them. The process of moving the images to the computer is called *downloading*. It involves transferring the digital data stored on your memory card to the hard disk in your computer. The computer is your digital darkroom, image catalog, and print manager. Give the computer the digital "film" and you can take advantage of all the tools that your system provides.

### Why Should I Download Images from Camera to Computer?

Because your camera is limited in the number of images it can store, you need to move them off the camera and onto a memory storage device. Memory cards can store a few images to more than a hundred, depending on the capacity of the card and resolution at which you are shooting. Memory cards are not cheap, so you wouldn't want to use them as permanent storage solutions. To keep reusing a memory card, you need to download the images from the card to another memory device, such as a handheld computer, a laptop, or a desktop computer, so you can erase the card and start shooting and storing again.

The computer is also the best way to manage your collection. You will be surprised at how fast you can build up a significant library of photos. The computer makes it a breeze to arrange your photos into albums, which makes finding a photo as quick and easy as a few mouse clicks—instead of having to rummage through old shoeboxes of snapshots.

After you load the images onto the computer, you can begin the real work of editing the images. Because the computer can display the full resolution of each shot, you can see and manipulate all the detail you captured.

Image-editing applications provide easy-to-use tools that help you enhance your digital images. With these tools, you can adjust color, size, and many other elements. In some applications, you can even produce templates for items you print on a regular basis, such as cards, calendars, newsletters, and scrapbook prints (see Chapter 14). You can also set up your printer to produce the best possible prints of your digital images.

## What Is a Direct Transfer?

A *direct transfer* sends information back and forth between the camera and the computer through a direct cable connection. With this connection, the camera acts as the card reader so the memory card remains in the camera. You should familiarize yourself with your camera's options for output (see Figure 8-1). Older and low-end cameras commonly use a standard serial connection, which is slow. Newer and more expensive cameras often use faster connections such as universal serial bus (USB), Small Computer System Interface (SCSI), and FireWire. USB is quickly becoming the more accepted standard in consumer cameras, even though FireWire is much faster and favored by professionals.

Serial port

USB port

**FIGURE 8-1**   Typical output ports on the camera

## Why Use the Direct Method?

The cable and software used to perform direct transfer are usually provided with the camera, and the receiving ports on the computer are typically standard equipment, so there is nothing extra to buy. You also get the flexibility of being able to connect to many different computers so long as they have a compatible port and the software is loaded, and you have to carry only a simple cable with you. With the new, high-speed connection standards like USB and FireWire, it can take just a few moments to download the contents of your camera to your computer. This is a far cry from the standard serial connections, which can take up to a half hour. USB connections can be made while the computer is still running and allow your computer to *sense* the camera when it is connected, bringing up the download software automatically in some cases.

Performing direct image transfer can drain the batteries on your camera quickly, so if you are performing transfers in the field, you will need to have extra batteries on hand. When you can, you should use a power adapter to avoid draining the batteries. The connections for USB and serial ports are often in the back of the computer, making them less convenient to connect. With the standard serial connection, you must shut down the computer before connecting and disconnecting or risk damage to your camera or computer.

## How Do I Perform a Direct Transfer?

1. Load the software that came with your camera and follow the instructions in the install program (you need to do this the first time only).

2. Check your manual to determine what type of connection your camera supports and where the ports are located on your camera and computer (see Figure 8-1).

3. Locate the cable that came with your camera. If it is a standard serial cable, check with your vendor to see whether higher-speed options might be available.

4. Connect the cable to the port on your camera and then to the matching port on your computer. With a standard serial connection, make sure the computer and camera are turned off when you connect the cable or you risk damaging your equipment.

5. Plug in your power adapter if you are in a place where you can use one and you happen to have your power adapter with you.

6. If you are using a standard serial cable, power up your system and camera.

7. Run the software you loaded for your camera and download the images from your camera to a folder on your hard disk. Some cameras repeat the same file names for each download session; this means that if you download new images to the same folder where old images are stored, you will overwrite the older images. If your camera writes unique names for each session, you will avoid this problem. Double-check that all your pictures transferred properly before erasing the memory card.

8. If you need to download other memory cards, you can insert them into your camera and continue to download them in succession.

9. Power-down to disconnect a standard serial cable.

10. You can now erase or reformat the memory card(s) in the camera (check your manual for specific instructions) and you are ready to shoot again. Check your battery levels.

> **NOTE** *Although your camera's memory card looks to your computer just like a removable drive, it's usually a bad idea to erase or format image cards from the computer. The camera often uses special headers that include specific instructions for each file and these won't be included unless you let the camera format the drive.*

## 44. Use a Card Reader to Transfer Images to a Computer

A *card reader* is a small solid-state electronic device that lets you insert a memory card into a slot and read it as a disk drive on your computer screen (see Figure 8-2). It works in much the same way as the slot that reads the card in your camera. External card readers are small and portable, and unique card readers are available for each type of memory card. (See Tip 10 in Chapter 2 for more on memory cards.) Card readers either mount internally or they are attached to the computer through a parallel, serial, USB, SCSI, or FireWire cable connection. If your computer(s) have FireWire ports, get FireWire card readers. They will transfer a card full of files in seconds. In addition, SmartMedia adapters, which look like floppy disks, can be inserted into a standard 3.5-inch disk drive. Adapters are also available for PCMCIA slots, most commonly found on portable computers, that will accept SmartMedia and CompactFlash cards. If your card reader takes CompactFlash cards (the most popular format), make sure it takes Type II so that you can move up to the higher-capacity format as prices continue to fall.

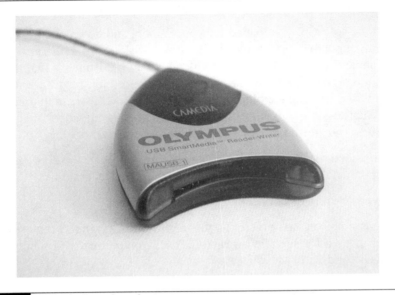

**FIGURE 8-2**    Typical card reader

*You can obtain multiple-format card readers that can read a number of card formats and offer the greatest amount of flexibility so that you can accept cards from other cameras and other devices.*

## Why Should I Use a Card Reader?

Card readers use less battery power by not using the internal card reader of the camera. You simply insert the memory card into the card reader to download the pictures, and the camera can be somewhere else entirely. This is ideal for business applications in which the camera needs to be out in the field while the office staff is downloading and managing images with the card reader. These memory cards are small and easily transferable. The card reader's interface looks like a regular disk drive. If you are familiar with working with a computer, you do not need to learn anything new. (Sigh of relief!)

## How Do I Use a Card Reader?

Card readers are easy to use. Install some simple driver software, connect the card reader to your computer, insert the memory card, and you are ready to rock and roll.

An extra drive letter will appear in your computer's main directory. Explore the contents as you would on a normal drive. If you are using an adapter, insert the memory card into the adapter and then insert it in the appropriate PCMCIA slot or disk drive on the computer. The card must be inserted correctly or damage may occur.

## 45. Move Images from One Computer to Another

You may need to move images from one computer, such as a desktop, laptop, or handheld device, to another computer that may be as close as the next desk or as far away as Timbuktu. The ability to move around these images in so many ways is part of what makes digital imaging exciting.

### Why Would I Move Images to Another Computer?

Digital images can be used in a variety of ways, and it is often useful to be able to share them with others. For example, your child may want to use one of your photos for a school project, or your boss may want to include a photo in a newsletter. Digital images are as portable as any other file on your system.

### How Do I Move Images to Another Computer?

You can transfer digital images to other computers in a variety of ways.

**Disk Transfer** The simplest solution is to use a standard 3.5-inch floppy disk that can be read by every computer. The drawback, however, is that a 3.5-inch disk offers only 1.4MB of space, so if you have photos of medium resolution, you will not be able to store too many images on a disk. With high-resolution photos, you may not even be able to store a single image.

A better approach is to equip your computer with a CD burner (a special CD drive that can use either write-once or rewriteable media). CDs can hold as much as 700MB of information, and blank write-once CDs are inexpensive, at just pennies apiece. Two types of blank, writeable CDs are available: CD recordable (CD-R) and CD rewritable (CD-RW). CD-Rs can be written to just once and cannot be erased (which makes them ideal for keeping permanent archives of original files), but CD-RWs can be erased and written to many times. Writing to CDs is quickly becoming popular due to easy-to-use software and the increased speeds of CD drives. With modern software such as Click 'n Burn or Roxio CD writing software, recording images is as simple as selecting and dragging the files into a window and then clicking the Record button.

Using a ZIP drive (from Iomega) makes sense if you are transferring large images or large quantities of smaller images. Several types of ZIP drives are available. Some offer 100MB of storage, while others offer up to 1GB. They are magnetic media, so they can be rewritten many times. Writing to them is also much quicker than writing to most CD recorders. The downside is that the disks cost approximately $10 to $12 apiece—about 30 times the price of a CD. Because ZIP drives are magnetic, they are not as reliable for long-term storage.

**Network Transfer**   A network is composed of hardware and software that link computers together. This link enables systems to communicate using a standard protocol. One good reason to use a network is to be able to transfer and share large amounts of data between systems efficiently. Systems connected to the network must have a network card and either a cable or wireless connection. You can move images to any shared space on other systems as easily as you can move an image to another folder on your own system.

Two things you must watch for when transferring images over a network. Be sure that you are using a high-speed (100 Mbps) connection—especially if you need to transfer several high-resolution files at a time. Also, if you need to transfer folders jam-packed with high-resolution files, even a small glitch in the signal is likely to freeze or abort the transfer. In that case, it's safer to write your libraries to a CD. Besides, you create an archival backup at the same time.

**Internet Transfer**   The Internet is a network that links computer systems globally. When you are online, you are actually linked to millions of other computers. This interconnected world gives you the ability to transfer your images to anyone who is connected to this worldwide network. As soon as you place an image on a Web page, it can be downloaded by anyone who views that page, no matter where they are. If you are looking for feedback on your work, the Internet is a good place to get exposure.

You can transfer images over the Internet in a number of ways:

- **E-mail**   You can attach small JPEG files to e-mail messages (see Tip 89 in Chapter 13).

- **Web pages**   Small JPEG images work well. If you want to download an image off the Web, you simply right-click the image and choose Save Image As. Be aware that images may be copyrighted, so you should read the terms of use.

- **Message programs**   ICQ (I Seek You), AOL Instant Messenger, Yahoo! Messenger, IRC (Internet Relay Chat), and other programs provide options for transferring files to other systems.

■ **FTP**   Using File Transfer Protocol, you can transfer and receive files that are stored on a *server* (a computer system that acts as a host for Web sites and is directly tied to the Internet). You will need to check with your Internet Service Provider (ISP) to see whether it provides this kind of service. You can use programs such as WS-FTP, a file transfer program designed to access these sites. This is commonly used to transfer information to and from Web sites.

## 46. Sort Images by Category on the Computer

Sorting involves rearranging the images in a logical order. Think of it as an organized filing system. Digital images can be sorted visually, which is really the only way that makes sense.

### What Are Categories?

The sorting categories can be anything you devise that helps you organize your images. Some typical categories could be family, friends, business, special events, and so on. You can also create subcategories to further refine your structure. If your category is flowers, for example, you might break it down further into types, such as roses or orchids.

### Why Sort Images?

Sorting is a time-saving device. As you build your library of photos, you may realize that the file names fall short of providing enough information to help you easily locate the images. If time is valuable to you, you may find it necessary to develop a better strategy for managing all these images so you can access those that you need in an efficient manner. This entails a process of going through your collection and moving images into groups with common themes. Who has time to sift through hundreds, or thousands, of photos every time you want to find something?

### How Do I Sort Images into Categories?

If your operating system allows you to view the images in folders as *thumbnails* (miniature images), you are a step ahead (see Figure 8-4 in Tip 47 in this chapter). If not, check the software that came with your camera. Most come with some sort of image-management software (see Tip 48 in this chapter). If the answer is no to both, you can buy one of many programs on the market to provide this capability.

Photoshop Elements file browser

Image editors are now getting better at image management, an example of which you can see in Figure 8-3. (Photoshop Elements 2 and Adobe Photoshop 7 ship with built-in image managers.) If you search the Web for *image management*, you'll find a host of available programs. There are even very capable shareware programs, such as ThumbsPlus and ACDsee, that you can simply download from the Web. Whatever image manager you choose, you should make sure it displays the image formats you use. It should also allow you to access the file system so you can sort, delete, copy, move, rotate, and rename your images. Being able to see a blown-up view of each image is another plus. Extra features that are also useful are the ability to perform simple image corrections and editing, make contact sheets, run slideshows, and perform batch operations (perform a task on many files at once).

After your images are displayed in thumbnail view, you can begin the process of categorizing them:

**1.** Navigate to where you want to store your images.

2.  Create a new folder. Type a name for a category you want to store and then press ENTER.

3.  Repeat step 2 for each category you want to create. If you want to create a subcategory, double-click a main category and then repeat step 2.

4.  Navigate to where the pictures you need to sort reside.

5.  View these pictures in thumbnail mode so you can easily identify them.

6.  Open the originating folder and the folder that you want to move your files to so that they are side-by-side.

7.  Drag the images to the appropriate category folder that you created.

If you don't like a folder system you created, try a file-naming scheme to categorize your files. This naming scheme makes it easy to find a file in any category, even if it has been misplaced. Simply name your files with a fixed prefix. For example, if you have a nature category, all files in this category could begin with *NAT*. After that prefix, you can add some descriptive text, such as *-Lake Mead*. So your complete file name will look like this: *NAT-Lake Mead.jpg*. When you need to find all image files within a given category, you could simply search for the category name.

## 47. Manage Images with Windows XP

Windows XP Home Edition is the newest beginner-level PC operating system from Microsoft. The Professional Version incorporates many of the features found in professional-level operating systems like Windows NT and 2000, but it's far more user friendly. Windows XP is much more stable and efficient than its predecessors—Windows 95, 98, and Me. It also provides many built-in tools for managing images. If you are serious about working with digital images on your PC, you should consider using XP.

### Why Should I Use Windows XP to Manage Images?

The nice thing about image management in Windows XP is that it is built into the file system. Past versions of Windows required that you load third-party software to get the same features that come standard with Windows XP—one less thing to worry about if you're a digital photographer. Windows XP allows you view images as names, icons, thumbnails, filmstrips, or slideshows. Windows XP's system for dealing with digital images can save you time and frustration in managing a large collection. Windows XP also provides a great foundation for working with image-editing programs.

*When you are working within a graphics application, Windows XP allows you to view images in various modes from any Explorer window. Just click the Views menu, and then choose a view option from the pop-up menu.*

## How Do I Use Windows XP to Manage Images?

Windows XP can help you view and manage digital images in a number of ways. You can view thumbnails within any folder by one of the following methods:

- Choose Views | Thumbnails.

- Choose Views icon | Thumbnails on the Standard Buttons Options bar and you will see the thumbnail views displayed in the folder window (see Figure 8-4).

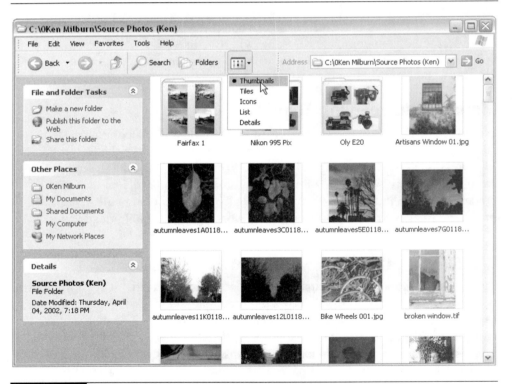

**FIGURE 8-4**    The thumbnail views in a Windows XP folder

You can perform any of the normal file operations on any thumbnail, such as copy, cut, rename, and delete, and you can drag the image to a new directory.

In thumbnail view, any subfolders with images inside will display four thumbnail samples of the images in that folder to help you identify the contents visually.

Here's how you can also enable any folder to view filmstrips:

1. Choose Views | Customize This Folder. The Properties window with the Customize tab will appear (see Figure 8-5).

2. Choose Photo Album from the pull-down menu under What Kind Of Folder Do You Want? This will activate the Filmstrip option on the Views menu.

3. The Filmstrip option allows you to scroll through a list of thumbnails at the bottom of the window and choose an image to display larger, as shown in Figure 8-6. You can also use the forward and back arrows to proceed one

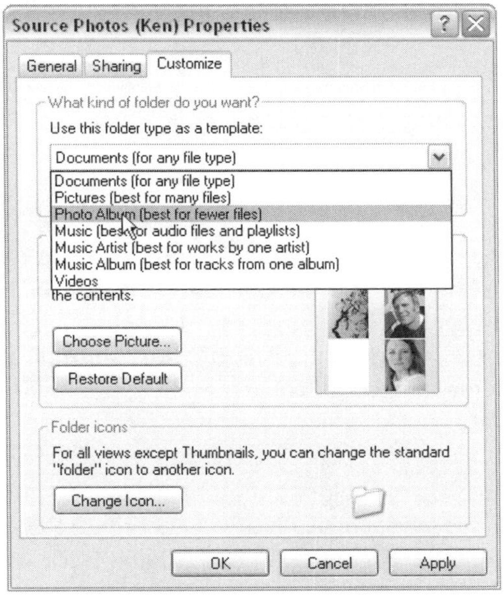

**FIGURE 8-5**   The folder Properties dialog box, where you can optimize the settings for photographs

**FIGURE 8-6**    The Filmstrip view

image at a time, and rotate the image with the rotate image buttons to the right of the arrows. This will permanently change the orientation of the image and will force resampling of your original JPEG file, which will cause some loss of image data. The file browser built into Photoshop 7 and Photoshop Elements 2.0 will rotate the thumbnail without resampling the original.

You can also double-right-click any thumbnail image to open the Picture and Fax Viewer to see a larger view of the image (see Figure 8-7). Along the bottom of the window are a number of controls: Forward and Back, Best Fit, Actual Size, Slide Show, Zoom, Rotate, Delete, Copy, and Print.

# EXCITEMENT

The slow shutter speed that caused some blurring in the child's hands actually serves to show his wonder and excitement. Deep shade provided soft lighting and it only took three Quick Fix adjustments to make this a perfect shot.

# COASTER CRUZ

The subtle colors illustrate the advantage of shooting in late afternoon on a winter's day. Color was manually rebalanced using the Photoshop Levels command. Shadow detail was lightened by painting in white on a transparent layer using the Soft Light command.

# BOTTLED UP

Keep your eye out for the shapes and qualities of light that you may have overlooked on account of familiarity. It sometimes pays just to explore with the viewfinder glued to your eye. This shot was romanticized a bit by isolating the Diffuse Glow filter to the view out the window.

# FRUIT STAND

This photo clearly demonstrates the advantage of using an extreme wide-angle add-on lens. Note that the image is in focus from the nearest orange to the farthest building, providing the viewer the feeling of being right in the scene.

# WAITING

This photograph was made in late afternoon on a slightly hazy summer day. The feeling of Rembrandt-like classical lighting was created with a Photoshop Elements built-in artistic effects filter, called Dry Brush, applied to a duplicated layer. The "dry-brushed" layer was then made partially transparent and partially erased so that details of the original photograph could be seen through it. Finally, the Burn and Dodge tools were used to emphasize certain areas of the photo.

# NEWS TODAY

Careful choice of a wide-angle zoom and kneeling to get a low point-of-view made for the strong composition in this picture of a couple reading the Sunday paper. Photoshop Elements 2.0 was used to progressively blur the background to reduce apparent depth-of-field.

# SUNSET HARBOR

Sunrise and sunset are two of the best times to take pictures. The lighting is dramatic and rich in color, yet shadows are open enough to show detail, and skies tend toward the dramatic.

# STAIRWAY TO JAPAN

This image was taken with a supplementary wide-angle lens, which greatly contributes to the feeling of depth. Two exposures were combined into one by sandwiching them onto separate layers with the lightest layer on top. I then erased through the top layer to reveal those areas that needed to be darker.

# MAGNOLIAS

Notice how much influence the play of light and the arrangement of existing objects can strengthen a composition. Part of the trick in making this work lay in taking pictures from several points-of-view. Remember, digital pictures are free—once you pay for the camera.

# SERIOUS BABY

This was one of those moments I couldn't resist preserving. Three Photoshop Elements Quick Fix adjustments corrected the color, contrast, and exposure, and the Clone tool removed some stray elements.

# FUN ON WHEELS

Sometimes the feeling of action is best captured with a slow shutter speed. This photo of a cycling couple was shot at 1/40 of a second while panning the camera to keep the girl's head in the same position, thus blurring the background.

# LIZ

Here is a photo of my friend Liz taken in a sunlit pasture. Fill light from the camera's built-in flash keep the shadows from being too harsh. The background was softened to decrease depth-of-field.

# ICE JUNGLE

A supplementary telephoto lens coupled with having the Nikon mounted on a tripod did most of the work to create this highly textured photo of ice plant and tropical foliage. The Photoshop Elements Auto Contrast command and a wee boost in color saturation did the rest.

# PERFORMERS

Because digital cameras are small, you can keep them with you at all times. I shot this when magician/contortionist/juggler/comedian Frank Olivier, his wife, and their brand-new baby stopped at my car to say hello. You just never know when the next generation of performers will come along.

# PURPLE PASSION

Flora and fauna never cease to be fascinating and beautiful. Keep your eye on the garden and you're almost sure to produce some lovely pictures. I set a Nikon CP5000 camera in automatic exposure mode using the spot meter settings to ensure sharp focus on the pistils of the flower.

# CAT'S EYE VIEW

It pays to get close to your subject, or to do anything else that gives you a fresh and unusual point-of-view. This picture was taken with a Nikon 995 camera, which can take very close-up pictures without a supplementary lens.

**FIGURE 8-7**   The Windows Picture and Fax Viewer

## 48. Use Your Camera's Image Catalog Software

Most camera manufacturers provide image catalog software that lets you control the download of your images from your camera, view your images as thumbnails, reorganize them to folders, rotate them, perform standard file operations, and in some cases perform basic image correction and image editing.

### Why Would I Use Image Catalog Software?

If your operating system does not support thumbnail views and image management, you can use the software features offered by the camera manufacturer at no extra cost. This software also supports the direct download features of your camera, so you will need it if you are planning to use that method.

### How Do I Use Image Catalog Software?

Image catalog software acts as an interface when the camera connects directly to the computer for downloading images. The software often has the added bonus of providing image-management abilities after you get the images off of the camera and onto the computer. Figure 8-8 shows such an interface for the Olympus Camedia.

Most of these programs operate in a number of modes. The exact functions will vary among manufacturers and from one camera model to another. The

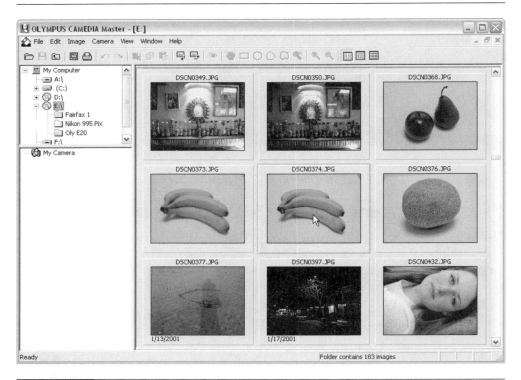

**FIGURE 8-8**    The Olympus Camedia Master interface

following discussion covers the general mode functions typically found in this type of software, but you'll need to consult your camera's user guide for more information.

**Camera Mode**    In this mode, the program is operating the camera remotely from your computer through the direct connection. You can download the images stored on the camera memory card, change settings in the camera, and reorganize and erase images on the memory card. Moreover, it is the camera, not the computer, that does the erasing.

**Image Mode**    This mode provides a full thumbnail view of all the images you have downloaded and lets you manipulate them in a variety of ways. This may take the form of file commands, image-editing commands, or batch-processing commands. File commands let you perform standard File menu functions such as move, copy, cut, paste, delete, rename, and so on. Image-editing commands let you resize, crop, change color and value settings, rotate, apply filters, and so on. Batch processing allows you to perform file or editing commands on a group of files at one time.

Another useful feature in most of the newer software is somewhat hidden, but valuable. It has to do with a new file format called EXIF (Exchangeable Image File Format) JPEG or EXIF TIF. This file format allows the camera to record all the pertinent information about each shot and place it in the image file itself. This information can be retrieved later by any program that knows how to read the file correctly. This format is catching on fast and provides a permanent record of the settings you used on each shot so you can avoid what went wrong and duplicate what went right. Figure 8-9 shows image file information provided by EXIF JPEG.

## 49. Rotate Images

Most of the modern software that helps you to manage images (such as Windows XP, Mac OS X, the new versions of Photoshop, and the software that comes with most any $200-and-up digital camera) provides you with the means to easily rotate thumbnails.

### Why Would I Rotate an Image?

As you will quickly learn, rotating the camera 90 degrees is something you do about half the time, in order to more precisely frame subjects that are vertical in nature, such as people and doorways. This doesn't affect the image quality, but when you download the images, you will see that those images are rotated sideways—which makes it difficult to judge the subject's expression and the quality of the image's composition.

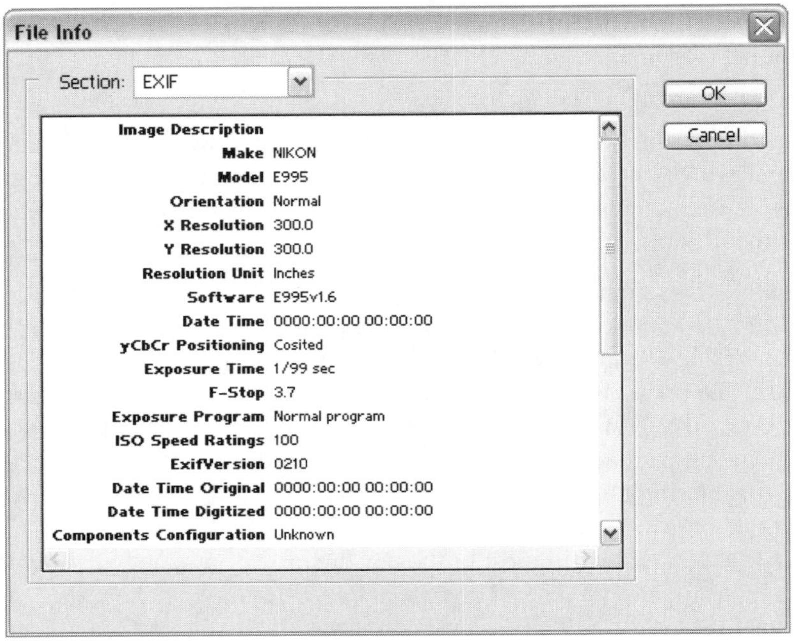

FIGURE 8-9    EXIF JPEG image file information

## How Do I Rotate an Image?

The location of the Rotate command varies from one image-editing software program to another, so it is impossible to give you exact instructions. The majority of programs let you rotate an image 90 degrees clockwise or counterclockwise by clicking a button with an icon of a curved arrow that points in one of those two directions. In some programs, the command can be found on an Image menu, and in others you'll be able to right-click an image and choose the Rotate command from a context menu. Some programs, such as those in the Photoshop family, let you do it in all of the above ways. Look at the orientation of the image and decide whether you need to rotate the image clockwise or counterclockwise to get it back to the correct position. If the image is completely upside down, you can use 180-degree rotation to correct it—or just click one of the 90-degree rotation buttons twice.

Figure 8-10 shows the rotation values for an image.

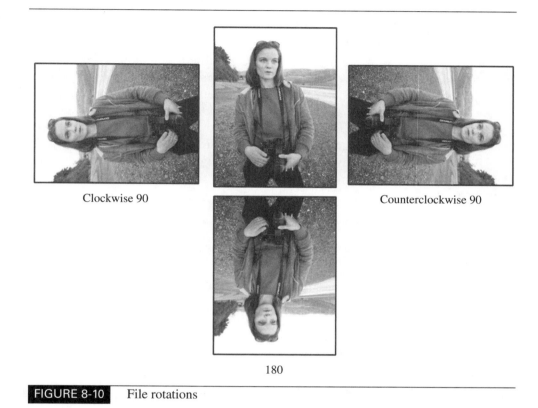

Clockwise 90        Counterclockwise 90

180

**FIGURE 8-10**    File rotations

## 50. Archive Images to CD-R and CD-RW

As mentioned earlier in this chapter, CD-R (CD recordable) is a blank CD that, once written to with a CD burner (a special drive that can record data to CDs), cannot be erased or overwritten. It then becomes what is called read-only CD, because the data on the disk cannot be altered. The CD-RW (CD rewritable) can be written to, erased, and then written to again; it's reusable. CD-RWs are slightly more expensive than the CD-R discs, so if you don't plan to reuse your discs, save yourself the money. Another issue with CD-RW discs is they are not as compatible with other CD drives, which makes CD-R a better bet if you are transferring images to other computers or want to put photos on an affordable medium that can be passed on to friends or clients. You can even put a whole portfolio or scrapbook of images on one of the business card–sized CDs, which can be burned on any standard CD burner.

### Why Should I Archive My Photos to CD?

Contrary to what a computer or camera salesperson may tell you, computer systems do have occasional problems, and you can lose information. Backing up important information is always a good idea. If keeping digital versions of your photographs is important, you need to consider a method for storing them safely.

Another consideration of archiving is the amount of space that digital images can consume on your system. Unless your system has large amounts of disk space available, your digital photographs can quickly fill up your hard disk.

CDs are one of the best ways to archive your photographs for a number of reasons:

- The discs are inexpensive—less than 50 cents apiece if you buy in bulk.

- They offer up to 700MB of storage space.

- The discs cannot be accidently erased like magnetic media, so your data is more secure.

- CDs enjoy universal support, so you can transfer information easily to others, regardless of what computer platform they use.

- New software for creating CDs is easy to use and reliable. It is also included with most all new computers that come with a CD burner built-in.

### How Do I Save Images onto a CD?

You'll need to purchase a CD burner. The average price these days is $75–$150. If you're buying a new computer, you're almost certain to get a CD burner with it. The CD burner usually includes software that manages the process of writing to the CD. Not all CD burner software is created equal, and it's important that you get a good one to get reliable performance.

You'll also need blank CDs. You can pick them up at any computer supply store or on the Internet. You get the best price per disc if you buy in bulk—usually 25–100 CDs per pack.

Read the instructions that come with the CD burner to download your images to the disc.

## 51. Create Wallpaper from Your Images

*Wallpaper* is a single image or tiled images that covers the desktop of your computer screen and acts as a visual backdrop. This is strictly a decorative feature and has no real functionality other than being a pleasing diversion from looking at a blank screen.

## Why Should I Use My Photos to Create Wallpaper?

If you like the photographs you take and would enjoy the opportunity to gaze into the lovely scene you photographed on that last vacation, making your own wallpaper gives you the chance to personalize your computer environment and put some of your photography on display. Photographs make a particularly good choice for wallpaper because they visually break the flat plane of the screen and can have the effect of looking out a window—which can be a relaxing experience not only for your brain but for your eyes as well.

## How Do I Create Wallpaper?

Creating wallpaper for your Windows XP desktop is an easy process:

1. Position your cursor anywhere in the desktop, except on an icon, and then right-click the mouse button. From the pop-up menu, choose Properties to open the Display Properties dialog box.

2. Choose the Desktop tab, shown in Figure 8-11.

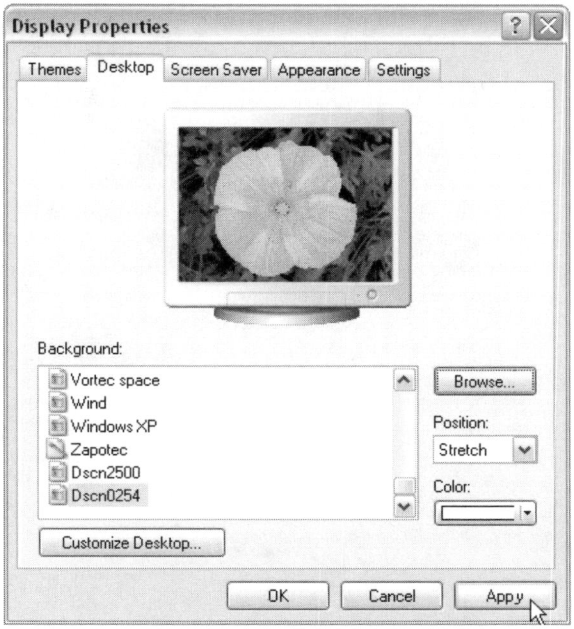

FIGURE 8-11  The Desktop tab in the Display Properties window

3.  Click the Browse button. The Browse dialog box displays the My Pictures directory by default. Locate the image file you want to use as the new wallpaper, and then double-click it.

4.  Select the appropriate option in the Position pull-down list to obtain the desired look.

5.  Click the Apply button.

---

**Try This:**    **Make a Desktop Slideshow, Using Windows XP or Photoshop Elements**

If you are running Windows XP, you can make a slideshow of your images. Gather all the photos you want to display into one folder. Choose Display Properties | Screen Saver, and then select My Pictures Slideshow from the Screen Saver drop-down menu. Click the Settings button to set the parameters for your slideshow.

Photoshop Elements will automatically make a slideshow that is a universally readable PDF file. You can attach the slideshow to an e-mail, put it on a Web page, or ship it to anybody on a CD. Then, with the Acrobat Reader installed (it's a free download from http://www.adobe.com/products/acrobat/), you just double-click the PDF icon and the slideshow starts playing—complete with transitions, such as wipes and dissolves between slides. Many other inexpensive image editors can create these slideshows as well.

# Chapter 9

# Correcting Images
# with the Computer

We would all like to get a shot right the first time. It would be nice to take the perfect picture whenever we pressed the shutter button. No one can do that, though, so relax and learn how to work with image-editing tools to increase your success ratio. Any photographer will tell you that the darkroom is where half the battle is waged. If you can get a decent shot with your digital camera, chances are you will be able to make it into something better in the digital darkroom. For the purpose of demonstrating image-editing methods, I will be using Adobe's Photoshop Elements program throughout this book.

## 52. Rotate an Image to Correct Alignment

One of the Rotate command's useful features is its ability to correct misalignments of the image, which is most apparent when you take shots of subjects with straight edges, like buildings or a clear horizon line. Sometimes you can tilt the camera as you're shooting, so the objects in the shot are not lined up correctly with the edges of the frame.

It's also common for photos to be aligned incorrectly after they are scanned, because it's difficult to get them positioned perfectly straight on the scanner bed. The Straighten Image command makes this a breeze to correct.

### Why Is Altering the Image in This Way Important?

When images are out of alignment, the viewer's attention is drawn away from the important parts of the photo and the composition is disrupted. The eye of the viewer wants to settle in with the photograph, not wrestle with trying to correct it. A misalignment will be the first thing that a viewer notices, no matter how good the photo is. The viewer's first impression will be that it is incorrect.

### How Do I Use the Image-Editing Software to Correct This Problem?

Following are a few commands available in the Photoshop Elements program that can help you correct your images.

To realign a photo with the Rotate command, do this:

1. Open the image you want to realign in Photoshop Elements.

2. Choose Image | Rotate | Custom to open a dialog box in which you can enter the degrees of rotation, down to fractions of a degree, as necessary.

3. Enter the amount in degrees. You might find it helpful to start with a small number like 1 or .5 to get a sense of what works best. This is a trial-and-error method, but it usually takes only a few tries to get it right. Then choose whether you want to rotate left or right.

You can also adjust the alignment with Free Rotate, which allows you to rotate the picture by hand and align it by eye.

1. Choose Image | Rotate | Free Rotate Layer. When the transformation box appears over the image, place your cursor just to the outside of any corner handle until you see the Rotate icon appear. This icon looks like a curved, double-headed arrow.

2. Click and hold down the left mouse button and drag to rotate the image in any direction. Release the mouse button to set the new position.

3. The image will now be tilted and the corners will be outside the canvas. Unless you like this (um, ugly) effect, you'll want to trim the image so that the borders are upright and perfectly rectangular. You'll do this by cropping, which I'll show you how to do in the next tip in this chapter.

> NOTE
>
> *If you open a JPG image in your image editor, make certain that you save it as a TIF file to prevent losing additional picture information.*

To realign a photo that was scanned crooked, use the Straighten Image command:

- Choose Image | Rotate | Straighten Image And Crop. The program will look at the angled edges of the image, adjust them to be parallel to the canvas, and then crop the image.

Figure 9-1 shows an image being rotated, and an image corrected and cropped.

## 53. Frame Your Shot with Cropping

*Cropping* is a method of cutting away portions of the image from any edge. Think of it as an electronic paper cutter or reframer. If, for example, you were standing too far back when you took the picture and captured detail that you really hadn't intended in the periphery, you can crop the shot to include just the subject you want in the frame. You may also want to crop an image that you've rotated, so that it will be straight again.

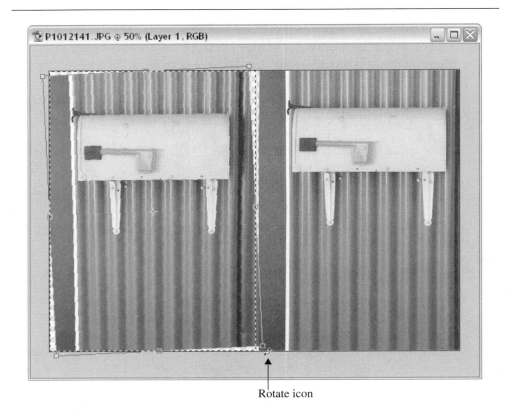

Rotate icon

**FIGURE 9-1**   The image on the left is being rotated to correct alignment; the image on the right has been corrected and cropped.

## Why Do I Need to Crop My Image?

Even with your best efforts, you may end up with extra subject matter that doesn't complement your composition. (The importance of good composition and framing your photos properly is discussed in Chapter 4.) The Crop tool and Crop command provide you with an electronic cutting board to snip off unwanted portions of the image and thereby improve the composition, giving you another opportunity to reframe your shot after the image has been taken.

## How Do I Crop an Image?

Here's how to crop an image using the Crop command:

1.   Open the image you want to crop in Photoshop Elements.

**2.** Choose the Rectangular Marquee tool from the Toolbox, and drag it to define the area of the image you want preserve after the crop.

**3.** Choose Image | Crop. The portions of the image beyond the crop border are cut away.

Here's how to crop an image using the Crop tool:

**1.** Choose the Crop tool from the Toolbox.

**2.** Clear the Crop options by clicking the Clear button on the Options bar.

**3.** Drag the Crop tool to outline the area of the image you want to preserve. The area outside the box is shaded so you can visualize the crop more clearly, as shown in Figure 9-2.

**4.** Click the Commit icon on the Options bar, or double-click inside the crop area to finalize the crop.

FIGURE 9-2   Cropping an image at left, and the final image at right

## 54. Use Quick Fix

The Quick Fix command is found in the Enhance menu of Photoshop Elements. Quick Fix is a virtual smorgasbord of tools you can use for correcting your photos. Quick Fix gathers basic and automated editing tools and presents them in a user-friendly way (see Figure 9-3). These tools include Auto Contrast, Auto Levels, Brightness/Contrast, Fill Flash, Adjust Back Lighting, Auto Color, Hue/Saturation, Auto Focus, Blur, Rotate 90 And 180 Degrees, and Flip.

### Why Should I Use Quick Fix?

Quick Fix is a convenience. You don't have to use it because all the commands are also listed separately on the Enhance menu. However, Quick Fix provides easy access to the most common tools, a before-and-after comparison thumbnail, and tips on how to use each command. This makes it faster and easier to do those things that are most likely to bring the image up to a quality point where you are

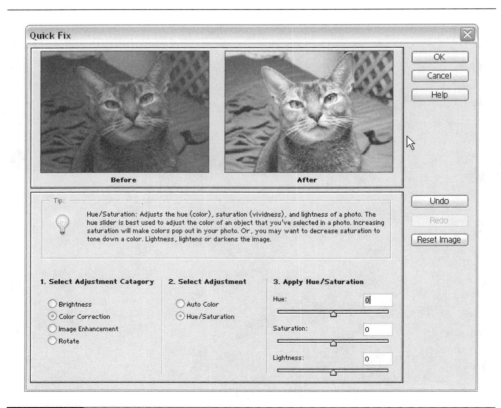

FIGURE 9-3    The Quick Fix interface

proud to show it to a friend or customer. That's important if you want to show off a few dozen pictures from an event or assignment in a hurry. It also offers a way to help maintain the quality of the image because the changes you make in the dialog are cumulative in their effect on the image, and that cumulative final effect is only used to change the image once, when you click OK, rather than once for each change you make. Finally, Quick Fix's ability to instantly preview the effect of any of its adjustments makes it a great learning tool that familiarizes you with editing features and the results they can produce. Of course, if you want a greater degree of control than the automated features can offer, you can always use the other commands available on the Enhance menu in addition to Quick Fix.

## How Do I Use Quick Fix to Correct Images?

The Photoshop Elements' Quick Fix interface is easy to use. Here's how to perform a Quick Fix on an image:

1. Open an image you want to edit in Photoshop Elements.

2. Choose Enhance | Quick Fix. The Quick Fix dialog box will appear.

3. You will see the image previewed in two windows at the top of the dialog box, labeled *Before* and *After*. They will appear identical when you first open Quick Fix because you haven't performed any changes yet. The After image will change to reflect your changes as you make them.

4. The commands are broken down into four categories: Brightness, Color Correction, Image Enhancement, and Rotate in column 1, Select Adjustment Category. Choose one of the categories to adjust your image.

5. You will notice that the items change under column 2, Select Adjustment. Each major category in the first column has a set of adjustments associated with it that appear in the second column. The commands are grouped for a particular kind of edit, such as color correction, to make your job easier.

6. Choose an adjustment and you will see the controls for that adjustment appear in the third column. (In Figure 9-3, you can see how the information appears in all three columns.) If this is an automated adjustment, Quick Fix will ask you to apply it. All other adjustments will provide a series of sliders to alter the effects.

NOTE  *You can undo any adjustment by clicking the Undo button, or you can reset all the adjustments you have made in the current session by clicking the Reset Image button.*

7. When you are satisfied with your corrections, click OK to finalize them.

## 55. Alter the Color Balance

You can alter the color balance and create a mood using the Photoshop Elements Hue/Saturation command.

*Correcting color balance* is the proper tuning of color in an image to match our perception of how it *should* look. Color balance can be used to make photos look more natural or to enhance ambiance and mood by changing the effect of color on lighting. The colors are balanced when the overall relationship and perceived quality of the colors in the image are optimized for the look you want. Color balance also refers to the editing system of changing the colors in an image to be more optimized.

### Why Do I Need to Adjust Color Balance?

We all know how environmental lighting in a restaurant or theatrical lighting at a live performance can affect our reactions and emotions. The same is true in color-adjusting a photograph. Lighting plays a significant role in how the mood in an image is set. The muted colors of a foggy day, the bright harsh colors of summer, or the soft glow of a sunset can help set the mood.

Because the camera cannot always capture the color as you envision it, it often becomes necessary for you to manipulate the existing color to achieve an effect. If the photograph is washed out, for example, you can bring up the color saturation to intensify the color and breathe new life into it. Shift the color hue, or perceived color, toward a cooler blue in a winter shot or add a touch more red to a photo of autumn leaves. This allows an ordinary photograph to produce more impact on our visual senses and emotions.

### How Can Color Balance Tools Alter a Mood?

The Hue/Saturation command is used to adjust the color balance of an image. You might want to experiment a bit with the controls of this command to get used to how they affect the image. Keep your preview on so you can visually follow the effect of the changes you make. That will be your guide. This is about getting the photograph to match your vision, not just what you actually captured.

### How Do I Use Color Balance?

Here's how to balance color with Hue/Saturation:

1. Open the image you want to color-balance in Photoshop Elements.

2. Choose Enhance | Adjust Color | Hue/Saturation. The Hue/Saturation dialog box, shown next, offers three slide controls:

- **Hue**   Shifts the color in the entire image or selected region.

- **Saturation**   Increases or decreases the intensity of the color. When the slider is shifted all the way to the left, all colors become gray. When the slider is shifted all the way to the right, the colors display their richest hue. Adjusting the saturation can add vibrancy to washed-out photos or surrealistic color to normal photos.

- **Lightness**   Increases or decreases the brightness without changing hue or saturation.

3. Choose a color range to work with from the drop-down menu at the top of the dialog box. Here, you can change all the colors in the image at once by choosing Master (the default), or you can choose preset ranges.

4. For a finer level of control, you can work with individual color ranges. You can choose individual color ranges from the drop-down menu.

5. You can also set up your own ranges using the eyedropper tools near the bottom of the dialog box to select colors from your image as a starting point, and then add or subtract colors with the + or − eyedroppers. Range sliders will appear over the color bars at the bottom of the dialog box, which can be moved to expand or contract the range. Ranges give you power to balance specific areas of color individually.

6. Another option is to choose the Colorize check box to convert the image to a color monotone, which gives you the effect of a tinted black-and-white photo. You can change the color of the tint by moving the Hue slider.

## Try This:   Reverse Time with Tinting

Use the Colorize option with a dark brown tint to achieve a good foundation for an antique photo look. Add some texture and a few torn edges and scratches to transpose a new photo into an "old" one. (Also see Tip 59, later in this chapter.)

## 56.  Eliminate Color Cast

In Chapter 3, Tip 12, you learned about setting the white balance to help your camera accurately interpret the colors in the scene. Although this works most of the time, sometimes unusual lighting will still produce an unwanted shift in color. This shift is called *color cast*. When this happens, a shot can appear as though a colored light was cast over everything in the photo. You have probably seen a photo affected by color cast, in which it looks too yellow or too blue, and the people look really awful.

### Why Do I Need to Eliminate Color Cast?

Although altering color cast can improve a photo, it can just as well make everything look unnatural and even downright unattractive. If changing the camera's white balance settings doesn't correct the problem, you can get a second chance at correcting color cast with image-editing software.

NOTE   *You can see color cast if you are looking through the LCD. If you are unsure of the light, check the LCD for color exposure. Take a few test shots to see if different white balance settings can correct the problem.*

### How Do I Eliminate Color Cast with Software Tools?

Photoshop Elements includes a handy tool called Color Cast, which makes dealing with color shifts as simple as a click of the mouse, provided you can find parts of your image that should be neutral (colorless). If there are no pure whites, grays, or blacks, you'll at least get some bizarre color cast effects. Here is how you do it:

1. Open the image in Photoshop Elements.

2. Choose Enhance | Adjust Color | Color Cast. The Color Cast dialog box appears.

> **Try This:**  **Click and Color**
>
> When using the Color Cast command, click the eyedropper on other colors in the image and watch what happens. You can get some interesting color effects this way.

**3.** Use the eyedropper tool in the lower-right corner to select a color in the image that would appear to be black, white, or gray if the colors were not shifted. This is akin to setting the white balance.

**4.** Check the preview to see the color change immediately as you select the color. If the result is not to your liking, simply try again. Sometimes a stray pixel of an odd color can affect the outcome. When the color balance looks pleasing to you, stop.

NOTE   *In portrait shots, if you can't find a good place to take an eyedropper reading, you can always use the whites of the eyes as a reference. White business shirts and black shoes or belts are also good references.*

## 57. Get a Visual Fix on Corrections with the Color Variations Command

*Color Variations* is a system for adjusting color, saturation, and brightness using an addition and subtraction process. Thumbnail references enable you to see the relationship of the changes as they happen.

### Why Should I Use This Command to Correct Images?

The Photoshop Elements Color Variations command provides an intuitive process for color correction that is ideal for beginners. This easy-to-use interface lets you see immediately how adding or subtracting color affects the image. You can also see how a number of changes alter the original image with before and after thumbnails. This makes the process totally visual, so you don't have to deal with separate processes that might be more difficult for the beginner to understand and integrate. The Color Variations command allows you to experiment with different combinations, and you can reset it as many times as you like before you finalize the changes. Just remember that the effect of each change is cumulative. That is, each change is made as an addition to any previous changes you made. Furthermore, the sum of these changes stays in effect until you click the Reset button to deliberately return all the settings to their defaults.

## How Do I Use the Color Variations Command?

Here's how to apply color variations to an image using Photoshop Elements:

1.  Open the image in Photoshop Elements.

2.  Choose Image | Adjust Color | Color Variations. The Color Variations dialog box will appear, as shown in Figure 9-4.

3.  Select an area to adjust under item 1. Midtones, Shadows, and Highlights limit the color changes to those general ranges with some overlap. The Saturation option adjusts the intensity of color for the whole image.

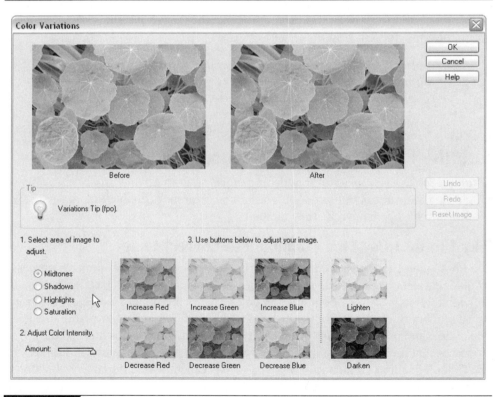

**FIGURE 9-4**    The Color Variations dialog box

4. Adjust the color intensity slider in item 2. This controls the amount of color correction that occurs when you click on one of the thumbnails. You can make subtle changes by moving the slider to the left and very obvious changes by moving the slider to the right.

5. In item 3, add and subtract color by clicking the thumbnails for each attribute, and observe the changes in the After box at the top of the dialog box. You can reset the image at any time and start again.

## **58.** Create a Perfectly Exposed Image

Simply stated, *exposure* is the amount of light that is used to expose the image on the light-sensitive chips in the camera. The shutter speed and aperture setting control the exposure of light (see Chapter 3).

### Why Do I Need to Get the Best Exposure?

The exposure of the image determines the quality of detail that can be properly rendered by the camera. If the image is overexposed (too much light), the details will be washed out. If it is underexposed (too little light), the highlights look dim and shadow detail drops out. A perfectly exposed image shows crisp highlights and good detail in the shadows, with a good contrast range throughout the image.

Perfect exposure is sometimes hard to achieve when taking pictures. The camera cannot always compensate for every lighting situation, and sometimes you need to go to the digital darkroom to correct the image.

NOTE *An underexposed digital image is easier to work with than an overexposed image. Details can hide in dark areas of an image and be brought out by image-editing techniques, but once details are washed out by overexposure, much of them will be impossible to restore.*

### How Do I Use Image-Editing Software to Optimize Exposure?

The Photoshop Elements Levels command is an advanced tool that offers a higher degree of control in adjusting your image than the Quick Fix and Color Variations commands.

Here's how to use the Levels command for correcting exposure:

1. Open the image in Photoshop Elements.

2. Choose Image | Enhance | Adjust Color/Brightness | Levels. You will see the Levels dialog box shown in Figure 9-5.

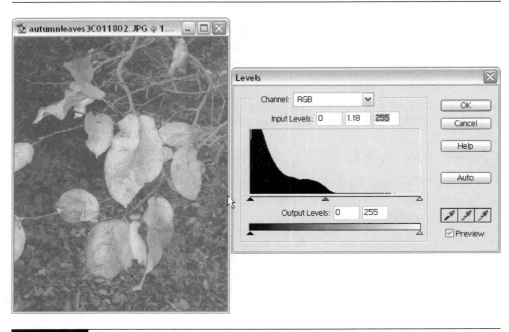

FIGURE 9-5    The Levels dialog box

**3.** The graph in the dialog box shows the distribution of pixels in the full tonal range from black (extreme left) to white (extreme right). The example in Figure 9-5 shows a dark, underexposed photo, in which most of the pixels are weighted to the dark side of the graph. If it were overexposed, the pixels would be weighted to the right side. This means that the vast majority of the pixels in this image are dark, and not much detail is available in the upper range. The leaves would be fairly bright if the image were properly exposed. The Levels command gives you ultimate control in correcting this. You want to shift some detail into a brighter range to increase the image range and contrast.

**4.** First, you should balance the exposure for each primary color: Press COMMAND-1 (Mac) or CTRL-1, or choose Red from the Channel menu at the top of the histogram. Then perform steps 5 and 6 that follow. Next, press COMMAND-2 (Mac) or CTRL-2, or choose Green from the Channel menu, and then do steps 5 and 6 again for that channel. Finally, press COMMAND-3 (Mac) or CTRL-3, or choose the Blue channel and repeat steps 5 and 6 one more time.

5. Slide the white triangle to the left until it is at the point where the graph starts to curve up (in this case, about halfway through the graph—see Figure 9-6). This is where the magic of levels takes place. When you change the slider, the program takes the newly defined graph segment (between the black and white arrows) and spreads it to cover the complete tonal range from black to white. This is shown in Figure 9-6. The image now has the maximum amount of value range to display detail properly.

6. Adjust the black triangle on the graph slider so that it just touches the histogram where it starts to rise.

7. Once you've expanded the brightness range to cover the entire histogram for each primary color, your image will have near-perfect color balance. Now, only now, and not one second before now, you can adjust your exposure. You should do that to all three channels equally in order to maintain color balance. So now and only now you will use the middle slider.

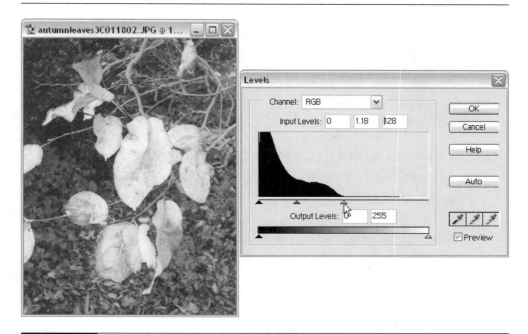

FIGURE 9-6    Adjusting the tonal range with the Levels command

First, choose the RGB (composite) channel from the Channel menu. Now, drag the gray (midtone) slider back and forth until you are happy with the overall brightness of the image. Your image is now color balanced and contains a pure white highlight, a solid black deep shadow, and perfect midtones. It's the digital version of Ansel Adams' famous Zone System.

**NOTE**   *If the histogram is taller than the level part of the graph at either the white or black end, do not move that slider yet … and probably never.*

## 59. Create Instant Effects

Photoshop Elements provides an Effects Palette that automates the process of applying special effects to your images, enabling preset routines that perform a series of operations on a selection, text, or a whole layer to produce unique effects.

### Why Should I Use Instant Effects?

Would you want to eat bland food every day, or would you rather add some spices to enhance the flavor so the experience is richer? Instant Effects can add some visual spice to your digital-imaging projects. Digital imaging is exciting because you can go beyond the realms of pure photography and explore a broader range of visual beauty and art than you can with a camera alone. The "why" of using these effects comes from your personal need to express a larger view than snapshots alone can communicate. These effects let you be adventurous. On the other hand, overusing effects and using them "just for the sake of it" usually produces tragically trite results.

### How Do I Use Instant Effects to Alter the Image?

Applying effects to your images is easy in Photoshop Elements.

1. Open an image in Photoshop Elements.

2. From the Window menu, choose Effects. The default menu will display, showing each of the effects in a thumbnail view so you can get a sense of what each effect does. Effect types are broken down into four categories:

   ■ **Text Effects**   Apply only to a text layer

   ■ **Image Effects**   Affect the whole image

■ **Textures**   Add a new layer with the texture applied

■ **Frames**   Alter the edges of the image

3.  To apply an effect, click and hold down the left mouse button on the effect thumbnail; or, if you are working in List view, click and hold down the mouse on the effect name. The cursor will change to a grabbing hand.

4.  Drag the effect over the image and release the mouse button. You can also select the effect and then click the Apply button at the upper-right of the palette. But wait! You can also apply the effect by double-clicking its icon in the Effects Palette.

## 60. Use Recipes for 31 Complex Solutions

In Photoshop Elements, recipes are lists of preset step-by-step instructions that perform a variety of tasks. They are an adjunct to the help system conveniently placed in an easy-to-access palette. These recipes are found in the How To Palette in the Palette well (at the right end of the Options bar).

### Why Should I Use Recipes as Solutions?

Recipes are an excellent learning tool because they take you through common editing tasks one step at a time, like a good cookbook steps you through a recipe. The recipe tells you what tools you need and how to apply them properly. They also provide links in the text that automatically bring up the tools and commands that you need as you follow the procedures. Recipes are handy reference guides and valuable aids for the new user.

As Adobe releases more recipes, you can download them from the link provided in the drop-down menu on the How To Palette.

## Try This:   Shuffle the Deck and Get New Effects

Try experimenting with the effects to see how they alter your image. Stack different effects on separate layers and adjust the layer opacity factor, blend modes (see Chapter 12), or layer orientation to see how combined effects change your image.

### How Do I Use Recipes to Achieve Solutions?

1. From the Window menu, choose How To. The Recipes Palette will appear.

2. From the Recipes menu, choose a category to access a list of recipes in a given category.

3. Choose a recipe, and then follow the step-by-step instructions in the wizard-type dialog that appears. Often, when the instructions might be a bit complicated, you're just told to click a button. Doing so performs several operations that will lead to accomplishing the effect you're after.

## 61. Draw Details Out of the Shadows and Highlights

When you take photographs in intense light, such as broad daylight, it is common for any dark shadows in the shot to hide some of the detail. Sometimes you can fill the shadows with the internal flash. The internal flash, however, does not deal with shadows that are farther away than the range of the flash—in some cases, they illuminate only up to 15 feet. If you end up with shadows that are too deep and hide detail, you can use the Fill Flash command in Photoshop Elements to help correct them. The beauty of this command is that it doesn't cast any unwanted shadows and all the shadows are lighted evenly, no matter how distant from the lens.

You can correct overexposed highlights with the Adjust Backlighting command. This situation occurs when foreground objects are lit from behind, and you increase the exposure to bring the foreground objects out of shadow, which overexposes and washes out the background.

### Why Do I Want More Detail in the Shadows and Highlights?

When shadows appear too dark and highlights are too bright, an unnatural lighting effect results. Without detail, the eyes perceive these areas as only shapes, which tends to flatten the sense of depth, form, and perspective. Restoring details in an image helps define the forms and adds dimension to the image, and produces the image you meant to shoot. The balance of detail in shadow and lighter areas allows the eyes to move freely throughout the picture with comfort and continuity.

### How Do I Get More Detail?

Use the Photoshop Elements Fill Flash command to bring out details in shadow areas.

1. Choose Enhance | Adjust Lighting | Fill Flash. The Adjust Fill Flash dialog box appears.

2. Check Preview so that you can immediately see the result of your adjustment in the image window.

3. Drag the Lighter slider to the right to lighten the shadows. An example of this effect is shown in Figure 9-7. Since you can see the result instantly, simply stop when you like the result.

4. Adjust the Saturation slider to intensify or subdue the color in the filled shadow areas.

**FIGURE 9-7**   Before (left) and after using the Fill Flash command

**FIGURE 9-8**    Before (left) and after using the Adjust Backlighting command

Use the Photoshop Elements Adjust Backlighting command to bring out details in highlight areas.

1. Choose Enhance | Adjust Lighting | Adjust Backlighting.

2. Adjust the slider to the right to lighten the shadows. An example of this effect is shown in Figure 9-8 (above).

3. Check Preview to see the changes immediately in the image window.

## 62. Open Up Shadows with the Dodge Tool

When you *open up* a shadow, you lighten it and expose the detail that was hidden. This is similar to opening the pupil of your eye to see better in the dark.

*Dodging* is a traditional darkroom technique. During exposure, parts of the photographic paper can be shaded to lighten those areas. The Dodge tool produces the same effect but works in a different way. Instead of holding light back, it adds light to darker pixels to raise their luminance. The tool is useful when you want to lighten only selected detailed areas of an image with a hand-brushed technique. Figure 9-9 shows an image changed by using the Dodge tool.

## How Do I Use the Dodge Tool to Open Up Shadows?

Here's how to use the Dodge tool in Photoshop Elements:

1. Open the image in Photoshop Elements.

2. Choose the Dodge tool from the Toolbox.

3. Adjust the brush size and Exposure Value on the Options bar. The Exposure Value controls how fast the effect builds up with multiple passes. Raising the Exposure Value to more than about 12 percent often causes streaking and grayed-out areas.

4. Choose Shadows, Midtones, or Highlights from the Range menu. The Range determines the luminance range where the effect is most dominant.

5. Paint over the areas you want to lighten, building up the effect with multiple passes over the same area.

**FIGURE 9-9**   The cat's eye on the left was dodged using midtone and highlight image-editing options.

## 63. Use a Soft Light Blend Mode Layer

Soft Light is the name of a blend mode (see Tip 84 in Chapter 12 for more on blend modes). By setting up a layer with a Soft Light blend mode, you can achieve some effective dodging and burning in an image. *Burning* is a traditional darkroom technique. During exposure, parts of the photographic paper are exposed to more light to darken those areas. The Burn tool produces the same effect but works by subtracting luminance from lighter areas.

### How Do I Use This Blend Mode Tool to Open Up Shadows?

The Soft Light blend mode burns in the underlying pixels if the brush brightness is lighter than 50 percent luminance (middle gray) and dodges the underlying pixels if the color in the brush is darker than 50 percent luminance. You can switch from dodge to burn by switching from black to white brush colors or shades of gray to reduce the power of the effect. Choosing middle gray will have no effect. Soft Light has no effect on areas that are pure white and pure black.

Here's how to use the Soft Light method of dodging and burning:

1. Open an image in Photoshop Elements.

2. From the Palette well, open the Layer Palette.

3. Create a new layer by clicking on the middle icon at the bottom of the Layer Palette. A new transparent layer will appear.

4. Set the layer attribute to Soft Light mode from the drop-down menu just below the Layer tab.

5. Set the Background and Foreground colors to black and white, respectively.

6. Choose the Paintbrush from the Toolbox. Size is arbitrary. Set the opacity at 100 percent. Lower the opacity to reduce the effect.

7. Use white to bring out detail in shadows and black to bring out detail in highlights.

NOTE
*You can press* X *to switch from foreground to background color. Use shades of gray instead of black and white to control the power of the effect. The brush does not affect black or white in the image.*

## 64. Create Your Own Shallow Depth-of-Field

*Depth-of-field* is the distance in front of and behind the center of focus in which everything is in reasonably sharp focus. (See Tip 15 in Chapter 3 for more information.)

### Why Do I Want to Change the Depth-of-Field?

Details in the foreground or background can often act as visual interferences to the main subject. Depth-of-field is normally changed by adjusting the aperture of the lens, but most digital cameras keep in relatively sharp focus almost everything that's more than a couple of feet away from the camera. The result is that, without the aid of a little digital image-editing magic, it's very hard to keep interest focused on the subject by letting the foreground and background blur out-of-focus.

So what do you do to get rid of the clutter when this occurs? Obscuring these unwanted details with the Gaussian Blur Filter allows the viewer to focus on what you intended and lets the other visual details act as a backdrop. In other words, you've created the illusion that you've shortened the depth-of-field of the shot. Blurring the detail can even enhance the main subject. This process mimics much of what your brain actually does when you are focusing with your eyes. For instance, when you are focusing on someone's face, the background is blurred. You suppress the extraneous details surrounding the subject and accentuate the facial details.

Figure 9-10 shows an image before and after the Blur Filter is used.

**FIGURE 9-10**   Before (left) and after the Blur Filter is used on selected background areas.

## How Do I Change the Depth-of-Field?

Use the Photoshop Elements Selection tools along with Blur Filter to achieve this effect.

1. Open the image in Photoshop Elements.

2. Use one or more of the Selection tools to select the areas of the image that you want to keep sharp. (The Lasso and Magic Wand tools were used in Figure 9-10. See Chapter 11 for more on selections.)

3. Invert the selection so that it is selected instead of the subject. Choose Select | Inverse or press COMMAND-I (Mac) or CTRL-SHIFT-I.

4. Choose Selection | Feather.

5. In the Feather dialog box, change the Feather value (see Tip 78 in Chapter 11) to increase the area at the edge of the selection that will smoothly transition so you don't end up with a hard edge.

6. Choose Filters | Blur | Gaussian Blur. The Gaussian Blur dialog box appears. Adjust the slider to change the amount of blur.

7. Click OK to apply the blur to the selection.

# Chapter 10

# Retouching Your Images

Photographs rarely come out perfect; that's why it is common practice for photographers to go in afterward and use image-editing software to tweak their photos so that they include and express just what they want them to. This chapter introduces image-editing techniques that can help you retouch your pictures and get them close to perfection. The extent to which you take retouching is entirely up to you—it can be as simple as covering over a few blemishes or as complex as giving someone a facelift or a hair-color change.

## 65. Fix Red Eye in Your Image Editor

When an internal flash is used, it typically aims the light directly at the person being photographed so the light actually bounces off the retina and back at the camera. This will produce pupils that are bright red in the photograph. This is called *red eye*, and it makes your subjects look like they're ready for Halloween.

### How Do I Use Image-Editing Software to Eliminate Red Eye?

Photoshop Elements makes it easy to eliminate red eye from your portraits by providing a special tool called Red Eye Brush.

1. Open the image in Photoshop Elements.

2. From the Toolbox, choose the Red Eye Brush tool. The Red Eye Brush Options bar will appear. Choose a brush size and style that is appropriate for the area you are working in.

3. Because in most instances you will be changing the color in the pupil, the default replacement color on the Options bar is black. The Current Color box shows you the color the cursor is currently over. You can set the Sampling option to be First Click or Current Color—First Click picks up the color from the first position you start painting from, and Current Color uses the current foreground color as the reference. The Tolerance level determines how many shades of the sampling color (in most cases red) will be affected by the brush. You want the Tolerance level to be set high enough to affect them all. Place the cursor over the red part of the pupil so you can choose the sampling color that determines which colors are replaced or use the Eyedropper tool to make the red the current foreground color.

4. With the Red Eye Brush, move your cursor over the region to be changed. Choose the sampling color, observing the Current Color box on the Options bar.

5. Drag to start replacing color over the red area. The brush will change the color but not the luminance value of the pixels, so the detail in the eye will remain unchanged. Adjust the Tolerance and resample as necessary until all the red is gone.

> **NOTE** *You can use the Red Eye Brush to change the color of other parts of the image as well. Just sample in other areas or choose a foreground color by changing the Sampling option to the Current Color. You could use it to change the color of someone's eyes or of the flowers in a dress pattern.*

## 66. Eliminate Small Annoyances with the Clone Stamp Tool

The Clone Stamp tool is one of the handiest image-editing tools ever invented, and you will use it time and time again. Do you have blemishes, specs, unwanted doodads, glitches, or just plain junk in your photos? The Clone Stamp tool can make all these pesky little things disappear.

The word *clone* means to reproduce with absolute fidelity. The Clone Stamp tool copies a section of pixels from one area of a picture to another. This section can be from the same image, another layer, or another image entirely. The Clone Stamp tool allows you to set a source and then target an area within the image and reproduce the pixels from the source to where you are painting.

### Why Do I Need to Clean Up My Images?

What if you didn't have time to get every piece of garbage off the lawn before you took the shot, or Aunt Clara had a speck of food on her wonderful smile? These might have been perfectly good photographs, had it not been for a few small flaws that marred the shots. Don't panic. The Clone Stamp tool provides an efficient way of removing all sorts of visual clutter and defects in your photo with great precision. An unwanted item can be removed by copying an acceptable similar area over the defective area.

### How Do I Use the Clone Stamp Tool to Edit?

Using the Clone Stamp tool, you can target certain areas of an image to use as a source for a brush stroke. The tool "paints" with the pixels that are part of the set target source. For example, to fix some blemishes on a subject's face, you could set the source target on a clear section of skin and then move the tool over the blemishes, painting over them with a copy of the clear skin at the source, and the blemishes would be covered. Setting the tool opacity at a lower setting would allow you to blend in the skin gradually so it looks seamless (see Figure 10-1).

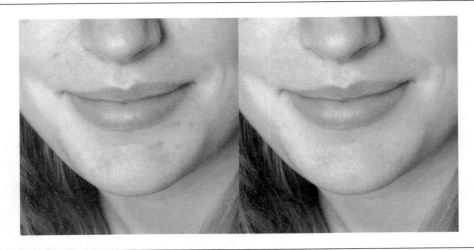

**FIGURE 10-1**    Before (left) and after using the Clone Stamp tool to cover blemishes

Also, be sure to clone from an area that is the same color and brightness as the area immediately surrounding the blemish you want to cover. Otherwise, you'll just create a different kind of blemish.

Here's how to use the Clone Stamp tool:

1. Open the image in Photoshop Elements.

2. Choose the Clone Stamp tool from the Toolbox.

3. Set the brush size, opacity, and blend mode on the Options bar.

4. Select Aligned if you want the sampled area to move with the tool. This keeps the source area in close proximity to the painted area so you can use similar local detail as a source.

   Deselect Aligned if you want the sampled area to reposition to the original target every time you stop and start painting again. Use this option when you want to keep reusing the same source image area in a number of locations.

5. Position your cursor over the source and OPTION-click (Mac) or ALT-click. You will see the cursor change to a target, indicating that the source has been set.

6. Position the cursor where you want to begin painting with the Clone Stamp tool and start painting. You will see the source location, indicated by a crosshair, maintain a constant distance and orientation as you move the Clone Stamp tool. The crosshair indicates the pixel area that the tool is using to paint with.

## 67. Smooth Out the Wrinkles

Wrinkles can occur in any surface—skin, cloth, earth, and water, for example. Anything with an undulating surface that might look better smoothed applies here.

### Why Should I Get Rid of Wrinkles?

People have been looking for the Fountain of Youth for eons, but nobody has been able to find one—until now. Using some simple smoothing and blending techniques, you can make wrinkles and hard texture vanish, adding a youthful texture to a face of any age.

### How Do I Use Image-Editing Software to Remove Wrinkles?

Welcome to the world of digital plastic surgery. Figure 10-2 shows what can be done with a good image-editing program. The trick with this method is to blur a copy of the image so that the very dark and very light tones in the copied image blend together, eliminating deep and high areas of the surface. This smoothed image acts as a source in painting in the wrinkles with an "erase-through" process.

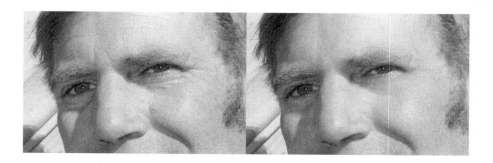

**FIGURE 10-2** Before (left) and after the wrinkles around his eyes and forehead and blemishes on his cheek were blended away

Following is a clever technique that will take 20 years off an aging face:

1. Open the image you want to "rejuvenate."

2. Duplicate the base layer two times. Select the second layer.

3. Choose Filter | Blur | Gaussian Blur. (I used a setting of around 20 to get a good spread and mix of light and dark tones in Figure 10-2.) Experiment with settings to get the best spread for your subject. Also, the exact setting will be dependent on the size of the image and the magnification of the wrinkles.

4. Choose Filter | Noise | Add Noise. The setting should be around 5. Choose Uniform and Monochromatic.

5. Select the third layer. You will use the Eraser tool to erase through the image on this layer to reveal the blurred image below. By erasing the wrinkle areas, you blend in the smoothed values from the image below, which makes the wrinkles diminish significantly.

6. Choose the Eraser tool from the Toolbox and set the brush size small enough to work in the wrinkles with a small amount of overlap. Set the opacity such that the effect builds up gradually.

NOTE    *You'll get the best results using a pressure-sensitive pen so that you can vary the transparency of the erased areas by the amount of pressure you put on the tip of the pen.*

## 68. Draw Attention to the Eyes

People make the most significant contact with another person through that person's eyes, so the more expressive and noticeable you make the eyes, the more impact the photo is likely to have. Focusing attention on the eyes is a powerful tool to hold the viewer's attention and draw the viewer into the subject. With a few simple adjustments, you can increase the vibrancy of the subject's eyes to make a portrait captivating and more alive.

### How Do I Use Image-Editing Software to Accomplish This?

To accentuate the eyes, you need to brighten the whites, darken the outer edge of the iris, and lighten the inner iris by boosting contrast. Boosting the color saturation of the iris can add punch, too, but be careful not to push it too far or it will look unnatural. (See Figure 10-3 for an example of a well-done enhanced eye.)

**FIGURE 10-3**    The eye on the right is much more captivating after being enhanced.

Here's how to enhance a subject's eyes:

1. Select the eye area with one of the selection tools that allows you to make a freeform selection, so that you don't include any more surrounding skin than necessary. Include the edges of eyelids and lashes. Also, make a separate selection around the eyebrows. (See Tip 77 in Chapter 11 for more on selections.)

2. Choose Select | Feather. Set the value large enough to get a gradual transition so any effects blend into the face seamlessly.

3. Choose Enhance | Adjust Brightness/Contrast | Brightness/Contrast. Adjust the sliders to raise contrast and brightness.

4. Select just the iris area with the Lasso tool and feather the edges for a smooth transition.

5. Choose Enhance | Adjust Color | Hue/Saturation. Adjust the saturation up to boost the color of the iris.

NOTE    *The key here is to accentuate but at the same time be subtle. If you push the enhancement too far, the eyes will look fake, and that will defeat the whole purpose.*

## 69.  Sharpen Eyes and Other Specific Areas of the Image

Before you can understand sharpening, you need to look at what causes softening. A sharp edge has a quick transition in contrast from one side of the edge to the other. This means that if you have a black edge on a white background, for example, it will go from white to black with few or no levels of gray in between, making the edge appear hard (sharp). If you take the same edge and transition it gradually so that many levels of gray are used, it will appear softer, like a fold or ripple.

When an image has mostly soft edges, it can appear to be slightly out of focus. To bring the image into tighter focus, you can use special routines to increase the contrast of the edges by removing some of those transitional colors.

### Why Would I Want to Sharpen Specific Areas?

Sharpening detail brings the image into focus and produces a more vibrant and powerful photograph. It is also more relaxing for the eyes of the viewer, which have to work harder to bring blurry or soft images into focus. This will annoy viewers, even if they don't understand why. Sharper detail also means more depth and definition of form, and it sets off the distinction of shape and color with more power. Clearly delineated edges and detail add more force to your composition and allow the image to come off the paper and reach out to the viewer. The sense of realism is greatly enhanced.

### How Do I Use Image-Editing Software to Sharpen Detail?

To sharpen key detail, use the Unsharp Mask filter. This Filter preserves the smooth transitions in the image and focuses its sharpening routines to areas of the image that are properly perceived as edges. This prevents unsightly pixel brightening in the middle of areas that should be smooth, which can be the byproduct of standard sharpening filters. Unsharp Mask provides a number of controls that determine which edges get sharpened and the extent to which they are sharpened. Figure 10-4 shows an image before and after the Unsharp Mask Filter was used.

Here's how to increase the sharpness of edge detail in an image:

1. Open a slightly blurred image in Photoshop Elements.

2. Choose Filter | Sharpen | Unsharp Mask.

3. Move the Amount slider to increase or decrease the contrast of the edges that are being sharpened.

4. Move the Radius slider to increase the area of sharpening effect around the edge.

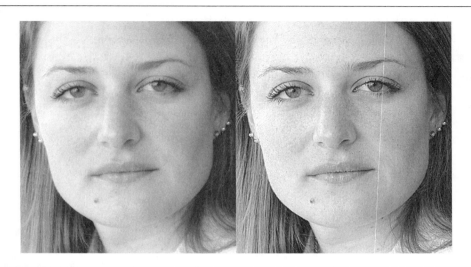

**FIGURE 10-4**   Before (left) and after the Unsharp Mask filter was used to bring out detail

5.  Move the Threshold slider to determine how different the pixels need to be in value to be considered an edge.

6.  View the results in the preview window. When you achieve the look you want, click OK.

## 70.  Spread Highlights to Achieve Glamour Blurring

The soft glow that appears around glamour shots can give the subject an ethereal quality. That glow is produced by spreading out the highlights of the image, adding an aura of light to the subject. This can be achieved with a special lens and lighting in a professional studio, or you can achieve it with your digital photographs by using some simple software techniques.

### What Are Highlights?

Highlights are the bright points of light in a scene that indicate reflection of the light source. They can brighten up reflections in chrome or general reflections that come from light-colored surfaces, such as a white shirt. Highlights are the brightest colors in the photo and are key to interpreting the type and quality of the light source. Sharp, intense highlights indicate a strong focused light such as a spotlight, while soft, diffused highlights indicate a more general light source such as an overcast day or flourescent lighting.

## Why Would I Want to Spread the Highlights?

By softening the highlights, you can change the nature and quality of the lighting in the scene to be soft and more intimate. It's like lowering the dimmer switch or adding a special shade to make the lighting more romantic.

## How Do I Use Glamour Blurring to Spread Highlights?

1.   Open the image you want to glamour blur.

2.   Duplicate the image to one more layer. Select the second layer.

3.   Choose Filter | Distort | Diffuse Glow. Move the slider to a value that spreads the highlights nicely, eliminates most edge detail, and makes the skin glow. Be sure to drag the Graininess slider to its lowest setting. When you like what you see in the preview window, click OK.

4.   In the Layers Palette, choose Soft Light from the Blend mode menu.

5.   Make sure the diffused layer is selected (highlighted) and drag the Opacity slider until you feel you have the right balance between the glow effect and the original image (see Figure 10-5).

**FIGURE 10-5**    From left to right—the original image, the image with enhanced highlights, and the merged image after adding the glow

## 71. Convert Color Photos to Black-and-White

Fundamentally, in the digital world, there is no difference between a black-and-white image and a color image with no color saturation. Every color appears as a pure gray in the black-and-white image. A color is *pure gray* when the color channels are all equal in strength. For instance, an RGB (Red, Green, and Blue) color value of 128, 128, 128 would give you a midtone gray; 0, 0, 0 would give you black.

When you change a color image to black-and-white, you move the RGB values to gray while maintaining the overall brightness of each color. You can convert a black-and-white image to a grayscale image, which strips out the color information completely and stores only the luminance level information, which decreases the size of the file. Converting your color images to black-and-white also teaches you about how light works in your photographs, because you can see the pure light values more clearly.

NOTE *Grayscale files cannot be colorized unless they are converted back to RGB.*

### Why Would I Want to Change a Color Photo to Black-and-White?

On the practical side, you may find it necessary to change a color photo to black-and-white for publication, to produce photocopies, or to create faxable documents. Converting color photos to black-and-white and then adjusting the brightness and contrast can increase the quality in reproduction, because some colors don't translate well when photocopied in black-and-white.

For a more subjective reason, black-and-white photos can be used to express a unique feeling and quality. By eliminating the color components, the image focuses on the value of the light and the interplay of shapes. If you are looking for an abstraction of reality, black-and-white helps detach the subject matter from the everyday.

### How Do I Convert the Image?

- Load a color photograph in your image editor, and then open the Saturation control. Reduce the saturation to zero and watch the color photo become black-and-white.

Another way to accomplish this task:

- Choose Enhance | Adjust Color | Remove Color.

And here's a third alternative:

- Choose Image | Mode | Grayscale.

You may notice that some colors that looked comparatively different in color may look similar in gray. This happens because even though the color values were different, the luminance values were close. You can adjust for some of these problems by changing contrast and levels to accentuate some of the differences in shades.

## 72. Color Tone Black-and-White Photos

*Color toning* is a process of tinting the image with a single hue. It is also called *colorizing*. If you were to shine a light on the photo through a colored gel, as is used in stage lighting, it would give the appearance of color toning. Color toning is an ambient effect that changes the overall color of the image. Color toning can give the appearance of an old-style photo with sepia tones, or it can be more upbeat by adding brighter and more radical color changes. It is an easy effect that adds another dimension to an image.

### Why Would I Want to Color Tone Black-and-White Photos?

- Color toning is an easy way to achieve an antique look in an image. Old photographs often have a brownish cast to them. You can simulate that using color toning.

- Color toning can also be used as a way of differentiating images used for a menu on the Web.

- By color toning your black-and-white photos, you can add another level of expression to accentuate a mood without giving up the simple but powerful quality of black-and-white images.

### How Do I Color Tone an Image?

Open the image you want to color tone. It doesn't need to be in black-and-white to begin with, as this process will convert the image to black-and-white at the same time it colorizes it.

**Try This:**   **Focus on Color**

Color toning can be used as a powerful tool for altering parts of a black-and-white image so they stand out from the background. Select areas you want to accentuate, then color tone the selected areas. This will focus the viewers attention on the color-toned portions of the image. This technique can be used on color photos also.

1. Choose Enhance | Adjust Color | Hue/Saturation.

2. Check the Colorize option, and you will see the image change to a color-toned image of the hue selected on the top slider.

3. Move the Hue slider to change the color tone.

4. Click OK when you're done.

## 73. Hand Color Black-and-White Photos

Hand coloring is a process of colorizing individual areas of an image with a brush and transparent color. Hand coloring maintains tonal values as you paint the color. It is much like the effect of painting a watercolor wash over a pen-and-ink drawing.

NOTE   *The first color photographs were hand-painted black-and-white photos. Transparent oil paints were used to color these early photographs. Actually Marshall photo-coloring oils are still in wide use today, primarily by wedding and portrait photographers who want to give their images a classic and timeless look.*

### Why Would I Want to Hand Color Black-and-White Photos?

Hand coloring can be used to create an interesting effect that mimics the hand-tinted photographs of years past, or to create the look of old postcards. You can scan old black-and-white photos and hand color them to achieve this affect. Relatives might find it exciting to see a scene from the distant past brought back to life in color, or you can use hand-colored photos to achieve an effect in a brochure or create an old-fashioned postcard.

You can choose to color portions of a photo to accentuate them or paint in every detail. When you are coloring by hand, you have precise control of where the color goes and how it should look. The choice of colors is up to you, so the whole process becomes much more about imagination and creativity and realizing your vision. If you have painting skills, this is a good opportunity to apply some of them to your photographic pursuits.

## How Do I Hand Color Photos?

There are two basic ways to go about this. The first method described is layer-based. The advantage of using layers is that if you don't like the result, you can delete the layer and start over. You can also try several other effects of blending the colors with the underlying layer by changing to different layer blend modes.

1. Open the image you want to paint. If it is in color, convert it to black-and-white (see Tip 72 in this chapter).

2. Create a new layer and make it the active layer.

3. Set the layer mode to Color.

4. Choose the Paintbrush tool from the Toolbox. Adjust the size and style to match the detail you will be painting.

5. Set the Opacity value lower to build up the color more gradually.

6. Choose a foreground color. You will notice the color conforms to the tonal values of the underlying image, so you don't need to worry about shading.

7. Begin painting with the Paintbrush tool.

8. When you're satisfied with the image, you can save it.

The second method for hand coloring is faster, but doesn't offer you as much flexibility as the layer-based method:

1. Open the image you want to paint. If it is in color, convert it to black-and-white (see Tip 72 in this chapter).

2. Choose the Paintbrush tool from the Toolbox. Adjust the size and style to match the detail you will be painting.

3. Choose the colors you want to use, then change the brush's blend mode to Color in the brush's Options bar. Then, when you stroke with the brush, the brightness values of the black-and-white image remain the same, but the picture is tinted with the current foreground color.

4. When you're satisfied with the image, you can save it.

## 74. Correct Perspective Distortion

If you hold your camera at an odd angle while shooting vertical or horizontal objects, you can produce perspective distortion in your image. If the camera is not parallel to those objects while the shot is taken, it will distort the object by exaggerating the perspective, causing it to look unnaturally squeezed at one end, as shown in Figure 10-6.

**FIGURE 10-6**    An example of perspective distortion

## Why Should I Correct Perspective?

When you took the shot, you didn't see the image in such a contorted manner, so if you want your photo to reflect the scene accurately, you'll want to fix this distortion.

Although there are artistic uses for purposefully distorting scenes, most of the time it is a problem. Your brain compensates for this distortion every time you tilt your head to look up at a building. This ability to compensate is what makes our brains different from the camera's brain. If you want your final image to match how your brain thinks an image should look, you will need to do some sort of correction.

## How Do I Correct Perspective Distortion?

The process of correcting perspective distortion involves stretching or distorting the image to re-form it back to the way it should look. Some wonderful tools are available to make this a fairly easy process.

Here's how to correct perspective distortion:

1.  Open an image that needs correcting.

2.  In the Layers Palette, double-click the background layer's Name bar. The New Layer dialog box appears.

3.  Enter a new name for the background layer and click OK. This will turn the background layer into an ordinary layer. Background layers cannot be transformed.

4.  Choose Image | Transform | Distort. The transform box will appear with handles on all sides and all corners.

5.  Click and drag the corner handles to correct the distortion. You'll want to make vertical lines parallel with the sides of the image frame and the horizontal lines parallel with the top and bottom edges, if possible. You may have to pull more than one handle to achieve this. Figure 10-7 shows how this process looks.

6. When you have corrected the distortion to your liking, click the Commit button in the Options bar (the big check mark on the right side) or press ENTER to render the transformation.

7. If necessary, use the Crop tool to trim any slanted edges that result. If you have dragged all the lines outside the Canvas (work area), this will not be a problem.

**FIGURE 10-7**    The distortion transformation handles being positioned so the image appears correctly proportioned

# Chapter 11

# Creating a New Reality with Composites

So far, you've learned what you can do to a single photograph to make it better, sharper, and brighter. Now it's time to enter the world of *composites*, the technique of combining multiple digital images into one. You're leaving conventional photography behind to immerse yourself in the world of computer imaging, where your imagination knows no bounds. At the core of compositing are the almighty layers that let you stack many images or parts of images in endless combinations and interlayer effects.

## 75. Stack Components on Layers

*Layers* are a function of the Layers Palette. You can use layers to stack a number of images or pieces of images within a single document and work each layer individually. Imagine a number of horizontal panes of glass that are stacked with a little space in between, so you can slip in image transparencies to rest on the surface of each layer. You can place images on the pane at the bottom, and then work your way up by stacking other images on other layers above. Some layers may include portions of images, so if you look down on the stack, you can see the stacked images below, where partial images let lower layers show through, forming a composite image. Digital layering is a complex process by which layers can change their transparencies and blend with other layers below in many ways.

The *components* represent all the pieces of a composite image that fit together to make the final image you see in the image window—text, gradients, textures, shapes, images or pieces of images, hand-drawn art, scans, special effects, or layer styles. You typically separate components into individual layers in an image.

### Try This:    Make a Simple Composite from Film

An easy way to understand the idea of components is to stack two or three slides or negatives (make sure they are not too dark) on a light box or in a slide viewer. The image you will see is a combination of all the stacked images—a *composite* of the *components*, which are the images on the individual pieces of film.

## Why Should I Stack Images in Layers?

Layers keep components separate, and stacking keeps them in order, from background on the lowest layer to foreground on the uppermost layer. When creating a composite, you are blending images from different sources. It is important that you carefully position, resize, and apply effects to blend the components into a unified composition. Stacking each component on a separate layer gives you maximum control over each part of the composite. If you are making a layer partially transparent, applying a blend mode, or erasing parts of an image, the effect of these operations allows the lower layer(s) to show through in some way. You can reposition layers to see how this affects the composite image. Consider layers the ultimate light box.

**NOTE** *If you adjust a layer to 50% opacity, it becomes like a sheet of tracing paper, showing the lower image while still showing the components on the active layer. This can serve as a handy reference for positioning and sizing.*

## How Do I Use Layer Stacking to Create Composites?

To get familiar with using composites, you can stack a number of photographs that include elements you want to combine on layers in a single document. Don't worry about which images you choose, as this exercise is meant only to get your feet wet. Place the image you want to use as a background on the first layer. The image components that you will cut from lower layers will be placed in the upper layers.

**NOTE** *If you don't like something you've done, remember that you can always move the layers around, partially erase them, change their transparency, and change the way their colors interact with layers below them.*

Cut out the image components from the background layers so you have a number of layers with image components on transparent backgrounds. An image component could be a picture of anything—a head, a flower, or a body of water, for example. The challenge is finding pieces that go together well and then figuring out how to merge them to make the image look like a single shot. That can take a little practice.

Figure 11-1 shows an interesting effect created by merging two images to create a composite.

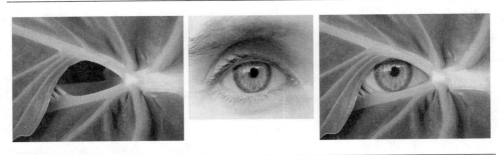

**FIGURE 11-1**    A composite of the two images on the left created the image on the right.

Transparency can be achieved by erasing unwanted portions of the image with the Eraser tool or by creating a selection and cutting away portions (see Tip 77 later in this chapter). Using selections will give you the added advantage of being able to feather the edge of an object, which makes merging components easier (see Tip 78 later in this chapter). You can hide layers by clicking the eye icon next to the layer in the Layers Palette. Making a layer active allows you to edit the images on that layer alone, so you can move from one component to another until you get them all edited properly.

NOTE    *You can make duplicate layers of components and then make the original layers invisible before you start to modify the duplicate layers. This way, you can go back to the original layer if your experiments go astray.*

## 76. Make Collages Using Layer Transparency

A *collage* is a form of composite that is unique in a stylistic sense. In traditional art, a collage is made up of image pieces that have been pasted together to form a conglomerate of images. The collage artist doesn't attempt to blend together these images in a seamless manner to create the appearance of a unified subject, but rather revels in diversity and contrast. Collages are viewed as visual conversations. The viewer's eye wanders around, picking up bits and pieces of the image just as the artist did when it was created.

Much of compositing is dedicated to producing unified images that you might not even suspect had multiple sources. Collages, on the other hand, make no bones about being loudly diverse. You can create a digital collage by using composite techniques to piece together all sorts of art and objects. You collect the objects with your camera and paste them together with your computer.

## How Does Layer Transparency Help Me Create Collages?

Because collages are made up of pieces of all shapes and sizes, it is common practice to lay them out so they overlap each other. To stay true to that way of working, you can cut out all the components from their backgrounds and place them on transparent layers. Transparent layers allow you to place objects on separate layers and the transparency lets you see where they overlap, like those shown in Figure 11-2. You can move around the layers to change the positioning of the image objects and you can change the stacking order of the layers. You can also transform the objects on individual layers so that they can be any size and proportion in relationship to the objects on the other layers. The combination of stacking and moving opaque objects on transparent layers and of being able to transform those objects makes it possible to get exactly the collage composition you have in mind.

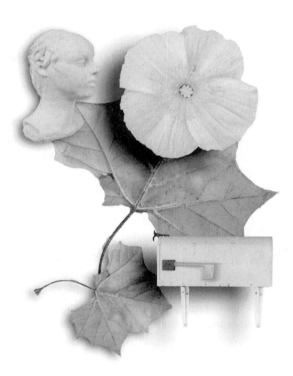

**FIGURE 11-2**   These image objects were cut out of other photographs and pasted into layers in one document to create a collage.

## How Do I Use Transparency to Create Collages?

Here's how to create multiple-image objects with transparent backgrounds:

1.  Open the image you want to cut out.

2.  From the Toolbox, use one of the Lasso tools to outline the portion of the image you want to cut out. When you have finished the selection, choose Select | Inverse to invert the selection.

3.  Cut the inverted selection (Edit | Cut). This leaves a transparent background around the image object.

4.  Repeat this operation for all the image objects you want to include in your collage.

5.  Copy all the images you have cut out and paste them into one document. As you paste them, they will be placed in unique layers with transparent backgrounds. You will be able to see the other objects through the transparent backgrounds of upper layers, as shown in Figure 11-2.

You can use the Eraser tool to create areas of transparency. You can also adjust the layer opacity, use blend modes, and add special effects (see Chapter 12). Anything you can photograph, scan, or draw can become part of your collage. And as a nice bonus, as long as you save your images in a format that preserves the layers, such as TIF or PSD, you can go back and modify your collage at any time. No glue to contend with.

### Try This:  Create a Family Scrapbook

For a nice family project, you can create a scrapbook in the collage style and add to it over time. You can create libraries of image objects by storing images on separate layers in documents that are named for the type of objects they contain. For example, you can name the library Family_Lib.TIF. You can drag these images from this document to any collage you are working on.

## 77. Make Use of the Power of Selections

Selections are one of the key components of any good image-editing program. A *selection* defines an area with an interactive tool and surrounds it with a boundary that is delineated by oscillating dashes that look like marching ants. Whenever you see those critters marching, you know they surround an active selection.

Selections limit the operation of almost every function of the editor to the area within the selection boundary. This containment lets you decide which selected areas of the image will receive specific operations. You can make selections with a number of tools in the Toolbox—the Elliptical and Square Marquee tools (geometric), Lasso tools (freeform or geometric), Brush Selection tool (freeform), and Magic Wand (freeform). (See Tip 79 in this chapter for more on the Magic Wand.)

### Why Do Selections Help Me Work More Efficiently?

A selection lets you isolate any command or action in Photoshop to just that part of the image that's surrounded by the selection marquee. Selections let you quickly move, copy, crop, stretch, rotate, and cut any portion of an image. You can also copy the selection to a new layer or document, where it can become part of a composite. Selections help greatly in creating components. Selections can also be inverted, with the result that what was formerly outside the selection (that is, protected) becomes the inside of the selection.

Masks and selections serve the same purpose. The difference is that masks are selections that were saved to a special type of image layer, where they become grayscale images. Virtually all image-editing programs permit making selections. Only more advanced image-editing programs, such as Photoshop Professional and Painter, also support masks. The advantages of masks are that they can be altered with any of the Toolbox tools and that it's easier to alter portions of them in transparency.

### How Do I Use Selections?

To select a portion of an image and make it a component in a composite, follow these steps:

1.  Choose one of the section tools from the Toolbox, according to the shape of the area you want to define.

2.  Select the object to define the outside edges of your selection. If you're using the Marquee tool, you will click and drag to make the selection. With the Lasso tool, you click and hold down the mouse button while you trace

the selection shape. You will see the moving dashes that define the border of the selection when you release the mouse button. The border will remain and the selection is active.

**3.** The selection can be repositioned while it is active. With the Marquee tool still active, place the cursor within the selection area. Drag it to a new location.

**4.** With the selection tool still active, right-click inside the selection area. From the pop-up menu, choose Copy Via Layer. A new layer with your selection appears in the Layers Palette.

**5.** Open a new document that is sized large enough to hold all of your components.

**6.** Select the Move tool from the Toolbox. Click the selection and drag it to the new document. You will see a duplicate of the selection copied to a layer in the new document.

Figure 11-3 shows a composite created by dragging objects to the new document. The apple and pear were cut from their background and dragged to a new document as a layer over the bananas. The bananas show because the area around the apples is transparent.

**FIGURE 11-3**    A composite created by dragging objects from one document to another

## 78. Blend Selections with Feathering

In conventional painting, *feathering* refers to a method of blending the paint from one area into another with fine bristles and soft, gentle strokes. Some painters actually use feathers to do this. The effect is much the same in the digital world, but you don't use a feather; you use the Feather command. The Feather command value determines how the edge of a selection transitions to the surrounding area. If you use no feather value, the selection will have a hard edge. The higher the feather value, the wider the area of soft transition at the edge of the selection. Figure 11-4 shows the effect of feathering a selection.

### Why Should I Feather Selections?

Feather selections when you want to blend selections into a new background. This effect causes the merged images to look more natural. Feathering is also useful if you have designated an area of an image for enhancement, such as someone's eye, and you want the effect to blend back into the face around the eye so it appears seamless.

> **NOTE** *Feathering edges to a transparent background produces edges with variable transparency built in, so it will blend easily with almost any background.*

| **FIGURE 11-4** | A selection that has been feathered with a value of 30 (left), and a feathered selection pasted into another image (right) |

### How Do I Feather a Selection?

1. Open an image from which you want to cut a selection.

2. Choose one of the selection tools from the Toolbox.

3. Select the area with the selection tool.

4. Choose Select | Inverse to invert the selection. You will see the selection border reposition.

5. Cut the inverted selection to make the area you originally selected transparent.

6. Choose Select | Inverse again to reselect the original image.

7. Choose Select | Feather. The Feather dialog box will appear. Adjust the value to indicate the pixel dimension of the area you want to soften. The border of the selection will smooth slightly when you feather it.

8. Drag the image. When you move the image, it will feature translucent edges that blend to the colors in any background.

## 79. Select Complex Areas with the Magic Wand

The term *magic* is not so farfetched for this ingenious little tool. The Magic Wand is a selection tool designed to select areas of an image based on similar color. The range of color is controlled by a tolerance value that you set. You can use the Magic Wand to select an area of sky, for example, or to select the petals of a yellow flower—the entire object will be selected as long as the colors in the object are fairly consistent. This saves you the time (and anguish) of tracing an outline by hand.

### Why Should I Use the Magic Wand?

In many instances, the Magic Wand can make selections that are next to impossible to do by hand, at least by any sane person. The Magic Wand lets you select complex areas, such as pieces of sky between tree branches. Try making a similarly complex selection by hand, and you'll learn to appreciate this tool. The Magic Wand does not perform well in areas that have a lot of color variations, but it can work miracles if you want to select clear areas of well-defined color. Even if the Magic Wand doesn't do a perfect job, it can often take you 90 percent of the way.

NOTE *It is often much faster to make a selection by hand if the majority of the area you have to select is already selected. Then you can zoom in, and just edit the edges of the selection for precise detail. You do this in most programs by pressing SHIFT while drawing with a selection tool when you want to add to the existing selection and OPTION (Mac) or ALT when you want to subtract from it.*

## How Do I Use the Magic Wand?

Here's how to select an area of similar color with the Magic Wand:

1. Open an image in which you want to make a selection.

2. From the Toolbox, choose the Magic Wand tool.

3. On the Magic Wand Options bar, set the Tolerance value you think might work for the area you want to select. You can experiment with this value to get it right. The idea is to get the value close enough to choose only the pixels that are in the area of color you want to select. If you want the edge of the selection to be smooth, click the Anti-aliased option. If you want all the pixels in the area selected to be adjacent, choose Contiguous. If you are selecting areas between branches, as shown in Figure 11-5, turn off Contiguous so it will find all instances of the color range, even though they are separated.

NOTE *If you turn off Contiguous so that you can make a selection, like the sky through the gaps in leaves, you may pick up lots of other areas you didn't want to include. It's easy to get rid of the superfluous areas. Choose the selection tool, press OPTION (Mac) or ALT, and make a loose selection around the areas you didn't really want included. Those areas will no longer be selected.*

4. Click in the area of color you want to select, and observe the selection the tool makes. If it is not to your satisfaction, you can adjust the parameters and try again until you get the selection to appear as you want. If the Magic Wand does not choose the entire area, you can SHIFT-click in the areas it hasn't chosen to add them to the selection. The selection can also be edited with the other selection tools.

**FIGURE 11-5**    This complex selection took only a few seconds with the Magic Wand.

## 80. Incorporate New Skies

You can use "sky replacement surgery" to insert some truly wild blue yonder, replacing a humdrum sky with a brand-new one of your choice.

### Why Would I Want to Change the Sky?

Photographing skies can be problematic. Often they appear uninteresting in a shot, because Mother Nature happened to move in that fog on the day you wanted to shoot, or because the sky was a dull gray overcast. Haze, smoke, or even the time of day can make it difficult for you to get a sky to look interesting or to add to the composition. Skies often appear washed out in a shot because the exposure was set to capture the foreground detail, which overexposed the sky. It is a shame to throw out a perfectly good photo because the sky doesn't look appealing. Image editing can let you create a replacement sky in your photo and possibly rescue it from the scrap bin. You can see an example of changing the sky in Figure 11-6.

FIGURE 11-6    The new sky on the right matches the excitement and dynamics
of the event.

## How Do I Insert a New Sky?

Before you can insert good skies into blasé photos, you need to capture some good
sky shots and store them into a "library of skies" to act as replacements. You can
shoot interesting skies when the atmosphere is clear and the clouds are dynamic.
Photograph clouds, moods, and colors that come with storms, sunsets, sunrises,
and other interesting times at their optimum. Collect lots of sky photos so that you
can easily match the direction of light on the landscape with the direction of light
in the sky. If the two don't match, try horizontally flipping the sky shot.

Here's how to replace one sky with another:

1.  Open the image you want to correct.

2.  Choose the Magic Wand tool from the Toolbox.

3.  From the Options bar, set the Tolerance level to 33 and adjust it as necessary.
    Raise the Tolerance value to increase the range of selection, and lower it to
    reduce the range. Try to choose a midrange value so the Magic Wand has
    the greatest latitude to capture the range of color above and below the
    reference pixel you selected. To do this accurately, you might want to use
    the Magnifying tool to see the pixels more clearly. Deselect Contiguous if
    the sky colors are not all adjacent.

4.  Click the Magic Wand tool in the sky area. The marching ants boundary
    appears, indicating the areas the Magic Wand selected. If the selection is
    not satisfactory, adjust the settings and try again. If no settings get it just
    right, it may be necessary to take the best one and then adjust it with one

of the selection tools (see the previous tip in this chapter for more about refining Magic Wand selections).

5. Choose Select | Feather and the dialog box appears. Set the Feather value to 5 to soften the edges of selection and help the new sky blend in. Adjust the Feather value as necessary.

6. Create a new layer by clicking on the New Layer icon at the bottom of the Layers Palette.

7. Open a new document with the image of a sky you want to use as a replacement.

8. Choose Select | Select All.

9. Choose Edit | Copy to place the new sky on the Clipboard.

10. Return to the original document. Make sure you are on the new blank layer you created. Choose Edit | Paste Into. This will place a copy of the replacement sky within the bounds of the selection. You can use the Move tool to move the replacement sky selection around and use the transformation handles to resize it to fit the area. The Magic Wand selection now acts as a mask, allowing only the new sky to show through where your original selection was made.

## 81. Add Texture to Your Photos

Virtual textures are achieved by creating patterns of lights and darks that are perceived by your eye as a pattern of texture. When you apply a texture over an image, you are superimposing or compositing the light and dark patterns into the image, giving it the appearance of texture. It is basically an illusion. Of course, if you want real texture, you can always have prints made on textured papers—such as artist's canvas or watercolor paper.

### Why Add Texture to a Photo?

Applying textural effects to your photographs can add visual interest and can also help blend components in a composite by providing a visual knitting of sorts. By adding a texture to areas of the photo, you can accentuate surfaces, such as stone, wood, or leather. This can take the form of enhancing a texture that is already there or adding a new one over an existing surface.

Photography is an exercise in illusion: you take a two-dimensional image and attempt to make the viewer believe it is really three-dimensional. Manipulating the rendering of light on form creates this illusion. The more of that illusion you add to the photograph, the more powerful the delineation and the more focused it becomes. Therefore, the photograph has more visual impact. Texture is key to defining the type of surfaces we are viewing. It is the visual cue the brain uses to say this is skin, or sand, or smooth silk. The textural quality of your photo can have a significant impact on the viewer's senses.

## How Do I Create and Add Texture?

The easiest method for adding texture involves using the Unsharp Mask Filter (see Tip 69 in Chapter 10 for more about sharpening) to accentuate the detail at the edges in the picture. This works best for hard-edge textures such as the chipping paint shown in Figure 11-7.

A second method involves superimposing textured patterns over existing areas of the image. This is accomplished with texture filters found in the Filter menu. A number of texture filters are available. In the example shown in Figure 11-8, the Craquelure Filter was used over the entire image to enhance the surface details and add a cracked look to the gourds. The Texturizer Filter lets you choose a number of preset textures, such as canvas, sandstone, brick, and burlap. You can also add your own textures, which you can load from any PSD file.

**FIGURE 11-7**    The image on the right shows the result of sharpening the details to accentuate the textural qualities.

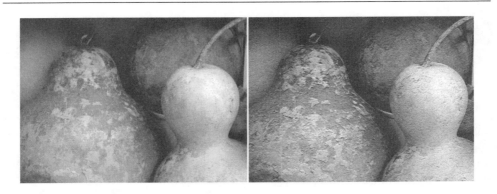

**FIGURE 11-8**    The original image (left) and the gourds with the Craquelure Filter applied (right)

If you want create a texture of your own to use in the Texturizer, you can create it in a separate document and save it as a PSD file. Keep the file size under 500×500 pixels for best performance. Keep in mind that textures need a fair amount of contrast (lights and darks) to work well and color is really not important. In fact, removing the color will help you adjust the contrast for the best result. You want a complete range from black to white.

NOTE     *You can create a whole library of textures by photographing real-life textures in macro mode and then editing them in Photoshop Elements to dramatize sharpness and contrast.*

When you open the Texturizer dialog box, choose Load Texture from the drop-down menu. Find the PSD file you saved, and load it. You will see the effect of your texture in the preview. Adjust the amount, the relief, and the direction of the light source to fine-tune it.

## 82. Match Grain

In conventional photography, the *grain* of film has to do with the fineness of the chemical particles that make up the color. When the negative is enlarged enough, you can actually see the particles, which give the picture a *grainy* look. With digital photographs, the graininess comes from noise ("visual static") in the circuits of the camera. The noise adds a color fluctuation that brands the file with a grain signature.

### Why Do Grains Need to Match?

As you combine images and transform them with various tools, it is possible to come up with mismatches in grain. This occurs because as you alter areas of the image, you are stretching and smoothing the pixels and therefore changing the noise patterns. Because your eyes and brain are exceptional at recognizing patterns, these mismatches are very apparent. You want your changes to blend back into the image seamlessly, so you need to adjust the grain to camouflage the differences.

## How Do I Go About Matching Grains?

The best tool for unifying textural mismatches is the Noise Filter. Although a Grain Filter is also available, this tool's results aren't as good as those of the Noise Filter, most of the time. You can try both filters and use the filter that works best for your situation.

Here's how to adjust the grain of a component to blend better into the original:

1. From the Layers Palette, make active the layer of the component you want to adjust.

2. Choose Filter | Noise | Add Noise. The Add Noise dialog box will appear, as shown in Figure 11-9.

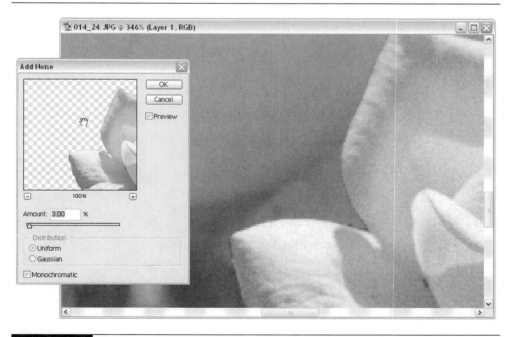

**FIGURE 11-9**    In the Add Noise dialog box, you can add noise to the rose in the foreground to make the textures match with the one behind.

**3.** Adjust the Amount slider to increase or decrease the amount of noise. Click the Uniform option to keep the distribution of noise constant over the area of effect. Click Gaussian to produce a high-contrast noise effect, and Monochrome will match the noise to the hue of the underlying pixels. With Monochrome turned off, you can produce RGB artifacts similar to the noise actually produced by the camera. Experiment with the setting until you get a good match to the original.

# Chapter 12

## Special Effects

This chapter is dedicated to some special techniques that take photographs beyond the everyday kind. You will learn how to add drama with lighting, blend photos to come up with unique looks, and even create your own weather effects. Special effects are fun to experiment with and easy to create.

## 83. Create Lighting Effects

Lighting effects are software routines that change the focus, quality, color, intensity, or spread of the lighting in the picture. You can accomplish these effects using filters or blends, or by hand painting your photos.

### Why Would I Want to Create Lighting Effects?

Each type of lighting has its own unique look. Many professional photographers search for or create unusual lighting that will accent the subject of a photo shoot. The type and quality of the lighting can make or break a photograph in many instances.

Because perfect lighting isn't always available when the subject matter presents itself to be photographed, you can use image-editing software to add special lighting effects after the photo is taken. This opens up a wealth of creative opportunities, such as adding a soft spotlight to a portrait that guides the viewer's attention to a particular area of the picture, or changing the time of day. You can even change the season of a shot by altering the light to indicate a particular effect—create a cold look for winter or a warm look for summer. Lighting effects can add a sense of mood and drama to your photos.

### How Do I Create Lighting Effects?

The Lighting Effects Filter is the most basic and easy-to-use tool in your image-editing tool kit. The filter allows you to create spot, directional, and flood lighting while controlling ambient (general) lighting at the same time. In Figure 12-1, I used a spotlight to focus a soft glow on the subject while darkening the general lighting to provide contrast.

To apply a lighting effect, choose Filter | Render | Lighting Effects to open the Lighting Effects dialog box shown in Figure 12-2.

In this dialog box, you'll see a circle and a radius line over the preview of your photo. The circle indicates the maximum diameter of the light and the radius line indicates the direction the light is shining. It is best to try and match the direction of the light to the existing light source, because the program needs to use the lights and darks to create the pseudo-lighting effect.

**FIGURE 12-1**    The Lighting Effects Filter can produce dramatic results as you can see with this before (left) and after.

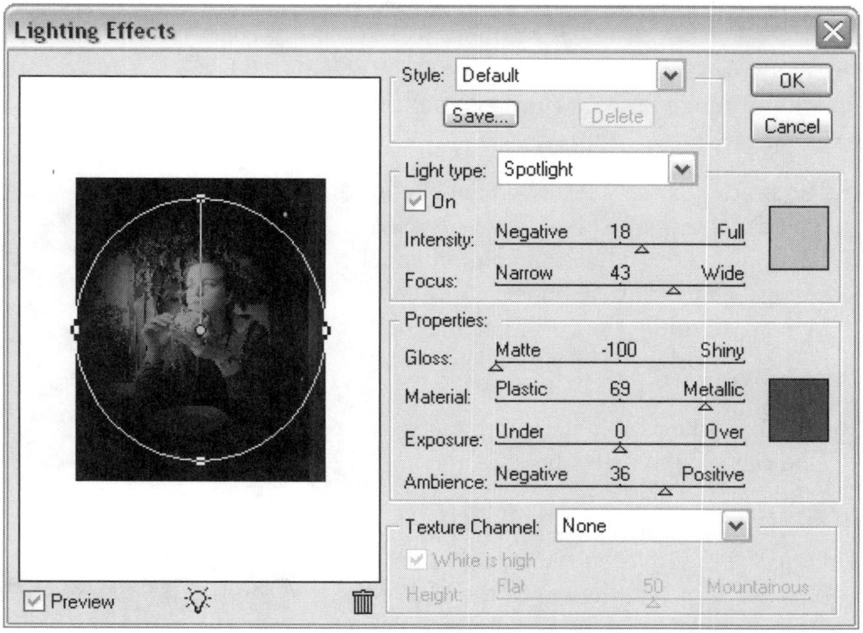

**FIGURE 12-2**    The Lighting Effects dialog box

The dialog box also includes the following features:

- In the Style drop-down menu, you can choose from a number of preset lighting configurations. You can modify the settings after you choose a preset and save the setting you like as a new item.

- Choose the light type from the Light Type drop-down menu: Spotlight, Directional, or Omni. Spotlight is focused lighting, Directional is flood lighting that has a light source, and Omni is similar to diffuse sunlight and doesn't have a strong directional component.

- You can also adjust ambient lighting by using the Ambience slider in the Properties section near the bottom of the Lighting Effects dialog box. (Ambient refers to general atmospheric, or overall, lighting.)

- You can set other lighting effects as well: Intensity affects the general brightness of the light, much like a dimmer switch. Focus works only for the spotlight and controls the area of illumination.

- Back at the Properties section, the first two sliders (Gloss and Material) control the relationship between highlights and shadows to make objects look shiny or flat. Exposure is another way to control the intensity of the light.

- The two colored squares on the right of the dialog box are used to set the color of the main light (top) and the ambient light. Click a square and the Color Picker will appear.

- The bottom is the Texture Channel control. You can use this to create an embossed effect based on individual color channel values. The Texture Channel drop-down menu determines the color channel that will be texturized. The slider determines the depth of the texture. Check the White Is High box to make lighter areas appear raised. You can see this effect here:

- Finally, you can add multiple lights by dragging the light bulb icon onto the preview screen at the left of the dialog box. You can set the parameters separately for each light. To remove a light, drag the center handle to the trash can.

## 84. Use Blend Modes for a Million Special Effects

Blend modes are one of the more powerful capabilities of Photoshop 7 and Photoshop Elements. Blend modes cause layers to interact and combine using mathematical formulas to create a variety of effects. These modes measure the differences between the layers in terms of color and luminosity and apply that information to the formulas.

The blend modes cause the layers to blend together in unique ways. You can darken, lighten, burn, dodge, create lighting effects, and also change hue, color, and intensity—to name a few. The results can sometimes be quite amazing and unpredictable.

Blend modes demand that you experiment with them, because no two combinations will produce the same results. The complex ways that they interact can produce millions of effects, partly because you can stack them up and have them cascade their effects through multiple layers. You can also combine blends with textures, gradients, and fills, giving you an even greater range. And if that's not enough, you can paint with blend modes, too.

You can find blend modes in the Mode menu in the Layers Palette and on the Options bar of the Paint tools.

### Why Are Blend Modes So Powerful?

Blend modes can be used to change an image in radical ways. You can create interesting effects simply by placing images on multiple layers and selecting various blend modes for each layer. The greater the diversity in the images you choose to blend together, the greater the impact of the effect. Blend modes thrive on the differences between the images used, so don't be afraid to try combinations

### Try This:    Using Blend Modes with Fill Layers

One of the more powerful things you can do with blend modes is use them in conjunction with fill layers. If you choose Layer | New Fill Layer you'll get a submenu asking if you want the fill layer to be solid color, gradient, or pattern. Choosing one of these opens a dialog box that lets you set options for that type of fill (such as which color, gradient, or pattern you want to use and which variables you want to apply to them). As soon as you click OK, a layer that has been filled as prescribed appears immediately above the currently selected layer. You can then apply blend modes to this filled layer for an infinite variety of interesting effects.

that are a bit extreme. When you apply blend modes to multiple layers, the effects combine to increase the range of effects. The more layers you add, the more complex the mode interaction. General descriptions for each blend mode are in the help section in Photoshop Elements, but you will gain a greater understanding of this feature by loading the images and trying them out.

## How Do I Use Blend Modes?

In Figure 12-3, I took a photograph of an iris and changed it into a soft outlined watercolor using blend modes and a few other tricks. This example gives you some idea of how you can use blend modes to create effects. This effect took only a few minutes to complete.

Here is how this is done:

1. Duplicate the background image twice and select the third layer.

2. Choose Filter | Stylize | Glowing Edges. Adjust the setting to get a nice, clean edge.

3. Choose Image | Adjustments | Invert to make the lines dark and the background light.

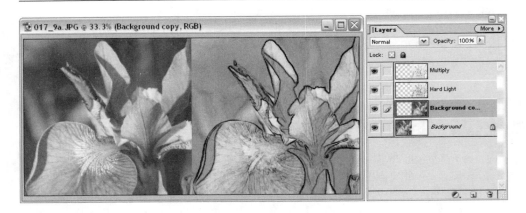

**FIGURE 12-3**    The iris on the left is transformed into a more artful image on the right with the use of blend modes.

> ## Try This: View a Blend Mode Slideshow
>
> Place two different images on separate layers. Select the top layer. Make sure you have dragged the Layers Palette out of the Palette well. Then you can press SHIFT-+ (plus sign) to cycle through all the blend modes and see how they affect the image.

4. Choose Enhance | Adjust Color | Remove Color so the outline is in grayscale.

5. From the Layers Palette Blend mode menu, choose Multiply. This will superimpose the dark outlines on the layer below.

6. Select the second layer.

7. From the Layers Palette Blend mode menu, choose Hard Light. Enter 50% in the Opacity field. The Hard Light blend mode uses a strong light effect to lighten the background image, while the lower opacity reduces the intensity of the effect.

The combination of the three layers gives the result shown in Figure 12-3.

## 85. Make Your Own Weather

Bet you didn't know that your desktop computer had a built-in weather generator. Your image editor can add some pretty wild weather effects to your photographs—rain, snow, fog, stormy clouds, and even lightning.

### Why Would I Want to Add Weather Effects?

Weather special effects add a sense of mood and/or season, and they can make an image much more dramatic and interesting. Weather is dynamic and instills the photo with energy. It can give the viewer a sense of motion and a sense of the environment. Interesting weather is not always there when you are, so you can use special effects to make it happen when you want it, and you don't even have to get your camera wet.

## How Do I Create Weather Effects and Add Them to My Images?

In Figure 12-4, you can see the same image with two distinct weather effects: lightning and snow. I wish I could show every weather effect available, but describing the snow effect will probably give you a pretty good idea of how to create a rain effect.

**NOTE**  *The lightning effect in Figure 12-4 was accomplished by painting the white by hand with a simple brush and then creating a layer underneath so I could paint in a blue glow, to give the photo that electric look.*

Here's how to create the snow effect:

1. Load an image that would look good with a little snow. Remember snow falls during a storm, so you should use a photo with cloud cover and a dark environment. And don't forget that you're going to create a winter scene, so no flowers should be in bloom or trees in leaf.

**FIGURE 12-4**    Two weather effects on the same scene

**2.** The production of snow is a layered effect, so create three new layers. The first layer will be the smaller background snow, the second the middle-sized snow, and the last the foreground snowflakes. Each layer will show successively larger and more spread-apart snowflakes to maintain the perspective so that you get a sense of depth as you would in reality.

**3.** From the Toolbox, choose the Paintbrush tool. Set the size at 2. Set the brush dynamics to Space: Maximum, Scatter: Maximum, Hardness: Maximum, and Jitter: 50%.

**4.** Set the foreground color to white and the background color to a very light blue. The Jitter control will oscillate the colors between the foreground and background as you paint. This makes the snow look more natural. Reduce the layer transparency to 50%.

**5.** Go to the next layer and enlarge the brush and continue to add flakes. Do the same with the third layer. You can use the Diffuse Filter, by choosing Filter | Stylize | Diffuse, to give the flakes a softer appearance.

NOTE *You can create rain with almost exactly the same procedure except that raindrops would be transparent, smaller, and more elongated than snowflakes. They also tend to have a highlight where light reflects off the shiny drop. Of course, you can make it rain harder or lighter by increasing/decreasing the density and blur in the drops.*

## 86. Combine Hand-Drawn Art with Photos

Hand-drawn art can be accomplished in two ways: the traditional way, by using pencil or paint on paper and then scanning the image into the computer; or the digital way, by using the drawing and painting tools provided in your image editor or paint program to create original works of digital art. Either one of these methods can be combined with a digital photograph to create an interesting effect.

### Why Would I Want to Combine Art and Photos?

As you have certainly learned by now, digital photography is about moving beyond conventional boundaries and exploring whole new ways of creating photographic images. So the answer to this question is, why not? This could range from something as simple as a hand-scribbled annotation to the sophisticated world of digital *photopainting*. There is really that much latitude.

## How Do I Combine Hand-Drawn Art with Digital Photos?

Combining digital photos and hand-drawn art is best accomplished by using layers and composite techniques. Most typically, the photograph is placed on a background layer and the drawing is done on a transparent layer above the photo. If you lower the drawing layer's opacity, you can still see the photo beneath even if you're using opaque paints. This is much like what animation artists do when creating cartoons. You could call this a "drawing-over technique"—in the animation industry it's called "onion-skinning" because onion-skin tracing paper is placed over the most recent frame of the cartoon. This allows the animator to properly position the elements in the next frame so that they will appear to move in the right degree and in the right direction.

In Figure 12-5, the tree was stylized from a photograph using the Threshold command and Sketch filters. The bird was drawn in by hand using the Paintbrush tool. This shows a simple, straightforward way to combine these two images.

**FIGURE 12-5**    The hand-drawn bird adds a nice touch to the bare trees.

Another way to merge hand-drawn art with photos is to paint or draw digitally onto the photograph itself. This takes you into the world of photopainting. If you are ambitious, this kind of art can let you explore your creativity. As you can see in Figure 12-6, you can take the level of sophistication as far as you want. These images were created using a paint program. The still-life photograph was painted over with digital brushes that have the ability to move color around like a physical brush.

## 87. Combine Vector Art and Text with Photos

The key to understanding vector art is to think of it as outlined shapes. *Vector* art uses mathematics to define shapes by way of straight lines and curves. If you want to transform these shapes, you can let the mathematics reformulate the shape. Vector art is primarily used for clipart and text, because vectors make it possible to size these shapes without any degradation of edge detail. Vector art can be filled with color, gradients, and patterns, but it cannot easily render the kind of complex interior detail found in photographs. For that you need the power of individual pixels, accomplished through *raster* art. You can combine vector art and raster art by placing them on separate layers. When the layers are combined, the vector art must be converted to raster art.

**FIGURE 12-6**   This still life demonstrates what can be accomplished by combining hand-drawn techniques with photographs. The detail on the right gives a closer look at the digital brushwork.

NOTE *Encapsulated PostScript (EPS) is a format that allows vector and raster art to reside in the same file and gets converted to pixels at the time of printing. This allows vector art detail to be maximized for the resolution of the printer.*

## Why Would I Want to Combine Vector Art and Text?

Shapes and text maintain a higher quality when you create them as vector art. Keeping them in vector format maximizes their visual impact at the time they are printed. Photographs maintain more detail when they're created with the individual pixels of raster art. By combining the two forms, you get the highest possible quality—the best of both worlds. Anytime you add text to your image, you are adding vector art. A good portion of clipart in the form of shapes is also vector art. This is useful for captioning and annotating, and for greeting cards, brochures, and more.

## How Do I Combine Vector Art with Digital Photos?

Photoshop Elements offers two ways to add vector art: via the Text tool or the Shape tool. To add clipart and text to a photograph, you will use layers to create the separate elements.

Figure 12-7 shows the results of combining text, shapes, and a photo to create an interesting greeting card image. The photograph used in this example is the background image, and the vector shapes and text reside in other layers above.

Here's how to add text to a photograph:

1. Open the image.

2. Choose the Text tool from the Toolbox.

3. In the Text Options bar, set font style, size, and color. Choose a color that will stand out against the background photo.

4. Click anywhere in the image to set a start point for the text entry. (Don't worry, because you can resize and reposition it later.) Type in the text, and it will appear on the screen. You can edit the text by clicking with the Text tool anywhere in the text. You can edit a block of text by clicking in the text with the Text tool and then dragging the mouse to select the text.

**FIGURE 12-7**   This greeting card took only a few minutes to create by combining text, shapes, and a photo.

5. If the text is the wrong size, you can enter a larger value in the Options bar. Or you can choose the Move tool, click the text, and then grab one of the bounding box handles and drag it to resize it. Hold down the SHIFT key to keep the resizing proportional.

Here's how to add custom shapes to a photograph:

1. Choose the Shape tool from the Toolbox.

2. From the Options bar, choose the Custom Shape icon, choose a Custom Shape from the Shapes menu, and then set the color.

3. Click and drag in the image window to create the shape. Use the bounding box handles to transform the shape.

NOTE

*If you like, you can easily use text and shapes (both are drawn with vectors) to frame the contents of a photo. Size the photo to fit the current document and place it on the top layer of the document. Then create your shape or text (such as the name of the city). It will appear on a layer immediately above the photo. Choose Layers | Group with Previous. The photo will be hidden except where it shows through the letters or shapes.*

# Part III

# Managing, Publishing, Printing, and Accessorizing

# Chapter 13

# Managing and Publishing Photos on the Web

P ublishing photos to the Web has become a popular activity among photographers. Now that you have taken the first steps into digital photography, you will probably want to partake in this rapidly growing phenomenon. With a few simple tools and some understanding of how to get your photographs in the right format, you can start sending your images across the world in no time. Consider yourself lucky that you are getting into this now, because the tools designed to help have come of age and make Web publishing much easier than it used to be. By the time you finish this chapter, you will be on your way to showing off your photos in style to anyone with a Web connection.

## 88. Optimize Images for the Web

The World Wide Web is commonly referred to as the Internet, or just the Web. The Web is a global network that consists of many computers, called *servers*, that are distributed across the planet. These servers maintain software that allows all computers to communicate and transfer information. Computers with Web access are linked by phone lines, cable, fiber optics, and satellites forming a web of connections—thus the name. Each server has a unique address that identifies it, so it can be located in a matter of seconds. You can purchase your own unique domain name and space on a server from companies that host Web sites. You can use these servers to store and display your images to the Web.

### Why Do I Need to Optimize for the Web?

All of the information displayed on your browser is transferred over electronic connections, such as your phone line. The larger the size of the file containing the information, the longer it takes to display on your system. Everyone knows what it's like to wait while a Web site takes forever to display. To avoid bogging down the system with slow-loading, gigantic files, you can optimize the information being sent to be as small as it can be, while still maintaining quality. You can use compressed data formats to reduce the size of the file and still allow for a decent image to appear.

Images, sound, and movies are some of the most data-intensive types of information you can send over the Web. If you were to send a full-sized digital photo over the Web, it could take more than an hour to display over an average connection speed of a regular modem.

## How Do I Optimize Images for the Web?

Photoshop Elements, as well as other leading programs designed to create Web graphics, includes some automated tools that can help you get your images ready for Web display.

NOTE    *Before you work on an image for use on the Web, be sure you resize it to the size at which it will appear on the Web. Otherwise, operations will be much slower than necessary and your optimization previews will be totally misleading.*

Following are the steps in optimizing a typical digital photo and saving it to a Web-ready format:

1. Open the image that you want to optimize for the Web.

2. Choose File | Save For Web. The Save For Web dialog box appears, as shown in Figure 13-1.

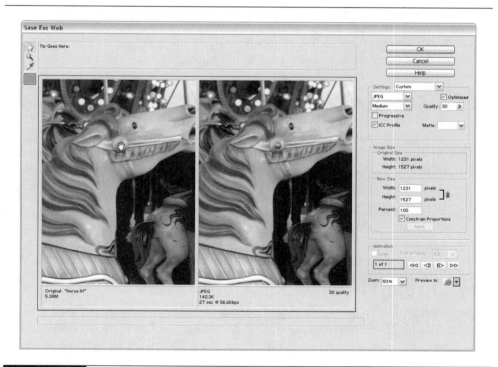

**FIGURE 13-1**    The Save For Web dialog box

Here, you choose how your image will be optimized and what format to use. The preview windows allow you to see before (left) and after images to evaluate the effects of compression and color reduction. In this exercise, you'll learn how to convert a high-resolution TIF photograph into a compressed JPEG file that loads quickly over the Web without losing too much quality. For now, we'll concentrate on the information in the Settings area of this dialog box.

3.  In the Settings area, choose a file format. For this example, because we are optimizing a photo, choose JPEG. (You could choose PNG, but this format is not as widely accepted yet. Photos are best represented in JPEG because it can display the full range of color values. The GIF file format works better for line art that does not use the continuous-tone color transitions that photos rely on for a realistic portrayal of the universe around us.)

4.  Below the file format setting is the quality level setting, which determines how much the file will be compressed. Start by choosing Medium, as this works best for most instances.

5.  Notice the annotation under the right preview, just below the format type (JPEG). This information displays the compressed file size and approximate load time over a 56 Kbps connection. Right-click the preview image to change the modem speed if you want to optimize for slower or faster connections.

6.  Adjust the quality levels until you achieve the optimum quality and load time. The name of the game is to get the lowest file size without overly sacrificing quality. Keep the view in 2-up mode (that is, both preview windows visible) so that you can visually compare the optimized version of the file with the original. You'll instantly know when you've compressed the file too much to give you a level of quality you can accept as adequate to your purposes. When you get to that point, move back up to the next highest level of quality.

7.  When you are satisfied with the optimization, click OK and save the file.

## 89. E-mail Your Photos

E-mail—electronic mail—has become one the most common ways to send messages today. E-mail works through your Internet Service Provider (ISP) and the browser on your computer (plus whatever e-mail software programs you may be using). You can send your correspondence to anyone else in the world who has an e-mail address.

## Why Would I Need to E-mail Photos?

One of the great attractions of e-mail, in addition to it being instantaneous (and not needing postage), is that you can attach many types of files to your message. You can attach image files as well as animation files. (Just be aware that many ISPs have limits on the size of an attachment.) You can send photos with your e-mail, which means that you need to convince all your relatives to get an e-mail account! With the proliferation of fast connections, fast computers, and high-quality printers, using e-mail to distribute images is becoming very practical.

## How Do I Prepare and Send Photos by E-mail?

Sending images by e-mail creates the same challenges you encounter in displaying them on Web sites. E-mail uses the same phone (or cable) lines used by the Web and is limited by the connection speeds of individual systems. If you simply intend to display your image on the recipient's screen, you can optimize the image, as described in the previous tip. If you are sending a file to a print service bureau or publisher, you'll want the resolution to be high. But transferring a high-resolution image can be excruciatingly slow using a standard 56KB modem.

NOTE    *Many e-mail providers place limitations on the file size of attachments. If the file is larger than 1MB, you may need to post it to an FTP connection instead of sending it via e-mail.*

The most popular e-mail programs allow you to send images with electronic messages in two ways: you can attach the file to the e-mail or you can insert the file in the body of the e-mail (as shown in Figure 13-2). If you attach the image, only its file name is displayed. To open or save the attachment, the recipient must usually double-click the file name. When you insert the file in the body of the e-mail, the image displays when the recipient opens the e-mail. You use an Attach button or Insert menu commands to perform these operations, depending on the e-mail software you are using.

Photoshop Elements has a convenient automated e-mail attachment program that can be accessed from the File menu. It prompts you to maintain the current size or automatically optimize.

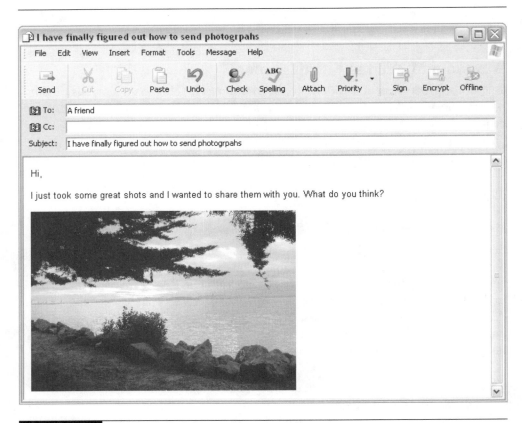

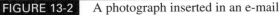

**FIGURE 13-2**    A photograph inserted in an e-mail

## 90. Turn Still Photos into Web Animation

Web animation is created in a file format called Graphics Interchange Format (GIF). Using GIF, you can stack multiple images of the same size into one file to display them sequentially in a browser—banner ads on Web pages commonly make use of animated GIF files. Because GIF files display a maximum of 256 colors, the images need to be converted from the format the camera produces. (This is discussed shortly.)

## Why Would I Use Photos to Create Animation for the Web?

Digital cameras can capture time sequences of motion (see Tips 18 and 19 in Chapter 3) that can be displayed in an animated GIF format. You can adjust the time interval between the display of each frame in a GIF file if you're going for a slideshow look rather than a movie-type animation. You can present your images in any sequence, to make them instructive, provocative, or just for fun.

## How Do I Take a Series of Photos and Create an Animation?

The tools for creating GIF animations are also included in the Save For Web dialog box (shown earlier in this chapter in Figure 13-1). Photoshop Elements makes setting up GIF animation easy by using the Layers Palette as a staging area. Each layer becomes an animation cell.

1. Start with a number of images stacked on separate layers. For best results, they should have the same dimensions.

2. Organize your layers so that the first image you want displayed is on the bottom and the last image is on the top.

3. Preview the transition between any two frames by making the upper frame invisible and then visible again.

NOTE   *If you are adding hand-drawn aspects, you can use the opacity value to make the upper layer partially transparent so you can see its relationship to the lower frame.*

4. After you have set up the layers, choose File | Save For Web (see Figure 13-3). This time, we will focus on the Settings and Animation sections.

5. Choose the GIF file format under Settings. Set the color quality to Adaptive. This causes Elements to choose the best 256 colors for display based on the original colors of the images.

6. While in the GIF optimization dialog, from the Dither drop-down menu, choose Diffusion (100 percent). Dithers create color patterns to simulate colors that are not available. Diffusion works best with photographic images. Select 256 from the Colors drop-down menu. This will let the file be optimized with the maximum amount of colors available for a GIF file.

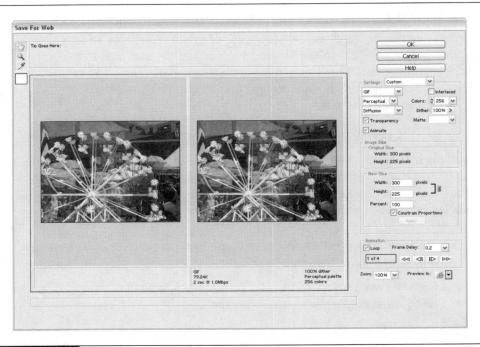

**FIGURE 13-3**    The Save for Web dialog box with GIF animation options

7. Check the Animate option in the Settings area, which becomes available only after you choose the GIF format. This will enable the Animation section at the bottom of the dialog box. You use these controls to set up the parameters for the animation.

8. Advance through each frame of the animation and make sure it is correct. Use the Frame Delay setting to control the time interval between frames.

9. If you want the animation to play continuously, check the Loop option.

10. Preview the animation in your browser.

11. When you are satisfied, click OK and save the file.

NOTE    *When you stack images in a GIF animation file, the size of the file grows accordingly. It's good practice to make GIF animations small in size or they may not load or play properly on the Web. Banner ads are a fairly typical measure of the maximum size of a GIF animation.*

## 91. Make an Instant Web Portfolio with Elements

You've set up your new Web site, and you're wondering how to get your photos displayed on the site in a good interactive fashion. Now that you know how to optimize your photos, you will learn how to get them onto a Web page by creating a Web *portfolio*. A portfolio provides you with a thumbnail menu of all your works. When you click a thumbnail, you see an enlarged version of that photo (or any other scanned artwork you care to display).

Photoshop Elements, and other software programs, provide automated routines that make putting together portfolios (or scrapbooks or catalogs) for the Web as simple as a few clicks. All the code, thumbnails, and images are placed automatically after you specify the style template, image and text sizes, and other options that seem most suited to your purpose. Photoshop Elements and many other programs come with style templates that provide a variety of theme interfaces.

### Why Should I Use a Portfolio?

Creating from scratch an interactive album or portfolio on Web pages is a laborious job, and updating it is difficult, too. Unless you really need a custom design, you can use automated software to put together a decent portfolio. Not only does it take time and resources to learn to do your own Web page production, but you also need specialized software to develop Web pages. Another big plus with automated portfolios is that updating is a breeze. This will encourage you to post your work more often.

### How Do I Create a Web Portfolio?

Photoshop Elements provides a nice routine for portfolio development called the Web Photo Gallery.

You will be surprised at how much work this program does in a short period of time. Building a Web portfolio from scratch can take you hours—or even days. Building such a portfolio in one of the programs that does it automatically takes only a few minutes ... maybe half an hour, if you're really a picky person.

NOTE

*As soon as you create a portfolio in Photoshop Elements, you can see, read, and modify the HTML that makes up the page. If you already have even a cursory knowledge of HTML, you can then do anything you'd like to modify the portfolio and can easily change the backgrounds, headline banners, and other styling touches to make it your own.*

1. Create a new folder in your operating system's Explorer or Finder and give it a name that reminds you of its purpose (for example, Web Portfolio Images). Place all of the images you want to use in this specific portfolio into that folder. There is no need to resize or optimize these images—Photoshop Elements automatically does all that tedium for you.

2. Choose File | Create Web Photo Gallery to open the Web Photo Gallery dialog box shown in Figure 13-4.

3. Choose a style from the drop-down menu at the top of the dialog box. A thumbnail of the style will appear in the preview window on the right.

4. In the Folders area, click the Browse button and navigate to the source folder in which you placed all your images.

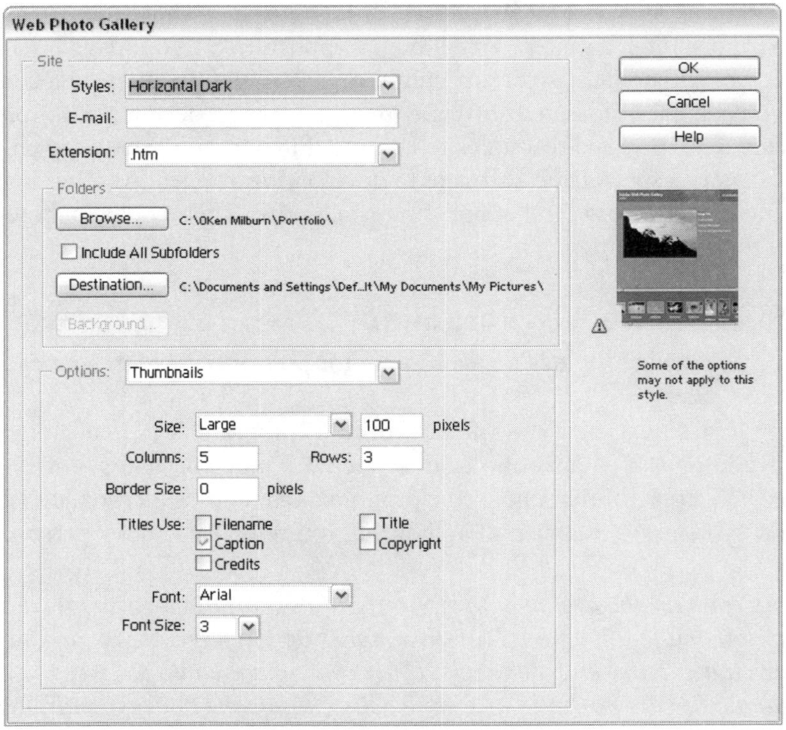

**FIGURE 13-4**    The Web Photo Gallery dialog box

5.  Click Destination to select the path and folder where all the Web files will be stored. The program will then create a number of subfolders in which to store the different categories of files it has created for the portfolio site: large images, thumbnails, and Web pages. This makes it easy to find and modify them once the site has been generated.

6.  In the Options area of the Web Photo Gallery dialog, you will find a pull-down menu that will bring up separate options dialogs for each of the following: Banner, Large Images, Thumbnails, Custom Colors, and Security. The banner (should you choose to use one) is the heading you want to appear on all your gallery pages. Large images are the images that display after you click the thumbnails. You can set their size, optimization, and captions. Thumbnails are the small images that help the viewer of the portfolio navigate to the larger images. You can set their size and location (top, bottom, or side of the page—or on a separate Web page as a "contact sheet"). Vertical row or column thumbnail styles will automatically scroll the thumbnails if there are more of them than will fit on one screen. The Custom Colors option sets the colors of the text and hyperlinks. Security defines the information you want listed with the images, such as copyright and credits.

7.  When you are through setting the parameters, click OK.

8.  The program opens, optimizes, and saves each image in sequence. The program is also creating Web pages, thumbnails, and all the code to make the gallery function on the Web. Figure 13-5 shows the finished Web gallery page.

9.  Copy the file directory structure on your Web host server, and your gallery is ready for prime time. Contact your Web hosting service for specific instructions about uploading your files.

## 92. Caption and Frame Web Photos

*Captioning* is the process of placing a title or descriptive text next to the photograph or inside a border. *Framing* is the process of applying a decorative border to an image. You can create many types of frames by hand, or you can use some of the automated features for framing images found on the Layer Styles Palette.

**FIGURE 13-5** The completed Web gallery page

## Why Would I Want to Frame and Caption Images?

Framing a digital image is much like framing a piece of art. It provides a visual separation from the background environment and keeps the viewer's focus within the work. If the background color for your Web page is similar to that of your photographs, a frame will help set off your pictures. Borders, such as torn edges, can also add a stylized look to the image.

Captions are used mostly to provide information to the viewer. Captions can provide the file name, photo title, artist name, copyright, date, size, price, type of camera, settings, a description of where or how the shot was taken, identities of the people in the shot, personal thoughts, and pretty much any information you want to convey.

## How Do I Frame and Caption Web Photos?

Captions are applied with the Text tool in the Toolbox (see Tip 87 in Chapter 12). As you can see in Figure 13-6, text can be applied in a number of different ways and in different positions.

**FIGURE 13-6**    Photograph with stylized border and a number of caption types

Here's how to apply text to a caption:

1. Choose the Text tool from the Toolbox and click anywhere in the image to start typing the text. Type in the text.

2. Adjust the text style, color, and size in the Options bar. You can also move the text by dragging it to another part of the page.

Here's how to apply the annotation circle and line:

1. From the Toolbox, choose the Elliptical Marquee tool. Hold down the SHIFT key while making the selection to draw a perfect circle.

2. Choose the Pencil tool from the Toolbox. Hold down the SHIFT key while drawing the line to constrain it to a horizontal line.

3. Choose Edit | Stroke. The Stroke dialog box will appear. Set the width at 5 pixels and the color to white (or whatever color shows distinctly over your image). Location should be Center, blend mode Normal, and Opacity 100%.

Here's how to apply the black border:

1. Choose Image | Resize | Canvas Size. The Canvas Size dialog box will appear. Select the Relative option.

2. Type **200** in both the Width and Height fields. This will create a black border of 100 pixels wide on all sides.

Here's how to apply the frame:

1. From the Palette well, open the Effects Palette. Make sure All is selected in the drop-down menu.

2. Find the Brushed Aluminum effect. Drag it over the image. The program will run through a few automated routines and then apply the frame.

## Try This: Captioning for Copy Protection

If you are concerned about people downloading your photographs and making copies without your permission, you can use captioning to prevent that. You can superimpose translucent copyright text over part of the image, which will discourage unauthorized use. It is not the most elegant solution, but it can help to discourage image piracy. There are also numerous watermarking programs sold for this purpose. Watermarks can be embedded invisibly and can be extracted even from images that have been cropped and edited.

# Chapter 14

## Printing Pictures that Look Good and Last

Now that you know how to get images into the camera, onto memory cards, out of the camera, onto your computer, and up on the Web, you need to learn some important issues about printing a digital image. One of the most significant changes to the digital imaging world is the advent of high-resolution color printing that can produce photo-quality output at an affordable price. These new printers give you a much higher degree of control over how, when, and where your prints are created. The world of digital printing is continuing to change dramatically and getting better all the time. Finally, the creation of photographs is totally in your hands.

## 93. Choose the Right Printer, Paper, and Ink

The plethora of printers, paper types, and ink types you'll find available at an office supply store or computer discount retailer can be daunting. When you're looking at a bank of 20 printers for sale, it might seem impossible to choose the right one without taking it home and trying it out. Short of that, you'll do yourself a favor by reading up on the various types of printers that are out there today to find out what services they offer and how they might fit your needs. The following information provides a primer to help you start out in the right direction.

### What Kinds of Printers Are Available?

A number of printer technologies can be used to produce digital prints: inkjet, thermal-wax transfer, dye sublimation, laser, and film recorder printers. These are described in the following sections.

Of all these choices, the inkjet stands out as the most practical choice for the average photographer who wants to print photos. Desktop inkjet printers have moved to the forefront as the printer of choice, and for good reason. Inkjet printers deliver excellent quality and ease of use for an exceptionally low price. With the advances in inkjet technology, the prints can rival the quality of conventional photographic prints. The high cost of supplies has been an issue, but the proliferation of other manufacturers of paper and ink continues to bring prices down.

**Inkjet Printers**     Inkjets are inexpensive and versatile, and they produce good-quality prints. Inkjets spray a dithered pattern of microscopic ink dots on the paper to produce a printed image. They can print on a variety of materials, such as art papers, canvases, T-shirts, and ceramic transfer materials—even mouse pads. Inkjet printers are the leading printers used by consumers at this writing.

NOTE     *Inkjet printers, thanks to a great deal of pioneering work by Epson (and more recently Canon and Hewlett-Packard), have begun to be capable of producing prints of both long life (surpassing a type-C photographic print) and archival quality. If you plan on exhibiting and selling your digital photographs, it is imperative that you use such a printer. Ordinary inkjet prints will last for only a few months to a year.*

**Thermal-Wax Printers**   These high-quality printers transfer wax-based ink onto specially treated paper. They are used for photographic proofing and technical printing. Thermal printers are a bit more expensive than inkjets, and supplies are not as readily available. In general, they can match the quality of inkjet, but they are not as versatile.

**Dye Sublimation Printers**   These printers are capable of producing prints that are nearly indistinguishable from photographic prints, and they have a comparable life span. They produce rich color with no perceptible grain and are limited to tabloid and smaller print sizes. Used by professionals for color proofing, these printers and supplies are relatively expensive. This technology is used in a number of snapshot printers, but the cost per print is higher than standard photo prints.

**Laser Printers**   Laser printers are mostly used for high-speed, high-resolution, black-and-white printing. Color laser technology is very expensive and does not match the quality of any of the other print technologies.

**Film Recorders**   Film recorders transfer digital images to either positive or negative photographic film at very high resolutions. The slides are used for slideshows and the negatives can be printed by conventional means. Film recorders are commonly used for business graphics and cinematic frames.

## Why Do I Need to Use Special Paper and Ink?

The quality and type of paper you use to print your images can make a world of difference, sometimes more than the printer itself does. Photo-quality, coated printing paper can be purchased at most office supply and photography stores. On some photo-quality inkjet printers, if you use regular paper to print your photographs, you'll get a soggy print without a lot of definition.

Inks, like paper, are not all created equal. Using quality, well-tested inks is also important to the performance of your printer.

**Special Paper**   Printer paper comes in all shapes, sizes, and types. You should use paper that has been specially treated for photographic printing on an inkjet printer. Look for papers that are clearly labeled for use with inkjet printers.

The surface quality, density, and texture of the paper determine how the ink takes to the surface. Whiteness, resistance to moisture distortion, and longevity are also important considerations. Thicker papers and papers with more rag content (the amount of cloth versus wood pulp content in the paper) will take large amounts of ink without distorting or wrinkling. Some papers are absorbent, which diffuses the color, while others keep the ink on the surface to allow for crisper detail. Each paper will affect how the color looks and can change the actual color of the print, often drastically.

If you are printing text and simple graphics, you can use a less expensive paper, because the demands on the coverage of ink are much less. On the other hand, if you are printing larger, complex color images like photographs, you will need paper that is stable (acid free), that is coated so that it can hold the minute detail, and that is white enough to provide clear, saturated color. You can get that kind of quality only by using the more expensive papers that are designed expressly for printing photographs.

**Special Ink**    Inkjet printers can use a number of types of inks, depending on your intended final product. Dye-based inks (most common because of their ability to produce a wider range of brightness) are chemically derived, pigment-based inks that use natural pigments like artist paints (longest lasting, but compatible only with very specific printers), and hybrid inks that combine both and are compatible with a somewhat wider range of printers. Hybrid inks are the latest generation of inks and are designed to optimize printer performance while also offering permanent color. (See Tip 97 later in this chapter for more on archival inks.)

The print head nozzle openings in an inkjet printer are microscopically small, so the ink needs to be very refined to pass through without clogging the nozzles. Color concentration and accuracy are also important to the color quality of the final print. You want ink that is going to be consistent from one cartridge to another. The final color result is always going to be a combination of the inks and the paper you print on. Each printer manufacturer calibrates its printers to a particular ink standard, so you need to use ink that is approved for use with your printer.

NOTE    *Inkjet printers use a variety of ink cartridges that can change with every brand and model. You must use the appropriate type of cartridge for your printer, so make sure you have printer model and/or cartridge model number handy when you want to purchase new ink cartridges.*

## How Do I Select the Right Papers?

Selecting the right paper can be a confusing task if you don't know what you need and what's available. When in doubt, carefully read the manufacturer's recommendations included in your printer's manual. Also, be aware that changing papers requires a change in printer profiles if you expect to maintain color accuracy. When you find a paper you like, stick with it so you won't have to adjust your print settings each time you use a new brand of paper.

Papers come in varying textures and thickness. The thickness of paper is often stated in pounds. This term comes from how much a ream (500 sheets) of paper weighs. You'll find a paper weight number on the package. One might guess that the higher the number, the thicker the paper will be. However, the density of the paper stock plays as much a factor as its thickness, so different types of paper can give the same weight rating even though the thickness varies. The best bet is to ask the paper vendor to let you test a sample if you are unsure.

Following are some general categories you can use as guidelines when looking for the right paper for your printing needs.

**Plain Paper**    This is the standard type of paper you would use in any copier or fax. It is not treated in any special way for inkjet printing and absorbs ink at a fairly high rate, so it will wrinkle (and get soggy) if you print large, solid areas of color. Even if you're only printing text, the edges of the type will be fuzzy. When you set your printer parameters, choosing plain paper will cut back on the ink flow to help compensate. Plain paper will not produce quality color printing and should be used only for proofing text and simple line graphics printing.

**Coated Paper**    Coated paper is designed to work with inkjet printers. If it says "inkjet paper" on the package, you know that it is coated with a special kind of clay compound that reduces the ink absorbency and allows the colors to stay on the surface without polluting one another. The result is a richer print. Even with this coating, letter-weight office papers are still not good for printing images that have large areas of color. Coated paper is good for printing brochures, flyers, and other illustrated documents, but it is not optimal for pure photographic prints. It is, however, a good low-cost solution for testing positioning and size before printing the final image on higher-quality paper. Remember, though, color proofing isn't worth much if it's not done on the same paper on which you'll make the final print.

**Photo Paper**    Photo paper is also coated, but the coating is much heavier. It comes in glossy, semigloss, and matte finishes. Photo paper is of a much higher quality than regular coated paper and is processed to have a whiter appearance, so printed colors are more accurate. Paper with more rag content will tend to stay whiter longer and doesn't deteriorate with age as quickly. This is a good choice for printing home photographs.

NOTE    *Make sure you print on the coated side of the photo paper. If you print on the wrong side, you'll get nothing but a gooey, inky mess.*

**Premium Photo Paper**    This glossy, semigloss, and matte photo paper is the highest-quality paper you can use for digital photographic prints. These papers tend to be heavier stock and therefore more stable (and more expensive). The printed colors will appear rich, and the prints will have the same finish you get from standard photographic print processing. Premium acid-free papers are designed to last and maintain color for the longest period of time. These papers are pricey, so use them for prints you plan to keep.

NOTE    *If you really want prints that last long enough to be sold and collected, read the upcoming Tip 97 on archival printing.*

**Other Materials**    Since the advent of inkjet printers, paper manufacturers have scrambled to deliver all sorts of specialty printing substrates. You can buy a wide array of materials, including canvas, linen, plastic film, and watercolor paper—to name a few. You can also find specialty papers to use for specific print projects, such as calendars, cards, and labels. Remember that each new paper or material will take ink differently, so you will need to test them and adjust your print settings to get the best print.

## How Do I Select the Right Ink?

If you use the inks that are recommended by the printer manufacturer, you can't go wrong. These inks are not always the cheapest, but they are the safest bet in terms of printer performance and image quality. If you do a lot of printing, the cost of ink cartridges can start to outpace the price you paid for the printer. In answer to these high costs, some ink manufacturers have started making ink that is marketed to be replacement alternatives to the name-brand inks.

NOTE    *The quality of these second-party inks can vary. Be careful when changing ink cartridge brands, because they can sometimes react with the ink already in the system and cause clogging. It is a good idea to flush your printer before changing to a new brand of ink. Cleaning kits are available for this purpose. Also, bargain inks of low quality may damage your printer— especially if your printer prints more than 1200 DPI or more than four colors. Be sure you've done your research before you buy such inks ... or at least have a friend who has the same printer as yours and can report a positive experience.*

## 94. Create and Print Projects

A *project* is the process of printing layouts on special-purpose materials. Some examples of "projects" would be greeting cards, mouse pads, coffee cups, aprons, scrapbooks, portfolios, invitations, announcements, calendars, newsletters, labels, postcards, brochures, business cards, and most other common layouts into which you can place a photo.

A number of products on the market provide a library of print projects for you to work with. You don't need to be experienced with graphic design or layout to put together a nice project. When it comes to special materials, such as coffee cups, there are many online services that will both acquire and print them for you. The automated process used in these products is designed to walk you step-by-step through building a project, making it easy for the amateur to accomplish fairly complex layouts.

Microsoft Picture It! (Figure 14-1) is an inexpensive and easy-to-use application that features extensive project libraries which make it very easy to incorporate your photos into the appropriate special-purpose layout. Other programs provide good project templates, including Canon Home Addition, Adobe PhotoDeluxe, ArcSoft PhotoStudio 2000 (one of the few that works on either Mac or Windows), and Ulead Photo Express 4.0. Most of these programs sell for less than $50 or can be had as part of the purchase of a product such as a camera, printer, or scanner. At those prices, you can afford to build a collection of them. Most of these programs also have other capabilities, such as panoramic stitching or mosaic photos.

### Why Would I Need to Create a Project?

After you have taken some great photos, you may want to include them in a publication, such as an invitation or maybe a calendar. You could choose to take your photos to a print shop and have them lay it out for you, but that is complicated and expensive.

Print projects can help. Print projects automate the process by providing a modifiable predesigned layout and then walking you through the all the steps necessary to produce that project. Using print projects, you can use your photo collection to develop many practical printed pieces, transforming your home photo studio into an in-house publishing enterprise.

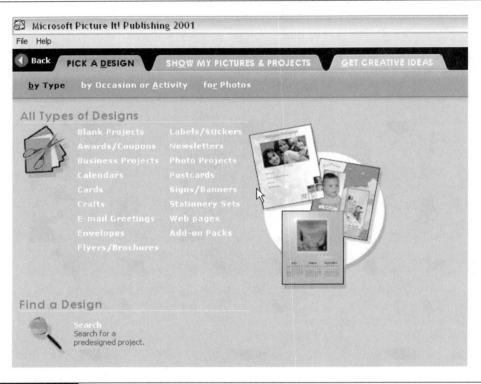

FIGURE 14-1     Microsoft's Picture It! Publisher 2001

## How Do I Go About Printing a Project?

Because every print project application approaches this process a bit differently, the following procedure provides a general idea of the kind of things you can do with print projects software.

1.  Decide what kind of project you want to lay out. The program will provide you with a list of categories. Choose one.

2.  Within the category will be a range of templates, which were laid out by top-notch graphic designers, to give you a creative range of choices (as shown in Figure 14-2). These designers have made some preset choices about the decorative components of each theme. Pick a theme you like—or if you don't like what you see, you can modify one or start with a blank template.

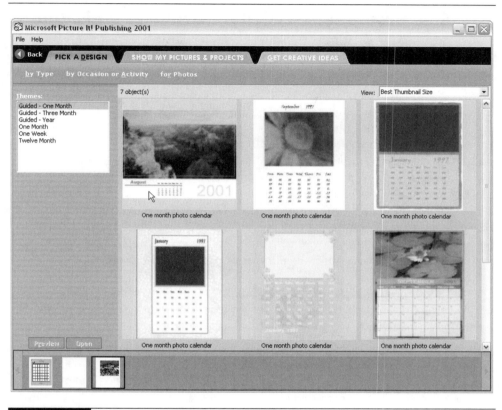

**FIGURE 14-2**    Some sample templates for Microsoft Picture It!

**3.** Next you have the option of accepting what has been provided or changing or modifying any of the components.

**4.** Adjust the sizes and shapes of the project's components (such as photos, headlines, and copy), as necessary.

**5.** Browse, select, and add your photos to the template. You can edit them in the process if necessary.

**6.** Type in and edit the copy.

**7.** Save or print the project.

It is really that simple. The help functions in these programs are extensive, so you will have plenty of help along the way.

## 95. Calculate Resolution Needed for Printed Publication

You will see the terms DPI (dots per inch) and PPI (pixels per inch) commonly used in relation to resolution. PPI is often referred to as *pixel resolution* and always refers to the pixel dimensions of the image. DPI refers to the *printer resolution*, which is always three times the PPI resolution.

Chapter 1 covered pixel resolution of the camera and digital-image files. This section focuses on resolution as it applies to printers.

Because printer resolution is a bit different than image resolution, you need to do some conversion to equate the two. All printers produce color using four colors: cyan, magenta, yellow, and black. The printer creates all the colors you see by placing individual dots of each of these four colors over or next to each other. This is similar to the way color in magazines is created. For every color pixel in the image, the printer has to put down three dots of color (black is not counted because it only determines how dark a color will be). So, ideally, you want the image size to contain one-third the number of pixels that the printer prints at its lowest resolution.

When you print at higher resolutions, most (usually, all) of the extra dots are derived from the image's base resolution—that is to say, they are *interpolated*. So having more than one-third of the printer's base resolution won't do you much good.

### Why Do I Need to Calculate Resolution?

There is no benefit to having more resolution in an image than the printer can handle effectively. Extra resolution will just increase the size of the file, take up space on your hard disk, slow down the printing process, and cost you lots of extra money for ink. Calculating the correct resolution you will need allows you to size your project to be the most efficient. It also tells you if you do not have enough resolution for maximum image definition. Printing an image with less resolution than is required will force the printer to interpolate the image to the minimum size necessary to match the output size, in inches, that you specified. Interpolation will soften the image. Matching the required resolution of the printer with the actual resolution of the image file will give you the sharpest print.

You should also understand how printers are rated in terms of resolution. The *base* resolution is the lowest resolution rating; this is the actual resolution of the printer. Any higher resolution than the base resolution is interpolated and does not actually increase detail—it just increases the apparent smoothness of the transition between dots (because there are more of them, crowded more closely together). Printing at higher resolution also puts more ink on the paper and this can have the effect of making the colors appear to be more intense. It's a little like using thicker oil paints.

### How Do I Calculate Print Resolution for My Project?

The easiest way to think about calculating printer resolution is to understand that the image resolution in PPI should be one-third of the printer resolution in DPI. For example, if a printer has a base rating of 720 DPI, it can place 720 distinct color dots per inch of output on the paper. Because it takes three dots to realize one pixel, the print resolution will need to be 720 / 3 = 240 PPI. If the printer resolution is 720 DPI, the PPI will need to be 240 (720 / 3 = 240).

> **NOTE**
>
> *The dot and the pixel are not equivalent. A dot represents a single micro drop of ink. Inks come in only four colors, so a dot can be only one of those four colors. Pixels, on the other hand, can be any of 16 million colors. The combination of those color dots produces the millions of colors we see in pixels. These terms are often interchanged and misused.*

When you are sizing your image for print, pay attention to the dialog box that controls image size. In Photoshop Elements' Image Size dialog box the Resolution setting, in pixels per inch, needs to be set to match your printer's resolution using the method just described.

You determine the image resolution as it relates to the size of the final print in your program's Image Size command. The first thing you want to know is: How big a print can I make given the real pixel resolution of the image? To find out, open the Image Size command's dialog box (in Photoshop Elements, choose Image | Resize | Image Size). The first thing you do is turn off Image Resampling. Then enter the resolution you need for your printer in the Resolution field. The Image Size for your document will change immediately. This is the maximum size you can print that image without resampling. If that dimension is larger than you intend to make the actual print, you're in good shape. If not, you're going to lose some image definition. You will lose too much image definition if you have to print at a size that's more than twice that of the original. It's as simple as that.

> **NOTE**
>
> *It's a very good idea to set the image size to its maximum resolution when you save your file for archival purposes. Then you have a perfect starting point any time you're ready to make another print.*

## **96.** Make Your Photos into Gifts

Photographs are a wonderful source to use for making all sorts of gifts. Many online services can apply digital photos to several products. MSN Photos, for example, shown in Figure 14-3, offers a number of options for photo gifts. By

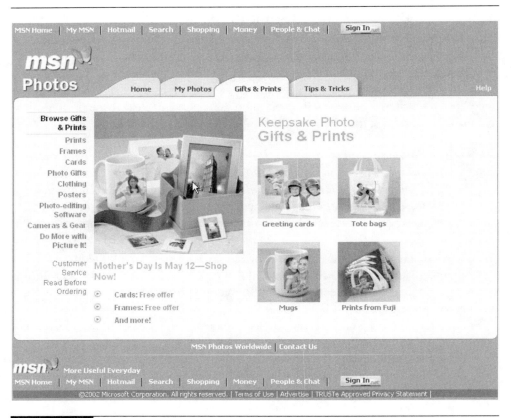

**FIGURE 14-3**    MSN Photos has a full line of gifts.

adding some text, you can personalize these gifts with names, dates, special messages, or sayings. You can create mugs, posters, T-shirts, cards, tote bags, puzzles, photo cubes, mouse pads, magnets, coasters, clocks, hats, key chains, and ties. Search the Web for "photo gifts" and you'll find many sites that offer these services. Kits for making most of these types of projects are available through such stationery manufacturers as Avery and many are available at your local office supply retailer, computer store chain, or online. However, it's often easier and cheaper to have such gifts made for you through an online resource, such as MSN Photos (http://photos.msn.com/).

A new-generation product called a *digital frame* is a unique item available from Digi-Frame, Nikon, Sony, and others. These frames are designed to look like typical picture frames, but the image area is a flat-panel display that can display any digital image. Imagine a framed photo that you can change as often as you like, just by slipping your camera's memory card into a slot on the frame. Some digital frames let you connect to the Internet through a phone line and download images from there, allowing you to network and send images to others.

## Why Should I Create Personalized Gifts?

After you have captured digital images in your computer, you can turn them into true mementos by adding personal touches with your image editor. Take a photo of a birthday, wedding, new baby, pet, or graduation; add a personal message, name, memorable date, saying, or even poetry, and you can create a one-of-a-kind gift. If you run a small business, you can make promotional gifts by including a logo and contact information. All this can be done through the Web from the comfort of your home or business.

## How Do I Use My Software and Printer to Make Gifts?

If you are using an online service, you will need to follow the instructions and provide any information the service requires to manufacture the products to your specifications. This can be as simple as uploading your digital photo and letting the service handle the rest; or you can do some magic in your image editor first. Most services require that your images conform to a certain resolution and file format, which you can easily create with your image editor. Add the text, frames, or any special effects you want and then save the file in TIF format, which is universally accepted. You will then need to upload your pictures to the Web service.

If you are more ambitious and you want to take over the whole process of creation, you can do a few things on your own. Some decal and iron-on materials can be used in your inkjet printer. You can then apply the decals or iron-on art to various items.

As mentioned previously, you can purchase special paper sets that are prepared for print projects such as calendars, greeting cards, and invitations. Use these in combination with project software to become your own print shop. The paper packages usually come with setup specifications, making it easy to configure the print area in your software to print them correctly.

NOTE    *When you use these specialty paper packages, be aware that they don't supply extra paper for testing purposes. I always cut some cheap paper to the same size and perform printing tests on that paper so I don't waste any of the expensive stock. Even so, I often mess up a few. It's a good idea to buy some extra paper when you purchase these packages so you are not left short.*

## 97. Archive Printing Techniques

*Archiving* is a process of maintaining important documents, images, clippings, and other objects for posterity. An archival print is created in a way that maximizes its potential to stay in good condition for a long period of time, so it can be enjoyed in the future.

Archival prints have everything to do with the materials from which the prints are made. The digital information has no effect on it other than the fact that you are using digital printers to produce the print. The substrates, inks, dyes, and pigments all interact to determine how long the photographic image will last. Many of the materials used for digital printing are treated to make the ink, dyes, and pigments look better. The chemical interactions among paper, inks, and environmental conditions—such as light, humidity, and air pollution—can have dramatic effects, causing colors to fade and papers to yellow or disintegrate in a relatively short 2–24 months. With the advent of higher-resolution digital cameras, powerful desktop computers, and advanced image-editing software came a demand for printing technologies that would produce digital prints that were at least comparable to conventional photographic prints and, preferably, of archival museum quality. The result is that with some careful shopping for all the right elements, it is now possible to make digital photographic prints that are rated to last longer than any traditional artistic medium. At this writing, such printers costing less than $2000 are made only by Epson.

Within the last few years, printer manufacturers have developed papers and inks that met the standard and went beyond it for prints that are considered archival quality. The most important development to make this a reality came in the form of pigmented inks. These inks are formulated from raw pigment, not from chemical dyes like earlier inks. Pigments are much more stable and will not break down in light and humidity as will many chemical dyes.

### Why Do I Need to Create Archival Quality Prints?

Some prints are not meant or made to last—such as magazines, posters, or food labels, for instance. Other types of images, however, are more·important, and it is desirable that they last through many years, or even generations—think of family photos, art, and historic pictures. When you are printing photos that you want to last, it is important that you understand how to make them archival prints so those who view them decades later can enjoy seeing what your world looked like. If your photographic interests become more serious, you can make your digital prints collectible. This demands that you print with archival methods.

> NOTE *Remember that the digital photos themselves, as long as they are stored on media that remains stable or doesn't become demagnetized, will never deteriorate. As long as the data is intact, you will be able to reproduce a digital image with perfect fidelity in 10,000 years. So just because you have already made prints with short life spans doesn't mean you can't make better ones as the technology continues to improve.*

## How Do I Create Archival Prints?

If you want your prints to last more than 50 years, and in some cases more than 100 years, you will need to use some form of pigmented inks. Epson is one of the leaders in developing pigmented inks for its line of desktop inkjet printers. The company succeeded in developing inks that work with select printers like the P2000. New pigmented ink, called Generations Enhanced Micro-Bright Pigmented Inks, is being marketed through http://www.Inkjetmall.com and http://www.Inkjetart.com. This ink is rated at 100-years-plus and will work in most of the Epson inkjet printers.

> NOTE *Each of the sites mentioned above is a great place to learn more about archival inks, papers, and advanced printing in general.*

If you want long-lasting prints, your choice of printing papers and other substrates is just as important as your choice of inks. No sense putting inks that will last 100 years on paper that will fall apart in 5. Premium photo papers are acid and oxidant free, which means that when the paper was manufactured, certain chemicals were not used in processing the paper, eliminating acidic residue in the fiber. Acid content can react with sunlight, air, and inks to cause deterioration. Archival papers are made from 100 percent rag (cloth fiber) and will stay whiter and hold together much longer than other papers made from a mixture of rag and pulp.

The last option is to go to print service bureaus that use professional-level printers and inks to provide superb color and archival prints. Search under "Giclée printing" (the name for high-end inkjet printing) to find a printer near you. This is an expensive solution, but it might be worth it for a treasure you want to display and keep for a long time.

NOTE

*There are also very expensive (mostly in the quarter million–dollar range) photographic printers that use lasers to print a digital image on photographic papers (the longest lasting is Fuji Crystal Archive). The Durst Lambda and Cymbolic Sciences Lightjet are the printers in this category to look for. You have to see a print made by one of these printers to realize how stunning it can be. If you need ultimate detail and photographic quality in your landscapes and studio still-lifes (and you have clients who will pay for it), look for printing services that use these printers. The average cost will be between $8 and $16 per square foot.*

## 98. Print Without a Computer

It is possible to print digital photographs directly from camera to printer, bypassing the computer. Some models of printers are equipped with special input adapters that accept direct printing from the camera, memory cards, or wireless communications.

### Why Would I Want to Print Without a Computer?

If you need to produce prints at a remote location, this method can make that possible. Portable-size printers that print directly from the camera, such as the Canon Card Photo Printer CP-100, can print 4×6 dye sublimation prints for super high quality, and they work on batteries. This turns you into a walking photo studio. This setup is ideal, for example, at gatherings where you want to hand out (or sell) photos as you take them. This is as close as you can get to a Polaroid, except the quality is better, you can make duplicates, and you have a digital photo which you can edit and improve on once you're back at the computer.

### How Do I Print Directly to the Printer?

You will need to purchase a printer that is fitted for direct printing. Printers like the HP Photo Direct 100 and the Epson Photo 895 come with memory card slots that allow you to insert your SmartMedia, CompactFlash, or PC Cards right into the printer and print directly from the card. Other printers also offer direct cable connections from the camera to the printer. The HP Photosmart 1215 color printer uses a system called "Beam and Print," which employs an infrared wireless connection (but of course, you have to use their camera).

## 99. Print Without a Printer (Online)

If you have an Internet connection and you want to make prints of your digital images, you can send your images to online service centers, where they can be processed and printed to your specifications.

Online photo centers work through Web sites. Some of the top sites can be found at http://www.ofoto.com (see Figure 14-4), http://www.snapfish.com, http://www.shutterfly.com, http://www.photopoint.com, http://www.zing.com, http://www.photonet.com, and http://www.photoworks.com.

## Why Would I Want to Print Directly Online?

For those who do not want to get into image editors and desktop printers, the online printing solution is the answer. Getting photos printed correctly and consistently on your own printer can be tricky, especially for those who are not too familiar with computers. Online services offer an alternative that can make the task of getting prints a breeze.

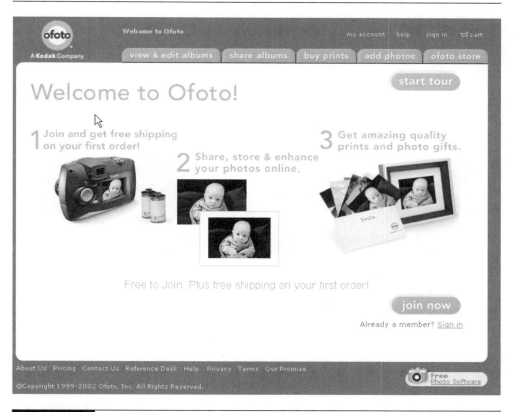

**FIGURE 14-4**    Ofoto is a typical online photographic service center offering albums, galleries, online editing, prints, and gifts.

## How Do I Connect and Print Online?

To access this type of service, you open an account, upload your images to the site, and then indicate what you want. Based on your instructions, the company prints your images on high-end printers and mails the printouts to you. Most of these companies use automated interactive menus that allow you to indicate options and even edit your photos online if you want. You can designate a crop, reduce red eye, add borders, or enlarge the image. You can also indicate how many photos you want and the size you want them. They can mail or e-mail duplicates to other people as well.

Features, prices, and delivery times vary significantly from one service to another, so do some research first. One of the best ways to compare is to test each service with small orders. Make sure that you keep duplicates of the files you send, in case the company loses them. Many of the online photo services also offer a variety of print projects and products, such as cards, albums, and framing options.

NOTE

*Many of the online services will allow you to put the photos on their site so that others can order prints for themselves. Beware of doing this if you plan to make any money from those photos. Nobody's likely to pay much for something that they can easily get for the price of a print.*

# Chapter 15

# Handy, Affordable Accessories

It's surprising how many small (and mostly affordable) pieces of additional hardware are available to help you solve problems. These items include everything from close-up lenses for extreme macros to bags that protect your camera in inclement weather. When I know of a way to help you create or improvise one of these gadgets, I've mentioned that, too.

## Close-up Lenses

Close-up lenses are magnifying optics that screw or slip on to your camera's main lens. You can use a close-up lens to photograph a subject that is closer to the camera than the built-in lens's minimum focusing distance allows. These lenses are ideal for shooting *macro* (extreme close-up) photography. You probably would like a close-up lens if you love to examine small details in nature, such as a butterfly's eyes, or if you want to photograph a collection of small items such as postage stamps or seashells.

### Using a Close-up Lens

How close will you have to be before you need a close-up lens? That's a tough question to answer because every camera's minimum focusing distance is different. It's best to look it up on your camera's specification sheet or in the manual. You'll usually see a minimum focusing distance listed there. Typically, digital cameras will focus down to about 18 inches without requiring an accessory lens. However, some will focus down to 2 or 3 inches. Some Nikon Coolpix-series cameras will focus down to less than 1 inch and are unlikely to ever need an add-on close-up lens.

Close-up lenses are rated in *diopters*. You can think of diopters as "degrees of magnification." A 1 diopter close-up lens will get you half again as close as not having a close-up lens. A 2 diopter close-up lens will get you another 50 percent closer than that, and so on. You get the picture (pun intended). The diopter numbers are handy references, because you can add diopters together to get the total number of diopters of magnification. So if you add a 1 diopter and a 3 diopter lens, you get 4 diopters.

To take pictures using a close-up lens adapter, you will need to keep the camera rock steady, because the slightest camera movement will be exaggerated in the shot. Using a tripod is a good idea. Frame your picture through the LCD viewfinder instead of the optical viewfinder eyepiece (unless you have a single-lens reflex, SLR, camera). Your optical viewfinder simply won't give you accurate framing, and *parallax error* (the difference between the position of the optical viewfinder and that of the picture-taking lens) will be more exaggerated as you move closer to your subject. In fact, in macro photos, your picture may hardly be in the viewfinder.

## Extension Lenses

Extension lenses are larger, multiple-element (several stacked optics) lenses. Like close-up lenses, they screw or slip on to the front element of your camera's main lens. Extension lenses aren't used to move you physically closer to the subject, but to widen or narrow the camera's field of view. That's why they're generally called wide-angle or telephoto extension lenses. You can buy extension lenses that give you anything from a 180-degree fish-eye, to a 600mm (or longer) telephoto that gives you a mere 5-degree angle of view.

Extension lenses give your camera a wider (wide-angle) or narrower (telephoto) field of view than is normally possible within the zoom range of your camera's built-in lens. It is important that you precisely frame your pictures in the camera in digital photography—especially if you're using the more popular and affordable 2- and 3-megapixel cameras—because cropping the picture after the fact can result in unacceptable image detail and sharpness.

### Using an Extension Lens

The mechanical techniques for using extension lenses are much the same as those for close-up lenses. Wide-angle extension lenses make camera movement blur less obvious, but telephoto extension lenses are likely to require the use of a tripod. You're also going to need to frame your pictures using the camera's LCD monitor, because the camera's built-in optical viewfinder can't broaden or narrow the frame beyond the limits of the built-in zoom lens.

Because extension lenses are heavier than close-up lenses and filters, cameras that allow them to be screwed on will be much less likely to have the picture go out of focus because the supplementary and primary lenses are too far apart. They also protect your investment by making it much less likely that your extension lens will fall off the camera and into the lake or onto the railroad tracks.

## Filters

Filters are optically transparent materials that cover the lens. Filters come in three basic types—color balancing, special effects, and polarizing—and in a number of configurations. They may be round screw-on/slip-on glass or they may be gelatin that fits into frames. As accessories go, filters are fairly inexpensive. Most cost well under $50.

### Color-Balancing Filters and Gels

Filters can be purchased for either black-and-white or color photography. Those that are made for correcting the color of light are most important to digital photographers.

Although your camera will balance for the color of light automatically, you will get less noisy (grainy) images if you balance indoor lighting for daylight. To change the color of indoor (incandescent) light to the color of daylight, simply buy an 81A filter at your local camera store that will fit into your camera's screw-in filter threads or into a slip-on adapter made for your camera. If you are shooting indoors with incandescent lights on stands, you can also find much less expensive 81A *gels* (sheets of gelatin) that you can hang in front of your lights.

You can easily re-create the effects produced by the color-balancing filters made for traditional black-and-white photography if you are shooting digitally. To do that, you either simply add the color of the filter to tint the image before converting it to black-and-white or use one of the color channels—whichever comes closest to the effect you are after.

### Special-Effects Filters

Special-effects filters give a specific "look" or character to an image. Traditional film photos that you've most likely noticed as having been taken through a special-effects filter are those of old movie stars whose skin seems to glow or car ads in which every bright highlight seems to glisten like a little star. If your image-editing program is compatible with Adobe Photoshop plug-in filters, you can get much more versatility in the intensity and variables in effects from such third-party vendors as Andromeda and Corel's KPT series of digital filters.

### Polarizing Filters

Polarizing filters are used to cut the excess reflection of light from reflective surfaces. Their principal use is to darken the skies in color photographs, to cut reflections from the surface of water, and to kill reflection from the glass covering framed artwork and documents. Polarizing filters are available as both glass accessory lenses and as gel sheets for polarizing studio lights.

You can polarize either the light entering the lens or the light sources themselves. Of course, the latter is possible only if you are in a controlled studio lighting situation. For most purposes, just ask for the least expensive circular polarizing filter that will fit your camera's lens.

> NOTE    *To use a lens-mounting polarizing filter, view the picture you are going to take through the LCD monitor and turn the polarizing filter until you see the effect you want—then take the picture.*

# Tripods

Tripods, as most readers of this book are likely to encounter them, are three-legged telescoping camera stands that hold the camera rock steady when you are shooting at shutter speeds of less than 1/125 of a second (or shorter, if you're the jittery type). Tripods are also useful for holding the camera while you're doing something else, such as positioning a flash or holding a reflector.

Pictures taken in existing lighting conditions are, for the most part, more likely to reproduce what you saw and the emotions you felt when you were there. Provided the subject isn't moving rapidly, you can take pictures in next to no light. However, you'll have to keep your camera still as Mt. Rushmore. This is especially true of photos taken indoors in dim light and outdoors during twilight and evening hours.

## Choosing the Right Tripod

Tripods come in all sizes, weights, and prices. Still, it's easier to choose the right one than the variety might make you think. The most important things to look for are quality components and good engineering. Nothing is more annoying than a tripod head that won't stay exactly where you positioned it.

In addition to quality, look for as much versatility as you can get for the money. The tripod should extend to at least 6 feet with the center post up, but you want it to collapse to as short a length as possible. You also want it to be as lightweight as possible, but still rigid when it's fully extended. It won't do you any good to own a tripod if you refuse to take it with you because it's too big. On the other hand, a tripod that gets wobbly in a strong breeze is next to useless.

When it comes to taking pictures in the sort of lighting conditions that require a tripod, you need to keep a few tips in mind. As lighting conditions dim, it's more likely that a few bright lights will mislead your camera's built-in meter. Take a few pictures, review them on your LCD screen, and then set your exposure manually to match the exposure of the best shots. If your camera has a bracketing mode, so much the better for taking the test shots. In addition, dim light exposures are often quite long, which increases the noise (grain) in the picture. If your camera has a noise reduction feature, use it.

## Other Devices to Steady Your Camera

In addition to the tall, telescoping tripods, there are also table-top tripods. Many of these are too cheesy to be useful, but some excellent ones are available for under $30, and they'll fit neatly into your camera bag. Table-top tripods can be braced against almost any type of surface—even vertical walls and posts—so they're amazingly versatile.

Two other "gadgets" that are handy are C-clamps with ball heads (see Figure 15-1) for mounting the camera, and bean bags. C-clamps can be attached to tall ladders, tree branches, all sorts of railings, the edges of tables—the list goes on and on. Bean bags are great for irregularly shaped but steady surfaces, such as the hood of your car, a rock, or a fallen tree trunk. The camera stays steady because it can be nestled into the bag until it is level.

**FIGURE 15-1**    A ball head can be used on most tripods. Ball heads are comparatively inexpensive and adjust the camera to any angle with a single twist.

## Cases

So many types, sizes, prices, and styles of camera cases are available that one could write a (very boring) book on the subject. However, you should keep a few tips in mind when considering a case for your digital camera and equipment:

- Is it big enough? Will it hold everything you want to have with you when you're shooting, especially the things you need most—a supplementary lens or two, an LCD hood, a table-top tripod, and an external flash? It's also nice if it's roomy enough to hold other personal belongings (checkbook, PDA, and so on), so you have to carry only one case.

- Is it strong enough? If you are going to check it as luggage, it should be made of some rigid material, such as plastic or aluminum. If it's going to stay on your person, it should be made of sturdy, bulletproof (read indestructible), and waterproof nylon.

- Is it padded? If it's made of nylon (such as a shoulder bag or backpack, as shown in Figure 15-2), be sure that it's foam padded. Then when it accidentally swings into a lamppost, your delicate digital camera may still be usable.

- Does it keep the camera dry and dust free in rainy or windy weather?

- How easy is it to steal? Like any really cool techno-gadget, digital cameras are favorite targets of thieves in airports, big cities, and vacation lands. At the very least, place the strap around your neck, and not just over your shoulder.

## External Flash

If you like to shoot indoors, an external flash is the least expensive way to double the appeal of your photographs. External flashes come in a variety of sizes, shapes, powers, and prices. Some people make a whole sideline of their expertise in using external flash. Fact is, you can and should keep it both simple and affordable. Look for an external flash that has a built-in slave unit and that calculates exposure automatically—that way, you won't have to take the time to measure distances and figure out exposures. You also won't need to worry about physically connecting the external flash with your camera because it can be triggered by your camera's built-in flash, which will also provide fill light.

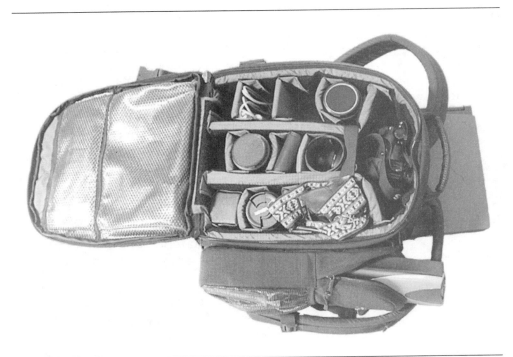

**FIGURE 15-2**    This backpack made for travel photography has room for several camera bodies and supplementary lenses, and even has space for carrying a laptop.

On the other hand, if your camera does provide a means of connecting to and synching with an external flash, you can turn off the built-in slave and operate the external flash that way. Such hard-wired synchronization lets you use the external flash when other photographers are present and using flash—and triggering your slave flash as a result. Hard-wired synchronization is also useful when you want to turn off your camera's built-in flash because you want deeper shadows than you'd get if the built-in flash were filling them.

Sunpak's external strobe, shown in Figure 15-3, is made especially for digital cameras, has a built-in slave unit, and can calculate exposures automatically. It also costs less than $50 in many stores.

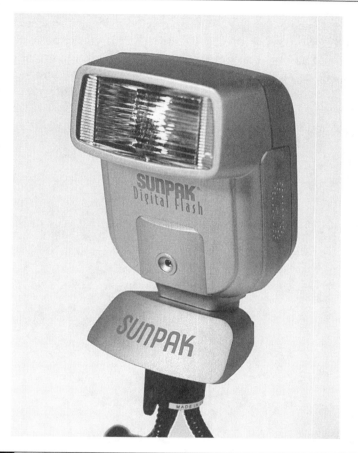

**FIGURE 15-3**    Sunpak's external strobe

## LCD Hoods

We could almost do without optical viewfinders if only LCD monitors could be seen clearly in lighting bright enough to permit handheld photography. On the other hand, if you're going to take carefully composed and framed digital photos, you want the previewing accuracy that you can only get from the LCD viewfinder. What to do, what to do? Simple: spend an extra 20 bucks and get a Hoodman LCD hood (http://www.hoodmanusa.com). It's a foldable nylon shade that attaches to your LCD monitor with Velcro strips or an elastic strap (better if you're borrowing someone else's camera) and makes your viewfinder viewable—even in bright sunlight. If you want to spend just a bit more, Screen-Shade (http://www.screen-shade.com) and Opt-X make somewhat fancier LCD shades that use a bellows to make them expand and contract. Or, if you really want to go the budget route, you can make your own LCD hood by cutting off the frosted plastic part of a slide viewer and holding it over the LCD. This is shown in Figure 15-4.

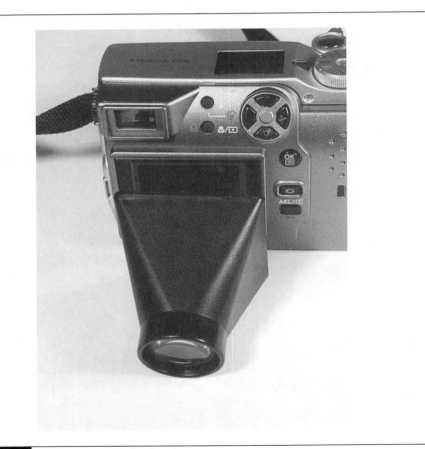

**FIGURE 15-4**     A homemade LCD hood

## Be Prepared

You'll always need to carry a couple of extra items with you, although they aren't really "accessories" in the strictest sense of that word. You need extra digital "film" and camera batteries.

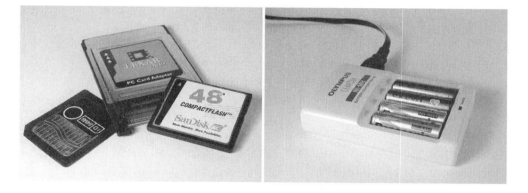

- **Ken's Law**   You will always need to take the most important picture just after you've run out of space on your camera's memory card.

- **Ken's Other Law**   Your camera will run out of power just before you need to take the most important shot and when you forgot extra batteries. (Battery chargers are also small enough that you can easily slip one into your camera bag.)

# Index

Note: Page numbers in *italics* refer to illustrations or charts.

# INTERNATIONAL CONTACT INFORMATION

**AUSTRALIA**
McGraw-Hill Book Company Australia Pty. Ltd.
TEL +61-2-9900-1800
FAX +61-2-9878-8881
http://www.mcgraw-hill.com.au
books-it_sydney@mcgraw-hill.com

**CANADA**
McGraw-Hill Ryerson Ltd.
TEL +905-430-5000
FAX +905-430-5020
http://www.mcgraw-hill.ca

**GREECE, MIDDLE EAST, & AFRICA
(Excluding South Africa)**
McGraw-Hill Hellas
TEL +30-1-656-0990-3-4
FAX +30-1-654-5525

**MEXICO (Also serving Latin America)**
McGraw-Hill Interamericana Editores S.A. de C.V.
TEL +525-117-1583
FAX +525-117-1589
http://www.mcgraw-hill.com.mx
fernando_castellanos@mcgraw-hill.com

**SINGAPORE (Serving Asia)**
McGraw-Hill Book Company
TEL +65-863-1580
FAX +65-862-3354
http://www.mcgraw-hill.com.sg
mghasia@mcgraw-hill.com

**SOUTH AFRICA**
McGraw-Hill South Africa
TEL +27-11-622-7512
FAX +27-11-622-9045
robyn_swanepoel@mcgraw-hill.com

**SPAIN**
McGraw-Hill/Interamericana de España, S.A.U.
TEL +34-91-180-3000
FAX +34-91-372-8513
http://www.mcgraw-hill.es
professional@mcgraw-hill.es

**UNITED KINGDOM, NORTHERN,
EASTERN, & CENTRAL EUROPE**
McGraw-Hill Education Europe
TEL +44-1-628-502500
FAX +44-1-628-770224
http://www.mcgraw-hill.co.uk
computing_neurope@mcgraw-hill.com

**ALL OTHER INQUIRIES Contact:**
Osborne/McGraw-Hill
TEL +1-510-549-6600
FAX +1-510-883-7600
http://www.osborne.com
omg_international@mcgraw-hill.com

# New Offerings from Osborne's
## How to Do Everything Series

**How to Do Everything with Your Digital Camera**
ISBN: 0-07-212772-4

**How to Do Everything with Photoshop Elements**
ISBN: 0-07-219184-8

**How to Do Everything with Photoshop 7**
ISBN: 0-07-219554-1

**How to Do Everything with Digital Video**
ISBN: 0-07-219463-4

**How to Do Everything with Your Scanner**
ISBN: 0-07-219106-6

**How to Do Everything with Your Palm™ Handheld, 2nd Edition**
ISBN: 0-07-219100-7

**HTDE with Your Pocket PC 2nd Edition**
ISBN: 07-219414-6

**How to Do Everything with iMovie**
ISBN: 0-07-22226-7

**How to Do Everything with Your iMac, 3rd Edition**
ISBN: 0-07-213172-1

**How to Do Everything with Your iPAQ**
ISBN: 0-07-222333-2

McGraw Hill
**OSBORNE**
www.osborne.com

Orders: McGraw-Hill Customer Service 1-800-722-4726 fax 1-614-755-5645   For more information: Karolyn_Anderson@mcgraw-hill.com 1-617-472-3555   www.books@mcgraw-hill.com/library/html